# Madam President

*June Mwikali*

Worlds Unknown Publishers

# PROLOGUE

It was on a Friday the last day of January and the sock-shaped tropical country of Kawemppe was as hot as it could get. The capital, Wemppe City, was in the chokehold of a heavy vehicle presence. Long tentacles of cars stretched for miles, billowing petrol fumes into the hot dusty streets. The end of the Wemppe month was known to prompt vehicles owners to drive them into town just in case the weekend spree of "wiping dust off one's throat" went into the wee hours of the night, when taxis were hard to find. The pavement was no better. Sharp eyed hawkers were laying their wares in the already crammed streets in pursuit of the elusive wera, as Kawemppe's local currency is called.

"Special offer: sieves, roach poison, and apples, one hundred Weras," the traders shouted in an effort to attract the hustled women and men pounding the pavements to their wares. Their repetitive calls synced with the blinking lights from the exhibition stalls, inviting customers to pop in and shop at enticing ninety percent discount prices. It was barely midday. The normalcy of the day belied three events taking place in three different venues. Though seemingly unconnected, their joint impact would alter the political landscape of Kawemppe land forever.

On the fourth-floor offices of the red brick Kasoro pavilion, a serious environmental crime was about to be committed. Senator Marko Virunga positioned his bulbous frame in a leather recliner uneasily. He was chairing the annual Select Environmental and Communication Board (SECOB) meeting. The board had been constituted to award licenses to private and public investors interested in investing in the country. This had been after careful scrutiny of the environmental impact of their proposed development.

Barely keeping awake, the senator sank deeper into his chair and began doodling on the writing pad a secretary had placed before each of the fifteen members. The boardroom bore the hallmarks of a nineties senior government personnel office which had aimed at conjuring a shock and awe effect on any visitor who set foot on it. Its padded walls had a bright red leather finish, which matched the thick red carpet on the floor and complimented the dark mahogany furniture. Three portraits of Kawemppe's presidents hung on the wall. They were composed of the founding president, the late Kavango Nzhuu, the dictator, the late Harvester Ochao, and Meshack Jabali the sitting president.

From the wall, President Jabali eyes seemed to be staring down at the dark suited board members, who were crowding around the oval mahogany table, like pall-bearers serenading a coffin.

Old Seth Pasakhwa was holding court at the opposite end of the oval table. "Honorable chair, we cannot ignore this work of research and permit an alteration of the course of River Maru," Seth said and slapped a fat file on the table. "If the course of river Maru were ever to be changed for whatever reason, millions of people would be seriously affected. Right from Amusitu County to parts of Makutano County and Ufuoni County on the Indian Ocean. Chair, the impact on the wildlife habiting that ecosystem will be disastrous." Seth the oldest board member paused to catch a breath, before continuing his argument. "I have been around since independence, when our founding father, the late freedom fighter Kavango Nzhuu emerged from the forest with our independence in one hand and the constitution in the other and pointed this country in the right direction. Yet, despite the suffering he had endured in the thickets of Kawemppe fighting for our freedom, he did not annex any part of nature for his own personal use." Seth paused to stare at the committee. His eyes shone with sincerity. "You all know how the madman President Ochao, was possessed by strange lust for wealth that saw him cling to power for years, but still, not even he thought of slicing a portion of nature for his personal use. Now, President Jabali has to a good degree cleaned up the corruption nightmare and baffling impunity left by Ochao and brought this country back on the road. Why do we want to do the unthinkable? We cannot sign this permit unless we want history to judge us as murderers." "Honorable members, if you are going to ascend to the change the course of river Maru, my resignation letter is ready." Seth reached inside his coat and removed the envelop bearing the resignation letter and placed it on the table.

Although thoroughly corrupt, Senator Virunga's conscience did not spare him the occasional stab of remorse. Virunga looked at the old lawmaker in disdain. Seth was not to be taken lightly. Over the years, he had garnered a reputation as being a highly impeccable individual. The power-hungry dictator, President Ochao, unable to take Seth's criticism of his corrupt government, had once charged Seth of treason. Seth had fled to the neighboring country of Gumbotswi, where he had spent ten years in hiding.

To wash away the guilt pangs, Senator Virunga, snapped open a bottle of water and took a noisy sip. Under normal circumstances, he would have cut off Seth's speech and ordered him to sit down, but more pressing needs held back the urge. His position was compromised. His re-election to the senate was dependent on Mrs. Victoria Maarufu, the wife of the current deputy president Honorable Ronald Maarufu. Her friend, Mr. Cho, the chairman of Hoangz Conglomerate, wanted the course of River Maru altered to suit his new upcoming hotel projects. Virunga's reelection was intimately tied to his ensuring that SECOB approved the change of the course of river Maru.

Accomplishing the controversial feat was bound to set the board on a collision course with the citizenry. It would invite the wrath of Wemppeans, Kawemppe's citizens. Opinion leaders and especially the Amusitu county Governor Dr. Risper Fundi, would be up in arms. Shuddering slightly, the senator acknowledged that he would rather face the wrath of Wemppeans, which he could sidetrack by creating endless smokescreens, than face Governor Risper Fundi. That woman was a different force altogether. He knew she would fight tooth and nail to have the permit revoked. After all, changing the course of the river would adversely affect her constituents and turn her county into a desert.

Sweeping his sleepy eyes lazily across the all-male panel, Virunga identified three individuals, who would attempt to block his intentions—the current speaker included. But he had done his preparatory work well and was ready for them. He was backed by the fully paid support of the other twelve members whom he had met secretly earlier in the week (bearing a heavily stuffed envelope for each of them). As for Governor Fundi, he remembered a quote he had read somewhere: "In politics there are no friends, just a lack of permanent enemies". Reenergized by the quote, the senator slowly brought his thoughts back to the meeting.

The second event was unfolding at the Supreme Court. It was airing live on various T.V and radio stations. A protracted battle between the giant mobile communications company Xamcom and the citizens of Kawemppe was drawing to a close. Xamcom was accused of fraudulently obtaining billions of Weras from the citizenry through illegal surcharges. The newspapers had predicted that the court might award unprecedented payoffs to the affected people.

Lead counsel lawyer Deborah Binti Nzingha, representing the over eight million aggrieved Wemppeans, walked up and down the court as she presented her case.

Her arguments were being followed across the country by her keen clients who were glued to their TV and radio sets. Shortly before midday, the judges deliberating the case emerged from their chambers and fixed a final ruling date for a fortnight away. Long after the ruling had been made, it was lawyer Deborah Binti Nzingha that people would recall. Not because of her clear alto voice or her natural shoulder-length hair which was the envy of many a woman. Unknown to her and the many watching her, a cosmic wind was moving Deborah towards the center of Kawemppe's politics. It heralded a change that would confront and transform the country's political landscape forever.

The third and final event was being lived out in the densely populated Mabanda Moors slums five kilometers east of Wemppe City. Phyllis Mngamata Jones lay in bed sweating in pain. A violent fit of coughing racked her thin body, leaving her breathless from the effort. Fatumatta, her neighbor, groped for more clothes from the dirty heap on the floor and propped Phyllis into a sitting position. Moving fast, Fatumatta deftly scooped out a cup of hot water from a pan on the kerosene stove and began administering little sips to Mngamata to relieve the congestion. The kerosene fumes mingled with the putrid stench from the sewer trenches outside made Mngamata's labored breathing even worse. In her feverish mind, she knew she did not have long to live. Her drawer-sized mud shack had nothing of value. Feebly, her eyes turned towards the tiny TV set parched on a rickety stool at the foot of her bed and began following Xamcom's proceedings. Her eyes refused to stray away from the lawyer Deborah Nzingha.

"Fatumatta, if something were ever to happen to me you should contact her. She was my seatmate in high school." Phyllis said as she pointed a shaky finger at the image on the TV screen.

Fatumatta, who had been running a cold towel on her neighbor's forehead to cool the out of control fever, turned around to see who she was pointing at. A lady who looked composed and smart was on the TV screen talking about a company called Xamcom.

*How could the lady on TV have been Mngamata's classmate?* Fatumatta wondered before asking. "Which school were you in?"

"Kilele Girls Government School."

"You mean you are a Kilele girl, get out of here" Fatumatta gasped.

Mngamata nodded her head weakly before going on, "I know, my dear. It's unbelievable. I even made national headlines when I clinched the highest possible points in my secondary school entrance exam. Just tell Deborah to bury my remains. That is all I ask of her. She will know what to do."

"Mngamata talking death. You will outlive a lot of people. Prepare for the long haul." Fatumatta hoped her words sounded more hopeful than her faith.

Turning her face towards the mud wall away from Fatumatta, Mngamata pulled a threadbare sheet over her head and let tears fall freely down her bony cheeks. Fatumatta, convinced that her neighbor had fallen asleep, gazed at the empty maize flour tin near the stove and began contemplating which shopkeeper was likely to be kind enough to part with a two-kilogram packet of corn flour on credit, so that she could come and make porridge for her dying neighbor.

Dusk eventually enveloped Wemppe City. Predictably, Wemppeans retired to their favorite Friday past times. Many went to the pubs, and a few disappeared into all night church vigils while the bulk of the women went home to their families. Seth Pasakhwa handed in his resigned letter and left the SEBCO meeting. The VIP lift in Kasoro Pavilion opened and let out a tired Senator Virunga clutching a black briefcase. Moving his hefty body with speed, he ignored his own four- wheel cruiser parked under a nearby tree and moved towards a dark limousine parked at the far end of the near empty car park. As he approached, a muscular chauffeur eased off the driver's side and opened the back door for the senator. Grunting, the senator managed to squeeze his girth into the back seat, where he rested on the cool leather seat next to Mrs. Victoria Maarufu. An arm rest divided the space between them.

"Ah, Senator, from the look on your face, I know you have good news for me," Victoria gushed out and enthusiastically pumped Virunga's offered hand. From the corner of her eye she could see the glowing cigarette her chauffer held, as he kept guard of the parking lot.

"Madam, I am yet to encounter something that defeats me," Virunga said pompously and opened his briefcase. In reply, Victoria chuckled admiringly and reached for the photocopy of the permit for the alteration of river Maru that the senator was proffering to her.

For several minutes Virunga watched the woman he admired and loathed with equal measure read the document. Victoria, who was on the plumb side of size eighteen, was dressed in a smart purple dress. Her head was covered by a curly calypso wig, which made her already plain features look duller. But Virunga knew that Victoria was not a woman to mess with. Victoria had an astute business mind that had seen her climb from being an untrained teacher to a respected business woman. It was rumored that she was the force behind her husband political success. Her lobbying and networking skills had helped Honorable Maarufu catapult his once obscure party to national prominence.

Satisfied with the wording of the document, Victoria leaned towards the passenger front seat and hoisted up a heavy briefcase.

"Here is your balance," she said while struggling to pass the briefcase to Virunga.

Virunga opened the briefcase at once. Bundles of crisp five-hundred Wera notes arranged in neat rows stared back at him. A triumphant smile began to play on his lips.

"Madam, this is why I love doing business with you," he said.

"You are welcome. Off course I don't need to remind you that your direct nomination ticket awaits you when you are ready," Victoria said in a business tone.

Moments later Virunga exited the limousine. Anyone watching him would not have detected anything amiss, save for the labored manner in which he hauled his briefcase towards his cruiser.

On reaching his car, he rapped the window with his knuckles imperiously. "Simon, are you asleep? Move! Move! You young people really surprise me," the senator bellowed at his driver. "You lack the stamina of our generation. If you had spent the whole day in a meeting as I did, you would have been carried out on a stretcher." Simon had fallen asleep in the back seat of the large cruiser more from hunger than anything else.

"Sorry sir," Simon said as he jumped to open the back-left door. With his boss situated, he reversed the vehicle expertly from the yard. He didn't need to ask his boss where to drop him, Fridays were reserved for the senator's second wife.

# CHAPTER

# 1

F RANCIS, YOU WON'T BELIEVE me, but they have done it." Honorable Carey Francis Fundi listened to his wife's distraught voice from miles away. A sense of despair engulfed him. When the news of the change of the course of River Maru hit the newsstands on Sunday morning, Wemppeans were stunned at first. Then reality sank in. Amusitu and other counties nestled on the banks of the Maru fell into a state of paralysis. They were mute with disbelief. By sunset, Governor Risper Fundi had begun mobilizing people to oppose and seek a revocation of the permit.

"The bulldozers are already on site, and they have started digging away." The last thing Governor Fundi wanted in her life was to disturb her sick husband with any news that could hinder his recovery. The first time the cancer had attacked her husband was after he had assumed office as President Meshack Jabali deputy. That had been almost eight years ago. The disease had forced Francis to step down to seek medication. Luckily, his doctors had carried out a successful operation on his prostate. Subsequent chemotherapy had taken care of any malignancy in his body. By the time he was fully recovered, the political scene had moved on without him. President Jabali had already appointed Francis's rival, Honorable Ronald Maarufu, as his new deputy. With nothing else to do, Francis had gone back to his businesses and over the years had thrown his weight behind supporting his wife's political career until the deadly cancer cells had reared their ugly heads again.

The Fundi's, together with their grown children, Faraja and Dr. Neema, had retired to the coastal town of Ufuoni for the December holidays and were lounging by the swimming pool when Neema had noticed a benign-looking lump behind her father's ear. Alarmed, the Fundi's had suspended their holiday. His daughter Neema, a research doctor, had decided they fly their father to a cutting-edge nutraceutical health clinic in Costa Rica, from where Francis was now listening to his wife.

"Senator Virunga is not picking my calls," Risper added.

"Go see Virunga in person, and tell him to restore River Maru at once, he should listen to you." In desperation, Honorable C. F. Fundi advised his wife unconvincingly. He had spent several hours trying to reach his onetime boss President Jabali in vain. Thus his advice.

"Ok, I will do that," Risper said. "Do not worry yourself with the matter for now, love."

"I am not going to do such a thing dear," Francis assured her.

"You take care of yourself, girl. I am doing the same here. The doctors think I might be a second time lucky.

From the last tests they carried out, they believe the cancer might be gone," Francis added.

"It is not just luck, Francis. We are blessed, and I love you very much."

Francis heard his wife's breath catch on the other end and wished he could see her face. The health farm never allowed any form of modern communication gadgetry. Only an old-fashioned telephone down at the nursing station sufficed for all patients. After filling her husband in with news of how their wheat and maize farms were doing, Risper ended the call.

Worry is exactly what Honorable C. F. Fundi did when he returned to his room. Analyzing his wife's call, Francis acknowledged that Risper must have been really frustrated to call him.

When faced with uncertainties, Wemppeans took leave of reality and left their leaders to single-handedly fight whatever was being flung their way. Francis had observed this trend over the years. The learned helplessness could get even the most determined of leaders exasperated, he thought. Foregoing a scheduled physiotherapy session, Francis put on his walking shoes and began pacing about the health farm compound to sort out his thoughts. It was obvious that his beloved sock-shaped country—the foothold of Africa as it was fondly called—was under threat. Corruption and impunity were attaining a frightening notoriety. It was like the cancer that ravaged his body. Twice it had robbed him of the opportunity to serve Kawemppe.

Francis acknowledged Kawemppe's problems had been sparked by the British colonizers. The uncaring thugs had carved up the country in total disregard of its history and culture. Kawemppe's seven communities, the Amusitu, the Makonge, the Mnazi, the Lokamiko, the Makutano, the Solanga, and the Ufuoni, which co-existed amicably for centuries had found themselves suddenly displaced and segregated by artificial boundaries. Choosing the central most part of the country to build the capital city, the British had displaced the nomadic Solanga community, who had raised their cattle on the central plains for centuries, to the northern-most part of the country.

The beautiful plateaus of Makutano County were turned into ranches for the colonizers' exotic cattle. The areas occupied by Lokamiko, Amusitu, Makonge, and Mnazi communities, where rainfall was plenty, were turned into agricultural lands, thus effectively rendering the natives squatters on their own land. The only reason the British had bothered with Ufuoni County along the coast was because of the port of Changu. It was the gateway that would ensure that the loot they raked out of Kawemppe was loaded into the waiting merchant ships and transported to their motherland.

With traditional values, the checks and balances which had kept the peace and order now replaced by alien rules and religions, a sense of suspicion had crept between the communities. In his mind, Francis acknowledged that all the mess in Kawemppe could not be squarely blamed on the colonizers. After independence, subsequent regimes had failed to deliver the independence promises of good education, world class health care systems, good governance, and water for all. Elected leaders who were expected to instigate the country's development agenda had started arguing about who got what slice of the national cake. Now, only a select and privileged few enjoyed the so-called national cake. This they did by forming iron clad cartels, which had infiltrated most sectors of the economy.

Francis felt that President Jabali was not to blame for the problem in Kawemppe. Having deputized him almost eight years before, Francis knew firsthand the chaotic state of affairs the president had inherited. Corruption cartels had been running the country. From controlling commodity prices in the shops to deciding who got employed where, when and at what wages. President Jabali had set up a committee that had painstakingly managed to free most of the affected sectors. However, the twenty million people of Kawemppe had yet to acknowledging the difference.

Reluctantly, Francis started walking down the well-trimmed grass towards the nurse's station and requested the old telephone for the tenth time. Yet again, he called president Jabali's private number. The call went unanswered. Returning to his room, Francis summoned Consuela, his personal nurse, and set up an appointment with his doctors. Generally, he felt great. His body felt energized by the combined therapy of nutrition and pharmaceutical products his doctors had rigorously adhered to. Unfortunately, this regimen was about to be disrupted. Francis had made up his mind. Whatever else his doctors thought was necessary for his healing was to be continued at home in his beloved Kawemppe.

By Tuesday morning, Governor Fundi had no clear answers about how to tackle the tension the diversion of River Maru's was causing. She and her friend Praxedes

Tangazo managed to track down Senator Virunga at his private offices, a bungalow located on the edge of Wemppe City. There had been rumors that Senator Virunga kept the bungalow to hide his clandestine operations away from prying eyes. The only guest waiting at the lavishly furnished reception was the legendary journalist, Paa Isaya. His newspaper, The Weekend Dossier, had carried comprehensive coverage of River Maru in its latest edition. Paa had published several reports by environmental experts depicting how the quality of life among the people, animals, plants, and birds who relied on the Maru was about to change for the worse. There were several pictures showing battalions of workers milling around the site engaged in various activities. In fact, it was the front page of The Weekend Dossier that had driven the message home. It had a full- page color photo of a bulldozer felling a sacred, ancient fig tree to create the detour. His report had inflamed the ire of the entire country.

Ever the gentleman, Paa eased out of his seat and greeted the women. "Governor Fundi, Madam Tangazo, it is nice to see you," Paa said as he shook their hands.

"Nice to meet you too, Paa, and thanks for the Maru report. It was spot on," The Governor replied.

"It is the least I can do for now," Paa said.

The senator's secretary, a middle-aged lady named Janet, was now by their side. She greeted them politely and looked hurt when the ladies declined her offer of drinks. Reluctantly, she retired back to her desk, which stood where there had once been a fire place.

The ladies took a corner sofa. Momentarily, they got lost in the décor of the room. *Whoever had decorated the four-roomed bungalow must have been guided by a strange enthusiastic energy when it came to decorating the waiting area*, Praxedes thought. Other than the sober secretary's desk placed where once a fire place must have been, the rest of the room was a scream. Carved sofas covered in gold cloth and fiery silver chintz contrasted with the glass coffee tables bearing an assortment of magazines. A giant earthen vase containing a mix of green, yellow, and pink plastic flowers stood in a corner. The whole ensemble, though expensive, left an infuriating taste in one's soul and failed to invite the eyes back for a more detailed look.

"I believe the Maru issue has brought you here," Paa said as he took a seat facing the ladies.

"Absolutely. If this is not pure madness, I don't know what is," Praxedes replied.

For a while they discussed the Maru issue candidly. They knew the senator was watching them on his CCTV link.

An hour went by. To make the waiting easier, the two ladies picked up some magazines from the table and began flipping through them listlessly. Bored, Paa rose and began pacing around the room. Although he had run out of patience waiting for the senator to grant him an interview, he was shocked by the senator's crassness. How long was he intending to keep his senior colleague Governor Fundi and media mogul Praxedes Tangazo waiting? Praxedes Tangazo owned Wanaichi Media WAMO which held a large stake in the country's mass media. Her radio and TV empire covered sixty percent of the nation.

When the clock behind the secretary's desk chimed eleven o'clock, it announced their second hour of waiting.

Governor Fundi's patience was wearing thin. She stood, ready to barge into the office. Just as she touched the door handle, a group of fifteen women arrived. Their noisy entrance disrupted her. She turned around to look at them.

"Madam Risper, thank God we have met you in person. You are our hero. We admire you so much," the chairlady, a large-bosomed woman named Maggie said as she approached Risper with her hands extended in greeting.

Praxedes sat back watching the effect her friend Risper had on people work its magic. Risper was a natural at connecting with people. Over the years, Praxedes had watched Risper, then a politician's wife, listen to people in an empathetic way that left her audience comforted by her assurances. Now a governor in her own right, her commitment to Wemppeans knew no bounds. If she wasn't sinking a borehole, she was fundraising for slum people to rebuild after a fire or a flood. Her face was as recognizable in remote villages as in the city. For five years in a row, Risper had been ranked the best-performing Governor in a survey that gauged voter satisfaction against projects implemented by county governments.

Her anger slightly abated, the Governor sat down and got into a conversation with Maggie, the chairlady of Nuru Women's Group. She and her associates wore green t-shirts that identified their organization. Praxedes turned her attention to the magazine she had been reading, but she couldn't avoid overhearing the loud whispers from the other women.

"A borehole is what we want", one woman whispered as she began fanning her sweating face with an exercise book.

"No way. Our personal projects must come first. Boreholes will come later," said a petite lady with huge spectacles balanced on her nose.

"There is no way Maggie will agree to deviate from our borehole agenda," the first woman replied. Her answer caused the whispering to escalate into a spirited discussion, which was disrupted by the appearance of the senator at the door of his office. Virunga leaned on the door frame. His fleshy face bore an indulgent smile. The whispering stopped.

"Alilililililililili" Maggie ululated, her voice piercing the afternoon air sharply. "Who is our Carpenter?" she began singing.

"Honorable Virunga," the group responded.

"Who has the power saw?" the soloist went on.

"Honorable Virunga" The group responded.

Our Guide! Our axe!" the soloist sang while advancing towards the door of the office.

"Honorable Virunga," the group replied.

Virunga who was soaking in the praises of the women looked at Governor Fundi's riotous face and attempted a smile.

"Governor Fundi, let me finish with these ladies first. You are next."

"Next indeed! When are you planning to see us, Senator? We don't have the whole day to waste," Risper replied.

Ignoring the comment, Senator Virunga turned his attention to the journalist, Paa Isaya. By then, his smile had turned into a scowl. "Paa, I don't think we will meet today." The senator's tone was dismissive.

"Sir, I just wanted your comment on two issues. One, what informed the decision by SECOB to divert the Maru River? And two, are you defecting from the Democratic Democracy Party DDP to the SASA Party?"

"Who is telling you those stories about me?" the senator retorted as he slammed the door in Paa's face. Paa rocked on his heels for a while. He stared at the door briefly and bade the ladies goodbye, then left. Praxedes made a mental note to buy the next edition of The Weekend Dossier. She knew the editorial would be unforgiving of the senator.

"Madam, I am very sorry for the wait. The Senator controls who goes in and in which order. Please allow me to serve you some tea or soda?" Janet, the senator's secretary asked.

Declining the drinks, Governor Fundi accepted the apology and sat down next to Praxedes.

"We might have a motive now. If Virunga is defecting to SASA, then he needs real money for his campaign. I hear that a SASA Senatorial ticket is retailing at twenty-five million Weras," Governor Fundi whispered to Praxedes.

"Once I get the facts right, my team will broadcast SECOB dealings immediately," Praxedes Tangazo whispered back

Governor Fundi's reply could not be heard over the ululations emanating from the senator's office.

"The handouts have been given and accepted," Praxedes said to no one in particular as she rolled her eyes. She glanced at her watch, picked up her mobile phone, and cancelled yet another meeting with a client.

An hour later, the women group spilled out of the office. Their exit was punctuated by loud cheers. Maggie, their chairperson, had a large brown envelop clasped in her hands. Anyone could have guessed its contents.

"Let us find a restaurant, sit down and plan what to do with this," Maggie told her followers.

"Listen, Maggie," the petite lady with the large spectacles shouted at the chairlady. "You are not the one to tell us what to do with the money. It is ours. We are splitting the money here and now. We own handbags and can capably carry our share."

"Yeeesss!!" The group shouted in response. Everybody was speaking at once. The well-mannered whispering observed earlier was crumbling fast.

Embarrassed, Governor Fundi watched the scene in shame.

Rising from her desk, Senator Virunga's secretary tactfully maneuvered the women towards an outer corridor to save the waiting guests from the unfolding drama.

"This is where matters have reached in our beloved Kawemppe," Governor Fundi commented in dismay.

"If I can divert the country's budget to my own use and get away with it, then I must be smart. If I can siphon money meant for a village borehole and buy a piece of land for my personal use, then I must be a hard-working Wemppean," she continued dejectedly, but Governor Fundi's words were cut short by the secretary who ushered them in.

Unlike the gaudy decor in the reception, the senator's office had less clatter. Painted a light cream color, it looked welcoming. The senator sat behind a mahogany desk, which was flanked by two comfortable chairs on each side.

Behind him, a glass wall unit bore some crispy volumes, which had clearly never been thumbed through. A sheave of files he seemed to have been working on lay on top of his desk.

"So, ladies. What can I do for you? "Senator Virunga asked as he rose up to welcome the ladies. The buttons of his ill-fitting coat were straining to contain his flesh. Refusing to greet the Senator's extended ham of a hand, the women lowered themselves onto the chairs.

Looking at the Senator, Praxedes couldn't help but see where the cartoonist at The Weekend Dossier got his inspiration from. He always presented Virunga's head in the shape of an avocado with two tiny eyes and a large mouth. Two knitting needles represented his legs. The caricature never failed to elicit laughter.

"Senator, we demand to know why you authorized a private investor to change the course of River Maru. This decision contravenes expert advice that such a move will affect human and animal populations adversely," Governor Fundi began.

In response, Senator Virunga leveled his eyes at the women. Slowly he drew out his mobile phone and proceeded to make a personal phone call. The two women stared at him in disbelief as he went ahead to hold a conversation in total disregard of their presence. A long ten minutes later, he turned to them and said, "You very well know that my hands are tied. These decisions are made by the board."

"SECOB has broken the law under your watch. You don't just wake up and change the course of a major river," Praxedes responded.

The impervious look on the senator's face gave the impression that he wasn't paying any attention to her. "You are not the ones to tell me how I should perform my duties," Virunga replied. His voice was laced with mockery.

Governor Fundi could not hold her anger any more. Pointing her finger at Virunga's face like a loaded gun, she exploded. "We know what they paid you to sign that permit. No wonder you have the audacity to so casually determine the fate of millions of Wemppeans using your big stomach."

The slap came from nowhere. It left an imprint of the senator's hand on Risper's light brown face. Reflexively, Praxedes picked up her hand bag which was loaded with phones, cosmetics, keys and other feminine paraphernalia and smashed it heavily on Virunga's head. Despite his bulk, the Senator shot up with unexpected agility. With his face contorted in anger, his beefy hands took hold of Praxedes weave and began to yank it off.

"Wuuuuweeee!" Praxedes screamed at the top of her lungs. Governor Fundi, still stunned by the slap jumped out of her chair and reached for a miniature flag which had been standing on the edge of the desk. Using both hands, she plunged its spiky end into the perfectly positioned butt of the Senator, who yelped in pain and let go of Praxedes's weave at once.

The first person to get into the office was the Senator's secretary, Janet, closely followed by several members of the Nuru Women's Group, who had heard the cry of alarm. Frightened by what they saw, they stood shell-shocked, surveying the turbulent scene in front of their eyes. Praxedes's flawless complexion was darker than a starless

Kawemppe night. Senator Virunga stood near his chair in a peculiarly awkward stance. Files and papers lay scattered on the floor around him. The women group stared at the governor in disbelief. The Senator was clearly at a loss. He didn't know what to say or do in order to pacify the situation. Realizing he was out-numbered and outmaneuvered, his cunning mind kicked into gear.

"Janet, get these women out of my office. They have started fighting each other in front of me."

A disbelieving Janet starred at her boss, her eyes travelling accusingly up his coat lapels. A few buttons were missing. His disheveled look belied his statement.

"Thank heavens, members of this women's group are my witnesses. Otherwise, people might conclude that Virunga is a woman batterer," the senator went on in an attempt to shift the women to his side of the conflict.

Despite the red imprint of a hand on Governor Fundi's face, she turned to the women and spoke coolly. "Ladies, don't listen to his nonsense. This man wants to ruin the livelihoods of millions of people who rely on the waters of River Maru. As if he is not satisfied with that, he wants to start by maiming their leaders when they protest. He has just beaten us in his office. Look at Praxedes's hair and my face. We are calling the police," Risper concluded. She regretted not bringing her bodyguard along.

"No one is stopping you from calling anybody you wish to call," Virunga said brusquely. Turning to his secretary he bellowed out, "Janet, stop standing there like a statue. Summon my bodyguard. I have been hurt." Janet fled the room.

"You mean you can hit us, insult us at will, and attempt to downplay your actions. Do you know that we can grind this office of yours into powder? Praxedes asked, staring dangerously at the Senator.

"Senator, with all due respect, I think we should call the police," Maggie ventured politely. "They are best placed to deal with these matters."

"Shut up, you leper. I have already sorted you. What more do you want?" Virunga roared. His shouting made Maggie and her women cringe in shock.

"I have always suspected that you two secretly admire me," Virunga said while wagging his finger accusingly at Governor Fundi and Praxedes.

"Nonsense," Praxedes retorted angrily before sending her hand bag sailing towards the senator. Virunga ducked expertly, and the handbag cruised past him and crashed into the glass bookshelf, sending glass and books spewing to the ground.

Suddenly, all the women began screaming. "Uuuuuiiiiii, uuuuiiiiiii."

Flustered, the senator yanked open his top drawer and drew out a pistol. He began brandishing it menacingly at the women.

"Kill us now, senator. If you think by so doing this basket stomach of yours will remain well-fed by your corrupt deals. I dare you to shoot us," Governor Fundi shouted, standing in front of the pointed pistol to shield the other women.

Charged, Maggie, the Nuru Women's Group chair, took two bold steps forward and confronted the senator. "A while back, we thought you were a useful person in society.

But look at you, pointing a gun at unarmed women. You are a coward and a bully who preys on the helpless. We don't need your money," she concluded and threw the hefty brown envelop the senator had given the group on the table.

"Risper Fundi, get out of my office now, and take your choir of women with you," Virunga shouted. He looked fit to have a heart attack.

Employing all her skill to remain calm, Governor Fundi stared the senator straight in the eye. In her most authoritative voice, she said, "Women choirs are not heard during the daytime for nothing. They make preparations and practice before they sing. There is a Kawemppe proverb that warns people against throwing stones at a bee hive, lest they be stung. Virunga, you will pay dearly for what you have done today." With that, Risper led the entire group of women out of the bungalow.

A shaken Virunga hastily shoved his gun inside his briefcase and stepped gingerly around the broken glass to look for his secretary.

After leaving Virunga's office, the women piled into their van and followed Governor Fundi's car to Mambo Leo hotel, where she had offered to buy them lunch.

"Men have taken women for granted for too long. If the senator can assault leaders like you, madam, what will prevent him from grinding ordinary people like us into dust? Call the police. We are ready to testify about what we have witnessed," Maggie said spiritedly.

The hotel manager had seated them in the hotel's conference room. Waiters scampered about taking their orders.

"We cannot say that all men are bad, but there is a level of disrespect accorded to women for no reason other than the fact that they are women," Governor Fundi said. Her eye had almost swollen shut. The hotel manager had supplied her with an ice pack to soothe it.

"My grandmother had a proverb that women should always keep their ears on the ground. That way, they would be able to detect an approaching underground animal and prepare for it. Ladies, before this weekend is over, Maggie your chairlady will inform you of the action we intend to take against the Virungas of this country. Keep your ears open."

The food arrived. It matched the anger and hunger they felt. Platters of sizzling roast goat meat accompanied by steaming *posho* and avocado salad. They fell on it at once.

Later as governor Risper and Praxedes rode home, they began to weigh their options. Praxedes wanted to summon her reporters and expose Virunga's misdeeds. Instead, Governor Fundi called her lawyer and explained their predicament.

"No problem, madam. We will file this case at once," The lawyer said. Risper's phone was on speakerphone for Praxedes's benefit.

"But before I do so, I want us to think through this action critically," The lawyer continued. "Being an election year, Virunga can resort to desperate tactics to wiggle himself out of the mess. He can fabricate dirty lies that could end up spoiling your reputations."

"What do you mean?" The two women asked in unison.

"Look at it critically, ladies. If Virunga senses that his political future is compromised, he will resort to using dirty tricks. Excuse me, madam Governor, for being this candid, but suppose he accuses you of wanting to rape him?"

"That would be nonsensical" Risper replied.

"Exactly my point," the lawyer said before continuing. "I want you to understand that it is not the accusation that will hurt you the most, but the images left in people's minds. To wipe off such rotten gob from the public psyche can take years. I strongly suggest that we think through this case more carefully before filing it in court," the lawyer concluded.

Not believing that they had so few options to access justice because of who they were, Risper called their lawyer and friend Deborah Binti Nzingha who agreed to meet them later in the day.

After parting with the Nuru Women's Group, Praxedes and Governor Fundi had spent the entire afternoon in the latter's home garden, strategizing on how best to secure revenge. Deborah Binti Nzingha arrived at Governor Fundi's Mansion shortly before sunset. She looked elegant in a simple grey suit. A double-stringed white and black bead necklace complimented her earrings. After greeting them, she surveyed the physical damage meted on her two mentors by Virunga in shock. A chef brought out a flask of mint tea and freshly baked cupcakes. As Deborah took her tea, the women told her about their unusual day.

"We need to get this bully arrested now. We are driving to the police station now to report this incident," Deborah said firmly. When she had started out as a lawyer, her two mentors had generously given her substantial business and even referred their friends to her law firm.

It never failed to impress the two ladies how Deborah, whom they had met in her twenties, had blossomed into such a success. Risper could vividly remember the fateful day, twenty-five years ago, when she had met Deborah. Then a law student at Wemppe University, Deborah, had appeared in Risper's obstetrician and gynecology clinic seeking to procure an abortion. Immediately, Risper had sensed that Deborah was no ordinary girl. Apart from being intelligent, Deborah had appeared thoughtful and reserved unlike her peers. Risper had taken her under her wing and mentored her over the years.

"We did think of going to the police initially, but we have changed our minds," the governor said. A sinister smile played on face.

"We have decided to do something earth-shattering. Virunga and others of his ilk who think that Kawemppe republic is their playground will be sorry." Praxedes said this as she applied a generous blob of Vaseline to her painful hairline.

Deborah's curiosity was now aroused.

"This country needs some tender, loving leadership to put it back on track. We are going to field a woman to contest for the presidency in the coming elections," Governor Fundi said resolutely. Deborah's eyes opened wide as the gravity of the words sank in. She knew from experience that the two women never spoke in vain.

We know it is already February and elections will be in December, but we will manage. Even if it means racing all the way to the ballot box, we will," Praxedes added with determination.

The three women looked at each other with no doubt in their minds about the fact that a female presidential contestant was going to be on the ballot paper come December. But who was it going to be?

"I am with you. We do need a lady CEO," Deborah concurred. Having lived with the Fundis, Deborah knew that they planned their campaigns with military precision. She would have loved to help with the planning, but she had no time to spare. The ruling of the Xamcom case was in a few days' time, and every spare minute she had was occupied with the preparations.

"If you change your mind about suing that bully, I am only a phone call away," Deborah said and rose to leave.

"We won't," Risper said.

After Deborah left, Risper flipped open a clean page on her note book and wrote with firm strokes. The making of Madam President.

# CHAPTER

# 2

S O LADIES, DOES IT mean that the only way a woman can sleep inside the Kawemppe Presidential palace is if she is the president's wife?" Governor Fundi asked as she banged her dining hall table. She now had the attention of the fifty women drawn from the eight counties of Kawemppe republic sitting around of her. Her big sitting room had been converted into a mini conference room. A corner table was heaped with appetizing trays of sliced arrow roots, sweet potatoes, and pastries for her guests. Flasks of mint, black, and hibiscus teas stood next to jugs of assorted juices.

"You are saying something, madam." The encouragement came from Mrs. Ziphorah Lengo, The chairlady of House Managers Association (HMA), a house wives lobby group. She was a close friend of the hostess.

The Governor went on. "When I was a small girl, my mother used to say that if you saw a star during the day time, you must ask yourself why. Four days ago, my friend and I woke up in good health and went to SECOB's office to enquire why River Maru's course was being changed without proper consultations. By now, you must have heard what happened to us. As you can see, my eye was almost torn out. Thanks heavens my friend Praxedes still has some hair on her head."

When the rumors of their assault by Senator Virunga reached them, their unbelieving friends demanded that she call them together so they could chart some course of action. Governor Fundi had expected lawyer Deborah Binti Nzingha to be present, but the latter had called with an apology. Preparations for the upcoming Xamcom ruling were at a crucial stage.

"If someone calling himself a leader can kill entire communities of people and wildlife without a backward glance, then as women we need to rise up and scream that we do not need that kind of leadership. That is why we are gathered here. This country needs someone who will nurture it back to the unity we had sixty years ago at independence. I have been thinking around this matter for some time, and I believe that that someone must be a woman," Risper concluded to loud cheers from the women.

"Alilililililililililili," several women ululated.

"Ladies, let us never forget how the women of this country laid down their bodies to gain independence. As you can see by the nearly white skin God gave me, I don't know my father, because my beloved mother had to lure a white man into a compromising position so that the freedom fighters could steal their sophisticated guns to aid the fight. What a sacrifice? Who has ever acknowledged what women gave our independence? No one." Risper mock-plucked an incisor and cast it to the ground to signify the absolute nothingness. "I have called you here because a star has been seen in broad day light. The fate of this country hangs precariously in the hands of bullies. It is time we took resolute action to liberate ourselves.

Maggie the Nuru Women Group chairlady stood up next. "Fellow ladies, it is time we took action. If we are waiting for a man to urge us towards the presidency, then let us bury the idea in the tomb of the forgotten. Why am I saying this? I have noted that as women we have a special liking for lower echelons of leadership. We need to contest for the bigger posts too." Maggie paused and took a sip of water. "This past Monday, when I witnessed Governor Fundi being assaulted like a common criminal by a man we refer to as a leader, I got scared. Then I thought to myself, if Governor Fundi could face such contempt at this time and age, what about our daughters ten years from now? Things must change." Maggie wound up her speech and was met with thunderous clapping.

The next speaker was the towering 'no holds barred' Mrs. Ziphorah Lengo. She was the chairlady of HMA and hailed from Mnazi County, as did Senator Virunga. The bluish kitenge dress she wore gave her the distinguished look of a college professor. Ziphorah had a rare common sense and distinct earthy wisdom. The only thing she lacked was a college degree. Praxedes looked at Ziphorah in admiration.

"That creature you keep calling Virunga is a bully that Kawemppe can do without. I am not going to waste my time talking about him. We have more important matters to attend to."

"Yes," the women replied. Ziphorah's speeches were always captivating, and the women sat upright so as not to miss a word of it.

"I am going to talk about getting one of us into that palace," Ziphorah said as she pointed eastward where the Wemppe presidential palace was situated. "Let us strike this iron while it is hot. We cannot claim to be twenty-first century women yet, while acting as flower girls and cheerleaders for our male counterparts as they take the powerful position."

"Yeeeesss," chorused the gathering.

"If we are good enough to become members of parliaments, senators, and governors, then we are also good enough for the presidency."

"Speak, Ziphorah," came back a reply, 'speak' the women shouted.

"We have been good and loyal party officials, activists, campaign messengers, and grass root mobilizers. We have the experience. We can manage the presidency. We are the millennial women—women who have been to Beijing and back . . . women who have benefitted from affirmative action. By the way, let no one imagine that affirmative action is a token to women. It is only the beginning of the balancing of the play field." Ziphorah paused briefly. Her face bore a thoughtful look. "I say we are going for the presidency because we always post a larger voter turnout compared to men. It is time we put these numbers to work by installing a woman inside that palace."

"Tell them!"

"Tell them!" followed the echo.

Ziphorah paused to adjust her blue head gear then continued.

"Are we together women?"

"We are together, Mama Ziphorah!" the women chorused.

"Then the moment has come for us to move from the sidelines to the center stage. We will no longer watch the men declare their projected leadership line up to the year three thousand and its uncle while we are sitting down." Ziphorah's lips had tightened to a thin line.

"You all know that I can speak till Christ comes. I am very passionate about this venture. As I wind up, I say this without any apologies. It is time a woman became president in this country. It is up to us women to see that this happens. Will we be like the USA, which with over two hundred years of democracy can still be so misogynistic when it comes to the presidency? It is hard to imagine that the most developed and democratized country on earth cannot see through that. Uh! Women, wake up."

"Yeess," the women shouted back.

"Then I urge you as we go back to our localities—to go back and stir up a storm of votes as we have always done. But this time it will be for one of us." Ziphorah waited for the enthusiastic clapping to die down and dramatically said, "I am done. Let the next speaker take the floor."

The chairlady of the Federation of Women Teachers, Mrs. Mary Msalaba, a stout no-nonsense lady in a cream skirt suit, spoke next.

"From the way you have demolished Governor Dr. Risper's finger liking delicacies I know you are fine," she began, causing much laughter, "so, ladies, I am not going to bore you with greetings. My take is that as women we have to stop our incessant bickering and assassinating each other's character. Let us stop fighting each other and work for the common good, and Kawemppe will remember us for years to come.

"We don't need to be given a chance to prove anything. We are capable of steering this nation forward. The political stalwarts may not be ready for us, but the presidency is not a reserve of the bearded and trousersed. Recent research indicates that forty-nine percent of men and fifty percent of women are ready to vote for a female president if a serious contender is fronted." Mrs. Msalaba's voice rang with a conviction. "The wait is over, ladies. Do we have an agreement or not"? she asked authoritatively.

"We do," the women replied.

"Is this wedding on or is it off?"

"It is on."

With her arms akimbo, Mary slowly began shuffling her shoulders in dance and belted out a popular wedding song.

"Is the wedding on or has it been called off?" she began.

"It is on, it is on, it is on," they replied.

"Is the wedding on or has it been called off," she continued

"It is on, it is on, and it is on."

"We are waiting for the bride."

"We are waiting for the bride."

"Indeed. that is the state of affairs as at present. We need a capable and inspirational candidate. One who will not let us down." Having emphasized her final words, Mary sat down to a thunderous applause.

Other women spoke, provoking and motivating the women to run with the vision. Lastly, Mrs. Praxedes Tangazo stood. She was sporting a new wig which was expertly combed to cover were Virunga had almost plucked off her hair. "Governor Fundi, I feel that you are preaching to the choir. By a show of hands, let me see how many of you ladies feel that this presidency is ours for the taking?"

All the hands in the room shot up.

"Then let the Governor tell us what she wants from us."

Risper stood up once again. Her heart could barely contain the happiness she felt. "Friends, I thank you once again for your unwavering support. We have about ten months to execute this mission. This is what I ask of you. Let us go talk with our God, our friends, and our men. I hope you are aware that men are not our rivals. They are an integral part of the equation. Find out who they think is the best-placed woman in Kawemppe to become president. We will meet this coming weekend and compare notes. Do not come here with the names of your relatives or friends. Bring names of women who are qualified and can command country- wide respect."

The meeting broke up soon afterwards, and a late lunch was served. The chef had laid out fresh-baked tilapia fish served in a coriander sauce accompanied by steamed cabbage and jacket potatoes slathered with butter. As they took their lunch, the women broke out into small groups and discussed their new quest in-depth.

# CHAPTER

# 3

DEBORAH BINTI NZINGHA LOOKED forward to driving from her home at Wemppe Meadows to the town center. Perched on a hill, the serene forested Meadows housed the diplomatic corps, reknown doctors, senior lawyers, basically the cream in the land. At five in the morning, the streets were almost dark, save for a few vehicle headlights on the road. Deborah drove downhill and, before long, drew near the Wemppe Stadium roundabout. It was already gridlocked with traffic, and she had to slow down. Wemppe County's entire population seemed to have convened at the same spot. The sidewalks were busy with a silent throng of determined people walking to work. The majority of them were from the sprawling Mabanda Moors slums. It was the slum that supplied the city and its industries with cheap labor.

Frustrated, Deborah switched off her car engine for the sake of the environment and looked at the passing pedestrians. When caught by vehicle lights, the shadows splintered into bizarre images. As she observed the pedestrians, Deborah thought the emerging scenario resembled the great wildebeest migration she so loved watching on television. Only, this time it was of cars and humanity. The rich and the poor would for hours engage in a vicious fight for resources on the streets of Wemppe City. The fight would be surrounded by the threatening crocodiles of tribalism, cartels, corruption, gun-wielding thieves, drugs and alcohol, and terrorism. In the evening, the people would once again retreat to the suburbs. The cartel kingpins would post guards around their mansions and share their loot. The poor would eat whatever morsel they had managed to salvage during the day, tightly bolt their doors, and sleep after praying for a better tomorrow. At dawn, a rerun of the vicious cycle would start afresh.

"Something needs to change," Deborah said aloud, her soul burdened.

The first rays of the sun tinged the horizon with a fiery orange color. It was a sure promise of the heat that would follow later in the day. To create some circulation of the stagnant air in the car, she cracked the windows open as she twiddled with the radio dials in the hope of getting a traffic update. She landed on Radio Five's Ananias and Sabina Breakfast Show.

"TGIF. Thank God it's Friday, people. I hear the traffic out there is a complete nightmare," Ananias said. His rich baritone voice made him the darling of his female fans.

"So, unless you really must go to the town center today, try to avoid it," Sabina chimed in. It was useless advice. The masses were on the road and already stuck in the traffic jam.

"Sabina, this traffic jam reminds me of a conversation I had with a lady friend of mine last week. She was distraught by the feeling that she had become a stranger to her children. The jam makes her leave home at five in the morning to avoid getting late for work. At that time, her kids are still asleep. In the evening she reaches home when the poor kids have already gone to bed. She was really miserable. It had gotten to a point where she wanted to quit her job. Were it not for the bills awaiting her, she would gladly have forsaken her job to spend more time with her children."

"Quite true, Ananias. In fact, we may have lost a generation of our children to cartoons and house girls. "Sabina agreed. A popular local tune followed.

Sabina's observation of lonely kids left at the mercy of cartoons made Deborah feel guilty. She thought about her daughter, Golda, and son, Amani Junior, whom she fondly called Goldie and AJ. They rarely saw her. Khavere, her charming house girl, and her grandmother ably filled the parenting gap for her. For Deborah going to work was a necessity. When her husband, Nzingha, had been shot dead, her in-laws had descended on her property like vultures. They had taken everything away, forcing her to rebuild her life afresh. But things were about to change. Today was her last day at work. The Xamcom case was going to be her last trial before she retired. She had drawn up the papers needed to sell off her practice to her partners. Nothing was going to reverse her decision. All she wanted was to concentrate on raising her kids.

"Anyway, traffic matters aside" Ananias butted in as the lyrics died down. "There is a silver lining to every dark cloud. This is the day that the Xamcom ruling will be made, and I am looking forward to a refund of sorts."

"Sure, baby," Deborah quipped. As the lead counsel for Nzingha and Co. advocates, she was the one responsible for getting Wemppeans their stolen monies from Xamcom. The comprehension of how eagerly people were relying on her to deliver a favorable ruling filled her tummy with a flurry of butterflies. She knew that even though her team had covered all the legal angles, surprises did spring up in the Wemppean judicial system. To diffuse her apprehension, she switched off the radio and gazed at the walking masses.

When she saw him, there was no time to pretend otherwise, Paa Isaya detached himself from the walking humanity and walked towards her purposefully. Despite her discomfort, she unlocked her car doors and Paa jumped in. His musky cologne led the way as he folded his five- foot eleven frame into the passenger seat. "Early bird," he said.

"Could have been earlier were it not for all this traffic," she replied before asking, "Still trekking to work?"

"It is my way of keeping grey hair away," Paa answered.

Twice a week, Paa Isaya walked the twenty odd kilometers from his house at Wemppe Meadow to the city center. It was part of his health regimen. The irony of it was that on his walks, Paa encountered thousands of his father's transportation trucks but never bothered to ask for a lift.

His father, the billionaire Isaya Hekima, of Isaya and Son Logistics, owned eighty percent of all transportation trucks in the East and Central Africa region. Paa, too, had a small fleet of fast racing machines parked outside his home. But he religiously stuck to his routine.

"Big day, ah", Paa said referring to the Xamcom case.

"Yep," Deborah replied. From the corner of her eye, she could make out Paa's profile. For a fifty-year-old man, Paa looked fit. A tiny belly was discreetly settling on his frame, giving him the compactness of a retired boxer.

"The grapevine has it that you are running."

"Running? Running from what?" Deborah asked in surprise.

Paa chuckled, a throaty laugh that crinkled the corners of his sharp eyes and brought out his irresistible lone dimple—one that once used to drive Deborah crazy. The apprehension that had been assailing Deborah began to cool down, and she felt her body begin to relax. Paa always had that effect on her. Yet she yearned to be alone rather than with this man who had almost ruined her life.

Their romantic relationship had been short and steamy and had ended rather abruptly. They had met on the first outing Deborah had ventured on after joining Wemppe University as a naïve twenty-year-old village girl. Paa had then been twenty-five years old and a junior political writer for The Wemppe Gazette. He had also been working on the side to establish his own paper and break away from the shadow of his billionaire father. After weeks of relentless pursuit, Deborah had finally agreed to a date. A whirlwind romance had followed, but it did not last for long. Paa had secured a scholarship to study for his master's degree in the coveted North West University, America. It was a perfect chance to break away from his father's shadow. He had flown off to America without knowing the predicament he had left Deborah in. She had written a letter via his mother explaining the situation, but he never replied. After waiting for three months to hear from Paa, a fearful and pregnant

Deborah had contemplated having an abortion. It was then that she had met Doctor Risper Fundi, her liberator.

She was woken from her reverie by Paa's throaty voice.

"I would be honored if you granted me an interview for the next edition of The Weekly Dossier," Paa said. In the past, he had cajoled Deborah to pen several lawyerly articles for his paper which had been well-received by the readers.

His request went unanswered.

The morning sun bounced off Deborah's dark cocoa complexion, making it glisten like an evenly stirred cup of chocolate drink. Paa unabashedly ogled the woman he secretly loved. He wondered why she always seemed to avoid him. When he left for America, he had religiously written to her through his mother for the first four of the seven years he stayed there. After that, he had given up. It was then that he had met beautiful Gail, his dead wife. Gail had lost her life to drugs. Paa's marriage had been one continuous nightmare of rehabs followed by brief, shaky periods of abstinence before Gail went back to using. The bitter struggle had come to an end three years ago when Gail went to visit her parents in America. Her parents had found her comatose in bed. Gail had overdosed, and the paramedics who had responded to the emergency were unable to revive her. The only solace Paa got in all this tragedy was the son Gail had given him: thirteen-year-old Lee.

"Getting time away from work will be tricky. But if all goes well in court today, I will have a party at Mambo Leo hotel. Come by, and we can squeeze in an interview," Deborah said.

"What about tomorrow"? Paa countered. He wanted to have her to himself and the crowded party would not do.

"Tomorrow is packed. I have a CLEAN event" Deborah said triumphantly. CLEAN was countrywide communal cleaning initiative she had started years ago and was carried out after every two weeks.

"Oh! I almost forgot tomorrow is a cleaning weekend. Then, in that case, I will meet you at the Mambo Leo Hotel."

Paa swallowed his disappointment. He had hoped for a more private venue away from prying eyes where he could ask Deborah why she avoided him so much. The two then lapsed into a comfortable silence. From his shared history with Deborah, Paa knew that she guarded her mornings jealously. She reserved them as her reflection time. A passerby looking at the couple would have gotten the picture of a smart married couple, comfortable in each other's company.

Minutes later, they watched as several traffic policemen, their luminous green overcoats screaming authority, walked up the road, disentangling the mess one car at a time. Soon, the traffic started flowing. Deborah dropped Paa near the building housing his Weekend Dossier, and she sped off to the valley where her offices were located. Her nine partners were waiting for her so that they could go over the closing arguments for the Xamcom case.

Praxedes Tangazo and Governor Risper Fundi were following the Xamcom case in Praxedes's fifth-floor office at her WAMO Media headquarters. A TV screen placed on a coffee table was beaming the proceedings live. They had been compiling a list of credible men they could bring on board once the women caucus agreed on their presidential flag-bearer the following day.

"I wonder why Xamcom took so long to realize the danger they were frolicking with. Their rivals have begun inheriting their disgruntled clients," Praxedes said as she took a sip of the freshly made mango juice that her personal assistant had placed before them.

"They must have underestimated the gravity of the case. Deborah is going to wake them up." Governor Fundi was like a proud mother. Her eyes which were focused on the screen connected with the presidential candidate they had in mind: Deborah Binti Nzingha. She looked quite outstanding in a simple navy-blue skirt suit which hung snugly on her body. Her hair was swept into a tight bun to reveal a clear face with just a hint of brown lipstick on her lips.

"I hope she will accept the proposal," Praxedes said warily.

"For days I have been sipping milk to quiet my ulcers. Suppose she turns us down?" Risper asked.

"We have to convince her. She is the only viable ticket in town. She has the skills, the education, and the presence. Most importantly, she doesn't have any dark secrets to contaminate her image." Praxedes's voice was confident. Were she not engrossed in her analysis of Deborah, she would have observed the alarmed look on Governor Fundi's face at the mention of people harboring dark secrets. Risper knew exactly where Deborah's secret was buried, and she held the only key.If it ever came out, the whole presidential idea would receive unwarranted publicity before it fully formed. God forbid.

A pensive silence hung over them until one of senior producers popped his head in and beckoned Praxedes.

"Pray and keep your fingers crossed" Praxedes said as she stepped out. Passing through the conference hall, she paused briefly to consult with the conveners of the River Maru demonstration. Five men and three women had spread a large map of Wemppe City on the table. With red marker pens, they were highlighting the roads from which different groups were to start the demo. Their aim was to inconvenience as many people as possible. This, they believed, would stir people to empathize with the people of Amusitu whose water supply had been tampered with. They expected their efforts would force SECOB to revoke the license for the project.

"I think it looks good already," Praxedes said as she turned to face Amos Juma, the chief campaigner and convener of The Save River Maru Demonstration.

"Any sign from the middle-aged male bracket? Praxedes enquired. Lately the pursuit for justice in Kawemppe seemed to have been left in the hands of women and youth.

"Madam, don't even ask. They have been neutered into complacency," Juma replied sadly. Despite being wheelchair bound, Amos never shied away from controversy. He led from the front. Twenty-five years ago, he had led his comrades at Wemppe University in the infamous week-long protest against hiked tuition fees. To break the stalemate, the university administration called in the riot police, at which point a trigger-happy police officer had left Amos permanently paralyzed from the waist down. A bullet had shattered his spinal cord. He still had a bullet wedged in his spine. A team of surgeons had agreed that it was best left as it was; any tampering could cause neck-down paralysis.

"It is sad to see grown men go mute in fear. All the same, do not forget that we start the demo after the Xamcom ruling has been made."

"Absolutely," Juma replied. When the Save River Maru group approached Deborah to take the case to court, she had suggested they go the demo way. "Wemppeans have a tendency of ignoring their rights to rot and decay before they run to the courts for remedy.

"It is about time they felt the plight of their brothers and sisters," she had said.

Deborah Binti Nzingha was to lead the protesters once she was through with the case. Her aim was to deliberately drag the same media covering the Xamcom ruling into the heart of the demo.

In Praxedes's office, Governor Fundi watched the panel of three ladies and the four men file into the courtroom in their customary Supreme Court red robes. The court room was brimming full with lawyers and eager Wemppeans who did not want to miss the ruling of the classic case. After the preambles, Deborah took to the floor confidently.

"Your Worships, Xamcom knew all along that it was breaking the law," Deborah opened in a firm but polite tone. For the many months that the Xamcom trial had been on, Risper had heard people comment that Deborah had educated Wemppeans on the law. Her knack for breaking down legal jargon into simple understandable language was unparalleled. But it was her character that the Governor Fundi admired the most. Deborah's demeanor conveyed empathy and respect—the kind that forced people to improve on their own manners.

For thirty minutes, Deborah Binti Nzingha outlined Xamcom's malpractices. They were shameful. For over a year, Xamcom had deliberately disconnected customer's calls ten seconds after they had thumbed the end call button on their mobile phones. The fraud had netted the company billions of weras in profits from their eight million subscribers. Deborah proceeded to inform the court how millions of customers had raised the concern over the discrepancy, but the dissatisfied subscribers had been tossed between Mbilia, Pierre, and Quyakhu's customer care teams. The complaints had been in vain, as no answers ever came back. For the record, Deborah pointed out that Xamcom's customer care office was based in the neighboring country of Gumbotswi, to cut down costs, while educated Wemppean youths were idle at home and on the streets. "Why did Xamcom find it necessary to locate these offices abroad?" she asked.

In their defense, Xamcom had blamed a defect in their software which their technicians had only recently discovered. Governor Fundi could not help but laugh aloud as she observed Xamcom lawyers begin to jot furiously in their notebooks. The defense was a stern looking group of three men and a lady dressed in expensive navy-blue suits.

Governor Fundi cheered Deborah on. "Flatten them, girl!"

In conclusion, Deborah accused Xamcom of secretly subscribing over five million of its customers into unsolicited services, including trivia competitions, sports updates, and daily horoscopes without their authorization. To illustrate the malpractice, Deborah cited the case of an eighty-year-old grandmother from Solanga County who had gotten unsolicited British premier league football updates daily and been diligently billed for the same for three years. The Xamcom lawyers attempted to cite grandchildren playing with the elderly woman's phone. The old lady had never had children, let alone grandchildren. Xamcon's excuse prompted loud grumbling to break out in the courtroom. It was effectively silenced by the legendary "You can all be tossed out of this court room right now look" of the no nonsense chief justice.

"How is it going?" Praxedes asked as she walked back into her office.

"Deborah has them. I think it's a clear win."

"Fantastic. So far, so good. The analysts are already in studio," Praxedes said. The analysts were trusted men and women ready to exploit Deborah's victory in the Xamcom case until every Wemppean, young or old, could spell the word Nzingha backwards in their sleep.

Satisfied, the two women listened to the lengthy verdict keenly. At last, the court awarded the plaintiff two hundred billion weras. The court award was unprecedented. Risper and Praxedes leapt out of their chairs, shouting in joy. Louder shouts and honking vehicles could be heard on the streets below.

"She has done it!" Risper said choking with emotion.

"I think fate has placed Deborah at center stage where her services are needed," Praxedes said. "Put on your sneakers, Risper. We have a demo to attend."

The demonstration started twenty minutes later at the Madiba Park. Deborah arrived on time towing a pack of journalists behind her. Each was dying to ask her questions. After the pandemonium had died down, Deborah had made the obligatory victory statements on the court steps. When the journalist began calling out more questions, she had abruptly excused herself and disappeared into the wash rooms with her team. They had emerged a few minutes later donning sneakers and white T-shirts with Save the Maru River stenciled on the front. The journalists' curiosity had grown wilder.

"You have just won a land mark case on behalf of the people. Are you going to sue the developer interfering with the Maru?" Anita Mzinga of Reke TV asked, prompting a forest of microphones to be thrust in front of Deborah's face.

"I believe that as Wemppeans we need to get involved in our destinies and learn that not every problem has to wind up in a court room when we can do something about it. I will be taking more of your questions once we reach Madiba Park," Deborah said before she eased into the waiting multitude that began chanting and waving placards. Amos Juma rolled his wheel chair and led the way.

# CHAPTER

# 4

EVENTUALLY, A WEARY DEBORAH trudged into her sixth-floor office as darkness descended on the vibrating Wemppe City. The vigorous Save the Maru River walk had left her sweaty. Flinging her body onto a settee, the only remaining piece of furniture in the office, Deborah looked at her personal belonging, which had been packed and boxed up by Geraldine, her assistant. Geraldine had been having difficulties about moving on with her life and Deborah summoned her.

"Have you decided what you want for yourself?" Deborah queried.

"I am stuck between taking up a teaching course, pursuing my modeling career, or retaining my slot here. Without you, it will not be the same," Geraldine said. She was a slender and stunningly beautiful woman. She had two lotion commercials under her belt and could be dithery at times.

Deborah smiled as she remembered the few boyfriend dramas that had pursued Geraldine all the way into the office. "You know my phone number. Get in touch once you make up your mind," Deborah said and rose, indicating the meeting was over, but Geraldine remained seated. When Deborah looked at the young lady, she saw tears in her eyes.

"Deborah I just wanted you to know that you were the best boss I have ever had, and I will surely miss you," Geraldine said as she stood and gave her boss a hug.

"Thank you, Geraldine. If you have any difficulty in charting your career path, there is this life coach I know who can help you prioritize."

When Geraldine left, Deborah exhaled with relieved gratitude for having enjoyed a short but successful career. It was a relief for her to know that when the clock struck midnight, Nzingha and Co. Advocates would belong to her nine partners who had bought her off. She had signed all the necessary transfer papers in advance. The ten percent commission she would retain from the Xamcom payout meant she could retire comfortably and raise her kids in peace. Rising up, she opened the mini fridge and reached for a bottle of Majani iced tea and uncorked it while swiping her vibrating phone.

"Mummy, you are all over the TV." AJ's voice was incoherent with excitement.

"What about?" Deborah asked her seven-year-old son.

"The man on TV says you have caught a tiger called Xamcom by the tail. Will you bring it home?"

"If you promise to build a cage for it," Deborah replied. She could hardly contain her laughter. From the background, she heard a slight tussle before Goldie, her eleven-year-old daughter, sounding all grown up, took charge of the phone.

"Hi mum. You are all over the news. A bit of you in court and a piece of you at the demo. We are almost going blind from staring at your face," Goldie said proudly.

"Is it a good or bad thing?"

"The bomb! All my friends are calling me up, wishing their mums were as cool as you are."

"Oh, thank you. You are my BFF," Deborah responded.

"You're welcome mum. Can we come for the party?" They had talked about this and Goldie knew that Deborah's retirement party was an adult-only affair. The little girl knew how to get pushy.

"You know the answer, girl," Deborah said. She heard her grandmother Nana Tabitha say something from afar.

"What is Nana saying?" she asked.

"Oh yeah. Nana says you are not to kill yourself with work."

"I won't. Tell her not to wait up on me tonight. I might be very late. Let me have AJ now."

"He is not nearby, but I can hear him hammering away somewhere. It is just a matter of time before he hammers his finger." Mother and daughter sighed knowingly. After AJ had watched a handyman construct their chicken coop, he had developed a strong affinity for the hammer and could be found hammering nails all over the place.

"Then please ensure he tackles his homework."

"Sure, Mum. Bye. Don't forget to bring us a piece of the cake." Like her late father, Goldie had a sweet tooth.

"Ok. Back to your books," Deborah said. In response, she got her a fake groan from her daughter. Goldie loved her studies.

At peace with her children's welfare, Deborah took a sip of the iced tea and felt the cumulative tiredness of the day came rushing at her. Lately she had been sleeping for less than four hours a night as she prepared for the case with her loyal team. She knew she was going to miss them. Her thoughts went back to the early days at the firm. Her late husband, Nzingha, had started it from a rented cubicle in downtown Wemppe twenty years before. The determination and hard work he had sowed in the early years was just beginning to flower when his life had been cut short. A whimper of pain escaped Deborah's lips. She reached for a tissue and dabbed away the tears in her eyes. *Nzingha had deserved to live and enjoy the fruits of his hard work,* she thought. Her crying escalated as she thought about the dark period shortly after Nzingha's demise. His relatives, led by her mother-in-law, Rael, had turned against her and forcefully grabbed all of her properties. She would have lost her mind if her grandmother Nana Tabitha had not consoled her with her earthy wisdom.

"Have they cut your hands or stolen your brains? Give them the things they are demanding. What are material things in comparison to losing a gentle giant like Nzingha?"

Deborah had moved to an apartment and rebuilt her life from scratch. If only Nzingha could wake up now and see her new mansion and the six-story ultra-modern glass and stone plaza housing the law firm. He surely would be proud. Wiping her tears, Deborah listened as the offices hummed with activities. To her, it seemed that the hum was persuading her not to severe her ties with it.

Afraid of the lure of nostalgia, she kicked off her dusty sneakers and padded barefoot into the bathroom.

The senior partner's offices had all been designed as mini suites, complete with a kitchenette, a bathroom, and a sleeping cove. After a brisk shower, she stepped out in a terry robe. Expertly she unclasped her hair and combed it gently before slipping on a simple knee-length red dress. They had spotted it while shopping with her friend Josephine. Both had simultaneously approved of it. Sparkly ruby earrings matched the large red and blue Masai bead choker. The set had been a valentine gift from her late husband. Straightening up in front of the mirror, she agreed that she looked good, even if she was only telling herself. Happy with the results, she aimed the nozzle of her favorite perfume generously behind her ears and under her armpits, giving a final, fast swoosh up and down her entire body. "I don't regret the decisions I have made," Deborah said aloud.

"Whom are you talking with girl? Open up this door." It was Aphia, one of the partners in the firm. She was jabbing the door handle impatiently. Jossy and Salamaa could be heard laughing outside Deborah's office.

"A minute, girls" Deborah said and flung the door open. Her three friends breezed in. They were all dressed in party mode.

"I knew it! You weren't locking yourself here for nothing. Pinch me if you don't cause some man a heart attack," Aphia announced as the three women circled around Deborah approvingly.

"You look like a young Diahann Carroll," Jossy said as she took out her phone and clicked a few snaps.

"That perfume smells like a combination of roses," Salamaa declared. She sucked in deep breaths of the intoxicating perfume before reaching for the bottle and dousing herself liberally. Salamaa had worn a smart black knee-length kitenge dress with large leafy golden prints. The tailor had played with the pattern at the bust, making it appear like one continuous golden leaf.

"You really are serious about this retiring thing" Aphia said. She was short and plumb and had a big burst. The stretchy black dress she wore hugged her calves flatteringly. Jossy, a pediatrician, was arguably the most beautiful of the quartet. She looked like a pop star in a leopard print dress that had thigh-high slits. Her feet were encased in high-heeled ankle-length velvet boots.

"I have talked with Nana, AJ, and Goldie and told them to expect you sometime next week. They are so excited that you are on all the TV channels," Jossy, who happened to be AJ and Goldie's doctor, announced. The women were like aunts to Deborah's kids. She could not have wished for better friends. Losing Nzingha would have been unbearable were it not for her friends, who had stepped in and given her the solace she needed. They had stayed in her house in shifts until she found her feet.

"Deborah, we are running late for your party and don't forget that we are walking to the hotel courtesy of your demonstration. It has gridlocked the town." Jossy's voice was accusatory

"It is not my demo. It is our demo. We need to sharpen our social consciousness."

"Sorry, I had forgotten I was talking with a lawyer." Jossy's mockery cracked the ladies up. Deborah grabbed her hand bag and sprang out the door determined not to look back at her past life. She had a retirement party to attend. Thankfully, Mambo Leo Hotel was only three blocks away. As she turned to the lift, her phone rang. It was Governor Fundi wondering whether they could meet by Tuesday. She had something urgent to share.

"Aich! Whose frozen hands are those?" Deborah asked as she shivered. Very cold little hands were burrowing at her back like earthworms.

"Mine" AJ answered and giggled naughtily at the effect his cold hands were having on his mother. Every Saturday morning the children tip-toed into her room and snuggled under the covers close to her like little pups. This was her way of making it up to them for being absent all week long.

"Mum, how was the party? Did you bring us some cake?" Goldie asked.

"Yeah, fetch my hand bag from the dresser." Deborah lovingly observed her daughter Goldie. She looked taller than her eleven years. The kid took long steps towards the dressing table. *This girl will be a beauty one day*, her mother thought. The sharp cheek bones and high forehead inherited from her father had mixed with Deborah's mop of hair to great effect on the girl. Retrieving the little square cake wrapped in a serviette, Goldie broke it up into two uneven pieces and gave AJ the smaller piece.

"This is unfair Goldie. You always give me the smaller piece," AJ cried out while looking at the miniscule piece of cake.

"Yes. That is because you are also little," Goldie answered.

Deborah loved to listen to her kids bickering. Goldie's arguments came thick and fast like a lawyer's. AJ was slow and reflective in his thinking, just like his grandfather Mzee Abraham had been.

"Mum, is it true that little kids should get smaller shares of everything?" AJ asked.

Deborah felt Goldie pause from her chewing to hear the reply. Out of all the complicated cases Deborah had handled in her law career, her children's spats challenged her the most. How could she remain fair without taking sides?

To avoid a direct answer, she changed the topic.

"Be careful now. Do not spill cake on my bed," she said and drew up the covers to shield her brood from the morning chill. The chill normally set the stage for the blazing sun later in the day. The two children snuggled closer to their mother. They were soon lulled by their mother's warmth and fell asleep again.

A senseless dream Deborah had had that night resurfaced in her memory. She vividly remembered how it had started. She had been sitting at a crowded bus stop when a bus pulled up. Having hoisted her suitcase to the carrier, the bus conductor had urgently beckoned her to get on board. But she could not move. Her legs had become heavy like lead poles. Irked by her hesitancy, the crowd milling around the bus stop had started shouting at her, but she'd remained rooted to the spot. Annoyed, the bus driver had threatened to drive off without her. But her legs could not move. The crowd had begun jostling towards her. Pulling and groping, they had propelled her aboard unceremoniously.

What baffled Deborah most about the dream was that once on board, her feet had become lighter. She had even taken over the steering wheel and started driving the bus. Mulling over its meaning gave her no clue, and she decided to forget it and start the day.

Careful not to wake her children, she slowly extracted herself from bed and pulled on a pair of jeans and a white t-shirt. Her three phones lay on the side table like guard dogs. She ignored them and disappeared downstairs to start breakfast.

"Have you slept at all?" Nana asked. She never slept a wink before Deborah's car had crunched up the driveway. "The time I heard you crawl in last evening was past midnight. You should be sleeping."

"Nana, you are forgetting one of your sermons. That a woman should sleep with one foot on the ground, ready to spring into action," Deborah countered as she looked at her grandmother fondly. At eighty-one years old, Nana still looked strong. The slight limp on her left foot caused by stroke a year ago was hardly noticeable.

"Ah, that was said to ward off laziness in young girls. Thank you for flattening them in court yesterday. They sung enough praises about you yesterday on television," Nana said. She had only acquired a grade two education which afforded her a limited repertoire in the English language. Still, that did not stop her from sensationally deducing the news on the TV. "So, how was the party?" Nana asked.

"Fantastic. Everybody I know came."

"How did you get here, considering the city was clogged up by your demonstration?" Nana's voice carried some mischief. She must have heard Paa's powerful motorcycle roaring in the dead of the night.

Paa had arrived at the party early, clad in a midnight-blue suit and a baby pink shirt. Deborah recalled how Paa's good looks had sent the wicked Aphia gasping in envy. Paa's intoxicatingly sexy cologne and good rumba moves were still fresh in Deborah's mind. After longwinded speeches and a mountain of gifts, the city was still paralyzed by traffic. Paa had insisted that he drop her off on his powerful motorcycle. He had deposited her home long past midnight.

"It was not my demonstration, Nana. How come people are accusing me for it?" Deborah countered spiritedly.

"Because we prefer to bury our heads in the sand rather than face reality."

Deborah thought about Nana's comment for a while. Nana's summation was true.

"Let me brew some tea," she said.

"You had better. Khavere has been serving us reddish river water and calling it tea."

Khavere, who had just walked in laughed at the chiding. She was hopeless at cooking and house work, but the kids loved her, and that is what mattered most to Deborah.

"Nana, criticize my cooking as much as you want because there is an alternative chef today. Next week, I will feed you raw *posho*," Khavere answered the old lady. The two women continued their good-natured bickering as they walked out to feed the hens.

Deborah walked into her spacious modern kitchen and put a pot of water on the gas burner. Other than her bedroom, her kitchen was her other favorite place in the house. It was neat and clutter free. Neat rows of kitchen utensils were arranged at eye level. It made cooking a joy. Why hide stuff in cupboards where cockroaches would fester when a few hooks and shelves would do? Loading the table with the tea and a hot pot full of pancakes, Deborah went to fetch her grandfather. On Saturdays the nurse who took care of her grandparents came at ten for his weekly checkup.

Mzee Abraham looked semi dead in his bed. What remained of his once muscular body were bones and wrinkles. Relocating her grandparents from their farm in rural Makutano County to Wemppe City a year ago had not been an easy decision. The relocation had occurred after Mzee Abraham began having recurrent episodes of memory loss. At first, it had been small things. "Who has taken my money from my shirt pocket?" Mzee Abraham would ask. Nana had wrongfully begun suspecting the farm workers Deborah had hired to help on the farm. It was not until she recovered the money within Mzee Abraham's orbit of operations that she realized that something was amiss.

As his memory deteriorated, Mzee Abraham would continue to ask for his lost money. Like a newly recruited police corporal, Nana would pat him down and recover the money from his trouser pocket or under the mattress.

"Somebody is playing tricks on me," Mzee Abraham would say with his eyes glaring accusingly at Nana. The dementia nearly broke up the loving couple. The forgetful episodes would be followed by long spells of lucidity that would cause Nana and the workers to drop their guard.

Then farm tools had started disappearing.

"Where is the machete that I kept here?" Mzee Abraham would ask, his face furrowed in anger. "Someone is stealing my tools."

"Might there be a machete you are be looking for other than the one you are holding in your right hand?" Nana would ask. By then, she was completely vexed by the devil of a disease that was robbing her kind man of his memory.

Mzee Abraham would stare at the guilty hand. A look of disbelief and shame would come to his face.

All along, Nana had been managing the situation, wishing not to burden Deborah and her young family with her woes. When contingents of excited village children began escorting Mzee Abraham home after finding him wandering and lost, Nana had decided enough was enough and called Deborah.

Deborah had suggested they move to the city where she could care for them around the clock. It was not an easy thing convincing her grandparents.

"I am not a town person. Who will look after my cows and my sheep? Mzee Abraham had asked.

"I will never plant and harvest any crop on my farm again if strangers take charge," Nana had protested.

Hell had broken loose one day when Nana suffered a mild stroke. A farm worker had called Mzee Abraham with the news. Mzee Abraham, who had been enjoying a clear spell of health, had gone to sell his bull in the neighboring Soda Baridi market.

The villagers would later conclude that the phone call was what had muddled the old man's fragile mind for good. In a state of panic, Mzee Abraham had boarded a coast-bound bus, paid up his fare with the money from sale of his bull and shuttled six hundred kilometers to Ufuoni County. He was found on the beach, disoriented and dehydrated, by a man who'd recognized his face from the numerous lost person adverts on TV and newspapers Deborah had put out. Deborah hadn't been able to take it anymore. Reluctantly, Nana who was by then recovering from the stroke, gave in, and the couple had moved in with Deborah.

Gently, Deborah woke her grandfather and began undoing the side barriers, which protected the old man from falling off the bed." Babu, we need to smarten you up for breakfast," she said. Unraveling a wad of gauze, she dipped it in warm water and began wiping his face, talking and smiling with him all the while. It was of no use, for Mzee Abraham's brain had stopped registering such things. He would never walk or talk again. As she dressed him up, Deborah made a mental note to replenish the Dettol and the massage oil for the Nurse. She then wheeled the now clean Mzee Abraham to the breakfast table.

"Mum, is today a CLEAN day? "Goldie asked while taking charge of the feeding of her great grandfather.

"You bet. My friends should be here any moment now," Deborah informed her daughter.

"Do we really have to go sweeping all the filth people carelessly discard every day?" Goldie asked as she reached for a napkin to wipe the porridge that was dribbling down her great grandfather's chin.

"Yes, as long as we keep disposing trash carelessly, we owe it to Mother Earth to clean up our mess so that she can sustain us."

Goldie pulled a face.

The first person to arrive was Josephine. She wore a pink bosom hugging t-shirt and a knee-length navy skirt. Goldie and AJ ran towards her and relieved Josephine of a carton and a large jar of honey she had in her arms. The children considered Aunt Josephine more indulgent than their own mother. When they visited her, Josephine allowed them to watch cartoons without disruptions, unlike their mother, who was always on their backs over homework and getting outside to kick a ball. Their joy escalated into yelps of delight when they unveiled the contents of the carton. Out came a cute little black puppy. The looks on their faces were priceless.

The kids were still racing after the bashful puppy, whom AJ had christened Blackie, when Dina and Zaituni drove in. Zaituni was glowing and had put on weight. In contrast, Dina looked gloomy.

"Get out of her. Someone is not pregnant!" Deborah squealed in delight as she hugged Zaituni and patted her slightly protruding stomach.

"Whatever happened to menopause at forty?" Josephine quipped as she too patted Zaituni's tummy. After checking on Deborah's grandparents, the women marched into the kitchen and demolished the remaining pancakes. Thereafter, they walked up stairs into Deborah's bedroom to snoop around and "shop" from her Wardrobe. Josephine flung open the doors of the walk-in closet. Her eye expertly ran up and down the neatly arranged clothes. She was looking for whatever new edition she could walk away with. The women never tired of shopping in each other's wardrobes this way.

"So, when did we decide to have a baby," Josephine asked while looking at Zaituni who was reclining on Deborah's bed and spooning ice cream into her beautiful mouth like there was famine.

"We didn't decide. It just happened," Zaituni replied truthfully, sending her friend rocking with laughter.

"By the way these things happen. A lady we work with thought she was past it at fifty. Last year, she developed serious stomach pains while at work and we rushed her to hospital, only for the doctor to declare that she was in advanced labor," Dina added. She was sitting on Deborah's makeup table, examining her collection of unique African ethnic earrings.

"I am happy and so is my Musa. We both look forward to baby number four," Zaituni said contentedly.

"Am happy for you. As for me, my husband would have to kidnap me and cart me off to an isolated island . . . and still things would have to be done at gun point," Josephine said. In her hand was Deborah's favorite dress, which she flung to a growing heap on the floor.

"Wee Josephine, that green dress is out of question. Girl you want to leave me practically naked," Deborah protested.

"Get used to it girl. With Xamcom's money you can buy all the factories selling green dresses," Josephine added grudgingly. She meant no harm. They all knew that the ten percent commission Deborah had gotten from the Xamcom payoff had left her a billionaire.

"By the way, what is wrong with being naked every now and then?" Josephine rejoined. Josephine, being a teacher, could be candid at times.

"Because Deborah has been auditioning for celibacy for years," Zaituni added in a sassy voice. The ice cream was gone, and she was mopping up the leftovers with her finger.

"That won't last long. There is a guy we teach with whom I want to introduce her to next time she comes by my place," Josephine added slyly.

"Let Deborah be. Who needs a guy to confuse your world and cause unbearable heartache?" Dina's voice conveyed the pain she had been carrying in her heart.

"What did Tafrija do now?" Josephine asked as she turned around to stare at Dina. The treasure hunt had lost its lure. Dina's husband, Tafrija, was an unpredictable man who had a weakness for women.

"I haven't seen him for five days now. What hurts the most is that his phone is on, yet he isn't picking my calls," Dina replied bitterly. The four women all sat on the bed and moved closer to their distraught friend. They were ready to shoulder Dina's pain.

"Sometimes I wish he would drop dead or something." The ladies listened quietly as Dina vented her disappointment.

"This time round you should leave him," Zaituni advised without thinking.

"I don't think so, Zaituni. Simply because your Musa knows the art and science of romancing a woman doesn't mean the rest of us should give up," Josephine said in reproach. The women had once tried to hammer some advice into Tafrija but it had been in vain.

The sound of an approaching car broke the huddle. Josephine, who was nearest, moved towards the big windows to see who the new arrival was.

*It must be Aphia and company*, Deborah thought. It would be a miracle, considering the state she had left them in at the party the previous evening. A tipsy Aphia had been dancing shoeless on the stage while Jossy was cuddled up in a corner with her boyfriend.

"Come and see the man Deborah has been hiding from us." With tears forgotten, Dina moved across the bed swiftly and joined the other women in time to see Paa being introduced to the new puppy by the kids. He squatted down and picked up the offered puppy, sending taut muscles rippling up and down his arms. He looked quite handsome in a grey T-shirt, faded blue jeans, and dirty cowboy boots

"Woweee! What a hunk! I don't blame you-oooh Deborah for hiding him," Josephine said in an exaggerated Nigerian accent and smacked her lips wickedly like she had tasted something tangy.

"He is not my boyfriend," Deborah began protesting. Her friends were giving her disbelieving looks.

"Great. Then let me have him if he is not your man," Dina taunted.

"Okay girls. It is not like we are tight or anything. He is just a guy I happen to have known for ages"

"Tell us another lie. Are you going to introduce us, or are we to stare through the window all day long and forget that we have some cleaning to do?" Dina asked. Coyly, Deborah led them down the stairs and into the outer yard.

"Here I am, hoe and spade ready for today's CLEAN event. Where do I begin?" Paa said sincerely and gazed at Deborah.

Deborah looked at her friends and her curious children standing eagerly around her. She cast a desperate look at her grandmother who winked at her and discerned that she was outnumbered.

"Okay, people. Meet Paa Isaya, a friend of mine."

"The guy From the Weekend Dossier" Josephine Dina and Zaituni cried out simultaneously.

# CHAPTER

# 5

T HE OVER THREE HUNDRED women began trickling into Governor Fundi and Honorable C.F. Fundi's residence shortly after nine on Saturday morning. The sun was already up, and the sweltering heat had prompted the house keeper to arrange the chairs on the well-tended lawn under the purple bloom of the jacaranda trees.

The Fundi mansion sat on a ten-acre piece of land. It was a three-story house, and its high-pillared entrance evoked a sense of calmness as one approached it. Climbing ivy clung to the pillars and proceeded to encompass the entire front wall, softening the stone structure.

Several ladies sat near a stylish gazebo that was garlanded by a climbing pink rose. A table next to them groaned under the weight of delicious snacks made by Rukia Zawadi, the legendary TV chef.

"If I'd known that Rukia was going to kill us with her baking, I wouldn't have contaminated myself with breakfast at my house," Mrs. Ziphorah Lengo, HMA chairlady, quipped as she approached Praxedes Tangazo. A plate piled high with mouthwatering pastry was delicately balanced on her left palm—several pistachio biscuits, a large slice of lemon curd cake, a slice of banana cake stuffed with cashew nuts, and her all-time favorite, chocolate éclairs.

She sat her plate down and picked one éclair and stuffed it in her mouth. "Uuuuhh, that woman can cook" Ziphorah declared as the airy pastry dissolved in her mouth and released the chocolatey goodness.

"Rukia is at another level," Praxedes concurred before going on. "So, who do you think is our candidate?"

"Who else other than me? I am as capable as the next woman," Ziphorah answered haughtily before pirouetting around like a model on a runaway. Praxedes dissolved into laughter and collapsed into a sofa, pulling Ziphorah down with her.

The place was abuzz with women conversing in small groups scattered all over the lawn.

"As your president, I will streamline Wemppeans to respect women," Ziphorah replied. "The hours that we the women put into making our families comfortable need to be respected, appreciated, and supplemented with some financial or social assistance from the government."

"I agree with you totally. A woman's labor deserves respect and support," Praxedes agreed.

Becoming serious, Ziphorah looked straight at Praxedes and said, "The woman I have in mind is Deborah Binti Nzingha. I have been following her career, and I must say, she has done well for herself. Not only that, she is a smart and tough woman. I have always been impressed by how she motivates people to keep the environment clean. The way she handled the Xamcom case proves that she is not faint-hearted. This is the kind of a person we need in the presidential palace: someone who will put things right. It is Deborah for me."

Barely containing her pleasure, Praxedes's eyes automatically began combing through the crowds of women, hoping to catch sight of Deborah Binti Nzingha. They had invited her for the meeting. Unfortunately, the scheduled CLEAN event meant she could not attend.

"I was thinking about Senator Lydia Masumbuko," Praxedes countered loudly and deliberately. Her remark invited several curious glances from the women at the neighboring tables. "Zhuu," Ziphorah clicked and twisted her neck sideways. The look on her face was that of one forced to take a cup of freshly extracted bitter aloe Vera juice."Those are the kind of women that give women in leadership a bad name," Ziphorah countered.

"Tell me about it," Praxedes said as she moved closer. "When Senator Lydia Masumbuko opens up her mouth, she spews hate, bitterness and unnecessary aggression."

"What do you mean?" Praxedes urged Ziphorah on

Praxedes's likability stemmed from her ability to connect with diverse people. Her more sophisticated friends viewed Ziphorah as an illiterate loudmouth, yet Praxedes had maintained a lasting relationship with her.

"So, don't tell me to vote for Lydia. She is a bright lady but lacks manners. Deborah Binti Nzingha is the one," Ziphorah concluded. She then drew a long sip of *ukwaju* juice from her glass. The talk around them was growing louder.

"Deborah caused the CEO of Xamcom, a powerful company, to apologize for his mistakes and compensate his customers. That, Praxedes, is my kind of woman. Hey! Receive my five."

Ziphorah laughed and smacked a sharp high five onto Praxedes's waiting palm. "Do you remember what she did to Sailor's? Ziphorah asked challengingly.

No person could forget the fate that befell Sailor Supermarkets five years ago. According to newspaper stories, an aggrieved old man had appeared at the offices of Nzingha and Co. advocates, complaining about the irregular pricing of goods at Sailor supermarkets. Deborah and her husband, Nzingha, had taken up the case.

Investigations had revealed that the shelf price of goods at Sailor's was different from the till price. Further enquiry had revealed that customers had been duped into purchasing counterfeit electronics at exorbitant prices. The supermarkets were also running a charity campaign dubbed "Save a School." They had invited customer support through collection tins placed at the till. This had turned out to be a hoax. Forced to pay for their mistakes, Sailor Supermarkets had fallen into bankruptcy and had finally folded up. Vowing revenge, the owner, Joel Malimali, had hired the lone gunman who had shot senior advocate Nzingha on the steps of St. Patmos church as he led his young family home after church service one cold morning in July.

"We are in agreement on this, Ziphorah. Deborah is our person," Praxedes said. She was happy with the way the vision was unfolding.

"Then let us mingle and sell Deborah to the other ladies," Ziphorah said while gathering the straps of her brown handbag and placing it on her shoulders.

Governor Fundi watched her best friend, Praxedes, work the room diligently. *Some decisions needed to be guided*, she thought. You leave room for wiggling around and the vision could take years to reach fruition. At ten sharp, retired naval Commander Pillar Shinyanga called the meeting to order. This she did by gently hitting her glass with a tea spoon. At five foot one, Commander Pillar's height almost matched Governor Fundi's, who stood at five feet. The diminutive sizes of the two women belied their trailblazing personalities. While Governor Fundi was a titan in politics, commander Pillar was a pioneer in the navy. Eight years before, as a three-star general, Pillar had commandeered the ship that had been ordered by President Jabali to go and rescue president Peters Sambadu of Kipepeo islands after a coup de tat. Twenty-four hours later Commander Pillar had returned to Kawemppe with President Sambadu and his family on board her ship.

It took five more minutes for the chat to die down and for the women to fully turn their attention to the commander.

"Women, are you awake?" Commander Pillar Shinyanga asked. Her strong voice automatically made people pay attention. Three hundred heads turned to listen to her.

"Yeeeesss," The women responded.

"Ok. Thank you all for coming, given such short notice. We have gathered here today to discuss weighty matters that will change the course of this country's history forever. Before we embark on the business of the day, I wish to request Bishop Priscilla Timotheo to lead us in prayer."

The Women Clergy Congress (WCC) chair, Bishop Priscilla Timotheo, took the microphone and began her prayer earnestly. "Heavenly father, this is Pricilla here, along with three hundred women gathered below your heaven today. We have come before you humbly for the sake of our families. Lord, we request you to listen to our plea. Father, you, more than any other being on earth, know what is happening to this beloved country you gave us. Corruption has skyrocketed our cost of living. Politicians have set brother against brother and sister against sister. Cartels have swallowed up jobs meant for our children. Lord, I know you have the full picture. I don't need to paint it for you. That is why I stand here with these women. Please let your hand come over us as we plan for this undertaking. Help us to put aside any weights that may drag us down. Let us view each other with tribe-less eyes. Help us discard useless gossip and self-mockery, Lord. Soften the hearts of our husbands and sons to join us in this fight." The Bishop beseeched God long and hard, confessing to any sin of omission or commission that may hinder the process. Eventually she wound up the prayer and handed the mike back to Commander Pillar.

"Our forefathers in their wisdom said that, "To hunt an elephant you require distinct skills," Commander Pillar Shinyanga began.

"We are gathered here to discuss two agendas. Firstly, we are to brainstorm over several proposals and arrive at a preferred presidential candidate. Secondly, we are to come up with our official party name. To mount a successful presidential bid in February and be on the ballot paper on December fourth is no mean task. To start us off, we are going to come up with five names through secret balloting. Thereafter, we will discuss the top three contenders and finally agree on the candidate. A word of caution, 'axes in the same basket cannot avoid knocking over each other.' Therefore, let us conduct our affairs with decorum." With that Pillar sat down.

Nominating the presidential candidate took lesser time than they had anticipated. Deborah Binti Nzingha was overwhelmingly voted in as the flag-bearer, deputized by Governor Fundi.

Agreeing on the name for the political party was a task that dominated the better part of the day.

"Ladies what do you think of PWP, Progressive Women's Party?" The question was fired by Anita Phillips, a millionaire businesswoman who had made her fortune in the aviation industry. She had promised to dispatch two of her helicopters for the duration of the campaign.

"We are a progressive and proactive group here. Our party should be inclusive of a both men and women," Bishop Priscilla Timotheo opined.

"How about UPPFENA?" This came from Mrs. Clementine Kinga Nzambe. Her presence was highly suspect, considering that her husband, Dalmas Kinga Nzambe, was the chairman of the Democratic Democracy Party which was fronting the obnoxious Mitambo Mitambo as their presidential candidate. Clementine was the chairlady of the Independence Women's League (IWL), an impactless women's institution which was heard from every five years during the electioneering period.

"Clementine, before we even hear what the fancy initials stand for, the word is too much of a mouthful. It sounds like an instrument used to brand cows. I don't think it will capture the imagination of the nation," Mrs. Ziphorah Lengo said.

There was a long history of hostility between the organizations led by the two ladies. Ziphorah's HMA had a mammoth following made up of everyday women. On the other hand, Clementine's IWL was comprised of rich society ladies who were out of touch with reality, just as the press claimed.

Smoldering, Clementine sat up more upright and gave Ziphorah a scalding stare. To forestall the impending squabble between the two women, Commander Pillar called for a lunch break. A long table set buffet style creaked with assorted Wemppean cuisine. The sight of endless jugs of assorted juices—red pomegranate juice, tangy tamarind bombed with organic honey, and rich orange juice squeezed from the irresistibly sweet oranges from the farms in Makutano County—got the ladies moving. Chef Rukia glanced at her catering crew and they lifted the foil covering the dishes. The smell of pilau wafting alongside barbecued goat ribs with the meat practically falling off the bone brokered peace and improved the general mood immensely.

After a long lunch, the debate resumed and raged on until the first stars appeared in the darkening February sky when the caucus came to an agreement. Kawemppe People's Movement (KPM) was the party that would drive Deborah Binti Nzingha and Governor Fundi to political victory.

Mission accomplished, most of the ladies left, and the remaining few retired into the house and sat in clusters as they engaged in political gossip and helped themselves to the bottles of wine a waiter had placed on the table.

"Let the girls have some fun. You know all work and no play makes Jane a dull girl," Governor Fundi teased Commander Pillar as she popped a rhumba CD into the stereo.

Risper was grateful the meeting had gone as planned. Earlier, she had spoken with her husband as he changed his flight in Amsterdam. Carey Francis had recovered his health and was on his way home. Risper glanced at her watch. Francis's plane would be landing in two hours' time. She had wanted to pick him up at the airport, but Francis would not let her leave the women unattended. Instead, she had dispatched her driver to the airport to pick him up.

As the wine mellowed the ladies, the discussions heated up and become louder. The Governor's chef wisely began circulating side plates loaded with roasted chicken drumsticks, spicy wings, and crispy potato chips.

With a glass of orange juice in hand, Praxedes began working the room, catching snippets of conversation from different corners of the vast sitting area. People were clearly in favor of a Deborah presidency.

"Did I tell you that my husband has been keeping a useless girl who is yet to know how to take a proper bath? Well, he is in for a surprise. I am not going to take this lying down. I am going to get myself a proper gigolo. What is good for the goose is good for the gander," said Uanita Phillips, the millionaire.

"Hahahahaaaaaaaa . . . wuuuuiiii." The unbridled laughter emanated from a respected high court judge who had been having her wine glass refueled a tad faster than Uanita's.

***Indeed, the girls need to have some fun***, Praxedes thought. As she moved on, she overheard a woman say, "Had God made the mistake of having men give birth and raise children, we would be extinct by now." Praxedes could not place the speaker. Furthermore, they had invited their friends who had in turn brought their friends along.

"Why should a market woman like Ziphorah Lengo contradict me? I do not belong in the same class with her." Without looking, Praxedes knew that it was the snobbish Clementine, who seemed not to have gotten over her tiff with Ziphorah.

"Politics can be painful at times," a lady in a beautiful yellow hat stated to her group of listeners.

"What pain?" Mrs. Ziphorah Lengo queried of her tipsy friends before standing up unsteadily. Praxedes stopped in her steps, expectantly waiting for what was to come.

"Who can describe pain better than women? Can men bear the labor pains women endure child after child?" Ziphorah asked and shook her rather generous tummy violently.

It was into such a scintillating atmosphere that the man of the house, Honorable C. F. Fundi walked into, having just returned to the country after a year-long break seeking treatment in Costa Rica. Behind him was his daughter Dr. Neema, hardly containing her grin as she surveyed the room full of hilariously happy women.

# CHAPTER
# 6

WHEN MITAMBO ANNOUNCED HIS intention of becoming the next president of Kawemppe republic on his Facebook and Twitter pages last November, the idea had not been well-received. It was like asking a man to wear two left shoes. Mitambo had risen fast through the ranks at the Ministry of Future Planning. He had retired as a senior economist at the youthful age of forty-five. This had left many of his peers baffled. His Bachelor of Economic Planning degree, purportedly awarded by Makonge University College (MUC), was suspect. But the great puzzle in Wemppeans' minds arose when they compared Mitambo's career as a civil servant against his massive wealth. The discrepancy was glaring. After retiring, Mitambo had gone into football management and was the secretary general of Wemppe Football Clubs (WFC).

Mitambo's declaration of presidential ambitions would have disintegrated were it not for David Tshambangala, a.k.a. Shah, his banker and Luke Anini an IT Manager in a regional hospital. These two had emerged from the skeptical masses and stepped in to help their friend Mitambo, whom they fondly called M2, pursue his dream.

In late November, the two had paid M2 a visit at the WFC headquarters and discussed his presidential quest at length. It was there that they had learned the change of plan. The sitting deputy president, Honorable Ronald Maarufu of the ruling SASA Political Party, had offered M2 the opportunity to become his running mate. It wasn't really an opportunity, as it came with two caveats. To earn his stay as Honorable Maarufu's running mate, M2 had to pay one billion Wemppeans to prove his worth, as Mrs. Victoria Maarufu put it. Two, he had to come on board with a fully kitted political party. M2 had to either buy an existing political party, or jumpstart one from the grassroots—and fast. Mrs. Victoria Maarufu had assured M2 that he would recoup his expenses within a week of ascending to power. M2 tasked Luke and Shah the task of finding him a political party for sale.

The SASA Party headquarters was a campaign manager's dream. An entire floor of the building had been dedicated to M2 coordinating his affairs. Tucked away from the distracting noises of Wemppe town center, the four-story building was equipped with state-of-the-art gizmos. Efficiency seemed to ooze from every pore of the place.

"I hope we are not late," Shah exclaimed as he climbed the circular stairway leading to M2's office. Young administrative assistants sat in front of humming computers and telephone consoles, answering questions and cold-calling would-be voters. It was early in January, but Shah and Luke had not yet found a party for sale. The truth was that they had never bothered to look for one.

Shah surveyed the unfolding scene, all the while thinking of the plum position of the SASA's logistics manager. He was sure M2 would award the position to him. In his mind, he could almost see the fleet of vehicles he would command as he hauled campaign material from one venue to another just in time for the president in waiting, Honorable Ronald Maarufu, to use. Obviously, there was no way his friend M2 would give him a lesser post.

"I heard that to get the SASA senatorial ticket, you have to shell off at least fifty million weras. For a member of parliament, it's ten million while a governor's ticket is retailing in the neighborhood of one hundred million," Luke whispered to Shah as they paused briefly on the second-floor landing.

"Whuuuee!" Shah let out a slow whistle in surprise. "Where do people get that kind of money from? For the last twenty years, we have worked from dawn to night and still haven't gotten that kind of cash."

"These politicians must be siphoning from us one way or the other," Luke said. His joyful mood was waning quickly.

"But can you blame them? Is it not us who praise the politician who has "looked after himself" and castigate the one who slept while the national cake was being shared? "Shah asked rhetorically.

"Look at it this way, Luke. If an authentic African oath like the dreaded "Kamaliza" (finisher) oath concocted by the medicine men from Ufuoni County was to be administered to all Wemppeans as proof that they have never acquired wealth illegally, how many people do you think would survive?"

Luke thought briefly about his friend's sentiments. The dreaded Kamaliza oath was a complicated spiritually bound oath, which could mysteriously clear dead the entire family of the guilty party. In its history it has a zero rate failure.

"You are right. Our ancestral oath systems would be more efficient than the courts."

M2's office on the third floor was stunning. A giant TV screen was tastefully mounted on the wall, and several guests lounged on comfortable leather sofas. Luke recognized Senator Marko Virunga and two members of parliament. The politicians ignored the two. Three mean-looking boys sat in corner playing with their phones. They were M2's security.

Each accepting a cup of coffee from the smiling secretary, Luke and Shah sank into the cream sofas and waited. The politicians were quickly seen by M2 and left. Two hours later, Mitambo emerged from his office and looked at his former friends blandly. Shah began to appraise the price of his friend's grey suit and silk tie. His mental calculator was already crunching past seventy thousand Weras when he realized that M2 had walked past them and was headed for the stairway, his security boys in tow.

Shah and Luke jogged quickly and caught up with him.

"Gentlemen, is my assignment done?" Mitambo asked while nodding at his boys to leave the two alone.

"We are on it." Luke said endearingly, eager to reestablish familiar camaraderie.

M2 placed his hands on Luke and Shah's shoulders firmly. "I have given you only one job to do, and you haven't delivered. You have ten days to find me an existing political party which I can buy, or I will get someone more competent. Excuse me, I have an important meeting with Honorable Ronald Maarufu." With that, M2 pivoted on his sleek heels and jogged down the stairs with the self-assured air of a man whose political future was carved on granite.

Taken aback by the brusque reception, the two stood stupefied. The scent of an expensive cologne was all their disappearing friend left in his wake. They would have stayed there much longer if the same secretary, who had only a few hours earlier welcomed them with a smile, had not approached in a no-nonsense manner and shoed them out.

"So, it has come to this?" Shah, sore with rejection, grumbled as he trudged behind Luke into the parking lot.

"My friend," said Luke, "we either deliver the cargo or the bus will leave without us."

In silence, they drove in Shah's second-hand Toyota across Wemppe City until they arrived at their favorite watering point, the Tokyo Makkhuti bar. Gloomily, they ordered a kilo of roasted goat ribs and some beers from a bored barman.

"How can Mitambo treat us like kids?" Luke asked when a cook placed the succulent meat on a wooden board between them. If the truth was told, the only reason they had been friends with M2, as dim as they thought he was, was the fact that money seemed to sprout around him like wild grass.

For an answer, Shah savagely sank his teeth into the succulent ribs. It seemed like he was unleashing his bottled anger on them. With his free hand, he clawed off a thick wad of *posho* from a side plate and molded it into a ball. Dipping it into a salad of chilies and avocado, he tucked the mixture into his mouth. Across the empty bar, a television set was showing a football game; a striker had just scored an easy goal and was running about the field in jubilation. The bar man chortled contemptuously at the ease the goal had been scored. Even a baby would have saved the goal. Shah, a piece of goat rib suspended midair, stopped chewing. A light bulb moment flashed in his mind.

Luke, puzzled by his friend's sudden concentration on the TV, belched and asked, "What are you drooling at?"

"I just understood a proverb my grandfather used to tell to me when I was a small boy. A man sleeps best on a hide from his own flock."

A period of silence ensued before Luke prompted his friend further. "So, what did the old man mean?"

"As the hide's owner, you are bound to be privy to its history. You can thus choose the best hide. Separate it from the ones which might have suffered wounds, branding marks, or diseases. That sort of thing."

"I'm still not getting it."

"I don't even know why I hadn't thought of this before," Shah replied before pressing on. "I am the portfolio manager of Dalmas Kinga Nzambe."

Luke didn't need to ask who Dalmas Kinga Nzambe was. Honorable Dalmas Kinga Nzambe was the chairman of the Democratic Democracy Party and had been a famous politician ten years before.

"Right now, Dalmas is as broke as a church mouse. If properly approached, Honorable Kinga Nzambe can sell his party and even hand over his son as a bonus to any willing buyer. Imagine a political marriage between Mitambo Mitambo's money and Dalmas Kinga Nzambe's DDP party," Shah concluded. His eyes were shinning.

The two men stared at each other intensely for several seconds, before giving each other a crackling high five that startled the dozing barman.

"We are rich," Luke cried out.

"Do you think he will accept our proposal? He is a very proud man. How many times has the guy been in jail?" Shah rejoined,

"Several times. When we were in primary school, do you remember the time when he was a university student leader, together with his deputy Bishop Priscilla Timotheo? They were slapped with fictious sedition charges by dictator Harvester Ochao," Luke said.

"Yeah, they were jailed for ten months and forced to write an apology letter to the president. They refused to pen the letter and instead fled to Gubwatso, where Seth Pasakhwa, who was already in exile, housed them. They caught up with their education at Gubwatso University," Shah recalled. The stories had been all over the newspapers.

"That was much later. You are forgetting that as a university student leader, Dalmas used to live in the jails of Kawemppe. Before he went into exile in Gubwatso, he wrote a letter to dictator Ochao, asking him to resign from the presidency because he was incompetent and he went in jail for a year. He then came out and was sent back to jail for eight months with Hon Francis Fundi, Praxedes Tangaza . . . eeehh, former speaker Robert Harakka and former chief justice Solomon Ngome for agitating multiparty democracy. The guy suffered for this country, my friend," Luke concluded.

"Let us go and talk to him. the worst we can get is a no," Shah said airily.

Settling the bill, they snatched their jackets and jumped into the Toyota and headed towards honorable Dalmas Kinga Nzambe's office.

# CHAPTER 7

IF EVER THERE WAS a marathoner in Kawemppe's political history, it was Dalmas Kinga Nzambe. He was the founder and chairman of the once popular Democratic Democracy Party. Ten years ago, Dalmas had been poised to win the presidential election. All indications were that he would win in a landslide victory. That was until he committed the biggest blunder of his political career. In the tense political climate of hastily cobbled together political coalitions, Dalmas had made a mortal mistake. He had chosen the then less popular Ronald Maarufu as his running mate over the more popular Honorable C. F. Fundi. The decision was to become the proverbial last nail in Dalmas' political coffin. His main rival at the time, Meshack Jabali of the SASA party, sensing Dalmas's mistake, had quickly roped in C.F. Fundi as his running mate and won the election with a clear majority. Dalmas's political fate had been sealed.

When Honorable C. F. Fundi was taken ill two years into the term, President Jabali had delivered the final blow to Dalmas's DDP Party. Sensing the political chaos, the departure of his ailing deputy would cause, President Jabali had cunningly poached Ronald Maarufu from Dalmas's DDP party and made him his new deputy. The move had officially banished Dalmas to political Siberia.

"Tea or the usual sir?" Onessi, Dalmas' house boy, asked his boss.

"Usual," Dalmas snapped at his grinning house boy and turned his attention back to the pages of The Weekend Dossier.

At sixty-two years of age, the six-foot tall Dalmas was aging well. After disappearing from politics, Dalmas had shed that glowing sheen which many politicians acquire once in office. He was trim and light on his feet.

After a short while, Onessi placed the usual on the dining table. A thermos filled with millet porridge accompanied by steaming corn on the cob. Newspaper in hand, Dalmas relocated to the huge dining table. It had once served meals filled with hearty laughter to the Kinga Nzambe clan before his children left the mold. Spreading the paper at a distance from which he could still read as he ate, he reached for a cob of maize and started munching away.

Onessi leaned on the dining room wall farthest from his boss. He looked at Dalmas with approving eyes. In his mind, he believed his boss was the most down-to-earth millionaire. According to Onessi, millionaires ate cakes and assorted breads lathered with copious amounts of honey and other spreads for breakfast. His boss was different; he had no qualms about munching boiled maize and arrow roots for breakfast. Sensing Onessi's stare, Dalmas raised his head at Onessi with a cold gaze, which sent the youth scampering into the kitchen. Annoyed with himself for projecting his anger at the poor boy, Dalmas swallowed his despair. Who would not pity him? There was a time when Kawemppe's news bulletins would be incomplete without the listeners being bombarded with . . . Honorable Dalmas Kinga Nzambe while leading a rally in . . . or . . . Dalmas Kinga Nzambe, the Democratic Democracy Party chairman, was presiding over the graduation . . . Now he was a regular target of political jokes.

Hurrying through his breakfast, he swallowed the last of the millet porridge in one gulp. He had to brace himself as the hot liquid went down his throat. Onessi was too generous with the lemon. Dalmas didn't mind, though, as he had read somewhere that lemon juice was a body-cleansing agent. Done with breakfast, he pushed the tray aside and was surprised to see his wife, Clementine, walk down the stairs fully dressed. Clementine never woke up before ten.

"Are you heading towards town?" she asked abruptly. It came as a surprise to him. They had rarely talked for over a year now, though that was a minor matter. Four years ago, when Clementine had accepted the fact that Dalmas would never be the same man he used to be politically and financially, she had moved into her daughter's bedroom upstairs. She had taken her mountain of clothes, jewelry, and makeup leaving Dalmas to nurse his political wounds alone in their cold king-size bed. Physical intimacy was a closed chapter between them.

"Yes," he answered suspiciously. He was not particularly headed to the town center but he found himself provoked by the scornful way in which Clementine had asked the question. It was like the once mighty Dalmas had been banned from casting his shadow around Wemppe City. Grabbing the newspaper, he stood up. A trip to town would also give him an opportunity to pass by his office. Being an election year, he could not rule out a few political customers stopping by to shop for nomination tickets.

Thirty minutes into the drive, they joined the Wemppe City traffic jam at its worst. Public transport minibuses aiming to beat the traffic over-lapped on both sides of the road. Their action clogged up the entire highway for hours. When the fuel light of his vintage car began to beep urgently, Dalmas cursed inwards. He needed to refuel and nearly succumbed to the thought of grabbing a jerry can and the last two hundred weras in his pocket and beckoning one of the bored bus touts to fetch him two liters of fuel from a nearby petrol station. But his ego would not let him. There was no way the chairman of the Democratic Democracy party was going to be gossiped about in the tabloids and the internet of driving around Wemppe City in a fuel-less car. Flexing his broad shoulders Dalmas tapped his fingers on the steering wheel in tune with the soothing rumba beat playing on Radio Five. Beside him, Clementine sat stonily. Her lower lip was curled in disdain. She held her handbag tightly in a manner that made Dalmas feel like a thug. The idea of asking her for a small loan remained zipped inside his mouth.

Suddenly, the traffic jam eased. Minibus drivers, who had alighted to smoke, jumped back into their vehicles and started off with maddening aggression. Dalmas stepped on the accelerator and with two jerks the car stalled. A public service minibus rammed into his car. Without a backward glance Clementine flung open the passenger door, and in one fluid movement made her way past the stalled cars and melted into the crowds on the pavement. Despite his predicament, Dalmas suppressed a smile. Her Royal Highness Clementine walking!

It was unheard of. If the circumstances were different, he would have photographed her with his mobile phone camera and posted the photo as his WhatsApp profile photo with the caption, "For better times only!"

It took Dalmas a full minute to comprehend the situation he was in. What had been a fuel problem had now escalated into an accident. Fortunately, patience and calmness were Dalmas's strongest assets. Breathing deeply, he stepped out to inspect the damage.

A worried tout, whose hair was uncombed, stood perplexed, holding a piece of a broken bumper light. Beside him, his equally confounded driver had his hands clasped behind his head, staring at the damaged vintage car. He couldn't believe that the week's profits were about to be swallowed up by the hefty repair bill.

"Mzee sorry, I had done my mathematics that you were already moving but I don't know what happened." When he realized who he was speaking to, the driver adjusted his language.

"Honorable sir, me I had photographed that you were moving; then I heard vyangalalala."

"Lads, it's okay. I'll just call the towing company. Push me to that petrol station, and I'll wait for them there."

"Mzee, thank you." The minibus crew cried out in joy. They could not believe the outcome of events. Eagerly they pushed Honorable Kinga Nzambe's car to an empty parking space inside Maple Oils Station and effusively thanked him. They then took off in haste, lest he change his mind.

"That's the beauty of rich people. They don't waste time with small issues. If it was a hustler's car we had knocked, we would still be arguing," the tout yelled at the top of his voice for the benefit of the passengers. The passengers enviously watched the rich and powerful Dalmas Kinga Nzambe, with his dome of a head shining in the early morning sun, emerge from the petrol station and stroll casually into a nearby shopping mall.

An hour of walking brought Dalmas to his office. It was located in the industrial area of Wemppe City. Hard times had evicted him from his plush offices in the city center, and he now rented a large room from a decrepit old building. He had proceeded to divide it down the middle with painted plywood to create two spacious rooms. One side was the inner office, where he attended to the few guests who ventured by. The other was for his secretary, Bibiana. He kept Bibiana for the sake of appearances, so that when people called in they could get an official sounding "Hello, Democratic Democracy Party headquarters. How can I help you?" on the phone. That way, the party would seem to be in business.

Opening the door to his side of the plywood division, he let himself in. Bibiana was yet to arrive. The musty air propelled him to open the only window which overlooked the badly plastered back wall of an adjacent mall. Hanging his jacket on a nail on the wall, he flicked the tiny TV on the edge of his desk on. All the while, he refused to think of what he was going to do with his stalled car. If only he had not paid his golf club membership the previous week, he would have enough cash for repairs. The income generated by the rental houses he owned was barely enough to educate his four children in Australia. The balance was split into two equal halves. One half inadequately covered Clementine's' expenses, including her wardrobe, hair, lotions, perfumes, gym, taxi and dining out with the girls. Dalmas' half paid all the household bills. It left him with just enough to squeeze in the occasional round of golf.

Reluctantly, his eyes wandered to the wall where several DDP Party campaign posters hung. A gigantic group photo of his current top party members—one governor, two senators, and three members of parliament who had captured different seats on a DDP ticket—stared back at him. On the left was Governor Konde, a former college professor who, upon realizing how broke the party was, had ceased all pretenses of paying his membership fees. He rarely picked up Dalmas's calls anymore. Next to the Governor were the main traitors, Senators Marko Virunga and Lydia Masumbuko. Dalmas knew that banking on Senator Lydia Masumbuko for support was harder than attempting to catch a wild guinea fowl with one's bare hands. Chances of being left clutching its tail feathers were high. Smiling innocently at the camera were the party's three sitting members of parliament—greedy individuals who hawked their loyalty to the lobbyist with the heaviest brown envelop. Functionally, the whole group had decamped to his rival Honorable Maarufu's SASA Party. They were members of DDP in name only.

Dalmas was still contemplating the state of his affairs when his mobile phone rang. He reached for it, hoping it was Clementine, who had been mugged by thugs and was now in need of his help. However, it was his elder son Michael calling from Adelaide, Australia.

"There is this dude I owe some cash, Dad," Michael began immediately after exchanging greetings with his father.

"So?" Dalmas asked gruffly. He visualized his thirty-five-year-old giant of a son who claimed to be pursuing a PhD program but was yet to show any tangible evidence of his other degrees.

"What do you mean, Daddy? My life is at stake here," Michael went on.

"And so is mine, Son." Dalmas's testy voice seemed to stall Michael's pleas. "If you can't pay the dude his money, then let him kill you. I cannot miss an empty space here in Kawemppe to bury your carcass. And by the way, don't you ever expect another cent from me again and two, stop calling me daddy like a suckling toddler. At your age, I was married to your mother and feeding your greedy mouth"

"Shit,man.. I mean . . . sorry . . . dad, I really really need some cash."

Dalmas hit the end call button cutting off his son's pathetic whining and hoped the guy wasn't hanging out with drug addicts. A slight headache began hammering behind his eyes. He slouched on his seat and stared at the ceiling. He maintained that posture for a long time until he was roused by a firm knock on the door. Bibiana never knocked. She had her own set of keys. Unsteadily, Dalmas rose to investigate.

If the sight of his banker in the company of another man surprised him, he concealed the fact well.

"Shah, please come in." Dalmas ushered in his guests just as his secretary, Bibiana, came through the door. She proceeded to store her hand bag. "Bibiana, get us some sodas please." Dalmas requested as he watched his guests ogle at Bibiana shamelessly. She was a beautiful woman in her early forties. Her dark supple skin provoked one's hand to want to touch it to confirm it was real. The bewitching gap dividing her milky white teeth had tempted many a man to attempt to woo her. They had all failed. It was a fact that had made Dalmas look at her with a fresh eye.

"So how can I help you, gentlemen?" Dalmas asked after Bibiana had uncorked the soda bottles.

Well, sir, with all due respect, we have come to request the impossible," Shah began after introducing Luke to Dalmas. "A politician friend of ours is seeking an existing political outfit to jumpstart his political journey." Shah's voice was cautious. They had agreed with Luke to be forthright in their request.

"Does this friend of yours have a name? Dalmas asked skeptically. Suppose these two had been sent by his rivals to gauge him?

"His name is Mitambo the Secretary General of Wemppe Football Clubs. He is willing to compensate you for all the inconveniences that he will cause you," Luke said convincingly.

Dalmas was affronted but remained silent. How could a hooligan like Mitambo want to buy his party? He listened, ill at ease, as Shah and Luke, the two power brokers, made their presentation. The proposal was too good to be true. He became suspicious. How could he trust the two men? "What you have shared here is interesting. It pleases me to see young people interested in politics," Dalmas said cagily while ruthlessly weighing the situation. Suppose he let a genuine opportunity pass him by? "You all know that if you are interested in marrying a particular girl in Kawemppe, then you should start thinking of the dowry," Dalmas said.

Shah and Luke nodded their heads uniformly.

"Things have to be done in a procedural manner. So, before we embark on any further negotiations, gentlemen, we need to be reading from the same page. You have to subscribe and become official members of the DDP."

"How much is the subscription fee?" Luke asked eagerly.

"Fifty thousand apiece," Dalmas answered without missing a beat. He watched unbelievably as his visitors grabbed their wallets and began counting one thousand denomination weras. At the sight of the money, different thoughts began flashing through his mind. They even managed to push the headache away. Could it be that he was back in business? Censoring any enthusiasm from his voice, he called Bibiana to issue an official receipt.

For over three hours Shah and Luke negotiated with Dalmas the terms of engagement right down to the 'compensation for inconveniences' and who got what share.

"Gentlemen, I will meet Mitambo on Saturday," Dalmas stated and stood up. He walked his guests to the door and shook their hands firmly as they parted.

After his guests had left, Dalmas impatiently waited for some minutes to pass. With utmost control, he rose from his desk, pulled on his jacket, and sidled over to Bibiana's desk. She was playing solitaire on her screen.

"Give me seventy thousand and use the balance to pay any pending bills," Dalmas said nonchalantly.

Bibiana made a few more clicks with her mouse before pulling open the top drawer of her desk and handing Dalmas the cash. He arranged the notes carefully in his wallet, closed the door behind him and galloped towards his beloved Mercedes. He was back in the ring.

Saturday found Dalmas Kinga Nzambe waiting for Mitambo at Savannah Big Five Hotel. Dalmas had arrived early and secured a private suite at the farthest end of the ground floor. On the face of it, Dalmas looked like a millionaire. The expensive black and white golf shoes, a checked navy designer blazer, and a gold wrist watch had caused the waitress to flirt with him as she handed him the glass of red wine he had asked for. She then vanished and left Dalmas in the company of the blaring TV.

On channel five was the contented face of Honorable Ronald Maarufu, addressing a massive campaign rally in Makutano County. Dalmas stared at his nemesis with open hatred. Without doubt, Ronald Maarufu was poised to be the next president of Kawemppe, he thought bitterly. No wonder his DDP people had defected to SASA Party, leaving him as bereft as a pastor presiding over an empty church.

"No one writes off old Dalmas," He said to himself for encouragement. He felt no remorse for wanting to sell the party. Times had changed. He had studied Wemppeans over the course of many years. They were not keen on political processes. Therefore, party ideologies and integrity were no longer virtues admired by the voter. Voters seemed dazzled by scumbags—people like Senator Virunga, senator Masumbuko, and Mitambo Mitambo. Men and women who belonged to the abracadabra school of politics. Con artists who suddenly burst into the political scene with zero Ubuntu but with big money and endless razzmatazz to hold hostage the ordinary voter into thinking that they were about to be rescued.

His thoughts were cut short by the hotel supervisor who knocked and ushered in Shah and Luke accompanied by Mitambo and his gang of mean-looking thugs who acted as his bodyguards. Dalmas had forgotten about the security entourage Mitambo was known to surround himself with. In angst, he gazed at the four hoodlums as they took strategic positions around the luxury suite in a manner that reminded him of a Mafia movie he had once watched. Noting the dark frown looming on Dalmas's face, Luke whispered something to M2 that saw the bodyguards leave the room at once.

With the goons gone, Dalmas relaxed tremendously. He greeted the overdressed middle-aged man in front of him warmly. "Mitambo, Kawemppe is not such a big country, yet our paths have never crossed. I admire the commendable work you are doing with football across the country." The compliment was untruthful.

Mitambo took the praise in his stride and smiled at his host.

As the secretary general of Wemppe Football Clubs, Mitambo, ran his affairs in a corrupt manner. The annual WFC elections produced some of the most violent clashes ever witnessed in Kawemppe's football history. Luke had been nervous that Dalmas might not like M2, but upon noting Dalmas's charming reception, he began to breathe easier. Luke recalled a lecture his leadership and governance professor had once given during his campus days: "Political power lies with the financiers and the cartels. The general public is brought on board much later"

After a while the men got down to business. Shah and Luke took the sofa while Dalmas and Mitambo faced each other across the coffee table.

Dalmas, unaware of the mission Mitambo had to undertake for Ronald Maarufu, went on. "Honorable Ronald Maarufu thinks he has won this thing lock, stock, and barrel, but he needs to work harder. Young people want one of their own to lead them. Honorable Mitambo, you have history on your side."

Dalmas sounded earnest although he wished Mitambo had dressed in more discreet clothes. The plaid red suit and thick gold chains dangling from Mitambo's neck were spoiling the Zen of the deal.

"True" M2 replied.

It was becoming apparent to Dalmas that Mitambo's political experience was limited. Conjuring up some enthusiasm, Dalmas officially began the transaction.

Shah stood up with the prepared documents in his hands and hovered over the group like a deacon assisting his Bishop in a ceremony. He wanted signatures appended before anyone could change their mind. The money at stake defined everyone's future.

"Let us start off with the party business," Dalmas began. "The DDP presidential ticket goes for one hundred million weras non-negotiable," Dalmas looked coolly at Mitambo. He calculated the value of the gold hanging on his neck and realized that it could raise a half of the required amount. This first amount was to be split fifty-fifty between Dalmas, Shah, and Luke. Detecting no hesitancy on Mitambo's part, Dalmas proceeded. "We need to rope in the media and ensure DDP Party does not attract negative publicity."

"As in advertisements?" Mitambo asked bluntly.

"Not really. The media is composed of newspapers, columnists, editors, and producers of news, both on TV and radio. These people shape history by telling Wemppeans what they want them to hear. If we don't pay homage to the media, then you can become a non-person." Dalmas knew this first hand. He was the walking advertisement for media black outs. The news coverage he used to enjoy in his heyday was now but a memory. "That will cost another one hundred million just to keep those guys happy enough to award you three minutes on TV and several sentences in their newspapers."

The point made sense to Mitambo, and he nodded his head. Dalmas flicked his eyes towards Mitambo. There was no reaction, no opposition, and no bargaining. Dalmas could barely contain his delight. He began to wonder whether this was how he had been reacting to issues years ago when he was being fleeced of his money.

Dalmas's idea to pacifying the media involved a round of golf with Elijah Lmbatwa, who enjoyed a quarter-page opinion column in the Wemppe Gazette. Two million werras was all Dalmas was planning to give the seventy-year-old Lmbatwa. The rest of the media seemed too obsessed with Honorable Ronald Maarufu to notice whether Dalmas and his DDP party were alive or dead. Shah and Luke were not aware that the rest of the ninety-eight million Weras was Dalmas' and his alone.

"Last but not least . . ." Dalmas paused and smiled cunningly. It was the ace he had kept up his sleeve.

When Luke and Shah had negotiated for their cut, they had overlooked many aspects of the transfer. In his possession, Dalmas had an extensive database of men and women—a team that could be prodded to get up and running politically in a moment's notice if the money was right. He had built it over the years and it came at a cost.

"Mitambo, the DDP has over two million active members—capable men and women who can easily deliver the presidential palace into your hands." Dalmas spoke with emphasis.

That piece of news brightened Mitambo's face. He was sure Honorable Ronald Maarufu would be impressed if he brought on board two million votes in one swoop. Shah and Luke looked at each other, startled. They had underestimated Dalmas. The political veteran was about to exploit their political naivety by charging M2 a fee that they could not touch. They had not considered that angle in their negotiation.

"Honorable Mitambo, for six hundred million Weras I will deliver the DDP party to you, together with its two million members," Dalmas said quietly.

The statement caused Luke and Shah to stare at Dalmas with newfound respect. Trust a politician to be one corner ahead.

Dalmas had wanted to say two million "active" members, but that would have been an exaggeration. He reached into his coat pocket and removed a hard disk, which contained the said names, and placed it on the table.

Mitambo reached for the disk and looked at it gleefully.

"And how will I recover the money?" Mitambo enquired.

"That is not a question. The fee I am charging you is peanuts compared to the deals and contracts you will sign on behalf of Wemppeans. They come with handsome reward," Dalmas countered smoothly.

Victoria Maarufu had told him the same thing. As a life member of the corrupt cartel society, M2 knew it was true.

"What is the total? I want to deliver the money today." Mitambo enquired abruptly to every one's surprise.

"Eight hundred million," Shah replied.

"Wait here. I will be back with the money in two hours' time," M2 said as he left the suite. He was slightly disappointed. He had been prepared to spend at least one billion Weras to acquire the DDP Party.

As M2's personal banker, Shah was taken aback. M2 did not have that kind of money in his account. He had checked. *Where else could Mitambo be keeping his money?* he wondered. Such a hefty amount of money required serious paperwork before it could be released from any bank. Obviously, the dude had other vaults where he kept his cash.

The two hours was spent arguing over the six hundred million Dalmas's had negotiated for himself. Shah and Luke wanted a share, but Dalmas was not ready to hear any of that.

"For a very cheap price, I am offering you a ready-made historical outfit. I have labored to put it together for the last thirty years—paid blood, sweat, and tears for it—and you are still complaining?" Dalmas riled at them. His face had a dangerous look that deterred his audience from pursuing the matter further.

Thirty minutes after dismissing his body guards, M2 sat on his haunches, stirring up an underground water tank with a metal pole. He could feel the pole hit the precious cargo buried in the depths of the water. Glancing at his watch, he realized that he had less than an hour twenty minutes to bring the entire cargo to the surface and deliver it to the people he had left at the hotel before they began to think of him as a joker just like the rest of Wemppeans. It was about time people realized M2 was a man to reckon with.

He had run out of patience with the annoying Wemppeans who had a habit of ridiculing him—especially his endeavors as the chair of the football association. He desperately craved to have people fear and respect him. He wanted to be a man among men.

The idea to metamorphose and become a feared legend had begun when M2's former employer, the Ministry of Future Projects, was allotted a budget of fifty billion weras to prepare for the Common Wealth Games. M2 had smelled a rare opportunity. Quitting his civil service job, he had ruthlessly contested for the chairmanship of Wemppe Football Club and won. The post had enabled him to control the massive kitty of ten billion Weras his former ministry awarded the federation to upgrade stadia and other sports facilities in preparation for the games. Over time, he had quietly siphoned off over five billion weras and stashed the loot in his house. When it had become too risky to keep the money in his house, he had begun to look for alternative avenues. Innocently, he began to solicit advice from his friends.

"With the recent bank heists, I wonder how the thieves manage to conceal their ill-gotten millions from the police," Mitambo tested the waters one evening over drinks with his boys. Robbers had struck a bank the previous day, escaping with over one hundred million weras, so his question did not seem odd.

"Uuuh . . . easy, just get a trusted banker to wire it to the Bahamas," Sadiki, his friend, had advised.

"That will attract the cops or the tax man. Just bury it in a pit latrine," said Phillip.

They had all laughed at the latrine idea except Mitambo who had remained pensive. He had ordered another round of beer for his friends and probed the latrine idea further.

"You can't risk paper money in a latrine. It would decay from all that heat and the muck, right?"

Phillip defended his idea convincingly. "Not if you pack the cash in old car tire tubes and tie it tightly with non-corroding wire before anchoring it in the muck with a heavy stone."

Sadiki thought the idea could work. "I would improvise. If I were one of those thugs, I would buy an isolated piece of land somewhere. Let us say on the outskirts of Wemppe, and then excavate an underground water tank. I would then build a simple site house on top of the tank.

Once I was through, I would fill the tank with water and stash my tubes of cash safely.

"Then how would you spend it once the cops stopped looking for it? Mitambo had asked casually. If only his friends had known the amount of cash he was thinking of stashing away.

"Buy large tracts of land all over the country. A beach plot in Ufuoni or maybe a hotel. The options are endless," Sadiki said.

"No. That will involve paper work. Your name will pop up in the government systems, and people would start asking questions. I would do two things," Phillip advised.

"Start a church from scratch and gradually bank the loot as offering. Everyone knows that churches are tax exempt and keep poor records of monies received. Alternatively, one can contest an election. Nobody is keen about where political money come from," Phillip had concluded as the conversation had drifted to other topics.

Mitambo had settled for the latter idea. Over time he had buried five billion Weras in different water tanks on different plots on the outskirts of Wemppe City. Now, an opportunity had presented itself to launder the loot, and bank it with the rest of his money. The eight hundred million Weras Democratic Democracy wanted was a small cost to pay.

Twenty minutes later, with every muscle in his body complaining bitterly, M2 fished out the pallets of cash. He deftly cut off the metal anchor and wires binding the tubes with pliers. Crisp one-thousand-wera bundles smiled back at him. Rapidly, he shoved the stacks of money into eight large gym bags and transferred them to his minivan.

Getting rid of any telling signs on the site, he took a speedy shower and drove back to the Savannah Big Five Hotel.

Shah, being the experienced banker that he was, counted the cash in short order. Satisfied that all money agreed upon was there, he nodded towards Dalmas Kinga Nzambe.

"Gentlemen the Americans have a favorite saying, which I want to borrow. Let's roll!" Dalmas said and rose up. He boisterously pumped M2's hand and ushered him out of the door. With M2 gone, Shah divided the money as earlier agreed under Dalmas' hawk eyed supervision. Dalmas's share filled six gym bags, which he hauled to his car and left. Afraid of being followed by thugs, he cruised up and down deserted highways with his eye on the rearview mirror until he was sure that no one was following him. He then called his wife Clementine. She picked the call on his third attempt

"What is it?" Clementine shot back,

"Are you free for dinner?" Dalmas threw the olive branch.

"I am not hungry," Clementine retorted and disconnected the call.

"Well, Clementine, the tide has changed. I am sorry should I leave you behind," Dalmas said aloud to himself. He then dialed Bibiana's number. He had been thinking of a tool shed he had spotted in Bibiana's compound one rainy night when he had dropped her off at home. He could store the loot there as he contemplated how to make it legitimate.

"Can you serve a passing stranger with a late lunch?" he asked once Bibiana picked up the phone.

"Does the stranger happen to like fried chicken, served with *posho* and a side plate of greens fried in sour cream sauce?" she queried.

"Very much so," Dalmas replied. His taste buds were provoked by the picture of lunch Bibiana had painted for him.

"Then tell that stranger to be here in forty minutes. I have popped some malt beers in the fridge and I don't want them to get too chilled," Bibiana answered coyly. Strangely, Dalmas felt as excited as a little school boy. Apart from his excited taste buds, other parts of his body resurrected and become alert. He stepped on the fuel pedal and gunned the car towards Bibiana's, occasionally glancing at the side mirrors to ensure that M2 had not sent one of his goons after him.

# CHAPTER 8

GOVERNOR FUNDI'S HOME OFFICE was tucked in the mansion's attic. It offered a bird's eye view of the large estate. Its décor was a combination of cozy armchairs on one wing and an imposing library on the other side. The library held a large collection of leather-bound books, ranging from medical volumes to autobiographies. Risper was a voracious reader and kept abreast of new inventions in the medical field. She subscribed to several medical journals. A simple PC rested on her reading desk. Earlier in their marriage, the Fundis had attempted to share Carey Francis's mahogany-paneled office downstairs, but they had found the arrangement destructive. They had talked more and worked less; thus Risper had relocated to the attic.

The Governor and Praxedes sat on the cozy armchairs, their eyes riveted to the long circular driveway. They were waiting for Deborah Binti Nzingha to arrive. A tray of tea and sausage rolls lay untouched on the table. Apprehension had robbed them of their appetites. From the moment the KPM steering committee had left them with the onus of approaching Deborah Binti Nzingha with the offer, peaceful thoughts had eluded the two.

"When women have made up their mind, their combined spirit turns into something powerful and unbelievable," Risper said, her eyes lighting up.

"The numbers joining the new KPM party were unprecedented." Her husband, Francis, was constantly on the phone recruiting new and old friends.

The sun dipped behind the jacaranda trees, allowing a cool breeze to dissipate the heat that had been clinging to the air. Governor Fundi crossed the floor to switch off the air conditioner. Absent mindedly, Praxedes flipped through a fresh copy of The Weekend Dossier. The headline screamed "Courts Delays as Life in the Maru Withers Away." Below the headline were pictures of children fetching greenish stagnant water in Amusitu County. She did not bother to read the details, as she was familiar with the story. Her Media house continually gave the matter prime-time coverage on all the stations.

Praxedes began prowling the room. An old black and white wedding photo of the Fundis compelled her to stop and stare. Carey Francis's kinky hair was parted on the side in an imitation of the Patrice Lumumba look of the sixties. A slim Risper stood beside him in her white wedding gown. The look in their eyes clearly indicated the love they felt for each other. Praxedes's business mind was activated by the photo she was looking at. Suppose she introduced a thirty-minute documentary featuring the lives of the famous from their black and white glory days to their current polished sophistication? *Would the viewers love it?* she asked herself. Next to the wedding photo was a recent picture of Risper's grown children. Faraja, their son, stood proudly next to his sister Neema, on her graduation day. Praxedes thought it strange that none of Risper's children had inherited her near white skin. Lifting the portrait closer to her eyes, she noted that the Fundis' children did not resemble each other in any way.

Across the room, Governor Fundi observed Praxedes inquisitive frown with a slight shiver. She imagined what her friend would make of her, if the family's best kept secret ever came out one day.

Her thoughts were interrupted by the sound of an approaching car. From their different positions, they watched a red sports car park under the jacaranda trees and a grim-looking Senator Lydia Masumbuko alight and begin to briskly march towards the main house.

"What do you think she wants?" Praxedes asked in alarm. The visit was unusual. The senator had never been to Governor Risper's house before.

From the agitated manner in which Senator Masumbuko was talking with the house keeper, it was obvious this was not a courtesy call. Governor Fundi walked down the stairs to welcome the unexpected guest. Praxedes was close behind her.

"Lydia, welcome." The governor never bothered with the titles of fellow politicians in private. She extended her hand towards her hostile-looking guest. Her hand was ignored.

"I understand you had a meeting here in which you not only excluded me but also had the temerity to discuss unfounded rumors about me at length." Senator Lydia's tone was hostile.

"We don't understand you, Senator Lydia," Praxedes butted in.

"Praxedes you are a major Judas, and I know your plans very well. You may think that your media house will make Deborah presidential enough, but for your information, I have better qualifications." Lydia hissed back. "Governor Fundi, I thought you had better sense. You don't grab a novice like Deborah and plunge her into politics just like that." Lydia snapped her fingers dismissively. The snap hung in the afternoon air for a while before she spoke again.

"Presidential elections follow laid-down procedures. It is not just a mere anointing of any rookie by a select few. Deborah has no political experience. I will ensure that she doesn't become Kawemppe's next president. Mark my words". The animated senator shook her head vigorously. This caused a few Nubian braids to unfurl from their restraining pins and stand up like spikes.

"Lydia, Deborah has been legitimately nominated by men and women who believe that she is the best suited candidate to take this country to the next level. It will be a mistake to fight us". Risper spoke quietly, facing the senator. Risper had mentored Lydia when she first appeared on the political scene and was disturbed by her insolence.

"Then how come I was not involved in the initial planning?" Lydia asked. Anger seemed to radiate from her body in waves. It was obvious she would have loved to be the presidential nominee.

"From the way you are presenting yourself here today, you don't have even have a modicum of respect in you. I suggest that you leave now," Dr. Risper added with her finger pointing towards the gate. A familiar car was steadily making its way up the driveway.

A moment later, Deborah Binti Nzingha parked beside Senator Lydia's car.

Upon entering, she couldn't help but notice the stern looks on the faces of three women. "Am I interrupting anything?" she asked as she walked towards them.

"Ha! Madam President, indeed! Why don't you stick to lawyering and that rubbish-collecting NGO of yours and leave politics to those with the knowhow?" Lydia exclaimed sarcastically.

Deborah stared at Lydia surprised. She opened her mouth to reply back but instead she heard the ever-cautious voice of Nana whispering in her minds ear. "Simply because someone is drumming out a tune, you don't have to start dancing".

"Find me in the house, please." she said to Governor Fundi and disappeared inside the mansion.

Praxedes watched with mounting satisfaction as Lydia's combative demeanor fizzled away on realizing that Deborah was not joining the fight.

"My sister, Lydia, do not fight us," Governor Fundi recommended.

"I would if there was a worthwhile mission to begin with," Lydia said scornfully before walking to her car. She reversed rapidly, knocking down a potted red rose that was in full bloom as she zoomed off. Risper's guard and housekeeper who had been standing puzzled, unable to decide what to do with the unfolding drama, bent down to right the pot.

Deborah let herself into the sitting room of the mansion. The room had always evoked a sense of security mixed with remorse in her soul. It was the sanctuary where she had hidden her pregnant self many years ago. She would only venture out to send a reassuring letter to Nana. In the letters, she would lie that she had secured a job that did not allow her to visit home.

"Girl, you look devastatingly good," Dr. Neema, the Fundi's only daughter, said as she approached Deborah. The two women hugged excitedly.

"If am looking good, you are killing them," Deborah said pulling back to admire Neema's size-ten body. Neema wore a simple crumbled white linen t shirt and blue jeans, her feet were bare. She looked like a model more than the research doctor that she was. Dr. Neema was home from Atlanta, Georgia—America—on a short break.

"My aim is to look like you, Aunt Deborah." Neema barely hid her admiration for Deborah, whom she fondly called aunt.

"You will be and much more." Deborah meant every word.

Disappearing into the kitchen, Neema brought back a glass of fresh mango juice and handed it to Deborah. Risper and Praxedes were back and beckoned Deborah to join them as they mounted the stairs to the attic office.

"I am not going to keep you in the dark any longer about all this drama, Deborah." Risper began once Deborah was seated. "Senator Lydia's visit is connected to the matter."

"We have a very important message to convey to you. Take your time and mule over it carefully before you give us your answer." Risper added

Mystified, Deborah looked from one woman to the other. Risper was pressing her fingertips together like one in deep prayer while Praxedes was staring at the ground thoughtfully. She knew the two women well enough to realize that something momentous was bothering them immensely.

"Do you remember the day Senator Virunga assaulted us? We vowed to change the face of politics by fronting a female presidential candidate. Well, we have agreed on the aspirant," Risper continued.

Deborah's mind relaxed. Her mentors probably wanted her personal input and some campaign funds. She settled more comfortably into her chair, but Governor Fundi's next sentence almost made her jump back to her feet.

"That woman is none other than you, Deborah. You are the best-placed woman to vie for the presidency of Kawemppe."

Deborah felt her breath catch. Time froze. Her heart began thudding, owing to the sudden denial of air.

"What?" she heard herself squeak. The request was so unexpected that it knocked her senses off.

"We want you to contest for the presidency," Governor Fundi declared.

Deborah looked through the large attic windows. All she could see was a clear blue sky. A flock of birds flew leisurely in a V shape, unaware of the historic decision being made below them. So, this is what Paa had meant when he had asked her about running, Deborah reflected. Her mind began a review her life. From the days she used to help her Grandmother in her market stall back at their village in Makutano County to her days as a head girl in high school. She remembered her campus days, studying law, until the infamously violent Wemppe university riots that forced the campus to close for a year—the year her life had changed for good, when she gave away her first child for adoption. Then she'd embarked on her long and successful career as a lawyer. She thought about her late husband, Nzingha, and the love they had shared before he was snatched away by an assassin's bullet. With her mind locked in another era, she heard Praxedes's voice come to her like a distance echo.

"Deborah, we have spoken with various stakeholders and they agree with us. They believe that you are the one."

"I am not a politician," Deborah said fiercely. "I am retired. I retired soon after the Xamcom ruling was delivered. All I want is to raise my kids without the constraints of a daily workday," she pleaded.

"We will help you. Do you think all these male presidents spend all their time hunkered down at work?" the governor shot back.

"Why don't you pick Senator Lydia? She looks willing." Deborah proposed.

Nobody responded to her proposal.

"We all know that the world is experiencing turbulent times, socially, economically, and politically. Trusted systems that have delivered before are now failing or proving to be unsustainable. Why do you want to plunge me into such chaos? Your idea is crazy," Deborah said as anger took root in her mind.

"Then let 'Crazy' be your middle name from now henceforth," Praxedes fired back.

"Who can understand where the world is moving better than you? Deborah, you have the ability. Look at the way you have gone after the multinationals. Through CLEAN, groups of men and women, young and old, clean up the country voluntarily. You have rebuilt your life from scratch after losing your husband tragically and surrendering all the wealth to your in-laws. Many people would have given hope by then. How many people have accomplished that? You are a leader and a role model. Your lone fight for justice has benefitted more people than all the chest-thumbing politicians combined. You are what the leadership gurus are calling a transformational leader. You are fit to be president, period."

Deborah had never seen Praxedes' eyes mist before. Still, she crossed her hands in front of her chest. It was as if she had put up an impregnable wall to protect herself from the inconceivable proposal.

"Maybe all you want is a puppet who will be at your beck and call," Deborah countered. Even as the words escaped her lips, she felt embarrassed by the hurt looks that registered on her mentors faces. "Sorry, I take that back" she said remorsefully.

The long silence that ensued was broken by Governor Fundi. "There is an urgent need for the right person to take over the leadership of Kawemppe. We need someone who will bridge the gap between the rich and the poor, the pauper and the king, the young and the old. Let history prove me wrong, Deborah, if you are not that person."

The three women were thinking on different frequencies. All conversation ceased between them. They stared through the windows for a long time until dusk settled in and the stars became visible. Somewhere in the labyrinths of the now dark office, a clock struck seven, but no one bothered to switch on the lights. A weak moon shone through the windows and threw the women's shadows against the walls. Deborah's mind went back to the many days she had spent campaigning for the Fundis. She wondered whether she had been unconsciously auditioning for the presidency all along. The proposition was tempting, yet she had made a commitment to her children. How could she disappoint them? Attractive though the idea was, her family had to come first.

"I appreciated your confidence in me to deliver your vision. However, I am sorry. I cannot be your candidate." With that, Deborah picked up her hand bag and left.

Behind her, Risper and Praxedes's heads remained downcast.

# CHAPTER

# 9

A FTER PARTING WAYS WITH the emissaries, Deborah drove straight home. The trees and people dotting the highways seemed to have acquired a different dimension. They had become sacred. As she waited for the traffic light to change, she broodingly looked at the passing throngs of people. She could not imagine she was on the verge of taking charge of their destinies.

When she got home, sleep eluded her till the wee hours of the morning, when she fell into a deep sleep. This was interrupted by the heavy boots of her gateman jogging up the driveway. Behind him was a group of over one hundred people. Deborah quickly shook off her night dress and slipped into a blue truck suit. She slapped some cold water on her face and ran down the stairs and swung her front door open. The distinguished Honorable C. F. Fundi stood a respectful distance away on the cobbled yard. Behind him was Robert Harakka, the former speaker of the Wemppe parliament the legendary, Praxedes, Governor Fundi, Mrs. Ziphorah Lengo, retired Commander Pillar Shinyanga,

Bishop Priscilla Timotheo, her high school headmistress Madam Mary Msalaba, and many other familiar faces.

"Deborah, I must apologize for invading your house in this fashion. But we had no choice," Honorable C. F. Fundi said. Deborah looked at the distinguished delegation and tried to concentrate. She was tongue tied. The last time Madam Mary Msalaba had been to her house was when her husband Nzingha was killed.

"Personally, I have walked a long way with you, and I have come to think of you as my daughter. Your well-formed sense of justice as a lawyer and environmentalist is exemplary. Your intelligence and pragmatism in handling matters is unparalleled. The skills you have can benefit this country immensely. When my dear wife, Risper, and our friend Praxedes failed to convince you yesterday, we said we would not give up. We decided to give it one more time try. We have come to ask you to be our flag-bearer and serve this nation." Honorable C. F. Fundi paused before proceeding. "This group you see here is a representation of the many people who believe in you and your ability. Please think through the matter some more. We will come back in a week's time for your final answer." With their agenda executed, the group trooped back to the two buses that had ferried them. On her way out, Mrs. Mary Msalaba threw a casual eye around the compound. Seeing toys and bicycles scattered all over the place, she concluded that if Deborah was going to get tied down by politics, then the place needed a proper house manager. When that time came, she would get her one.

"Mummy, what did those people want?" Goldie asked. Her face was knitted with worry. The last time Goldie had seen so many grim-looking adults pay them a visit was when her dad had died. AJ and Nana joined in looking anxious.

"Have a seat." Deborah watched as her beloved family sat close together on the sofa. Wondering how to break the news to them, she decided that candidness was the only way.

"They want me to become the president of Kawemppe," Deborah said simply.

"Yippee! Mummy, will you have soldiers? And helicopters? And motor bikes following you with their sirens blaring?" AJ was beside himself with excitement. Goldie rolled her eyes in dismay.

"The God I worship is great. I knew you were special," Nana shrieked in joy and broke into a little jig. A proud look spread on her face.

"You will die like daddy," Goldie exploded and faced the wall.

"Is it true, Mummy? Will bad people hurt you?" AJ asked in alarm. His enthusiasm was soon overtaken by the looming possibility of danger. Reflexively, his little hands clutched his mum's track suit.

"No one will harm me or any of you," Deborah said firmly and bent down to hug Goldie. The little girl stood rigid in her arms.

Nana came to the rescue, whisking the kids out. "Let us go to church first. When we get back, we may have a better view of the matter."

After church, they went to a rambling pizza joint on the outskirts of the city. Bright pictures of roasted chicken, burgers, and pizza were plastered on the walls. Nana watched skeptically as families queued to be served. "Who owns this restaurant?" she enquired looking uncomfortable with the pretentious air of the place.

"It is a big franchise from America. It is very popular over there," Deborah answered while wheeling Mzee Abraham to a shady spot of the outdoor section. Unlike most families who preferred to leave their old and ailing grandparents locked in the house, Deborah took her grandfather to church every Sunday.

"So, how sure are we that they are not selling us poison fancifully wrapped in glittering papers?" Nana was unconvinced by the large boxes of pizza and paper buckets brimming with chicken drums. She came from a generation that believed in home-cooked food.

"Nana, it is very yummy. Wait until you taste it." Goldie loved junk food.

"Only famine can motivate me to eat anything served in paper bags. How do people survive in this city? Good food is the kind you cook yourself and serve on plates." Despite her grumblings, she liked the marinated chicken. Deborah carefully fed Mzee Abraham who sat absent-mindedly in his wheel chair, trapped by a disease he could not fight.

After lunch, she drove the family home, using a longer route. She was scouting for dirty places that her CLEAN team could attack next. At the railway underpass, near the populous Mabanda Moors slums, a frail woman was picking wild vegetables.

"What is she doing?" Goldie asked.

"Picking her dinner" Deborah answered and watched Goldie's shocked face register the realities of life.

"Yuck! Wont the veggies be poisonous?" she asked.

"You should be grateful we can afford clean food. Times are tough out there." As she said that, Deborah thought that something about the lady seemed familiar to her. Then realization hit home. She stepped on the breaks suddenly, nearly tipping her grandfather off his seat.

"Phyllis Mngamata Jones," Deborah called out as she pulled the car by the road side. Scrambling out the door, she ran towards her long-lost friend.

Mngamata turned around startled. She dropped her bag of vegetables and started towards Deborah. The two women embraced.

"Your mother always talked about that woman. She was her best friend in high school," Nana told the children as they watched the two women weeping unabashedly in joy.

"She looks funny. Like she is sick. What happened to her?" Goldie asked. Her voice was somber as she looked at the woman called Mngamata, who looked too old to ever have been at school with her mum.

Nana fought back her own tears at the sight. "You are right. She looks unwell. Don't show it to her face when she comes by. Your mother used to say that Mngamata was her best friend and a pacesetter in school before she was expelled."

"Why did she leave school?"

Nana was surprised by Goldie's sudden interest in other people. "The then headmistress was of the opinion that Mngamata came from the wrong tribe, so she denied her a bursary, and Mngamata had to drop out of school in form two. It made your mother so sad that when the new headmistress Madam Mary Msalaba, the one who was in our house this morning, took over, your mother told her about Mngamata's plight. They went looking for her in her village, only to find that she had already been married off. Those days, there were no telephones to say 'Hello, where are you?' like nowadays."

"Are we from the right tribe?" AJ asked innocently.

"You ask daft questions! Are we from the right tribe?" Goldie mimicked.

"Leave him alone," Nana admonished.

"Now behave yourselves," Nana cautioned the kids. "Here they come."

"Your friend never stopped looking for you, Mngamata," Nana said and hugged the sick woman tightly. Her face was full of empathy.

Goldie's greeting was full of respect, and AJ's handshake was eager.

Mzee Abraham held Mngamata's hand for the longest time, peering intently at her before he lost interest.

"Let me show you my place. It is not far from here," Mngamata offered.

Goldie ran and retrieved Mngamata's vegetable bag, and they all piled into the car and drove into Mabanda Moors slums. From the train underpass, the population increased threefold. Men, women, children, stray goats, handcarts, and wheelbarrows spilled onto the road, narrowing it into a single lane, which motorists fought over. Tin kiosks lined the road with shopkeepers peeping out from heavily grilled windows. Any remaining space was occupied by rowdy hawkers selling second-hand clothes.

Deborah drove between the traders and parked her car under the canopy of a dilapidated bus stop. A collection of youths sat haphazardly on the metal rails, listening to reggae music that was squawking from a mobile phone radio. Several of them held black paper bags from which they dipped their hands for green tea-like leaves and stuffed them into their already full mouths.

"Jonte, keep an eye on this vehicle," Mngamata called out to one of the youths who detached himself from the group at once. His face was beaming at the opportunity to earn something. Looking at the youth, Deborah sensed a street-smart aura around him. It was the kind of persona that had drawn her late husband Nzingha to strange young men, making him give talks in an effort to help them make sense of their lives.

"No problem, Mama Mngamata. No one will touch the car," Jonte declared territorially and immediately perched himself on the car's hood.

In such a neighborhood, it was not a surprise for a parked car to be stripped to the skeleton if the owner left it unattended for more than ten minutes.

Mesmerized by Jonte's bulging cheek, AJ watched him crunch the green leaves, full of curiosity.

"Go. I will be okay with your grandfather," Nana urged. Deborah realized that she was holding her children's hands tightly like they were about to be snatched away by passing thieves. Her fear was valid. Her smartly dressed family stood out like a group of pastors in a brothel.

Deborah followed the slow-walking Mngamata down through the labyrinths of hovels until they turned a corner and stood before a rickety mud house. The short walk had left Mngamata laboring for breath. Her frail body was so weak, a gust of wind could easily have toppled her over. She reached for her keys to open the door. On the opposite side, her neighbor Fatumatta, who was frying golden brown buns by the sewer line, called out greetings. A small baby playing in the muck stretched her dirty hand and picked a bun. Deborah watched her children cringe in horror and prayed they didn't utter something demeaning like "yuck."

***People should not be subjected to such a life***, Deborah empathized inwardly.

Despite the surrounding squalor Mngamata's one-roomed shack was clean and neat. Beautiful purple and white crotchet work covered the simple sofa set. A purple bed sheet divided the room into sitting and sleeping quarters.

"This is my home," Mngamata said and paused painfully as she waited for the wheezing provoked by the walk to subside.

"Do you have something for the cough," Deborah asked in concern.

Mngamata nodded at a flask full of warm water near the stove. Deborah took a glass, poured some water, and handed it to her. She scanned the empty food containers that lined the single shelf and compared them with her fully stocked ones back home. A pang of guilt stung her heart. *I must help my friend*, she thought.

Goldie and AJ got lost watching cartoons on a tiny TV set perched on a stool.

"I followed you on television when you were prosecuting Xamcom. I thought of coming to see you but wondered if you would remember me," Mngamata, now recovered, said weakly.

"Surely, Mngamata if you knew where to find me, why did you not come and pay a visit? Deborah asked accusingly. Mngamata smiled apologetically, her hollow cheeks stretching gauntly from the effort. Retrieving a photo album from a wooden box, Mngamata pointed to the picture of her husband, a handsome truck driver now dead for six years and two of her children who had preceded him. The two ladies' tears knew no bounds as they shared their stories.

"Where are my manners? Let me buy some milk we make tea," Mngamata said, her voice husky from the weeping.

"No, we are just from lunch, and don't forget, Nana and Mzee are still out there," Deborah protested before reaching for her purse. Pausing briefly, she wondered how to give her proud friend some money without offending her.

"My dear, please let me bless you with something small, so you can go see a doctor," Deborah said.

She reached for her purse and pulled out some money. They parted joyfully after exchanging phone numbers and vowing to meet the coming Friday. Little did they know that this was the last time they would talk to each other.

Back in the car, Nana looked at Jonte as he chewed his leaves for a while before she beckoned to him. "Young man, if you spend all your time chewing leaves, what will the goats be left doing?"

Jonte laughed in embarrassment like one caught doing something wrong, but unwilling to let go.

"You seem energetic. All your limbs are intact. Isn't there something more meaningful you can do with your time?" Nana was not about to drop the subject.

Jonte moved to the side and discreetly spat out the wad of green mass that was tangled up with chewing gum.

"Have you tried getting a job?" Nana persisted.

"There is no work for us to do, Grandma. I don't have a tall relative to help me secure one. So, I do any menial job that comes my way," Jonte said defensively. Opening the driver's door, he sat on the driver's seat and left the door ajar. A gust of putrid air blew in, cooling down the warming car.

"What kind of education do you have?" Nana's probing eyes were on Jonte's head, which spotted unkempt little spiky dreadlocks.

"I have studied environmental science up to degree level grandma, if you must know," Jonte added, piqued by the old lady's curiosity.

They talked for some time, and Nana advised Jonte to shave his head clean, stop chewing leaves, and to knock on several office doors. That way, he was bound to get a job.

Jonte told Nana that his hairstyle was not an impediment to acquiring a job. And that the green leaves were for inducing peaceful thoughts to help him cope with the hard economic times. Jonte was so engrossed with the exotic interior of the car, it prompted Nana to pray that he was not planning to carjack them. When Deborah got back, Nana had an assignment for her.

"Get this young man a job. Don't look at that nest of hair in his head. He is going to shave it. He actually has a real degree." After parting with a generous tip, Deborah advised Jonte to drop his CV at Mngamata's house before Friday.

# CHAPTER 10

L OKAMIKO COUNTY WAS THE result of natives being unable to pronounce the name of the first white man who had settled there in the middle of the eighteenth century. Lord Carmichael Montgomery Clark had owned a massive farm on the fertile plains surrounding Mount Kawemppe and built a mansion worthy of a king. Over the years, successive generations had imported the latest farm machinery from Britain and turned the land into a prosperous enterprise.

When the British left Kawemppe shortly after independence was declared in 1960, the ranch now called Acacia Breeze had bristled with acres of wheat and maize, and there had been dairy cattle inherited by Maarufu Skukii, a local paramount chief. Its present-day owner was his son, SASA Chairman Ronald Maarufu. Over the years, he had modernized and mechanized the farm into a successful business. An army of workers could be seen dashing into the green houses, cultivating rose flowers. They emerged carrying packed cartons and loaded the refrigerated trucks, which took them to the airport for

European destinations. Where Lord Carmichael's maize had once stood, a pineapple plantation was in place. A processing plant on the farm supplied Kawemppe and the neighboring countries with pure pineapple juice. Thousands of dairy and beef cattle could be seen browsing on the plains.

Ronald Maarufu and his wife, Victoria, sat in the hunting room of their ranch, sipping wine with their guests: Mitambo, Ronald's running mate, Senator Lydia Masumbuko, Senator Marko Virunga, Kipesa Sampson, owner of the East Winds bank, and Smith Ossaka, the trade unionist.

"Chairman, from what I gather, Xamcom may go under. We have been having issues with them for outsourcing some of their services." Smith Ossaka always addressed Ronald Maarufu as 'Chairman.' "

Victoria ignored the affected concern creeping into Ossaka's voice on behalf of Wemppeans. She knew it was not real. Had Ossaka been overlooked by Xamcom's generous cheques, his union would have raised their concerns through the press.

"Xamcom will survive. Their apology was convincing enough. Since they are compensating, Wemppeans will soon forget about the matter. It is the lawyer, Deborah Binti Nzingha, we should be worried about," Victoria informed her guests.

"Rumor has it she is running for the presidency."

"What does a girl of yesterday have to offer people?" Senator Marko Virunga asked spitefully "Exactly the same question I asked Governor Fundi and Praxedes Tangazo the other day. Why are they forcing Deborah Binti Nzingha on the people?" Senator Lydia Masumbuko countered bitterly.

The conversation milled around Deborah's candidature as the group awaited the evening's chief guests, the industrialist Pramul Gupta and international business magnate Mr. Cho, to arrive.

"Did you see the ruckus she made over the Maru, as if it were her personal property? She is just being used by Governor Fundi and Praxedes. Some of you women need to be disciplined with a cane," Senator Virunga suggested and looked around the room for support before humming on. "My grandfather had eleven wives, and none of them dared to say *nghu* in front of him".

"Those days are long gone, Senator. You touch a woman today and you are met with fire," Victoria said dismissively. She disliked the print shirt Senator Virunga was wearing. It was a violent mix of green leaves and red berries which made the man look like a dressed-up orangutan. Swallowing her pride, Victoria realized that she had to put up with Virunga. It was the Virungas of this world who came up with the dirt required to soil political opponents. Most importantly, Virunga had delivered River Maru to Mr. Cho.

Ronald, who was tastefully dressed in a sky blue short-sleeved shirt and white khaki trousers, tactfully maneuvered the conversation to more amiable grounds. "What is happening with Dalmas Kinga Nzambe?" he asked tentatively. He wanted to get Ossaka's views first, but Lydia butted in.

"DDP party is dead. Dalmas is a dead man walking. Senator Lydia tone prompted Ronald to look at her askance. ***This lady can be a thorn in the flesh***, he thought. It was obvious to Ronald that no one knew that Mitambo Mitambo had politically neutralized DDP.

Ossaka noted the flicker of discomfort on Ronald's face and moved the conversation forward.

"Chairman, the only political party that might have a chance at challenging you is Bishop Epaphras's New Wine Skins (NWS). Otherwise, this is a one-horse race, and that horse is you." Ossaka laughed boisterously, emphasizing the unsightly pock marks on his face.

Victoria knew Ossaka occasionally resorted to flattery, but he was loyal to her husband. Ronald had helped Ossaka access influential friends. People like the industrialist Pramul Gupta who occasionally showered him with gifts. Brand new SUVs and expensive watches—not to mention the hefty envelopes full of crisp bank notes. In return, Ossaka ensured that employee protests at Gupta Industries and Refineries were dealt with quickly and quietly. There had been no strike in any of Gupta's companies for the last six years.

"Bishop Epaphras's campaign looks well-oiled." Ronald was fishing again. He knew where the Bishop was getting his funding from but wanted a confirmation from Kipesa Sampson, the banker.

Kipesa lowered his expensively barbered head for a moment to contemplate the question. "I heard from a friend of mine that during one of his crusades in the American Midwest, the Bishop stumbled upon one of those Dallas billionaires who tend to think that Africa is a country in the Angolan continent. He managed to convince him that Kawemppe has huge deposits of oil and diamonds waiting to be mined." The group interrupted Kipesa's tale with loud laughter. Kawemppe's yet to be exploited mining potential lay in Mnazi County, and diamonds were not part of it.

"So, the billionaire is bankrolling the venture, hoping to reap the diamond mining rights in the near future." The impeccably dressed Kipesa was careful not to betray himself. He had not heard from any friend. His bank was channeling Dwayne Kirby Hershel's dollars to Bishop Epaphras's party, but he was not a man prone to proclaiming his business in public.

Across the room, Ronald's running mate, Mitambo, who had been left from the conversation, sipped his wine thoughtfully, mentally appraising his host's luxurious hunting room and wondering how he could replicate the same in his home. The oval room had large windows through which guests could view the ranch. The mahogany easy chairs they sat on had plump cushions that coaxed the occupants to luxuriate in the comfort. When the helicopter had flown them onto the ranch earlier, Mitambo had observed how the old mansion dominated the surrounding plateau. The mansion's elaborate chimneys that jutted into the sky matched a picture he had seen in a history book of eighteenth-century Britain's architecture. Inattentive to the conversation, M2 was the first person to spot the approaching maroon helicopter as it circled the farm before landing. The initials SASA were prominently displayed on its sides and underbelly.

Wine glass in hand, Ronald led his guests out to the helipad a hundred meters away, to welcome the new arrivals. The first guest down was Mr. Cho, who was squinting at the setting sun. Pramul Gupta wore his signature meek veneer that hid the industrialist's ruthless business mind. After Honorable Ronald had introduced his guests, the group stood arrested by the sun as it began its rapid descent behind the Lokamiko hills. There had been talk about listing the Lokamiko sunset as one of the wonders of the world. Its beauty was unparalleled. It must have been the reason why the colonialist Lord Carmichael had chosen that site for his mansion. Mesmerized by the vista before him, Mr. Cho grabbed his camera and began snapping away at the setting sun

"Excellent, excellent," he said, turning this way and that way to capture the sunset against the backdrop of the pine trees.

His enthusiasm roused the other guests, and they soon followed suit. They whipped out their mobile phones cameras and began clicking away. Victoria looked at Mr. Cho cautiously. The heat he had caused them over the Maru River acquisition was almost becoming unbearable. Quietly, she detached herself from her guests and walked back to the main house to supervise dinner. She had flown in two chefs from the capital Wemppe to specifically carter for Pramul's vegan needs and present Mr. Cho with unmatched oriental cuisine. Though the professionals did not need her help, she felt a need to ensure that everything was in order.

"How about that at the end of a day's job," Ronald inquired while waving at the setting sun.

"You must slice some five acres for me. Vith a suuset like zhat, you only get younger and younger," Pramul Gupta sang out. Mitambo and Smith Ossaka guffawed loudly at Pramul's comment. Senator Lydia Masumbuko laughed along before turning her attention to Mr. Cho, the CEO of The Hoangz Conglomerate, who oversaw the company's shipping, mining, hotel, and retail empire.

"When I need an escape from the office madness, I now know where to go," Sampson Kipesa conceded. He was impressed.

Beside him, M2 was content to count his blessings. Among them was the fact that he was Ronald's Maarufu right-hand man, a post every Wemppean man was yearning for. He had joined the big boys' league. It was just a matter of time before other men would start bowing before him.

The group stood in the evening breeze, admiring nature, until dusk forced them indoors.

"Dinner is ready," Victoria announced as the guests came through the door. Without raising an eyebrow, she noted how Lydia was covetously looking at Mr. Cho. Discreetly, she changed the seating arrangement and put the two next to each other at the table. Then, the feasting commenced. Pramul's veggies were unrecognizable to the other guests. What mattered to Victoria was that he seemed to love them. The rest fell on the marinated guinea fowls served with naan and a side dish of fermented greens. One of the chefs dished out Platters of roasted gazelle meat curved straight from the bone.

M2 attempts to converse with Senator Lydia seated on his left were futile. The senator seemed to have awarded all her attention to Mr. Cho. Sinking his teeth into the tender gazelle quietly, M2 listened to the massive corruption dealings taking shape at the jolly dinner table. Pramul and Mr. Cho's contributions to the SASA cause were enough to bankroll the entire campaign.

"Weren't you in the same university college with Deborah Binti Nzingha?" Victoria Maarufu paused from eating and asked Mitambo.

"Yes," Mitambo said hesitantly. He had never been to any university, but he had papers that claimed he had been.

"Find a stain that will tarnish the squeaky-clean image she normally portrays, and let us know about it soon."

Mitambo realized that Victoria was not making a request. An order had been given, and it had to be executed. Wasn't the one billion weras he had paid SASA enough? He lost his appetite.

# CHAPTER

# 11

Y OU WILL MISS THE bus!" Deborah called after the kids, who had run upstairs to fetch their sports shoes, which they had left behind. From the bottom of the stairs, she could hear them rummaging through the shoe rack like two weaver birds fighting. The morning had been a blur of activity. The kids had taken quick showers, gulped down their breakfast, and brushed their teeth in record time. Impatiently, she began walking out of the door while lugging their backpacks along.

Several minutes later, the harried children emerged from the house and jogged down the driveway to catch up with their mother.

"Mum, this is as far as you can come," AJ said abruptly and stood blocking his mother.

"Why?" Deborah asked surprised by the sternness in AJ's voice.

"Because we are no longer babies. Bryan, Pendo, and Makini will laugh at us if they see you escorting us to the bus," Goldie answered.

Deborah was about to ask what they meant when the kids snatched their backpacks and raced each other towards the bus stop, where their pals stood in a little huddle.

As she stood watching them, a feeling of rejection came over her. Maybe she had made a mistake by selling the practice to be with the children. The kids seemed to crave their independence. Walking back to the house, she went straight to her bedroom and began arranging the already neat room. A pile of unread magazines lay on the table beside her bed. Gathering the lot, she took them to the balcony, pulled a chair, and began reading under the warm morning sun.

From the elevated balcony, she watched the nurse wheel Mzee Abraham around the compound. Nana was trudging along for the exercise. In the kitchen, Khavere, who shunned modern kitchen gadgets like the dish washer, was treating the household to the symphony of her attempts at dish washing. It sounded as if she was attempting to break the cups with the spoons. Her rate of breakage stood at a minimum of a cup or a plate per week. For several hours, Deborah randomly read different articles till midday, when she tired of them. Facing a long day of unstructured hours, she picked up a sponge and filled the bath tub with hot soapy water and vim and began to scrub her bathroom. As she scrubbed the walls, the events of the past week crept up on her like a thief. They seemed surreal. First, she had sold her share in the law firm so that she could settle down as a full time mum, only to tealise her kids were clamouring for their indepedence. Then had come the proposition: "We want you to become our president." The idea was mindboggling if not ridiculous. Straightening up, she caught her frowning reflection in the mirror and sternly said to it, "We want you to become the president".

The thought was like throwing a pebble into a stagnant pool of water. Waves of doubt started rippling through her mind. She realized that if she were to accept the offer, then she had to develop a tough skin and prepare to deal with Wemppeans and their views. Her widow status was likely to be viewed with suspicion. "What happened to the husband?" or, even worse, "I heard she was behind his killing." In fact, the inquiries would help validate her mother-in-law's assumptions. Rael, Nzingha's mother, had once come very close to accusing Deborah of her son's murder. But the icing on the cake, as Deborah perceived it, was the speculation that would burn in Wemppeans' minds as they pondered who she might be sleeping with. Deborah giggled at the thought.

She thought of the few occasions she had dressed up to humor her girlfriends when they had proposed blind dates. Nothing meaningful had come of it. There had once been an encounter with a younger lawyer, whose unbridled enthusiasm in bed had been too clumsy and fast. She had ignored him when he came looking for a rematch. Then there was Paa. Her feelings towards him seesawed between love and hate of what could have been but was not. Thinking about Paa brought a warm glow that began to spread all over her body until her inner voice accusingly asked, "Is this how you plan to spend your retirement? Cowering in the house and daydreaming about men?" Jolted by the admonishment, Deborah took a quick bath and toweled off. Slathering on some moisturizer, she slipped into a blue button-down denim dress and went to the kitchen to start lunch.

"The sun has descended a little," Nana quipped. She had just had lunch and was sitting under the shade of a mango tree, a rivulet of sweat coursing down her face. She wiped it off with the edge of her apron. Deborah watched her grandmother's hands moving rhythmically as they shelled pigeon peas expertly, swiped them into a clean basin, and cast the empty pods onto an old newspaper that she had spread on the grass.

"The sun is still where it used to be. It is we who have destabilized it with pollution," Deborah said while pulling a wicker chair close to Nana's and starting to help with the shelling. A jug of fresh mango juice she had just blended for her children to have after school sat on the cool verandah.

"You should have let the children eat the mangoes instead of juicing them, or even make some millet porridge for them. A strong child is the one fed on millet porridge mixed with sour milk straight from the guard or pounded pumpkins washed down with a glass of milk."

"Try convincing them to eat pumpkins yourself," Deborah said.

"That is why most people in your generation are lethargic because of feeding on lifeless bread plastered with margarine, and going everywhere in cars. Pthuu." Nana spat contemptuously. "Anyway, that is not what I want to speak to you about. I know that you are well educated— far more so than me. But sometimes there is a need for fools to say what they know so that wise people can sift the wisdom from the chaff." As Nana spoke, she stopped the shelling, and her voice grew solemn. "One cannot see one's own back without a mirror. Why are you not listening to what those people are telling you? Those people are seeing something great in you that you cannot see for yourself. They are holding a mirror up for you to examine your back. Stop minimizing your talents. You should go for the presidency. Stop wasting time babysitting old folks like us who are just whiling away the time before Jesus calls us home. Even these margarine-eating children of yours that you claim to look after will soon fly out of here before you have time to say hallelujah."

Deborah smiled and braced for more.

"You, more than anyone else, know that life is a risk. Imagine if I had not taken you to school, where teachers sharpened your brain to grasp a new world of possibilities other than the ABCs and one-two-threes, that I knew. Would we be sitting in such a beautiful place?" Nana swung her hand to encompass Deborah's large compound.

Deborah shook her head negatively.

"Let me tell you, the first time I saw a woman driving a car back nineteen fifty three, I thought it was the beginning of the end of the world. A woman controlling a moving metal, using a circular wheel? That was the height of audacity. Now, you have two vehicles of your own in the garage. Or do you want to go back to the days when a visitor would stop by our village wondering whether there was anybody home, and the women would honestly tell them that there was nobody? That it was only us and the children because we considered ourselves to be nobodies? Those days are long gone. If it was a man who had been offered this same position, we would not be having breathing space due to the din he would be generating on radio and television."

Despite herself, Deborah laughed out aloud. She loved Nana's humorous analogies.

They shelled some more peas as they sat under the sweltering February heat. From experience, Deborah knew that the old lady was not done.

"It would be to your advantage if you were to stop torturing that gentleman who comes here loaded with all manner of excuses. Give him a chance to blather out his intentions."

"Who?" Deborah asked defensively

"Who else other than Paa? Are you blind, child? That man has the kind of stature that can keep a woman warm and happy throughout the night. Don't be a fool. Take your chance before another woman grabs him."

Deborah laughed so hard tears sprung in her eyes. *What great timing*, she thought. She had grown up with an earful of advice from her grandmother, reinforced by Mrs. Mary Msalaba's closing day speeches, "Girls, don't be common and cheap women with brains no bigger than a chicken's and fall for every man you meet on the way." Now at forty-five years old, the coast was being cleared for her to do as she liked.

"Nana, I don't need a man to keep me warm during the day or at night."

"Nonsense. Get a man to hum and clear his throat around here. AJ needs a man around to help him build up his spine. There are a lot of women surrounding him, and he needs to man up. Goldie can also benefit from the mentorship of a respectable man like Paa," Nana said. A slight breeze rustled the mango tree and lifted the newspaper with the empty pods up.

Deborah stepped on the fleeing paper and anchored it more firmly with a big pebble.

"In case you have been too busy to notice, Paa has been following you around the compound obediently with his tongue sticking out like that of a dog in the hot sun," The elder woman said as she collapsed with laughter at her own joke. Deborah, feeling mortified, thought that her beloved Nana had gone insane.

"Anyway, Paa aside. What is so hard about accepting the presidential nomination?" Nana asked. She had a penchant for mixing up different stories without losing track of either.

"Nana, I am not a politician".

"What nonsense is that?" Nana rebuked. "If my son, Nzingha, were to wake up this minute, he would be proud that Wemppeans think so highly of you they want you as their leader. He might also wonder what you are waiting for before getting yourself a man. You are still young enough to have another baby," Nana added smugly. Deborah looked at her grandmother in horror.

"Stop looking at me like I have grown a beard. If you won't run for the presidency, then get yourself a man to quarrel with. Very soon, your grandfather and I will meet our maker. Who will you be left with?"

Deborah looked at her grandmother-turned-matchmaker fondly and debated within herself whether to share the one secret that she had never divulged. The daughter she had given away when she was twenty. She was saved from the agony by her ringing cell phone. It was Mabanda General Hospital.

"May I speak to Deborah Nzingha?"

"Speaking," Deborah's voice caught.

In a concise, professional manner, a nurse informed Deborah about Phyllis Mngamata Jones's predicament.

Briefly explaining the situation to Nana, Deborah grabbed her purse and jumped into her SUV.

It turned out that Jonte had taken his CV to Mngamata's house and found her lying deathly ill on her bed. With the help of neighborhood youths, they had carried her in a makeshift stretcher to the hospital. Mngamata had given the nurse a scrap of paper bearing Deborah's number. For hours the youths had been standing at the gates of the hospital waiting for the doctor's verdict.

"It is the meningitis," Sister Ann, the duty nurse, said to Deborah. "It has defied all the medication we have administered to her." Sister Ann's short stature did not prevent her from single handedly manning forty critically sick patients with the help of only one nurse aid. As efficient as a drill sergeant, she effortlessly loaded her trolley with IV fluids and medicines as her eyes scanned the scrawled doctor's instructions on the treatment charts. Pausing, she glanced at Deborah, whom she immediately recognized as the lawyer who had led the onslaught against Xamcom and the lady from CLEAN.

"Do you think it would help if I transferred Mngamata to St Luke's?" Deborah enquired. St. Luke's was the best and the most expensive hospital in Kawemppe.

Sister Ann looked at Deborah with mounting contempt at first but soon realized that she was acting out of concern for her sick friend and not in mockery of the humble services offered in the general hospital.

"I doubt you will even make it to the highway. We have taken good care of her here. Some assurances might help Mngamata feel at peace." Sister Ann was gentle but practical. Until then, Deborah had not thought that Mngamata would die. *How could Mngamata die when they had been planning a big surprise reunion for her with Josephine, Dina, and Zaituni?* She thought as they reached Mngamata's bed. Mngamata had been reduced to a mere skeleton. Drawing up the faded blue curtains around the bed, the nurse left a crying Deborah alone with her friend as she fought for dear life.

Mngamata was in a coma. She was in the high dependency unit of the hospital. Careful not to disturb the numerous tubes protruding from her friend's nose and mouth, Deborah reached for the bony hands and squeezed them. Fresh tears pricked her eyes and coursed down her cheeks. "Mngamata, my dear sister. This is Deborah. If you can hear me, I want you to know that I will never forget about you. Never doubt that." Deborah spoke aloud, hoping her words would comfort and reassure her friend. At that juncture, a strange wave of strength surged through her body like a lightning bolt. It felt like Mngamata was transferring whatever little energy she had remaining to Deborah. Gently, Deborah let go of the bony fingers, and like a candle in a dark room, a sense of clarity came to Deborah's mind. Mngamata's life would have been different if somebody's misguided decision had not robbed her of the right to an education. Her dear husband would not to have been assassinated if business was conducted legally in Kawemppe.

***I need to fight the rot that robs the Mngamata's and Nzingha's of this world of their life***, Deborah vowed silently as she watched her friend chest rise laboriously with each breath. Her friend was dying. Swiftly, she linked her hands with Mngamata and prayed the repentance prayer with her. Mngamata's chest rose up one more time and then went still. She had breathed her last.

Twenty minutes later, an orderly wheeled the lifeless body of the forty-five-year-old Phyllis Mngamata Jones out of the ward and down the long corridor to the cold mortuary.

Jonte, who had been hovering around, looked on, his face was knitted with throbbing veins to keep away the tears. Sister Ann looked at Deborah's bright red eyes. The lawyer looked frighteningly dangerous, like she might sue somebody. Dina, Zaituni, and Josephine, who had been caught in the traffic as they drove towards the hospital, pulled their car to the side of the road and began sniffling when Deborah called and told them there was no need for the trip. Their classmate was dead.

The filling of forms at the hospital took Deborah until eight o'clock in the evening. She had dismissed Jonte and his friends with instructions to call the next day and inform him about the funeral arrangements.

When Deborah got home, an inspired Khavere loaded the table with steaming ***posho*** and fried goat meat, red tomatoes, and a platter of greens. Despite the food being tasty, Mngamata's death had robbed Deborah of her appetite.

Excusing herself, she climbed up to her bedroom.

Nana, worried by the withdrawn Deborah, went after her.

"I wonder why God in his wisdom let you reconnect with your friend when he knew he would take her away so soon," Nana said, settling on the dressing stool.

"Tell me about my mother," Deborah requested of her grandmother.

Nana peered at Deborah's face with concern. Deborah had never sought the details of her mother before. After determining that Deborah was not falling into any sort of depression, Nana Tabitha began her story.

"Your mother, Inyaandu, as beautiful as the rising sun, ran away from home one school holiday and got married when she was barely sixteen. Your grandfather and I tried to talk sense into her, but she adamantly resisted our advice. Being our only child, we didn't want to raise controversy in the village, so we let her be. Eight months later, Inyaandu died giving birth to you."

Nana paused in pain. She was recollecting how the village had been flooded with rumors at the time. "How can an only child die during childbirth unless witchcraft is at play?" people had wondered.

"What about my father?" Deborah asked as she vaguely recalled a cruel joke a child had made in school—about her grandmother being a witch.

"He had married another woman while your mother was pregnant." Nana paused briefly and watched Deborah shoulders heave with pain. "After her burial, we begged our in-laws to let us take you with us. They did not object."

**How could they object when the stake involved only a useless girl?** Deborah thought.

"The night I took you home, my heart was bursting with unbearable pain. It was your grandfather who made sense of the whole experience. He reminded me of old Abraham and Sara in the bible and said that you were our Isaac, and did you not turn out okay?" Nana concluded with an optimistic ring to her voice. A period of silence stretched before them before Nana spoke again. "Find out what Mngamata's pain is telling you. Making sense of the pain I felt when I lost your mother is what held me together and gave me the strength to take care of you," Nana concluded. She rose up slowly and limped out.

Alone, Deborah felt numb until Goldie interrupted her with a bowl of fruit.

They took turns spooning the fruit into their mouth. Deborah preferred the avocado and the melon while Goldie speared the pineapples and the banana cubes.

"Mummy, can I tell you something?"

Deborah nodded.

"I have been thinking. Suppose aunt Mngamata's life had been swapped with yours. What would have happened to us?"

Deborah hugged Goldie reassuringly with her free hand.

"Nothing is going to happen to us," Deborah said firmly, looking deeply into her daughter's eyes.

"When you become president, will you ensure that people are not discriminated against for silly reasons?

Like who they are or where they come from like aunt Mngamata?" Goldie asked simply.

"Do you want me to become the president, Goldie?" Deborah gazed keenly at her daughter.

"Of course, Mum. Who wouldn't want their mum to be the president?" Goldie added importantly and pranced out of the room.

Deborah felt the heaviness that had weighed her down like a cumbersome anchor slip away. She reached for her mobile phone and called Governor Risper Fundi, who picked the call at the first ring. "Get the committee ready for a breakfast meeting tomorrow. We don't have much time before the elections."

"They will be here," Governor Fundi replied firmly. As they were talking, the skies opened up and let down fat rain drops that drove away the overpowering heat, which had domineered the entire month of February, and ushered in March.

# CHAPTER
# 12

A LONE HELICOPTER, WHICH WAS painted purple with two gold stripes running around it, nestled in Governor Fundi's compound, when Deborah squeezed her car in the crowded parking lot. It was eight in the morning on the first day of March. Alighting, she followed numerous shoe prints stamped in the wet ground and made her way to the front door. Carey Francis Fundi, looking healthier than before, ushered her into his sitting room, where a group of ten men and women were chatting over a cup of tea. The first people to note the strange look on Deborah's face were Praxedes and Governor Fundi. It was the unnervingly calm and steady stare that Deborah always had before annihilating a criminal in front of a judge.

Shaking hands all around her, Deborah did a double-take when she came across Seth Pasakhwa and Solomon Ngome, her law lecturer and the immediate former chief justice. Other guests included former House Speaker Robert Harakka, who was sandwiched between Mrs. Mary Msalaba and Bishop Priscilla Timotheo on a big sofa. Retired Commander Pillar Shinyanga was chatting with the indefatigable Ruthanne Kasi, Governor Fundi's campaign coordinator. The pint-sized Lumumba Abiola, a much-sought political analyst, whose wealth of experience in politics had helped Governor Fundi clinch the Amusitu gubernatorial seat twice, was also present. Lumumba, as usual, wore his trademark ankle-length jeans and white socks. He had never recovered from the eighties breakdance rage. His restless eyes darted cleverly behind a pair of Malcolm X spectacles as he conferred with Francis. Deborah knew Lumumba well. He had schooled with her late husband, Nzingha, and their paths had crossed at various functions.

Declining a cup of tea, Deborah sat down and launched straight into the business of the day. "Thank you for the honor you have bestowed upon me of vying for the presidency. I am ready for the task ahead," Deborah began and the group clapped heartily.

After tucking AJ into bed, Deborah had spent the entire night drafting the terms and conditions under which she was willing to work and compiled them into a file. She handed the neatly-typed file to Governor Fundi, who after reading and failing to understand the legalese it was written in passed it over to the former chief justice Solomon Ngome, who was now the KPM lawyer.

He read it thoroughly, all the while nodding his grey head sagely, as he flipped the pages. When he was done, he gave a simplified explanation to his audience. In a nutshell, Deborah had stated that democratic primaries needed to be conducted as soon as possible. The KPM steering committee was to embark on a country-wide exercise of mobilizing all communities together and identifying individual community development priorities. KPM was also going to identify credible individuals who would represent the party in various legislative posts before the end of March. Deborah had made it clear that even the presidential slot was open for contest. She also made it clear that her commitment was to serve the best interest of the citizenry. Any pressure for preferential treatment from any quarters and she would resign. The steering committee agreed to her terms.

With the ground rules laid down, Francis began the meeting. "Deborah, we cannot thank you enough for accepting the nomination. As a politician who has been in the game for a long time, I become afraid when I gazed into the future. Kawemppe cannot go on like this. The course of River Maru cannot be changed, and yet Wemppeans continue to carry on their business as if nothing has happened—or as if they have become numb with stress. I want to say this without scaring anyone: when numb people reach their saturation point, they can react unpredictably. That is why there is a need for change, and not just any change but equitable change. We believe that you are the best-suited candidate to bring about that change." There were unanimous nods of agreement from all. "Now, I will not take more of the little time. We thought it prudent to introduce you to the task at hand by giving you a quick aerial tour of the Republic of Kawemppe. But before we board the chopper, let my friend Solomon Ngome say something he wishes to share with us, if he has not forgotten about it already." The gathering laughed. The two men often made fun of each other on the state of their mental alertness.

Retired chief justice Solomon Ngome, tall and courtly, stood up briskly. "Don't listen to a boy I taught the other day pretend to be my age mate," he said admonishingly to a mischievously smiling Francis. After a moment of reflective silence, he embarked on his speech. "Most of you know that I lost my last-born son, Josh, late last year. The pain was and is still unbearable. For weeks, I felt that the pain was going to kill my wife, Jane. Josh was almost ready to graduate from medical school, something that his mother and I were looking forward to. But it never came to be. Heroine took care of that. Shrouded with grief and despair, a moment of poor judgment slipped into my mind. I hired people to find out who these drug peddlers were and get rid of them. My hired guns managed to track down the den where Josh used to get his drug supply and identified the peddlers hard at work supplying their wares to other kids. So, I ordered my boys to carry out the execution the next day." The room had become deathly quiet. It was unlike the retired chief justice to tell such a personal story.

Bishop Priscilla Timotheo closed her eyes in prayer.

"I was consumed with revenge, so I wanted to watch the execution of the thieves who had stolen my son's life. I accompanied the hitmen I had hired."

Deborah became alarmed that Solomon might have gone berserk with grief and was about to disclose something incriminating, but she held herself in check.

"On arrival at the dumpster where the drug den was located, we thought we were in the wrong place. There was no dumpster; it had vanished." Solomon paused briefly, his face twitching. When he resumed his voice was almost a whisper. "The CLEAN team led by Deborah Binti Nzingha had cut down all the wild shrubbery around the place and carted away the garbage." Solomon brought his palms together and let them slide in opposite directions. "The former dumpsite was now a football pitch complete with two goal posts ready for a game. The dealers where nowhere to be seen and they have not been back to the place since. "I then asked myself what kind of an animal I had allowed myself to become. Why had I not thought of just reclaiming the dumping ground and saving all the innocent children who were falling prey to those animals? As a one-time custodian of Wemppean law, how come I hadn't thought of such a simple solution to such a complex a problem?"

The anguish in Honorable Ngome's voice made Mrs. Msalaba to fetch out a white handkerchief and wipe away a stray tear.

"Later, I told—or rather confessed—to my wife, Jane, about my mission. I am still begging for her forgiveness to date." The comment was greeted by relieved smiles all round.

"Thank you, Deborah for graciously bringing about changes that are needed in this country—changes of which I am a direct recipient. Having taught and interacted with you over the years, I know that you can and will compete with the best of them. Don't be distracted by what SASA, Democratic Democracy Party or NWS have accomplished. We are here to help. When Francis ordered me to avail myself here today, I could not refuse. People, I have reported for duty at Kawemppe People's Movement today. I am ready to answer phones, sweep the floors, and hop into the campaign bandwagon whenever and to wherever you want me." With those remarks, Solomon sat down.

Moved by Solomon's emotional story, Deborah shared the sad plight of her friend Mngamata. "My friend's death is the deciding factor that swayed me to accept this nomination."

Mrs. Msalaba vividly recalled how Deborah had pounced on her the first day after she reported as the new headmistress of Kilele Girls Government School, disturbed by Mngamata's unjust expulsion. She had attempted to track Mngamata to her rural home in the hills of Mnazi County, only to find that she had gotten married and relocated to Ufuoni County.

In a short while, the group joined Captain Tanar in the helicopter. True to her promise, Uanita Phillips who ran a helicopter rental business, had dispatched the two choppers she had promised to the KPM party. They strapped their seats belts and were soon airborne. *What a way to start your first day of work*, Deborah thought. From her window seat, she watched the houses below reduce into orderly shaped matchboxes. The landscape looked cool and the soils dark from the rain, which had drenched the entire country.

Occasionally, Captain Tanar broke the silence over the headsets as he named the different counties they were flying over. The capital, Wemppe, looked crammed and packed tighter than a can of sardines. From the air, Deborah could see the traffic jam pandemonium below. This brought to mind the wasted hours which Wemppeans seemed to have become accustomed to. Soon, they passed large tea plantations, which looked quite picturesque from the air. Deborah thought of the hard-working farmers below—people like her grandparents, who relied on the soil for their livelihoods but were held hostage to the cartels that reaped where they hadn't sown.

After a short stop over to refuel, they approached Amusitu County in the southwest of the country. Deborah requested the pilot to fly alongside River Maru for a closer look. The team watched the spectacle below, spellbound. In an act of defiance, the raging flood waters had carried away the man-made barriers that the Hoangz Conglomerate had put up to divert the river's course. The river was back to its original course. Giant bulldozers could be spotted lying on their sides downstream. They looked like medieval monsters. An army of construction workers in red reflector jackets and matching helmets stood at a safe distance, watching the gorged river helplessly.

"Nature has avenged itself," Governor Fundi said over the head sets. The group gave a loud cheer. Praxedes was already filming the scene on her mobile phone for her WAMO viewers.

Elated, the pilot turned east towards the mountainous Mnazi County. There had been volcanic activity in the area thousands of years ago. The windward side of Mnazi County had rich soils that supported macadamia nuts and sugarcane plantations. The Lee side was bone dry. Its rugged ridges stretched into the extensive plains of Solanga County to the north. Deborah found her eyes scanning the ground, hoping to catch sight of the pastoralists as they moved their cattle in search of pasture.

Staring down at the shifting ground, Deborah felt the desire to serve her people overwhelm her. She remembered the recent dream in which she had been standing at a bus stop, unwilling to board the bus, causing people to shove her in. ***This is my biggest chance to bring change to Kawemppe, the foothold of Africa***, Deborah vowed, steely resolve in her eyes.

# CHAPTER

# 13

ABOUT THE SAME TIME Deborah was surveying the republic like a hawk from the skies, Bishop Epaphras was chairing a top management meeting at his private offices in the plush Kasoro Pavilion. He had just concluded a series of crusades with his benefactor, the billionaire Dwayne Kirby Hershel, who had been quite impressed by the congregation that had filled stadia wherever they went. Before leaving for America, Kirby had stuffed the Bishop's campaign chest with an additional ten million dollars.

As the founder of Our Father International Church (OFIC), Bishop Epaphras boasted eight county branches country-wide. They were headed by pastors he had hand-picked. All the pastors who had been duly summoned sat at the T-shaped conference table, waiting for their instructions. Four pastors sat on each side of the mahogany table, facing each other. The Bishop sat at the helm of the T.

Years ago, when Bishop Epaphras had begun to push his political ambitions, several established churches in Kawemppe had offered him unlimited support. Having taken matters a notch higher by forming the New Wine Skin Political Party NWS, the religious allegiances were now becoming slippery. The church had grown cold feet. The oldest and most populous Wemppe African Church (WAC) owed its allegiance to one of its members, the current President Meshack Jabali, and couldn't risk deserting their valued leader. To drive the point home, one of the BAC deacons had told Bishop Epaphras that they would still support president Jabali, should the Kawemppe constitution allow him a third term.

Archbishop Noah Jongoo of the Holy Trinity Church (HTC) was a tall, stooped man, seventy-seven years old. He had been warm to the idea of Bishop Epaphras serving Kawemppe as its next president but had also changed his mind. He wasn't sure that the country would be safe under the leadership of the unchecked charisma of Bishop Epaphras, who allowed women into his church without requiring them to cover their hair with head scarves. Archbishop Jongoo had shifted his allegiance to a more elderly and trusty man, Honorable Ronald Maarufu, of the SASA party.

With support from key stake holders dwindling, Bishop Epaphras had begun to court the widespread Indigenous Kawemppe Church of God (IKCG). Despite contributing generously towards their university project, a week before the church committee had with a blank face informed him that they had an issue with the manner his church conducted their baptism.

"We cannot have a person who baptizes his congregation in hotel swimming pools, where sinners go to fornicate, rather than in the natural rivers as our leader."

With his political prospects looking dimmer by the day, Bishop Epaphras had decided to rally his troops.

"You must start vigorous campaigns among the low-income brackets in your area, as they have the majority vote." Bishop Epaphras paused and examined his county pastors sternly. They were an interesting mix of men. To his left was the reliable and loyal Paul Saatgi, a thirty-five-year-old former jail bird whom he had rescued from street preaching. One lunch hour break, the Bishop had paused on a crowded street and listened to Paul preach without a microphone. Gauging the impact Paul had on a mass of people who had formed a ring around Paul, the Bishop had wrenched him from the sidewalk and absorbed him into the OFIC fold.

Next to Paul was Pastor Silas Gaawha. He was a refugee from the neighboring country of Gumbotswi, who had nowhere else to go and was therefore bound to tow the OFIC line. The other two pastors on that side of the table had been praise and worship leaders at OFIC, who had risen through the ranks. After acquiring a diploma in divinity, the church had promoted them.

On the right side of the table were more mature men: three pastors who were slightly older than the bishop and therefore harder to manipulate. Bishop Epaphras had poached the three from rival churches due to their experience and commitment to spreading the gospel. But it was the fourth man, Pastor Nehemiah, presiding over the Ufuoni County parish that the Bishop glared at. Unlike the other pastors, the forty-five-year-old Nehemiah, a former college tutor, was more prone to challenging his decisions.

The bishop watched unhappily as Nehemiah opened his mouth to speak.

"Bishop, with all due respect, I feel that you are asking Moses to become comfortable in Pharaoh's palace. Let me elaborate." Nehemiah's rectangular face was full of sincerity. "I think that the church has lost its original mandate. From the word *go*, the church should have been the country's unofficial shadow government. We should be the ones pointing out the evil in our society. We should also be supplementing the needs of our people. For example, Wemppeans in Solanga County have been oppressed by drought for years yet the church has never thought of drumming up resources to dig dams and sink boreholes for our brothers and sisters in that area." Nehemiah was about to elaborate further when Pastor Paul interrupted him.

"So how do we do that unless we campaign for leadership positions?"

The bishop nodded at Pastor Paul's question.

"By equipping Wemppeans to act with integrity in whatever space they operate from," Pastor Nehemiah countered before going on. "Instead of sending two reverends and three pastors to parliament to fix the problems, why don't we teach our congregations to render services with integrity? That way we will tackle the ills affecting us like corruption. In the past, when we have sent pastors and bishops into parliament, what have they achieved?" Nehemiah paused and looked at his colleagues who were diligently avoiding his eyes. Bishop Epaphras's face was tweaking with fury. Nehemiah knew that church tradition held it as anathema to challenge the senior Bishop. Despite this, he stoically went on.

"Our church headquarters borders the heavily populated Mabanda Moors slums. In fact, most of our members come from there. Why don't we help them ease the congestion in the overpopulated Mabanda Primary School by constructing another school to cater for them? As a church we need to do less telling of how we love one another and show it instead. Otherwise if we ignore the plight of our people, then we should not expect them to support our political ambitions simply because we are the clergy." Nehemiah's major weakness was his inability to read faces. Bishop Epaphras's face was now aflame with anger. Pastor Paul and Pastor Silas looked at each other with knowing glances before staring at the face of the naive Nehemiah. They wondered how far his lofty visions would go.

Several minutes of silence elapsed as the bishop stared at Nehemiah scathingly. Young Pastor Silas began playing with his moustache to cover a grin that was threatening to become a full-blown cackle. He looked at Nehemiah's innocent face and realized that unlike their senior Bishop Epaphras, the poor man would never acquire the art of preaching water and drinking wine. Pastor Nehemiah believed in practicing what he preached. The bishop, on the other hand, had already deployed Dwayne Kirby Hershel's money and had begun to build a private up market housing estate.

For one long hour, the Bishop gave Nehemiah a tongue lashing that left the elderly pastors in the group shocked. They were shamed by the words the bishop chose to use. "Just do as I say," Bishop Epaphras thundered at the group in the late afternoon before dismissing them with instructions on how to execute his strategic plan. Each pastor was to double the number of his congregation by the end of March.

After four days of whirlwind cross-country trips which saw Deborah meet the KPM grassroots supporters, she was back in the city to bury her friend. She had been sleeping less than four hours a day and was understandably tired when she arrived at the morgue on Friday morning. With her was Vumilivu, Mngamata's mother, now frail with age. Mngamata's brother, Msafiri, a poor peasant farmer, was present too. Jonte and Fatumatta, in the company of several neighbors from Mabanda Moors slums stood in the parking lot, observing Mngamata's in-laws, a quarrelsome looking group that had packed the morgue wearing grim faces. Custom dictated that Mngamata be buried by her husband's people, but Mngamata's brother-in-law and his people would hear none of it.

"This woman killed our son and his two children. She is cursed. We don't want her corpse anywhere near our village," He raged over Mngamata's casket, which had been bought courtesy of the alumni of Kilele Girls Government School. Honorable Solomon Ngome was trying to calm the tempers. Watching from a distance, Deborah felt like she was reliving the ordeal she had gone through with her own in-laws all over again. *Kawemppe's marital laws will be among the first to be changed once I become president*, Deborah vowed to herself as she watched Mngamata's in-laws gleefully walk away from responsibility.

"Of course, the lot of you never cared about my sister even when she was alive. We do not expect you to start now," Mngamata's brother, Msafiri, called after the retreating clan.

With the departure of Mngamata's in-laws, the burial plans were changed. Msafiri was going to bury his sister in his own compound, the following day, a Saturday, in their native county of Makonge. With the matter settled, Deborah who was sharing a van with Mngamata's mother, Vumilivu and her brother Msafiri, led the funeral convoy for the eleven-hour journey to Makonge County. Mngamata's neighbors from the slums followed in a hired bus. Josephine, Mrs. Msalaba, Dina, a clean-shaven Jonte and a pregnant Zaituni brought the rear in another van.

Ruthanne Kasi, who was spearheading the KPM campaign, was adamant that the funeral presented the best opportunity for Deborah to launch her presidential bid. Deborah had protested. She abhorred politicians who capitalized on gathered mourners to advance their agenda. But after some thought she had consulted Mngamata's kin and they had given their blessings for the undertaking.

Without wasting time, Praxedes began arrangements for the media to cover the event. Ruthanne rolled up her sleeves and organized numerous groups physically over the phone and on the internet. Mrs. Ziphorah Lengo's HMA WhatsApp group was already oversubscribed to unimaginable levels and had to be subdivided into regional cells. From the moment the germ of fielding Deborah's candidature in Kawemppe had been fronted, Ziphorah had marshaled her HMA members to start canvassing the length and breadth of Kawemppe, preaching the KPM gospel. The lawyers and medics who were excited by the prospect of having a lawyer for a president and a doctor as a deputy for the first time in the country's history were not left behind either. CLEAN had also mutated, and its members had formed a political wing called All on Board.

By late afternoon, the convoy began the dizzying descent into the ravines of the cactus-clad county of Makonge. A narrow road that had been hacked from the rocky cliff was the only access to Mawe Kubwa village, where Mngamata hailed from. Herds of emaciated cows that were slowly recovering from the prolonged drought could be seen by the roadside nibbling on grass shoots so short they seemed to be eating the soil. A group of excited children who were tending the herd gave the convoy a spirited chase, scuttling the few hens that were scratching the dirt for worms. Deborah could hardly remember the place, though she had visited once with Madam Msalaba when they had attempted to get Mngamata back to school. Msafiri directed the convoy down a stony path that led to a collection of three mud huts under the shade of a large acacia tree. Mngamata's mother disembarked from the van and stared at her compound like someone who was seeing it for the first time. Noting that no neighbor had come to light the mourning fire as per tradition, she walked unsteadily towards her hut.

"What has become of the world? All my life I have lived well with my neighbors, yet none could bother to light a fire and keep vigil for my daughter. It is true indeed that daughters are valueless?" Mama Vumilivu lamented as she opened the simple door latch.

"Mama, do not say that. It is our daughters who hold the families and the country together. They are raising their small children while taking care of their aging parents.

Without them there would be a disaster in this country. Maybe the villagers were not aware that Mngamata's in-laws had abdicated their duty. Let us give them time; they will soon be here," Mrs. Msalaba said reassuringly.

The inside of the hut spoke of crippling poverty. Though bare, it was nonetheless clean. The walls were plastered with a special mixture of white clay and cow dung which gave the impression of a cement finish. Deborah placed her handbag on the cot sized bed, sat on the thin mattress, and surveyed the room. Only two dresses hung on a sisal rope. The old lady's worldly possessions amounted to a tooth brush and a small tub of petroleum jelly placed on a simple table next to her bible. It was poverty she had grown familiar with in her early life as her grandparents struggled to educate her. The memory made the tiredness she felt desert her. She walked out and bypassed the table where Mngamata's casket had been placed and went into the bush next to the cow shed. Collecting a heap of dry sticks, she returned to the hut and began a fire.

"You won't know how to light a fire," Mama Vumilivu protested. She was surveying Deborah's manicured hands break the dry sticks with a remorseful look. Deborah noted the look of shame that crossed the old lady's face. She knew the feeling first hand. She had seen the look on her grandfather's face innumerable times when he could not pay her fees on time. She had seen the look register on the faces of her hapless clients as they fought faceless multinationals. It was the helpless look that hard-working people wore when poverty robbed them of their dignity.

"This is work for up-country folk, let me do it." Mama Vumilivu was already pulling her three-legged stool towards the fireplace. Zaituni, whose feet were swollen like those afflicted by elephantiasis, sat on a reed mat by the floor. Mrs. Msalaba sat on a rickety stool near the door.

"Mama, please rest. I was raised in such a kitchen," Deborah said, reassuring Mama Vumilivu. Within no time, big orange flames went up, and Deborah fetched a large pot of water to brew tea.

"Mama Vumilivu, don't be daunted by these girls," Mrs. Mary Msalaba said while gesturing towards Deborah and Zaituni, whose eyes were already tearing from the smoke.

"When I met them thirty years ago at Kilele Girls Government School, they did not even know how to apply Vaseline on their faces. I taught them. So do not let their long scarlet nails scare you." Mama Vumilivu was still unconvinced but her fretting had reduced.

Jonte watched in fascination as Deborah and her friends took charge of the compound. Dina's sophisticated hairdo soon disappeared behind a head wrap as she took charge of the cooking. Josephine and Jonte were helping Mngamata's neighbors from Mabanda Moors set up tents and get settled around the compound. A semblance of order was soon created.

Mama Vumilivu's neighbors were yet to show up on the scene, and Jonte decided to provoke them. He hooked wires to a car battery and strung some lights around that lit up the darkening compound. Hooking up his mobile phone to the loud speakers on the hearse, he swiped through his newly acquired smart phone, selected an immensely popular gospel number, and turned up the volume. Like moths attracted to a lantern lamp in the dark, the locals soon began to trickle in, drawn by the electric lights and the loud music. Several shamefaced women arrived and apologetically took over the cooking from Dina. Deborah held a private meeting with Msafiri and gave him a generous donation to help the family out.

Satisfied that Mama Vumilivu seemed somewhat relaxed to be surrounded by her neighbors, Jonte stepped outside and sought Msafiri. He needed him to point out the grave site. Long before bowls of meat stew, *posho*, and steaming mugs of tea were served, the energetic local youths had dug the grave. After dinner, the people began to settle down for the night, unaware of what was to hit them the next day.

The rhythmic drone of two helicopters approaching Mawe Kubwa village startled the villagers from their quiet morning. Shielding their eyes from the morning sun, they watched in disbelief as the choppers tumbled down from the skies and landed on Mama Vumilivu's stony farm. Praxedes and a six-person crew from her WAMO TV station emerged, weighed down by equipment. They were ready to broadcast an important live message to an unsuspecting nation. Governor Fundi alighted from the second chopper in the company of C. F. Fundi, Ruthanne, and other members of the campaign staff that Deborah was yet to get acquainted with.

The arrival of the helicopters elicited palpable excitement in the villagers. People began making their way to Mama Vumilivu's compound.

"Did Mngamata become famous after her husband passed on?" a scrawny man with bloodshot eyes, dressed in dirty farm clothes asked a friend.

"I heard, and don't quote me, that she was the mistress to one of the powerful governors," his gossiping partner shot back loudly.

"Women are lucky. They don't need proper education to snare a rich man," the wiry man said loudly and clicked dismissively. His statement drew the wrath of a middle-aged lady who sat nearby knitting a sweater.

"Charles, no one is denying you the opportunity of becoming a woman if you think it will make you rich," the lady said sarcastically, her fingers flying in rhythm with the yarn. Her voice was a decibel louder and the surrounding crowd cracked up with laughter.

"Bucket mouth, I am not talking to you. Did I say I wanted to become a woman?" Charles shot back.

"Good for you, Charles. Remain a man. It's no wonder you don't have a wife. No woman would accept to sleep with a skunk like you." The laughter that ensued embarrassed Charles. He waded deeper into the crowd and stood under a tree, creaking under the weight of young men perched on its branches in order to get a better view of the new arrivals.

Later, when a third helicopter was spotted on the horizon, the village wags began speculating that it was bearing President Meshack Jabali, a native of the area. People from the neighboring villages, who had resisted the temptation of the first two helicopters, stopped their activities and scampered towards Mawe Kubwa Village. Farmers carelessly dropped their hoes to the ground. Women fetching water abandoned their water cans by the stream. A choir from Mawe Kubwa Church of God quickly adorned itself in blue and white flocks and assembled near the makeshift dais and began singing. Flustered, self-appointed local party functionaries urgently began to summon their bosses on their mobile phones. From the meandering road to the ravines, a police car could be seen racing towards the village with its siren blaring and lights flashing. It was the local police boss. Hot on his heels, was the convoy of the area member of parliament. He had been attending the funeral of a more noteworthy person. He could not resist the curiosity to find out what the helicopters had brought on board.

As the speculative yarns of Mngamata's mysterious lifestyle were threaded, a fourth helicopter landed in a nearby field. It disgorged several known leaders.

"Is it true the president is amongst us?" somebody asked and peered at the arriving guests who were filling up the raised platform. The question prompted necks to crane longer in an effort to catch a glimpse of the president.

"I think he is the one seated near Honorable C. F. Fundi," a local pastor claimed loudly, pointing at the dais where Mngamata's family sat with the large group of KPM officials.

The burial service started at ten. A local pastor gave a brief and precise sermon before handing over the microphone to Mngamata's mother. Holding her pain with dignity. Other relatives spoke before Mama Vumilivu introduced the KPM caucus.

"You must all be wondering what all these people with aeroplanes are doing in my humble home when I am not a person to warrant such attention," Mama Vumilivu said humbly as she adjusted her white shawl.

"I want to introduce to you someone who honored my daughter in a way I cannot explain with words. She is not a stranger. You know her very well. It is only in the recent past that she got us our money back from the exploitive Xamcom. Deborah is the hope of this nation." Mama Vumilivu stepped back and reached for Deborah's hand. Ruthanne was pleased by the rousing welcome Deborah got from the gathering. Deborah stood up and linked her hand with Mama Vumilivu before the latter continued.

"This lady went to school with my late daughter many years ago, but they lost contact until they stumbled into each other only this past week. By then, my daughter was very sick. Deborah stepped in and helped her, like her own sister. Only God can repay her for this kindness. When the time for her to speak comes, please listen to her message very carefully," Mama Vumilivu said before she and Deborah took their seat.

Mrs. Mary Msalaba took over the microphone and in her eloquent style explained how thirty years before an injustice had been perpetrated against the bright and promising Phyllis Mngamata Jones on account of her tribe. "When I arrived at Kilele Girls Government School as the new principal, hardly had I settled down before Deborah came knocking at my door. With tears in her eyes, she explained to me how her friend Mngamata had been expelled from school. When I checked the academic records, Mngamata's performance was excellent. It matched Deborah's. A week later, we came here with Deborah and two other teachers to track down Mngamata and get her back to school. Mama Vumilivu can ascertain that. But our trip was in vain. Mngamata had gotten married and relocated to Ufuoni County.

"Mngamata broke the country's secondary school entry exam records and made national headlines, and that is why she was admitted to Kilele School. She deserved better." In closing Mrs. Msalaba chastised every one present to think twice when denying any child their God-given opportunity.

"As a leader, when you reallocate dispensary funds supposed to benefit people in Makutano County to Ufuoni County just to win a few votes, do you pause and think about the many women and children you have murdered by that single act?" Mrs. Msalaba posed reflectively before she sat down. The crowd's excitement seemed to have sobered significantly.

The next speaker was the political activist Amos Juma, who spoke from his wheelchair. Juma was a well-known Wemppean activist. Most people still remembered him from the River Maru conservancy demonstration. The year before, Amos had gone on a twenty-day hunger strike to protest buildings that weren't mobile compliant. As a result, a good number of buildings had altered their plans to cater to the disabled. Grabbing the microphone, Juma went ahead to blame corruption, tribalism, and poor governance for failing Wemppeans in general and Mngamata in particular.

Governor Risper Fundi spoke next and cautioned local governments to be vigilant enough not to lose the citizenry in the cracks of their mismanagement. "If the school management failed Mngamata, how come no one raised the alarm? Where was the local Member of Parliament? The village elder? And the pastor? Let us not to leave anyone behind simply because we are not related to them. No Wemppean should be ostracized by a fellow Wemppean by way of tribalism or whatever reason. The cost of making an about-turn forty or fifty years down the line to reach for their hand is enormous." Governor Fundi concluded and sat down to thunderous clapping.

The legendary Honorable Robert Harakka stood up next. "Democracy, like the body's immune system, should be self-correcting," he began somberly.

"Every generation of Wemppeans has a duty to hold the government accountable in order to improve the delivery of services. The government, like a tailor, is mandated by the people to make a cloth fit for them all while still considering their individual preferences." The crowd began clapping, but Honorable Harakka hushed them. "So, how can Wemppeans ensure that the tailor, who happens to be the government, is working for them?" Honorable Harakka asked while looking directly at the nearest WAMO TV camera. The proceedings at Mngamata's funeral were being broadcast live to an estimated six million Wemppeans.

In his heyday, Honorable Harakka had directed parliamentary proceedings with wit and decorum such that Wemppeans tended to tune into the tedious proceedings just to listen to his artistry with the spoken word.

"When credible men and women reflect upon our history, they should gather lessons that can be applied to guide us in the present. If in the past the country's resources have been inequitably distributed and misused with impunity, then that needs to be corrected. This will enable the country to move forward with fewer mistakes and more solid planning. That is prudent political husbandry." He paused briefly, allowing his words to sink in.

"Mngamata and other Wemppeans have been let down by systems, some of which I have been a part of for many years. It is time this came to an end. It is time to make a new beginning"

It was not easy for Honorable Harakka to take the blame on behalf of his generation. But after days of soul searching, he had recognized the existential need of rejuvenating governance by acknowledging past mistakes and planning for a better future. Deborah looked at the remorseful face of Honorable Harakka and felt the full weight of the job she sought. If she didn't deliver, the same look that Harakka wore would be hers in days to come.

"Ladies and gentlemen, I want to introduce to you someone whom I believe has the intelligence and skills needed to eradicate the discrepancies and ensure that no one is left behind anymore."

Harakka beckoned to Deborah, who stood up boldly. She was dressed in a knee-length purple and gold dress and a choker of white and bright blue beads. Deborah reached for the microphone.

"For days, I have been wondering why God planned that I meet my friend Mngamata on her final days on earth," Deborah began. "A month back, a group of people approached me with the proposal that I vie for the presidency of this nation. At first, I declined the offer until I met Mngamata. My friend Phyllis Mngamata Jones made me see things in a different light. Mngamata was the answer I had been looking for." Respectfully Deborah recounted Mngamata's last moments. A few people shook their heads in sadness. The crowd which had arrived mired with carnival excitement had grown somber.

"Who killed Mngamata? How many more Mngamatas are dying as we stand here marinating in political lethargy? When I stood next to my friend on her death bed, watching as her life ebbed away, I swore that I would never let another person slip through the cracks of the system if I could help it. For that reason and that reason alone, I ask you to join me as we make that change." Deborah turned her eyes to the nearest camera as she wound up her speech.

"I, Debora Nzingha, humbly submit my application to Wemppeans to join me as I vie for the presidency of our beloved country in the coming elections. Back me up, we seal the cracks in government systems and grow together. "Seal and grow" is our motto. Thank you, and may God bless."

The crowd was stunned and barely listened to the presiding reverend's last prayers. After the helicopters had disappeared into the skies, the mourners stood in small clusters, discussing the day's events. In their hands were plates overflowing with food. Jonte, who was supervising the catering crew, overheard the talkative pastor who was still holding court tell his captivated audience, "Honorable Ronald Maarufu we know. Bishop Epaphras we see on TV three times a day like medicine. All that I am asking you people is: who is this girl?"

He had not seen the woman with the knitting needles draw near. "What girl are you referring to, Pastor?" she butted in with gusto.

"That was not a girl. That is the next president of Kawemppe, believe it or not. For years we have supported Wemppean men who have served us badly fried governance. Now move over and witness a woman chop the onions of education, stir in a good amount of developmental fat, sprinkle just enough salt for health, and serve you a well-balanced government. Hee heeee," she taunted before sauntering away, holding her head high like a member of the royal family.

# CHAPTER

# 14

DEBORAH NZINGHA'S DECLARATION TO vie for the presidency televised straight from Mngamata funeral gathered momentum like a juggernaut. By Monday morning, most FM radio stations, internet personalities, and political columnists were talking about Deborah Binti Nzingha and attempting to sketch a biography about her. The newly appointed IT manager at KPM was a young chap in his twenties called Marcus Pilipili. He had recreated Deborah's Facebook account and was managing the Twitter and Instagram accounts for his boss while listening to Radio Five's Ananias and Sabina Breakfast Show.

"Would you vote for a female president?" Ananias asked his audience, jumpstarting a topic that was to dominate the media through the entire campaign period.

"A what?" a male caller spat out.

"Yes, a woman for president," Sabina reinforced.

"A woman?" the caller asked in disbelief.

"Yes, a woman. And one you know very well: Deborah Binti Nzingha, who got us a refund from Xamcom," Ananias countered.

"Oh, that one. I got my refund, okay. But, Sabina, politics is not like business, and I cannot accept being sat on by a woman," the caller reiterated with vigor before hanging up.

Celestine, who was calling from Mabanda Moors slums, was next.

"Ananias, tell those men who are bothered by the gender of the next president to grow up. Personally, I run a vegetable and fruit kiosk, and I have never encountered any customer bothered by whether the onions they buy had been planted by a man or a woman. Or if the paw paws came from a farm owned by a man or a woman. The same conditions apply when we fall sick and go to hospital. We simply want to be treated by whichever doctor we find there, be it a man or a woman. So, why should people have bellyaches when it comes to a woman seeking the presidency? Let me tell Wemppeans why some men are afraid of a female president. It is because they have been giving women a raw deal for far too long. They fear being given a dose of their own medicine."

"Well put, Celestine," Ananias concurred.

Other media stations were also working around the theme. By midday, total strangers stuck in traffic turned to each other and debated about Deborah Binti Nzingha, presidential candidature.

In the lush residence of Ronald and Victoria Maarufu, the weekend had been spent in discomfort. Victoria was disturbed by the article she had been reading from The Weekend Dossier. Paa Isaya and his diverse columnists had presented over twenty-five pages of heavily debated and varied opinions around the subject of Deborah Binti Nzingha's candidature. The pundits extolled her and the yet-to-be-launched KPM Party. What rattled Victoria even more was what Paa Isaya's had written in the editorial. Unwillingly, she let her eyes linger longer over the first few sentences.

*The Game Changer*
*By: Paa Isaya*

> *Two women have decided to forgo traditional party structures and forge a new party that will carry their quest to lead Kawemppe to the Promised Land. Deborah Binti Nzingha, who is seen as a competent problem solver, and her running mate, the veteran Governor Risper Fundi, are a potent threat to the established parties. The combination of youthful vigor and proven experience the two women bring to the political fray is not to be underestimated . . .*

Wearily, Victoria cast the paper on the sofa. Though thin, the Weekend Dossier was a deeply satisfying paper, and each edition (of over two million copies) never lasted more than two hours in the newsstands.

Victoria's worry was cemented by the fact that Paa's readers were intellectuals who were highly inclined to take his advice seriously, a fact that could spell doom for her husband's bid. In silent anger, she thought of the happy-go-lucky battalions of SASA hopefuls, who were content to let the party's political machinery do its own work without putting in a day's worth of work. Ignoring the tea her chef had placed on the table, she retrieved her mobile phone and summoned Alloys Faya, the SASA Campaign Manager, Senator Virunga, and Mitambo to her residence at once.

Without questioning the urgency of the summons, the three individuals converged in Victoria's palatial sitting room within an hour. Senator Virunga wanted to grumble about the short notice, but his few interactions with the lady had fostered good sense in him. He knew that Victoria Maarufu's decisions were above reproach. Mitambo had come because he had no choice. So far, he had not unearthed any juicy dirt on Deborah Binti Nzingha's past to appease Victoria. He made up his mind to engage the services of a professional detective.

Alloys Faya stared at Victoria's severe face and swallowed uneasily. For the fifteen years he had worked for Honorable Ronald Maarufu as his campaign manager, it was Victoria Maarufu whom he had come to dread the most.

"Don't underestimate those KPM ladies. We need to stop them in their tracks," Victoria informed her audience. "Gentlemen, tell those SASA hopefuls hanging around the party headquarters to disperse and go back to their villages to canvass for votes. Let them not expect Ronald to assemble the party's organs for them and travel throughout the country to drum up grassroots support while they do nothing. If Ronald loses, they will also lose." Victoria's face was stony with anger. Mitambo Mitambo cowered in his chair in discomfort, occasionally firing a contemptuous stare at Victoria when he was sure she wasn't looking.

Ego scratched by Victoria's chilly tone, Senator Virguna scowled dangerously for a minute. Then common sense kicked in and he realized that his political future as the SASA Governor for Mnazi County lay solidly in Victoria's hands.

"Don't worry madam" he said quickly as he adjusted his scowl to resemble a respectable-looking smile.

"I will personally get them to start working immediately."

# CHAPTER 15

THE MONTH OF MARCH was late for Deborah and KPM party to nurse any hope of winning an election come December. But the dogged KPM caucus was determined to do their best. Deborah arrived at the new KPM headquarters promptly at nine in the morning. The building was situated near the railways station that served Wemppe City. It had once housed a truck assembly garage and had been loaned to the party by Honorable Harakka. With care, Deborah walked past the chaotic collection of cables that were on the floor—red, white, and blue. Technicians were wiring the ground floor in readiness for the KPM delegates meeting scheduled for the next day.

Ignoring the lingering smells of fresh paint and old grease that hung heavily in the air, she made her way to the makeshift first-floor office. Carpenters had partitioned the space into two wings. One wing hosted the campaign staff offices, while the other wing housed the cafeteria, the sleeping quarters, and bathrooms. A stack of mattresses stood in a neat pile against the wall, ready to accommodate weary campaign assistants.

Deborah took her seat and attempted to block the din of the constriction going on around her. On an adjacent empty plot, construction workers were busy working on a helipad.

"So, people, let us review our readiness for tomorrow's launch," Deborah began and sneezed heartily as the pungent paint fumes hit her nostrils.

Automatically, Governor Fundi, her self-appointed doctor, handed her an anti-histamine tablet and a bottle of mineral water. The people Deborah was talking to were sitting on plastic chairs around a large dining table. They included Obed Jaribu, who was in charge of security and logistics; Jonte who had taken over as the CLEAN coordinator; the campaign's financial manager, Irene Cheupe; Amos Juma, who was deputizing Ruthanne as campaign manager; and young Marcus Pilipili, the IT guy. Ruthanne and Lumumba were present too.

Governor Fundi had been keen about enlisting Paa Isaya as their media consultant, but Deborah's vehement opposition to the idea had led them to settle for Jasper Hadithi, the veteran journalist. Jasper sat between Governor Fundi and Praxedes. Praxedes's role as KPM advisory manager was to smell trouble on behalf of the party and shoot it down before it grew out of hand.

Deborah began speaking, happy to be working with such a collection of professionals. "I have two unbendable rules that we are to abide by. First, no matter what part of Kawemppe we find ourselves campaigning in, I must spend time with my kids daily. If we are out in the field during the day and I get home late, then the mornings will be reserved for my kids. If I miss the morning time with them, then you are to get me home before five o'clock, when the school bus drops them."

Ruthanne knew that Deborah's success as a lawyer and environmentalist stemmed from the meticulous planning she undertook before every project. She waited attentively for Deborah to state her second condition.

"Secondly, for the sake of my family, no campaign matters should ever make their way to my home. All meetings are to take place here or at other venues. I want to thank Governor Fundi here. She has offered us her place, just in case any urgent meeting or private consultations are necessary. Now that I have given out my conditions, let us proceed."

"You got it, ma'am," Obed, the forty-eight-year-old former marine now in charge of KPM security and logistics, called out. He was perusing the campaign schedule he had drawn up for Deborah and realized that he would need to adjust the timings.

The group talked about pending concerns. Ruthanne assured everyone that the work around the hall would be finished by midnight and the hall would be ready for the meeting the next day. Jasper Hadithi and Praxedes had the media ready.

"The cash box is sound," Irene Cheupe affirmed. KPM main financiers were a growing number of low-income Wemppeans who were sending small but steady contributions. With nothing left to report, the meeting was just about to break up when Lumumba Abiola interrupted.

"Just a minute. I almost forgot," he called out theatrically.

"I insist that we do not call Madam Deborah "aunt" or "Debbie." No euphemisms whatsoever. It will steal the oomph from our candidate."

"I totally agree," Deborah added spryly. "Deborah Binti Nzingha will do fine. Furthermore, we are yet to hear about an Uncle Mbeki or Aunt Merkel."

"Now that we have a workable framework in place, allow me to invite you all to my residence, for your last decent meal before the campaign chaos overwhelms us," Governor Fundi said. The invitation brought the three-hour meeting to an end.

The meal turned out to be a reunion of sorts. Governor Fundi had invited Deborah's friends from her former law office, plus her dear friends Josephine, Dina, and Zaituni for the lunch. Josephine had in turn invited Paa Isaya. Deborah gave Josephine a reproachful look as Aphia playfully shoved Deborah towards Paa who caught her, his lone dimple framing his face at his handsomest. Fundi's daughter, Dr. Neema, who had been helping in the kitchen, entered the room and squealed with delight when she saw Deborah.

"People can easily confuse you two for sisters," Josephine exclaimed. She had immediately noticed the striking resemblance between Neema and Deborah. This prompted the small crowd to pause and marvel at the identical foreheads, oval-shaped eyes, and almost matching dark chocolate complexions. Honorable C. F. Fundi noticed simultaneous clouds of pain and discomfort come to the faces of his wife and Deborah. He judiciously steered the gawking guests towards the well-laid-out dining table.

Deborah excused herself and withdrew to the bathroom. She could barely contain the sob stuck in her throat. Standing in front of the sink, she began heaving painfully with guilt. "God help me," she whispered as a tear streamed down her face. Feeling selfish about her prayer, she rephrased it. "God help us all." *What would happen if Paa Isaya realized that he was sharing a roof with the daughter he never knew about?* Deborah pondered. The smell of lavender scent in the bathroom helped calm her down. Afraid that she might be delaying the luncheon being held in her honor, Deborah wiped her face and rejoined the guests. A chef dressed in starched whites moved around the table with his assistant supplying platters of sizzling goat roast, pounded *matoke*, tikka chicken, and yams. The tantalizing scents wafting through the air drove the guests to the food immediately. They totally unaware of the inner turmoil the luncheon's hostess and guest of honor were going through.

As promised by Ruthanne, the KPM headquarters were ready when Jonte, whom Ruthanne had christened the Manager at Large (MAL), strode in, flanked by his numerous friends from the hood. It was a lovely day. The rain, which had been pouring all around the country, had cooled the air and resuscitated the dry roadside grass and saplings to a luscious green. Armed with brightly colored *vuvuzelas*, the youths had walked all the way from Mabanda Moors. The small group that started off had grown into a sizeable crowd by the time they reached the KPM offices. A battalion of volunteers, mostly university students, were ushering in the delegates and handing out

KPM party manifestos. The conference room was filling rapidly with delegates dressed in the party's gold and indigo colours. Ruthanne moved up and down the aisles, her sharp eye missed nothing. She was constantly talking on the two mobile phones she held. WAMO TV and their rival, Reke TV, were airing the event live. Lumumba Abiola was chatting with the journalists, most of whom were well-known to him. Having been a journalist for many days himself, he knew that one of the worst mortal sins a politician could ever commit was making enemies with the media people. They either gave you poor and negative reporting or a total media blackout. There was a need to cozy up to them.

Deborah peered at the surging crowds on the CCTV monitor in her office. She spotted Nana seated with Goldie and AJ near the dais. Nana sat ramrod straight, her face full of pride and adoration. The children wore baggy purple t-shirts, whose front bore the picture of their smiling mother. The words Deborah Binti Nzingha for President were stenciled on the back. The children, mesmerized by the dance, had started their own shuffle. They were occasionally giggling in a manner Nana referred to as "fools who have caught the rabies."

Closing her eyes, Deborah rehearsed the notes she had made. She recalled the words that a woman had spoken amid the first meet-the-people tour. "If your government gives me water, I will practice agribusiness and take care of my children's school fees and give Kawemppe an educated child. If you make me feel that I belong to this country by distributing the government resources fairly, I will give you a peaceful, loving child who will not feel that his future ambitions are limited by the tribe he comes from. If you deny me the basics, in a few years' time, the government will have participated in the making of a hoodlum. A person who wants to eat and has no money, a person who wants to work but can't find a job, is a disenfranchised soul."

Her reverie was interrupted by some commotion in the hall's entrance. From the CCTV monitor, Deborah watched Mrs. Ziphorah Lengo, the HMA chair, walk in with an army of singing women dressed in a kaleidoscope of bright gold and purple gowns. The hall shook with song and stomping feet. The sound was louder than that of an approaching herd of buffaloes. Smiling, Deborah picked her way downstairs and joined the women.

"Ayiyiyiyiyiyiyiiiiii."

"Mama is a wonderful nurturer."

"She corrects her children with love and kisses."

"Mamaaaa."

"Mama is love."

"That is why she never dropped your big head on the hard ground?"

"Mamaaaa."

"Who wiped your little bottom clean?"

"When she could have neglected you?"

"Mamaaaa, ayiyiyiyiiiii."

"And who corrected and pinched you, siniii?"

"When you said that bad word?"

"Mamaaaaa, ayiyiyiyiiiii."

"So why are you doubting Mama?"

"When she wants to the president?"

"Ayiyiyiyiiiii, ayiyiyiyiiiii, ayiyiyiyiiiii."

The song was heavily embellished. The original version was different, but who cared when distinguished gentlemen like honorable Solomon Ngome, Seth Pasakhwa, and Honorable C.F. Fundi loosened up and joined the women in the jig?

When the music died down an hour later, the launch began with several speakers addressing the gathering. Before long, Governor Fundi took to the floor.

"Is there anyone in Kawemppe who does not know the people's defender, Deborah Binti Nzingha?" Governor Fundi asked with her eyes glittering under the spotlight

"Noooo," the hall thundered.

"She is fearless," Risper went on.

"Yeess," the crowd answered back.

"A defender of justice."

"Yeess."

"A woman of integrity."

"Yeess."

"A woman we can trust."

"Yeess."

"An environmentalist who inspires us to care for our habitat."

"Yeess."

"An inspiration to the youth." Risper paused before adding, "So, why should I waste your time anymore when she is in the house? Ladies and gentlemen, I give you Deborah Binti Nzingha, our president in waiting."

The welcoming applause was thunderous. AJ blocked both his ears from the din of the *vuvuzelas*. He watched his mother mount the dais with pride.

Experiencing an adrenaline, rush Deborah looked skywards and mouthed "Help us all," and as she had composed herself, she adjusted the microphone and began her speech.

"My fathers and my mothers, my brothers and sisters, citizens of Kawemppe Republic, the foothold of Africa . . ." The TV cameras zoomed in. The delegates sat mesmerized, watching brains and beauty at work. At five foot eight, Deborah had been blessed with two things: skin that made had her face look ten years younger and the extraordinary sense of a female at home with her power. It took twenty minutes for Deborah to request the country to back her presidential bid. When she was done, the crowd was still entranced and only began to clap when she took her seat.

After a brief interlude of music and dance, it was time for the official launch. A gigantic purple and gold cake was wheeled in, causing Goldie and AJ to hyperventilate with excitement.

"As I have said, this is not just politics as usual. It is politics for positive change," Deborah began. She moved to the side as a gigantic banner unfurled behind her bearing the word "WOMAN©"

" 'WOMAN' will be the KPM campaign tool," Deborah stated. The crowds stared at her, awaiting an explanation. Ushers materialized from the sides and walked down the aisles, dishing out saucer-sized indigo plastic badges, hats, and purple t-shirts with the word "WOMAN" stenciled in gold.

"'WOMAN', stands for Word of Mouth Advertising Network. It is a tool people have used for centuries. This tool requires every Wemppean man and woman of voting age to walk to their neighbors' homes and hold conversations about how we want this country to be governed going forward. It is from these discussions that you the people will come up with the representatives you want KPM to work with.

Paa was watching the launch on his office TV. He watched Deborah spellbind the delegates better than she ever did during the Xamcom trial. A pang of regret rippled in his tummy, and he thought bitterly of the fool he was to have given up on such a woman. Sipping some water to quell the rising bile in his gut, he listened as Deborah laid down the strategy KPM would employ to ensure that nominees for the civic, parliamentary, and gubernatorial seats passed the standards of zero tolerance for tribalism and nepotism that KPM subscribed to. Silently, Paa vowed to pursue Deborah to heaven and back. Whatever the cost, he was determined to have her back—this time as his life partner.

# CHAPTER 16

THE HEADQUARTERS OF OUR Father International Church, OFIC, occupied an acre of land whose front side bordered the busy Ring Road. The backyard which served as the church's parking grounds shared a boundary with the Mabanda Moors playground, a handkerchief-size piece of land that held the rapidly mushrooming slum in check. Paa Isaya's desire to gauge Bishop Epaphras's tenacity in the face of the fast-rising popularity of the KPM party had driven him from bed early one rainy May Sunday to worship at Bishop Epaphras church.

KPM had a following that was impossible to ignore. Deborah's feminine intuition was able to link with the masses in a way never seen before in Wemppe politics. Shepherded by the experienced Fundis, Harakka, and Ngome, hers seemed to be a surefire ticket to the presidential palace. A successful KPM primary had been conducted, netting a surprisingly fresh catch of candidates who had no scandals hanging around their necks. According to the latest polls from the reliable Mzalendo pollster, the

KPM party was jostling for the number two slot alongside Bishop's Epaphras's NWS party with twenty nine percent each. The SASA Party's popularity was at forty percent. Democratic Democracy Party was officially out of the race. Paa's assessment pegged the rising KPM popularity to the open and fair manner in which the party had conducted its primaries as the reason for such overwhelming public support.

He nosed his car towards the open parking lot, where a band of hard-looking youths sat in a cluster ready to serve as parking boys. With the help of a sinister teen with bulging arm muscles that screamed "ghetto gym," Paa squeezed his car between two pickup trucks. He fished a battered New Testament bible from the dashboard and alighted to the waiting reception of the muscled youth.

"Boss, your car is safe with me. Can I shine it for you?" the teen requested. Loosely interpreted, the ghetto language of the request meant, "Give me something little to guard your car; otherwise you are not assured of its security." Paa agreed to have the already clean exterior of his car washed again, with what he hoped was not sewer water. Happy for having snagged some cash legitimately, the youth dashed to fetch a bucket and a rag.

Sidestepping a used condom lying next to a plastic Sunny Set Vodka bottle, Paa fell into step with a lovely looking couple that was herding their teenage children into the church. A battalion of ushers, scanning batons in hand, frisked him before they showed him to a seat in the middle of the church. The church was a stone and mortar structure with grey iron sheets riveted to steel beams shielding the over six thousand members from the elements. It was obvious that the bishop hadn't spent much money on the building. The growing sea of humanity had to make do with four fans distributed around the building. Fan number one was at the pulpit, intended to cool the preacher. Another one whirled where "Mum," the bishop's wife, sat to the left of the pulpit. The remaining two were distributed between the deacons seated behind Mum and the choir to the right of the pulpit. The rest of the congregation suffocated over each other's breath in their blue plastic seats. They were fortunate to catch a blast of wind blowing in through the wide windows.

Although familiar with church worship procedures, Paa was an Easter and Christmas time church attendant. With shame, he noted that every other person was laden with heavy bibles and notepads. His wallet-size bible was attracting stares. Quickly he buried it in his jacket and instead downloaded the bible app to his mobile phone. A Sunday school class beautifully recited a memory verse from a tent somewhere in the church compound. Paa vowed to attend more church services and improve his spiritual life and that of his son Lee, especially when the boy came home from boarding school.

A choir stood up to sing as the offertory baskets were passed along. The TV consoles beamed a thin choir master flapping his hands in rhythm with the song. Paa thought the man looked like a giant stick insect. Leaving the insect man alone, he was taken by the soloist, an angelic beauty with an arresting voice.

"In the cross," the beauty sang to the accompaniment of the piano.

"Iiiiiiiiin the crooosss," the rest of the choir joined in, swaying in their yolk yellow tops and jungle green batik skirts and trousers.

"In the crooooooooooss," the beauty sang out in a pure voice.

She reminded Paa of Deborah. Involuntarily, Paa felt something stir in his loins, which he quickly shamed to death, due to the thought of the hallowed ground he was on. Paa remembered that it was Deborah's integrity and clarity of vision that had endeared her to him when they first met. Her practical approach to life came from her peasant farmer background. Her grandfather's faith in his farm to provide for their needs, and her grandmother's assiduous saving from her vegetable kiosk to educate her had imbued Deborah with an uncommon practicality at solving complex problems. He was still ruminating over Deborah's inspiration when Mum, Reverend Naomi Epaphras, rose to begin the Sunday service formally. Paa's journalistic enzymes kicked in, and he hit the recording knob of the old-fashioned recorder that was hidden in his jacket pocket.

Reverend Naomi wore a smart pink frock, which parted open to reveal hidden slits, as she walked towards the podium.

"Church, have you been living in the same country as I have these past few months?" Rev. Naomi asked the audience that had more women than men.

"Let me refresh the memory of some of you who are looking at me blankly."

The flock laughed.

"Women are created to be helpers," Naomi Epaphras said succinctly.

"Women were not created to rule and lord it over men," She added emphatically and paused to wipe nonexistent sweat from her forehead with a white handkerchief.

"Ladies in the house, are we together?" She leveled her eyes at the television cameras for the benefit of the ladies at home. The sermon was being broadcast live.

"When a woman walks in front of her man, she blocks his vision. If she walks behind him, she drags his vision. But when she walks besides her man, she becomes the neck which supports the head". Naomi fanned herself briefly with the handkerchief before continuing. "Can I talk now people?"

"Tell it like it is, Mum," shouted a lady in the front.

"I am not putting women down. Far from it. But when two ladies, one of them husbandless, claim that they can run this country, then we are in deep trouble."

Giggles and murmurs broke throughout the church. Mum let it go on for a minute as the congregation turned to each other to discuss the KPM party.

"Do you think it is right to vote those two women in?" Paa found himself accosted by his neighbor, a pretty lady who mimicked the same astounded expression Mum was projecting from the podium.

"Sure, why not?" Paa answered.

He was about to add some more insights when Mum's voice boomed through the state-of-the-art sound system.

"Be smart and wise people. Give NWS a chance to lead the people. Rise to your feet and put your hands together as we welcome our bishop, the presidential contender for New Wine Skin party, my husband Bishop Epaphras."

The congregation gave a prolonged clap.

"Okay, okay, okay . . . if you are clapping for Christ, keep it going" Bishop Epaphra's voice boomed through the microphone as he emerged from the back of the church, where he had been overseeing the counting of the church offerings. Bishop Epaphras never took chances with the offerings. It went without saying that OFIC offerings were better guarded than those who gave it. At eleven sharp every Sunday, an armored security van with an armed escort evacuated the hefty offering to the bank.

"I said if you are clapping for the Lord, keep it going." Despite being a short, pudgy man, his voice boomed like that of a giant. As he talked, his jowls shook in rhythm with his every word. To mirror his wife's dress, he wore a white suit with silver lines that contrasted well with his dark complexion.

Paa imagined that the attire must be a nightmare for the OFIC television crew, who were attempting to project their Bishop favorably to millions of viewers all around the world.

"I said, if you are clapping for the Lord, you can do better than that." The piano picked up tempo, and the clapping grew wilder as shouts and whistling came into the mix.

"Now, give Brother Timothy a clap for organizing such a wonderful choir.

The clapping continued until the insect man, whom Paa now knew was called Brother Timothy sat down.

Bishop Epaphras then began speaking.

"Brothers and sisters, there comes a time when the church must stand up and let its voice be heard." He jerked his head upward, sending his jowls quavering.

"I will preach in a moment. For those of you who are wondering . . . I have all the notes ready here," the Bishop said, shaking his iPad in the air. Changing his voice to a more endearing tone he went on. "For the longest time, the church, which makes up more than ninety percent of Kawemppe's population, has been looking outside its ranks for leaders. Are we together?"

"Get to it, Bishop," a deacon encouraged.

"No, no, no. You are not ready for what I have to say to you," the Bishop taunted as he broke into a fast-paced strut on the stage.

"What's on your mind? Unleash it, Bishop," several voices prompted him.

The bishop slowed down and leaned on the glass podium.

"There comes a time when we have to look into ourselves to get our answers. Remember Joshua and Moses. They were not just priests but also leaders in their day. Why can't the twenty-first century church in Kawemppe replicate the same?"

Paa observed that most people had their necks craned towards the front expectantly. He acknowledged that, indeed, in the not so far future, the church may have the clout needed to field a presidential candidate.

"During election time, don't we all see our politicians filling the front pews of our churches to dish out promises and lies?" the bishop went on. "But the moment they get our vote they disappear."

"Nail it, Bishop!" insect man said.

"Why am talking like this today?" Bishop Epaphras asked and shifted to the edge of the pulpit.

"It is because if you are not going to subscribe to NWS party in large numbers. You need be wary. Some two women are walking around the neighborhoods flaunting an apple. If you are not careful, we might have a repeat of the Garden of Eden all over again."

Paa watched unbelievingly as most women stood up to cheer the Bishop some more. He felt a strange urge to head to the front and defend Deborah. Slowly, he rose from his seat, careful not to drop his recorder and headed towards his car. The youth had already cleaned it and was casually leaning on the hood. Paa gave him a generous tip and drove off towards Wemppe meadows. He had to see Deborah.

# CHAPTER
# 17

Pʀᴇsɪᴅᴇɴᴛ Mᴇsʜᴀᴄᴋ Jᴀʙᴀʟɪ ʜᴀᴅ inherited the worst case of corruption and negative ethnicity ever witnessed in the Republic of Kawemppe since independence. The former president, dictator Ochao, and his cronies had plundered the country dry. Wemppeans had settled for a steady menu of ethnicity, old boy networks, gangster tactics, and the occasional assassination as the only conduits to power. Painstakingly, President Jabali had clawed through the muck to dismantle tribal networks, insane levels of impunity, poor use of Kawemppe's resources, and crippling corruption, and restored some sanity. He had gone ahead and instituted civic education in schools and places of worship to empower Wemppeans. His efforts to end corruption and wrestle Kawemppe from the clutches of calculated poverty had netted him many enemies.

Meshack Jabali was a grandson of the first generation of Christian converts, men who had preached the gospel with zeal and fortitude devoid of the enormous financial benefits most of the current crop of preachers could not do without. His parents had perished in the Great Famine of

1944. He had been brought up by his grandfather, who was a lay pastor. At nine years of age, Jabali had joined the local Makonge Mission School, whose entrance examination was determined by the ability of a child's right hand to curve over the head and touch the left ear. It was a queer way the missionaries deployed to assess child's efficacy skills. The Makonge Mission School, was run by the Wilberforce Missionaries.

The boy's knack for influencing others was spotted early on in his school days. No one could accuse Jabali of being dirty. At night, he would remove the only set of clothes he possessed—a pair of brown khaki shorts and a white shirt—and tie a loose sarong around his body. He would then proceed to clean the uniform gently, so as not to tear the seams. Before long, the other boys who were mucky most of the time, followed suit. His charisma was noted by the missionaries, who appointed him a prefect. Combined with his love for athletics, he became an outstanding example of what the missionaries, in their ignorance, called "the converted native spirit." They didn't know that Jabali's great grandfather was the chief priest's runner, a man who was appointed to relay crucial messages between the five tribes scattered across present-day Makonge County in a single night.

Under the guidance of his grandfather and the missionaries, Meshack's studies flourished, and he joined a teacher training college. Upon graduation, he was absorbed by the Wilberforce Mission Schools as a history teacher. By the time Kawemppe gained its independence from the British, Jabali had been groomed as the youngest African to head a mission school in Kawemppe. For thirty years, Jabali had traversed the length and breadth of Kawemppe, supervising the Wilberforce Mission schools which had been renamed Wemppe African Schools after independence. When politics beckoned, Meshack Jabali had received the support of generations of Wemppean students who had known him personally as their teacher and were tired of dictator Ochao brutality. Zealously, they had campaigned for him until he trounced his more popular rival, Dalmas Kinga Nzambe, in the presidential race.

The president sat, enjoying the rich fragrance infused air, filtering in from the indigenous forest surrounding the Makonge presidential lodge after his morning jog. At seventy years of age, he still ran ten kilometers every morning. The lodge, an old sprawling bungalow which had been inherited from a colonial district commissioner, held the charm of a bygone era. With his term almost coming to an end, President Jabali had formed a habit of retiring to the quiet lodge most weekends to work on his memoirs. This weekend had been special. He had brought along his forty-year-old daughter, Vizuri Jabali, a professor of political science at UuZala York University.

"Sir, may I shift the table to the shade?" Peter, requested as he approached the president.

"Sure, Peter," the president answered and followed his loyal aide-de-camp as he moved the table and nestled it under the shade formed by the umbrella like branches of an ancient mvai tree

Resuming his seat, he hunkered over the draft of his memoirs he'd been writing in longhand. A laptop the aide had placed on the table lay untouched. President

Meshack Jabali considered himself a B.B.C era man—Born Before Computers. He had a love-hate relationship with technology and had long discovered that without the ingrained connection of a pen and paper in his hand, his writing was much hampered. In public, the president was known to pose intelligently behind a computer screen. Only his close friends knew how he avoided modern gadgets.

Thirty minutes went by before he could think of anything to put down. He started wishing he had accompanied his daughter Vizuri to the village. (Vizuri ran several non-profit early child educational programs around Makonge County.) Frustrated, he threw down the pencil and watched a flock of crown birds sauntering near the edge of the forest. Intrigued, he rose up for a better view and began to walk after them, but they disappeared into the denser part of the forest. *What a great country we have here*, he thought while swatting a swarm of mosquitoes aiming towards him. The action made him feel like he had cut the surrounding June heat into halves. The heat made him wish he was in one of the cooler presidential lodges, like the Amusitu presidential lodge, which was nestled in the cool cascading falls of the Maru River. The thought evaporated quickly when he remembered the Maru River controversy, brought about by his deputy's desire to win the elections, had almost ruined his immaculate track record in fighting corruption.

President Jabali could not rule out the conniving Victoria Maarufu as the driving force behind the Maru debacle. Lately, Victoria had been boldly suggesting to the media that the president was endorsing her husband as the next president of Kawemppe. What disturbed

Jabali the most was the fact that the media had lapped up Victoria's words without questioning their veracity. It was an indication that the electorate had learned nothing from his ten years of civic education. Throughout his tenure, President Jabali had advocated that the king's child and the villager's child had the same chance of competing at any level of government, including the presidency. The last thing he wanted before he left office was to be sucked into the vortex of electoral fever, forcing him to take sides.

Drawn by a bush of well-trimmed bougainvillea, awash with purple flowers, the president ambled over to inspect it. A clever gardener, with the help of trellises, had beautifully shaped the shrub into a canopy. The president walked under and sat on a boulder. Absentmindedly, he snapped a small twig and shaped it into a tooth pick. His thoughts stole back to his memoirs which he had titled *The Transitional Man.* What would Alice, his late wife, make of it? Would she laugh at the utopian theory he was perpetuating? That he had inherited rotten power and almost succeeded in separating the wheat from chaff and made Kawemppe a better place? A little smile formed on his broad lips. It was at times like this that he missed his dear Alice, who'd now been gone for six years.

Dark clouds began gathering in the June skies. Jabali thought of calling his son Wilberforce who was working in the Kawemppe Embassy in Kenya for advice about his memoirs. But the president refrained from activating his mobile phones. He was sure his deputy, Maarufu, who had been expecting him at a rally in Lokamiko County, had called him numerous times. Peter, watching his boss discreetly from a window, thought that the presidential pose made him look like a monk.

This was the stance Vizuri found him in when she came back from her tour of the village. "A penny for your thoughts dad," Vizuri said as she handed her father a cold glass of orange juice and sat facing him on a boulder opposite. Her long white skirt draped around her feet like a theatre curtain.

Jabali never failed to be struck by the resemblance between his wife Alice and his daughter Vizuri. The round noses and high cheekbones made both women exotically beautiful. The only difference was that while Alice had been plump, Vizuri had maintained her slim figure, even as the mother of a teenage daughter. For thirty minutes, Jabali listened as his daughter enthusiastically updated him on her projects.

"Enough about me, Dad. What do you think of the current lineup of presidential contenders?" she asked as she drained her ice-cold juice in one gulp. The hot Makonge climate could not be compared to the cold weather she was used to.

The question caught the president off guard, and he took a few minutes to think his answer. If it were up to him to pinpoint who among the four presidential contenders, he would entrust Kawemppe's leadership to, it would not Ronald. He could never entrust him with the continuation of the changes he had affected. The man was too complacent. President Jabali could even bet that Maarufu was still hoping for a presidential endorsement. However, the same could not be said of his wife, Mrs. Victoria Maarufu, who could smell danger to SASA party while her husband was still cavorting with it. While the citizens knew that his deputy was Ronald Maarufu, the responsibilities of the deputy presidency rested solidly on the shrewd shoulders of Victoria Maarufu. President Jabali could himself testify to that.

When a power gap had been created by the sudden illness of his then deputy, Carey Francis Fundi, in Jabali's first term, it was Victoria who had sprung into action and suggested the merger between Maarufu's party and Jabali's party, resulting to the SASA Party. Jabali's interactions with Victoria over the years had left him with a clear understanding that Victoria was desperately in need of the presidency more than her affable husband, Ronald. Jabali knew that Victoria was greedy and corrupt. Her role in the Maru river saga had led Wemppeans to question his seriousness in reining in corrupt elements in his government. For a man who wanted to leave a clean legacy around his name, touching the Maru was an unforgivable sin Jabali could not condone, and he was waiting for the right moment to strike back.

"My opinion might be biased. You are the one with a fresh outlook. Who would you support?" Jabali said at last.

"I am with the KPM ladies. Come November, I will be back here to join in their campaigns."

Jabali looked at his daughter in amusement. He believed that he was a reasonably liberal man. The idea of two ladies attempting to secure the top executive jobs of a country was still too foreign of an idea for Wemppeans to grasp. Grudgingly, he admitted that Governor Fundi was widely experienced, being a two-time governor and a politician's wife to boot. She had the required skills to lead. It was the girl Deborah Binti Nzingha who was a hard sell. Despite the fact that Deborah's nerve for prosecuting wayward multinationals had in its own way helped the fight against corruption, the president felt that Deborah needed more grooming—probably as a governor. *The popularity of the two women should not be mistaken with the credentials necessary to win a presidential election*, he thought.

"What makes you support the ladies?" Jabali probed.

"Because they have been tried and proven to be worth their salt. I mean, you cannot compare them to Ronald Maarufu and that peacock Mitambo Mitambo or even the Bishop"

Scratching the day-old stumble on his chin, president Jabali shuddered as he imagined what would happen to Wemppeans if in the unforeseen future the country fell into the hands of Mitambo Mitambo. When his intelligence chief had handed him a brief that Mitambo had acquired the Democratic Democracy Party from Dalmas Kinga Nzambe, he had called the police chief and ordered him to investigate Mitambo Mitambo extensively.

Thinking about Bishop Epaphras, Jabali actually felt pity for the reverend. Personally, he liked the man's preaching on TV. But it would be a mistake for the bishop and his NWS Party to bank on the devoted church crowds to unquestioningly join his political cause. Religion and politics were strange bedfellows. Shaking his head, he reflected on the eclectic mix of characters jostling for the presidency.

"So, who have you been grooming to succeed you?" Vizuri queried. The intensity of the question jolted the president from his thoughts, and shame spread over his face. With regret, he realized that Vizuri's question was what his late wife would have asked him: "Who have you been grooming to continue to fruition the change that you have so scrupulously advocated?"

To give himself time to come up with an appropriate response, he changed the topic. The clouds had turned black. Capillaries of lightening lit the sky, followed by clapping thunder, and then it began to drizzle.

"Let us move away from the rain and have lunch." the president said and led his daughter towards the veranda. A steward was setting up a lunch table. In the surrounding bushes, armed guards discreetly changed their positions.

# 18

GOOD EVENING, VIEWERS. WELCOME to the Bandari Live Show. Senator Marko Virunga and Mrs. Ziphorah Lengo, the chairlady of the House Managers Association and a KPM supporter, are our guests tonight," Prost Bandari, the host of the Bandari Live Show, said.

The Bandari live show on WAMO TV was a program that brought together opposing political authorities for a face-off. KPM had sent Mrs. Ziphorah Lengo to spar with the Senator.

"Senator Virunga, what do you make of the rising popularity of KPM?" Bandari began.

Senator Virunga's left buttock cheek still hurt from the "injection" Governor Fundi had given him almost four months ago. "Bandari listen, I am not saying that women cannot be leaders, but there is a way in which things are ordained to be." The Senator's voice had acquired the sober tone of a father advising a defiant child. "We cannot have two women running this country. Unless all the men have died." His hands gestured wildly.

"Senator, unless you want to inform Kawemppe women that they have been wrong all along when they elected male presidents and deputy presidents, I don't see why women should be vilified.

"What is wrong with two women leading Kawemppe?" Mrs. Lengo countered before bestowing a withering look on the senator.

"Senator, I don't understand the double standards. We have always had two men gun for the same seats and no eyebrows were raised. Why now?" Bandari asked.

"Number one. This this is not Europe where their king is a queen. The senator's sober tone was getting garrulous.

"It is not that their king is a queen, but a lady who happens to be the queen is the head of the country," Ziphorah interjected curtly.

It was as if the senator never heard the interjection, and he carried on. "Number two. If we allow this trend of women wanting to becoming leaders to go on, Wemppean men will soon be strapping children on their backs and bending over stoves to stir up stew. Take it from me".

"Aaah!" Mrs. Lengo exclaimed, brushing off the comment. "Senator don't you think you are overreacting and undermining the strides women have made in this country? I am sure you have flown in planes piloted by women."

"Exactly. Now we are on the same page woma . . . eh madam Lengo. What I am saying is that there are levels of leadership that are acceptable for women to hold. But to tell us that two of them are gunning for the top seats in Kawemppe, that is unheard of."

"What is wrong with women leading a country?" Bandari protested.

"Young man, which part of Africa do you come from"? The Senator eyed Prost Bandari, who was in his late thirties, menacingly.

"You are talking as if those two women have paid you. Some things are not possible. Period," Virunga added, clearly dismissing the whole notion.

"Senator, where is the impossibility arising from? If Wemppeans feel that a capable lawyer like Deborah Binti Nzingha teaming up with the respected Governor Dr. Risper Fundi can run this country well, where is the problem?" Mrs. Lengo asked.

"My people have a saying: 'If a child does not taste cooking from its neighbor's homestead, it might grow up thinking mother is the best cook ever.' Senator, why are you not happy with the KPM presidential nominees?" Bandari asked.

Virunga, irked by Bandari's casual approach to matters of serious gravity like the presidency, shifted his corpulent body and angled his weight to a lesser painful position.

"Bandari, keep your twenty cents worth of proverbs to yourself. 'Imitation made the wasp build a comb without honey.' Politics is not for everybody. First, look at the little one, Deborah. She just lost her husband recently. Who is looking after the children as she wanders through the country hunting for votes? Eeh! I think she has her priorities wrong. She should be looking for a husband before the cold July season arrives next month." Virunga chortled at his own joke before proceeding. "Governor Fundi should also be looking after my ailing friend, Carey Francis, instead of leaving him in the care of maids. Bandari, do you still want to tell me that those two people have the qualities needed to lead us? Please," Virunga said out as he rolled his eyes.

Praxedes, who was watching the show from her office at the WAMO T.V studios, watched Mrs. Lengo tighten her mouth dangerously. She knew the woman could massacre the senator with her razor-sharp wit if she so wanted, but Ruthanne had coached her against appearing aggressive.

"Senator, if you are suggesting that women should get men for the sole purpose of shielding them against the cold July chill, then I have news for you. There are warm and soft blankets on the market for that. Furthermore, if the available men are of your irk . . ." Praxedes crossed her fingers, afraid that the conversation would turn into a men versus women debate. Luckily Bandari called for a commercial break.

After the commercial break, Mrs. Lengo talked about women's unique leadership qualities. She enumerated women's strengths. How women loved to co-exist in peace. How the collaborative nature of women was fueling businesses through table banking projects that were benefiting families all over the country. Virunga countered by shooting down every one of the qualities down.

"Let's be clear on a few basics," the senator said, "Women are good to look at. That is why people are warming up to KPM.

"What exactly do you mean by that statement?" Ziphorah enquired.

"What I am saying is that women are plain incompetent. I doubt whether those two at KPM have any idea of what it takes to manage this country's economy, foreign policy and the ever-present danger of terrorism. If Kawemppe was attacked with those two at the steering wheel, and God forbid, I can honestly guarantee you that the only thing those women can do is to take out their handkerchiefs and have a hearty cry. Therefore, Wemppeans cannot have two women being our leaders. There is need for a male voice in there somewhere," Virunga scowled at the cameras.

A moment of silence passed by as a furious Mrs. Lengo gathered her bright pink shawl around her neck. Praxedes knew that there was no way Mrs. Lengo would allow such a comment to pass unchallenged.

"Wemppeans, do not be misled. Just look at the world we live in today. In every direction you look, there is a man standing behind a missile aiming at innocent women and children. How can Senator Virunga claim that women don't understand war and foreign policy? We feel the effects of war and the so-called foreign policies right here in our hearts," Mrs. Lengo said as she touched her chest for emphasis before going on. "As a matter of fact, women have done far less harm to the earth than men."

Bandari knew a good interview when he saw one, and even his producer was giving him discreet thumbs up. He allowed the two to continue uninterrupted.

The next day, the internet was awash with copy and paste caricatures of the panelists at Bandari's interview. The KPM candidate, Deborah, and her running mate Risper, were illustrated crying their hearts out while clutching gigantic handkerchiefs. Senator Virunga was not spared either. His huge girth had been manipulated to look like an ogre chasing women.

# CHAPTER

# 19

THE MONTH OF JULY brought with it a bitter chill that saw many Wemppeans avoid outdoor activities. They preferred to watch the political rallies on TV from the comfort of their houses. The first seven days of the month were the requisite days under the Kawemppe law, in which presidential candidates were required to present their party nomination papers to KES, the Kawemppe Election Secretariat. The SASA party, led by Ronald Maarufu, had already presented their papers the previous day. On Wednesday, NWS, under Bishop Epaphras, was expected to present their nomination papers. KPM, under Deborah Binti Nzingha, was due to appear before the KES secretariat on Thursday.

Deborah woke up with a start, afraid that she might have missed the kids. The marathon campaign had left her energies totally depleted. She had slept like a log. After campaigning in Lokamiko and Solanga counties for weeks, the KPM team was taking a break in the capital Wemppe to await their date with KES. The campaign team had booked her for a series of interviews. On that Tuesday morning, she was to appear on *Your Good Morning Show* on REKE TV. The REKE media house was owned by Jamal Petro, the son-in-law to Kipesa Sampson, owner of the East Winds Bank and friend to Ronald Maarufu. The station was the surrogate media outlet for the Maarufu presidential bid. It had heavily promoted the SASA agenda to its audience. It was that audience which the campaign team at KPM, led by Communication Director Jasper Hadithi and Deborah, was hoping to sway towards her side.

Pulling on a track suit, Deborah ambled downstairs while twisting her hair into a knot. The new house help, Agrippina, sourced by the methodical Mrs. Mary Msalaba, was helping Khavere to bundle the children into heavy jackets. Slipping on an overcoat to shield herself from the cold weather, Deborah followed her children to the gate.

"Mum, you know the rules," AJ said sternly when Deborah tried to go past the Muthiga tree marking the midway point between the house and the bus stop. They had agreed she would be doing the U- turn at that point.

"But I feel like taking you all the way," Deborah protested.

"No way. We don't want to be called big babies."

"Yeah, Mum. Have a nice day," Goldie added and broke into a run with AJ following closely behind her.

Reprimanded, Deborah watched her brood disappear into the mist. She turned and started jogging back to the house. After taking a quick shower and a filling breakfast of tea and sweet potatoes, she joined Obed in the driveway, where he had just arrived with the team. He was as punctual as ever and held the door for Deborah, who slid onto the soft leather seat next to Ruthanne. Jasper Hadithi sat in front while Lumumba sat at the back.

Maneuvering the van expertly through the morning traffic, Obed delivered Deborah and her team to the sprawling bungalow that housed REKE TV station an hour later. Ndollah, Deborah's official stylist, had dressed her in a golden batik shirt and a straight A-line indigo skirt that he proclaimed would make any doubting Thomas's out there still calling Deborah a mere girl think twice.

"Be yourself, no matter what they throw at you," Jasper Hadithi whispered in Deborah's ear before joining Ruthanne and Lumumba in the audience. *Your Good Morning Show* was recorded in front of a live audience, mostly Wemppe City's jobless mob and university students absconding from adjacent Wemppe University for the free cup of hot cocoa and cake that the studio offered.

The show's host, Anita Mzinga, a vivacious thirty-five-year-old lady, greeted them out front and escorted Deborah to the studio.

Deborah waved at the audience as she took her seat. Television shows were not new to Deborah. She had done several televised interviews for her court cases and her CLEAN projects. Within minutes, a crew member handed Deborah a cup of tea. A tiny microphone was attached to her lapel, and she sunk into a comfortable armchair before storing her hand bag beside her chair. Anita Mzinga had a segment in the show where she got to ask her guests to share with the audience personal details like the contents of one's handbag or wallet.

"I will ask a few questions to start off the show. Then it will be a free-for-all with the audience participating," Anita informed Deborah over the countdown signature music. The assisting crew that had been attending to Deborah disappeared into the background like startled mice.

"Deborah Binti Nzingha, the KPM presidential candidate, is our guest today," Anita said once they were on air. The audience clapped.

"Let me start by establishing what name you wish to go by now and in the future. Do we call you Deb, Debbie, the Steel Lady, or what?"

"Thank you, Anita for having me. Well, there is the famous quote: 'What is in a name?' Just as we are used to calling you Anita not Annie, or even calling Honorable Ronald Maarufu as such, not Ronnie, I wish to remain Deborah as I have always been known," Deborah answered lightly.

Satisfied, Anita next asked Deborah about her family background. Deborah talked about her grandparents and children and briefly touched on her late husband.

"Nzingha would be proud of me for taking up this noble calling," she added.

"What issues will you tackle if elected? "Anita continued.

"Like I say at all my rallies, the reason I went into politics was not to fulfill some promises that I had thought up myself. When Wemppeans, who are the true reporters of their circumstances, asked me to vie for this post, they had two agendas for me. One was to have the sovereign right of every one of them respected by getting rid of power brokers, lobby groups, and non-elected individuals who are mismanaging our resources. The fate of Wemppeans should not be decided by few centralized decision-makers, politicians, or media outlets pushing misinformation."

Somebody in the audience clapped loudly, rousing a few sleepy members in the process. Deborah cast a friendly eye and connected with the clapping person before turning her face back to the main camera. Sensing no interjection from the host, she went on. "Anita, my team and I strongly believe that any form of poverty should be classified as an act of violence against humanity. Kawemppe is a rich country. Lack of basic rights like education . . . children missing out on simple nutritious foods or immunization . . . a mother dying in labour. In this time and age, all of these things should be criminalized. A KPM government will attend to such matters with immediacy. We cannot play politics with the core needs of the people. The days of dishing out tax money inequitably while favoring friendly voting zones and marginalizing regions that don't vote for us will come to an end. Taxpayers' money should never be used as a tool to marginalize sections of this country. The secrecy surrounding how revenue is spent will be a thing of the past.

"Expound more on that," Anita probed.

"Thank you, Anita. Wemppeans are well-versed in the different methods the government employs to collect revenue. That is through taxing our salaries, goods, and services. But do they fully understand how the collected revenue is used? A KPM government will be transparent and accountable. KPM will equitably distribute government revenue throughout the country.

"We will use the internet and notice boards outside every village headman's office to clearly show how our tax money will move from the central treasury down to the grassroots. The map will highlight the projects the people have identified and agreed upon, how much they cost, the tendering process, who won the tenders and the expected completion dates for the projects." The audience, now fully awake, clapped in earnest.

Ruthanne and Richard, happy with the manner Deborah was conducting herself, stole proud glances at each other.

"Anita, my heart goes out to the men and boys, our fathers and brothers, who are prone to turn to addiction and substance abuse to escape from the reality of unemployment. A KPM government will create resource centers for boys and men. These centers will equip them with the requisite skills to enable them get by in life." Noting that the host Anita was not interrupting her, Deborah went on to make good use of the free advertisement time.

Victoria Maarufu watched the *Your Good Morning Show* from her office at the SASA headquarters. Despite herself, she felt Deborah's unshakable passion pierce through her hardened heart. She wished that Ronald and his team had thought about creating a ministry for men and boys first. It was now evident that their only threat was not with the other contenders but with this girl. A wicked smile spread on Victoria's lips at the thought of the rude surprise that lay in wait for Deborah.

"Anita, a secure person is a productive person. The course of River Maru was changed by a few greedy individuals, and they ended up destroying millions of livelihoods downstream. When few individuals use us as expendables or props and dehumanize us to enrich themselves, when we feel abandoned by the police, the clergy and even the government, that is a dangerous feeling. That is how the seed of insurrections are planted. A KPM government will carry out its duties in a manner that assures each Wemppean that they belong to this nation and that they are safe wherever they maybe." Deborah concluded to thunderous applause from the audience.

Anita, realizing that time was almost up, invited the audience to ask questions. It was the last question that undid the thrust which Deborah had successfully built in the first twenty-five minutes of the show.

"My name is Dennis."

Deborah nodded warmly towards the youth, who was wearing a remarkably wrinkled brown shirt.

"In the past, we have witnessed episodes of the rich and powerful in society, especially women, fail to vote simply because they think it is the duty of the ordinary and poor people. My question to you is: do you possess a valid voter's card? Thank you."

"Thank you, Dennis. I am a registered voter, and as a matter of fact, I have my voter's card right here with me," Deborah reached for her handbag and extracted her purse. Confidently, she flipped the side pockets and perused through her neat row of credit cards before her face creased with worry. Slowly, she began extracting her credit cards one by one but her voter's card, which she had personally stored in her purse, was missing. She was sure she had put it there in preparation for her day with the KES secretariat. In Kawemppe, it was mandatory for every voter, and especially a presidential contender, to possess a valid voter identification card. Without the voter's card she could not contest anymore. Silent panic was taking hold of her. Where could it be? A feeling of déjà vu crept up her spine.

Deborah embarked on a more frantic search and ferreting through her bags various compartments. This caused the audience to start sniggering. Ruthanne's breathing became more labored as the minutes stretched awkwardly. She looked at the host Anita Mzinga and thought that the she was looking too cheerful at Deborah's misfortune. Pausing briefly from the search, Deborah remembered a peculiar scene that had happened the night before. After Obed and his team had deposited her home from a successful rally in Solanga County, Deborah had deposited her handbag on her bed. She had then taken a quick shower before descending to the kitchen to fetch a snack. On her way back she had bumped into the new house keeper, Agrippina, exiting her bedroom in a suspicious hurry.

"Madam, I was just checking for dirty laundry," Agrippina had said while holding up the dirty frock Deborah had been wearing.

Thinking nothing of the incident, Deborah had brushed her teeth and climbed into bed.

Seizing control of the situation, Deborah looked straight at Dennis who was still holding the microphone with a cynical look on his face, and addressed him.

"Dennis, I am sorry I changed my handbag this morning. It seems I left the card in the other bag. I definitely guarantee you that I am a registered voter. I will soon have the chance to display my voting card to the public." Deborah's face was flustered.

Anita wound up the show. Lumumba Abiola and Ruthanne were impatiently waiting in the parking lot for Deborah to finish greeting members of the audience. Behind the Malcolm X frames, Lumumba's face was a meringue of worry. His anxiety was heightened by the thought of what the lost voter's card coupled by a corrupt clerk deleting Deborah Binti Nzingha's name from the KES voter register could spell. It would be the end of the KPM dream. The many hours of campaigning and preparing Deborah for the presidency would become a waste. Most frightening of all, Lumumba thought, would be the wrath of their supporters.

"I suspect the new house help might be a mole" Deborah cried out to her anxious team once the tinted doors of their van closed behind her. Obed stepped on the fuel but a hundred meters down the road, joining the inevitable morning traffic jam. Deborah activated her phone and made an urgent call to Khavere. Her other phones began to ring incessantly with incoming calls from Risper, Praxedes, and even Paa Isaya

"Khavere, is Agrippina there?" Deborah asked.

"No, I was just about to call you. She has left, claiming that she is not interested in working here anymore," Khavere answered

"Did she say anything or speak to anyone before she left?" Deborah asked urgently as she hit her phone's loudspeaker for the team's benefit.

"Well, I heard her tell someone to meet her at Maroon House at nine o'clock" Khavere said. Automatically every one glanced at their watches. It was thirty minutes to nine.

SASA Headquarters was normally referred to as the Maroon House.

"It will take us at least two hours to get there in this traffic jam," Obed advised. A general mood of despondency gripped the occupants of van.

"Lumumba, take the wheel, I am heading there," Obed instructed as he alighted and flagged down a passing motorcycle taxi. A brief talk with the owner saw him take over the motorbike's handlebars and the owner become the passenger.

"Praxedes is the one closest to Maroon House. I am calling her," Ruthanne announced while frantically dialing Praxedes's number. WAMO Offices were situated a short ten minute drive from the SASA headquarters. Praxedes picked up the phone immediately, full of worried questions. Ruthann abruptly cut her off.

"Praxedes, it is the new house help Mrs. Msalaba brought to Deborah. Most likely, she is heading towards SASA quarters with the card. Can you intercept her?" Ruthanne shouted into the phone.

Praxedes had been in the company of Governor Fundi and Mary Msalaba planning for an upcoming KPM rally. They literally ran out of the office and piled into Praxedes's SUV and sped towards the SASA headquarters. Reaching for her phone, Praxedes made a rare phone call to her most secret source, a senior executive who worked for a telecommunication company and occasionally broke the law to tap into delicate phone conversations for her. The man was reluctant to tap into Agrippina's phone until he heard Praxedes mention two million weras as his stipend for the job.

Back in the van, Deborah was almost sick with worry. How could she have allowed a woman as evil as Agrippina to operate at such close proximity to her children? Fortunately, she had noted that her children tended to gravitate towards the more playful Khavere, while Agrippina labored with the cleaning. Anything untoward would have been detected by the hawk-eyed Nana, she reassured herself.

A feathery drizzle brought the jam to a total standstill. Left with nothing else to do, Lumumba twiddled the dials of the radio. Several radio stations had picked up on the missing card story, and a major public uproar was in the making.

"It is only the poor who waste their time voting," said a caller from Makonge County on Radio Five's *Ananias and Sabina Breakfast Show.*

Senator Lydia Masumbuko was among the first leaders to call in. Deborah listened as Senator Masumbuko, in her staccato voice, called her incompetent. "If we want people to be accountable, then it should start with us as leaders. You cannot order people to vote for you and yet you don't even possess a voter's card. I am not surprised that Deborah Binti Nzingha doesn't have a voter's card. She is ill-prepared for the job," Senator Lydia concluded.

"Women cannot be effective leaders. Deborah Binti Nzingha's unpreparedness is a true example that women in general cannot be entrusted with crucial leadership positions like the presidency. It is the same reason our ancestors never sent women to war." The sentiments came from a gleeful Senator Virunga.

"Thanks, but no thanks, Deborah, for leading us on a wild goose chase," added a caller from the capital, Wemppe

City. "I was really vouching for the KPM agenda, but now it is obvious that rich people and politicians are all the same," the caller concluded.

Jasper Hadithi stole a glance at Deborah. She looked like someone who had just been told that the porridge they had just consumed had been laced with finely ground glass. To shield Deborah from the onslaught, he switched off the radio and instead switched on the tiny TV mounted on the dash board. Several TV channels had the developing story news bar flashing in crimson red 'KPM presidential candidate Deborah Binti Nzingha is not a registered voter!' He thumbed the TV off violently, almost knocking it off its delicate stand. Roiling with anger, he reached for his laptop and logged onto the van's WIFI. What he encountered looked like an orchestrated SASA onslaught to cash in on the missing card hysteria

Wemppeans were responding to the story trending under the #Guess who hashtag.

Ruthanne, who had not spoken for a while, wiped her numerous phones and frantically gave instructions to the team. Marcus was to start devising a credible response to the negativity churning on the internet.

'I am not going to let KPM die,' Ruthanne thought determinately. The matter had begun to look like the archetypal campaign manager's nightmare, but she was determined to save it.

Across town, Praxedes's secret source had done his job well and managed to get the women tuned into a conversation between the fugitive Agrippina and a voice they instantly identified as Victoria Maarufu's.

Praxedes, Risper, and Mary looked at each other, surprised at the lengths Victoria was willing to go to secure the presidency for her husband. Praxedes was recording every word just in case it could come in handy later in the campaign.

"How far are you?" Victoria inquired

"I am about to alight" Agrippina answered back. She was on a bus, making her way to the SASA headquarters with Deborah's missing voter's card.

"Good. Come straight to the gate. A guard is waiting for you," Victoria instructed and disconnected the phone the call.

Praxedes pulled into the lonely road serving SASA and several other adjacent offices and left the car engine running.

"It is my fault entirely," Mrs. Mary Msalaba groaned regretfully. Her stomach was knotted with worry. "How do we convince Agrippina to give us the card?" she asked.

"We don't need to convince her. I will snatch that bag if necessary." Risper's tone was ruthless.

"What if it the card is on her body, as in stuck in her bra?" Mary enquired.

"I will run her over if necessary," Praxedes added without flinching. Mrs. Mary Msalaba stared at her two friends in alarm.

A hawker selling cheaply dyed wrappers passed by and Mary disembarked fast and bought several.

"We are not going to kill or hurt anyone. Ladies make good use of the wrappers" Mary said.

Their secret source called again. From his GPS reading, Agrippina was five minutes from where Praxedes was parked.

Three minutes later, they saw the lone figure of the suspect walking towards them. Her stubby legs were vigorously pounding the road. The women held their breath until Agrippina drew close and Praxedes rolled down her window.

"Young lady, we are a bit lost here. Might you know where the SASA headquarters is located?" Risper asked in her best Ufuoni accent. Most Wemppeans spoke Pidgin Swahili, but people from the coastal county of Ufuoni spoke a more refined Kiswahili, almost like the East Africans. The people from Ufuoni also loved to dress in the loose wrappers due to the hot costal weather.

"Agrippina looked at the ladies suspiciously at first but trust set in once she realized she was only dealing with kind Ufuoni women. She didn't even recognize Mary Msalaba who was so well covered only her eyes visible.

"I am heading there myself. I will show you the way," Agrippina replied.

"Then hop in," Governor Fundi looking like a sea of wrappers encouraged and casually vacated the co driver's seat for their guide and joined Mary Msalaba at the back. Praxedes reached for the suspects handbag casually passed it backwards to Mary Msalaba's waiting hands. Agrippina, who was busy fumbling with the seat belt failed to notice the move. Mary began working on it while Risper framed herself between the driver and the passenger seats to hide Mary's activities.

The teacher in Mrs. Msalaba was itching to discipline Agrippina, but she restrained herself and instead concentrated on the search. After a minute of riffling through Agrippina's handbag like a professional pick pocket, she pinched Risper and winked at her.

Taking the cue, Risper cleared her throat loudly.

"Hewooo! I have forgotten my phone at the restaurant where we just had tea. Please turn back we go for it," she said dramatically.

Unceremoniously, Agrippina was ejected out of the van and her handbag thrown out after her. The three musketeers spun their car swiftly and almost collided with a motorcycle taxi that was hurtling at break neck speed towards them. Before Praxedes had time to curse, she recognized Obed. He rushed swiftly to Praxedes side, a worried look on his face.

"Don't ask how we did it, but we have it with us," Praxedes briefed him.

After tipping the taxi owner generously, Praxedes requested Obed take over the wheel. She was too shaken to drive. Obed buckled in and sped towards the KPM headquarters.

"We got it" Governor Fundi roared down the phone like a detective who had captured a most wanted thug.

"How did you do it?" Deborah asked over the loud cheers inside the van.

"It was easy. We just ran over the thief flattening her to the tarmac like chapatti. Then, using a pair of tongs we pried out the card from her minced body." Deborah knew Praxedes was not that cruel, but she couldn't rule out the women might have done something illegal to get the card.

"Thank you and sorry for giving you all heart attacks. Let us meet at the headquarters. We see how we can contain the situation." Deborah's body was surging with relief.

By the time the nation tuned in for the midday news roundup, Wemppeans were full of scorn for KPM, Deborah in particular, and women in general. The KPM staff who had been flooded with calls all morning long took a break. They crowded around the nearest TV sets and eagerly waited for the news while nursing mugs of hot cocoa. After Deborah had recovered her missing voter's card, the steering committee led by Honorable Harakka had converged for an hour-long strategy meeting. A press conference was quickly convened for midday where Deborah would display her voter's card. A KES official had agreed to come by and verify its authenticity. All the news channels were covering the event live.

"Folks, do you know there was a time in Kawemppe when the nine o'clock news was the most dangerous news bulletin in this country for the politicians?" Lumumba Abiola asked. He looked woefully at his audience of young college graduates, who had no clue how far Wemppean politics had evolved, and sighed.

"Why?" Marcus volunteered. He was updating his ego wall where he displayed hilarious campaign posters he'd collected from the millions plastered on walls and electricity poles across the country.

"It was the edition politicians got sacked on. No politician worth his salt dared miss it," Lumumba explained before realizing that he was speaking with youngsters who were seriously out of touch and were not appreciating his reminiscences. Rising from his seat, he moved to Marcus's ego wall to inspect the latest poster additions. A youthful Abe Qkatula of SASA stood in a rubbish heap brandishing a huge straw broom. Next to him was Mrs. Njedi Thompson, of KPM, sitting regally while cuddling a hurricane lamp on her lap. Reverend David Saul, of NWS, flaunted a jar of anointing oil. SASA hopeful Patel Naggi, dressed in a three-piece designer suit, trailed behind a team of bulls with his delicate hands clutching the handles of a plough. A giant poster of Mitambo standing cockily with bank notes raining around him occupied the remaining space.

"Shuuh!!! Shut your beaks people. She is on!" Ruthanne shouted when the screen filled up with the picture of Deborah as cool, as a cucumber, still dressed in her indigo and gold outfit. Beside her was Governor Fundi in a free-flowing gold dress that was girded by a huge indigo belt.

"Those outfits will make people fall in love with KPM all over again," Ndollah, the stylist claimed proudly.

"It is not the dress but what the ladies represents that people love," Lumumba Abiola added possessively.

"Who asked you? By the way, why do you dress like a clown?" Ndollah asked exasperatedly. He had been itching to make Lumumba Abiola a Kaunda suit for a while.

"Ah! Shut up you two, we need to hear," Ruthanna's tone was playful. All the same, the group grew quiet.

"Like I mentioned earlier in the morning on *Your Good Morning Show* with Anita, I am a committed voter. Over the years I have voted five times since I came of voting age. Voting is such a fulfilling exercise, as it gives us an opportunity to express how we wish to be led to positive change. It also gives us an opportune moment to decide the individuals we want to lead us. I want to make it clear that a KPM government will not appoint any individual who has no voter's card, or does not vote, for any government post. That is how serious we are with this exercise."

"Yeah! Tell them," Marcus shouted loudly sending the group into laughter.

Ruthanne, satisfied with the terse briefing her boss was issuing, withdrew to her office. A minute later, Lumumba followed her and flung himself into a rickety sofa. They began brainstorming on possible comeback moves.

The press conference brought to an end the contempt Wemppeans were having towards KPM and especially its two leaders. By the time the cold evening crept in, Marcus and his team seemed to have taken control of the internet wars. The beauty with the internet era of news coverage was that floods of serious news items fizzled out easily and were forgotten in a matter of hours.

At the same time that Lumumba Abiola and Ruthanne were working over a new campaign strategy, Deborah was in her warm kitchen surrounded by her children, chopping vegetables for dinner. After a long day of uncertainty, cooking with her family had proven to be one of Deborah's best ways to relax. The kitchen's relaxed atmosphere offered the family the time and space to share their day's activities. Deborah had just explained to the children why Agrippina had suddenly left.

"She was mean," Goldie summarized while replacing the lid on the boiling pot of meat.

"So, why did you not tell me? I would have fired her a long time ago," Deborah said as she looked at Goldie with admiration. From the time her children had declared that they were not babies, there had occurred notable transformation. They could now make simple rice and stew dishes. AJ too had toughened up and could manage some kitchen duties like taking out the trash and shining shoes.

"Because we did not want Agrippina to become jobless," Goldie added defensively. She did not notice her mother's face glow with pride that her daughter was growing into a considerate citizen.

"AJ, stop wolfing down all the carrots. Otherwise we will have colorless stew," Goldie squealed at AJ who was crunching more carrots than he was grating into the stew pot.

Goldie's eyes were runny from onions she was chopping. Watching the children work around the kitchen made Deborah feel proud. Yet, she could not escape the "you are incompetent" mantra that had been repeating itself inside her head since losing her voter's card.

She was about to add the peas in the meat stew when the noise of a car pulling up on the driveway interrupted her. She stepped out to investigate.

It was her mother in-law Rael, who stood beside a taxi watching the driver retrieve her medium-sized suitcase. The woman had gall. After all the harassment her clan had meted to Deborah, she still had the guts to dare visit? Deborah stared at Rael's back with fury. Softening a bit, Deborah realized that the woman might have come to attend the impeding memorial of her son Nzingha that was scheduled for August. With the suitcase off- loaded, the taxi sped away, and Rael's bird-like face turned towards Deborah and appraised her with some degree of disproval.

How dare you disturb my peace? Deborah wanted to yell out at her but she instead dished out the expected customary greeting while curtsying for her mother in-law. Rael was an extremely short and self-possessed woman. She was swathed in a heavy poncho to keep the cold away. From the first day Nzingha had taken Deborah home for formal introductions, Rael's eye had been disapproving of her. Deborah had attempted to befriend her with freshly baked cakes and swathes of expensive Ghanaian materials whenever she visited, but Rael had remained frosty.

"Welcome Mama," Deborah said, leading the way to the house.

After a while, the children filled in and greeted their grandmother shyly before setting the table for dinner. An uncomfortably quiet dinner ensued. The children hastily gobbled up their stew and rice, afraid of their grandmother across the table. Deborah, strained by the negative energy that had been whirling around her all day long, could not stand the stilted conversation. Nana tried her best. Her attempts to converse with Rael were akin to a murder trial cross examination.

"So, how are people down in Lokamiko" Nana enquired.

"No one had died when I left this morning. Maybe during the day," Rael replied through pursed lips.

"I hope the good rains will give you better yields, like it is promising to do in Makutano," Nana continued, undeterred by her chilly in-law.

"The agriculture people are in a better position to answer your speculations," replied Rael. Deborah looked at her mother in-law critically and began to wonder how her late husband had turned out to be such a sweet man, despite growing up with this harsh tongued woman as a mother.

When Khavere brought the evening flask of tea, the children—who had been rather quiet—took the opportunity to clear the table and flee to their rooms. Nana, citing tiredness, wheeled Mzee Abraham to an early bed and left, leaving Deborah to face-off with her mother-in-law. Rael wasted no time before launching into her litany of woes.

"Why have you hated us so much such that you cannot even inform us to come to this presidency business you are carrying on?" Rael's accusatory voice was full of bitterness.

"What is there to love in you when you frighten little children into fleeing from you?" Deborah thought of countering. Instead she conjured up all the goodwill she could master and nailed a smile on her face.

Rael, mistaking the smile for encouragement went on. 'If you must drink hot porridge, then you should sip it from the edges.' It was a widely used Wemppe proverb to warn people about to embark on difficult endeavors, to walk with caution. Deborah stared at Nzingha's mother patiently. A mountain of paper work and emails needing her attention awaited her. Among Wemppeans and Africans in general, elderly people enjoyed a high degree of respect—even in overstepping their boundaries—so Deborah sat patiently.

"I am sure you must think that what happened to you today came out of the blue. That is not so. Your voter's card cannot just disappear and reappear in a matter of hours. There is something to it. That is why you need protection.

This is politics, not jokes," Rael nodded at Deborah knowingly.

"I am aware of the problem. That is why I have security around me all the time. I think I am well protected" Deborah replied. Obed and two of his beefy friends all ex-marine now lived within her compound. Jonte, too, had moved in to assist Obed with minor logistics.

"The problem with you is that you use English where English is not required. A person does not stay empty like this." Rael's said, her eyes critically sizing up Deborah's five foot eight frame.

"Meaning what?" Deborah pried.

"You may have physical security but don't be so green. You need security from unseen forces. Wemppeans are dangerous people. They can send kegs of witchcraft your way in a fashion that only kith and kin would know when they to see you running up the streets stark naked." Rael's bird-like face wore an ominous frown.

"Don't you know that evil people can gather your foot prints and cast them into the sea? And no one would ever hear of you again?".

Deborah, tongue tied, looked unbelievingly at her mother in- law, a self-styled prayer intercessor in her church. Rael mistook the silence for encouragement and went on.

"There is this woman—a diviner—I know who has surefire immunization against such things. She even divines using the Bible. She will pray for you and give you a vial of ointment to anoint your feet every morning. This will distract your enemies. Most politicians, business people, and pastors cannot step outside their doors in the morning without applying her powerful powder on their lips to woo their followers," Rael said. Her face shone in earnest.

"Furthermore, what is wrong with having someone take a peek around the corner of your life, to see whether something dangerous is hurtling towards you?" Rael concluded, missing the pithy look Deborah was directing her way.

Thunderstruck, Deborah sensed someone swiftly walking towards them. It was Nana her weak limb forgotten.

"My in-law, the moment I saw you placing your foot in this compound, I sensed trouble," Nana said. Her voice was trembling with rage. After tucking in Mzee Abraham, Nana had been unable to sleep. She was walking back to fetch her bible from the sitting room when she overheard her peer's advice to her grandchild.

"I wanted to send you away but said to myself that maybe you have changed and you have come to see your grandchildren. How wrong I was. Instead of visiting with your grandchildren, you have been talking like a person chocking from tobacco snuff." Deborah had never seen her Nana that incensed. She stood up, ready to intercept her in case she rapped Rael with her cane.

"What ails you as far as my Deborah is concerned? First, you accused her of killing your son, and because we said nothing you must have thought that we were fools. Second, you rallied your kin to snatch all the properties your son and my grandchild Deborah had worked so hard for, and we still said nothing because where I come from in-lawship is king. All that did not satisfy you. So, today you woke up, applied oil on that crow face of yours, and thought of inviting the devil to this home. I want you to leave this compound immediately using the same way you came through, unless my name is not Tabitha Nzingha." Deborah watched her Nana straighten her eighty-year-old frame threateningly.

Rael stood up, her chin jutting in the air. "I am leaving. Furthermore, what are you offering me that my son never gave me? But before I go, I want you to know that you can pretend that you know the bible better than me. No problem. Continue with your naivety. What you will find with this political ambition of yours has no name."

"Phuu!! Rael, get out of my child's compound before I curse you," Nana Tabitha screamed, attracting Obed and Jonte to the house.

Within minutes, Ken, one of Obed's boys, had Rael and her suitcase in a car ready for the long journey back to her home in Lokamiko County.

Deborah climbed up to her bedroom with frazzled nerves. She switched off her three phones and filled the bath tub with warm water. After sprinkling in a generous dose of lavender and ylang-ylang essential oils, she climbed in and attempted to block Rael's image. She needed to come up with a strategy to rebuild any political goodwill she might have lost from the voter's card saga.

# CHAPTER
# 20

Bishop Epaphras was beginning to realize that the united church support he had banked on to propel his political ambitions was quickly becoming a mirage. Calls to his peers, bishops, and pastors he had held many a crusade with over the years now went unanswered. Even the secretary general of the Federation of Kawemppe Churches of which his church, OFIC, was a member had gone quite on him. *Indeed, religion and politics do make strange bedfellows*, he thought. With a heavy heart, he downgraded his original goal of winning the country's presidential election to a personal vendetta on his cowering peers. He was bent on proving that the Wemppean church could hold a ringside seat in the country's politics.

Perusing through the stash of newspapers that his secretary had ordered for him, he picked up the latest edition of The Weekend Dossier and glared at the front page. The latest Mzalendo polls indicated that SASA had gained points to lead with forty-six percent. KPM had lost two points due to the lost voter's card saga to stand at thirty three percent. His NWS brought the rear at twelve percent. Deborah Binti Nzingha's lost voter card drama had introduced a frightening twist of voter apathy.

A flicker of hope began to take hold of the Bishop. If he stuck to his guns, there was a chance of reaping the wind fall of deserting KPM supporters in the long range.

It was that kind of reasoning that had him seated in his conference room in Kasoro Pavilion, freezing in the cold. He was waiting for his eight pastors to help him ruminate about the future of NWS. Sipping a steaming cup of tea his secretary had supplied, he turned to the middle pages of the newspaper, where the page long editorial was located. It would be perilous for any politician to ignore Paa Isaya analysis of the week long political goings on.

*To Vote or Not to Vote*
*By Paa Isaya*

> *Following the hubbub raised by the public over Deborah Binti Nzingha's "lost" voter's card, which she immediately recovered, the notion that economically secure Wemppeans have an inclination to exempt themselves from the murky business of politics cannot be ignored. The uproar has opened a discussion that has prompted many a Wemppean to pause and actually ponder how important this voting exercise really is.*
>
> *Many Wemppeans would be surprised by how our social,*

*economic, and spiritual wellbeing are interconnected to politics through the ballot box. To cast a ballot is to deploy a rare decision-making tool to work for you. If one lives to be seventy years old and start voting in their early twenties, they will have utilized this tool only ten times in their entire life time since the voting exercise in Kawemppe is carried out once every five years.*

*Many Wemppeans are still disgruntled by poor delivery of services and inequitable distribution of resources, despite President Meshack Jabali's determined efforts to fight corruption. It is paramount to pause for a minute and ask ourselves what the state of the country will be five or ten years down the line if we do not vote in ethical leaders to represent us in government.*

*If all that we can do as Wemppeans is to vent out our frustrations on radio talk shows and abandon the onerous task of propagating democracy through the vote, then we are setting ourselves up for failure.*

*Not to vote is selfish, irresponsible, and an act of injustice to the future generations. As patriotic Wemppeans, we cannot cynically observe our nation decompose, by refusing to become stakeholders and participants in the electoral process. Subsequently, refusing to vote robs one of the opportunity to stop a local thug from becoming an Honorable so-and-so. It denies one the opportunity to protest and get rid of Honorable XYZ, who went to parliament to advance his own business while neglecting the needs of the people who sent him there in the first place.*

*Whilst not blaming the voter entirely for being put off by politics. Politicians and established political parties are to blame for the disillusionment and despondency they cause among the voters. When party kingpins impose preferred candidates on the electorate, some of whom are social misfits, they only help to worsen the contempt of the masses in the voting process. They steal the rare chance afforded to the voter by the constitution to exercise their free will in making their political choices. So why should such a voter not feel compelled to watch a Naija movie on Election Day, rather than burn their skin in the hot sun waiting to cast an impact-less vote?*

*All said, Wemppeans need to feel a sense of belonging and to be reassured*

*that the elected government will cushion
them from the pressures emanating
from the global markets and unstable
world order . . .*

A soft knock interrupted his reading and the bishop looked up as his secretary escorted in his eight pastors. They were dressed in heavy jackets to keep warm. After pleasantries and a prayer, briefcases containing bibles and church pamphlets were put aside, and they faced one another. Bishop Epaphras had spent several days thinking about his comeback plan. It was ingenious enough to kill the proverbial two birds with one stone: shame his critics and, at the same time, explain his expenditure to his benefactor, Mr. Kirby. For two hours, he laid down his strategies. Each pastor present would forthwith canvass every corner of his allocated county, preaching the gospel and at the same time vigorously campaign for NWS. Secondly, the Bishop wanted OFIC to be the sole financier of the popular interdenominational crusade held annually, by the eccentric prophet Esau Phaladum in the coastal town of Ufuoni every first week of November. He was sure that during the crusade, Prophet Esau would definitely be thankful enough to point his audience to the NWS party.

"Any questions?" The bishop asked and watched in consternation as Pastor Nehemiah cleared his throat to speak

"Bishop, with all due respect, unless you want to kill this church faster than the devil, do not push your presidential ambitions down the worshippers' throats."

Pastor Nehemiah began his speech in his usual candid manner.

Rising from his chair, the bishop moved towards the window overlooking the parliament buildings. The cold July fog hung in the air like a continuous feathery mattress. "Why do you say so pastor Nehemiah?" he asked.

"Because, my bishop, my very humble observation is that modern day clergy is beginning to lose its credibility among its followers. We have taken for granted our having people voluntarily pack our church pews every Sunday year after year. We should at least be able to boast about some countrywide project undertaken to serve our followers. Having a member of the clergy occupying a political post doesn't necessarily guarantee integrity. Reverend Cain Dumakuwili sits in the SEBCO board, yet when the board agreed to have River Maru's course altered, we never heard him utter a word to oppose the evil move. So, my point is that when we as a church lack the love and grace to serve, then we lose the moral authority to ask our followers to vote for us because our works are just as dead as those of the politicians.

Bishop Epaphras moved away from the window and resumed his seat. The rest of the pastors avoided his eye except Nehemiah whose bluntness he had come to approve of, albeit privately.

"So, Nehemiah, short of telling the church to stand by and do nothing, what else are you suggesting we do?"

"I think we need to start by cultivating the right atmosphere. By teaching Wemppeans about quality leadership traits to look for in our leaders before we come to the specifics of who they should vote for."

"Let us take a vote. How many of you feel that we should forge forward with my original plan?" Bishop Epaphras enquired. Pastor Nehemiah watched the two jailbirds, Pastor Paul and Pastor Silas, shoot their hands too eagerly in the air. Four others followed suit. The six pastors whose hands were up had learned about the benevolence of Mr. Kirby through the bishop's secretary and were keen not to be left behind in spending the free dollars offered. Only the elderly pastor Yakubu of Makutano Parish was with Nehemiah.

"The majority of you agree. So, the plan stays. Pastor Paul, close the meeting for us with a prayer," a jubilant Bishop Epaphras said, rising up to signal the end of the meeting.

Undaunted, Nehemiah obediently rose up and bowed his head.

As the KPM campaign team waited for the lost voting card brouhaha to die down, Ruthanne and Lumumba took Deborah into the thickets of Kawemppe to shop for votes in provincial churches and village meetings. Any free day she had was taken up by Jonte and the CLEAN volunteers who had Deborah and the KPM fraternity sweeping and rehabilitating waste lands and dump sites. By the end of the month, exhausted but fulfilled, Ruthanne declared that things were near back to normal.

Their next rally was in Mnazi County. It was well attended and successful. But something had been unsettling Deborah's feelings all day long. Unable to put a finger to it, she ditched the helicopter and instructed Obed to drive her back to Wemppe City via road to buy some thinking time.

The KPM convoy began snaking through the mineral-rich Mnazi County in the twilight of the fading sun. Before long, a bizarre scene began to unfold. What had appeared to be exotic yellow, blue, and white flowers growing by the roadside turned out to be a kilometer-long line of carefully arranged old plastic water cans. There was no human being in sight.

"I wonder what that means," Obed, ever hyper vigilant quipped.

"Let's see whether we can solve the puzzle," Deborah pointed out.

Soon, the convoy came to a halt in a sleepy shopping center made up of several shops. It looked like it was a market day. Several women who had their fruits and wares displayed on the ground were haggling with customers.

An old man, a rare sight of a bygone era, sat alone on the verandah of a bar, watching cars pass by. He had a frothy drink in his hand. An enormous snow-white beard covered his face, contrasting with the red blanket tied around his shoulders, toga style.

"Pull over there," Deborah said, pointing to the old man. Obed pulled off the road and parked beside the pub. Curiously, the old man peered at Deborah and beckoned her to join him. Obed looked on disapprovingly. He hated unplanned stops and would have loved for Deborah to stick to the campaign timetable. So far, he had managed to get Deborah home on time and watched her play a very bad game of badminton with her children every day.

A group of women and brawny young men roasting peanuts by the roadside raced towards the convoy of cars and jostled at the windows, attempting to sell their wares.

Deborah noted a few had WOMAN badges pinned on their dress. Obed expertly slipped Deborah through the mass to the pub.

"Jonah, give my guest a seat," the old man said.

A short, stout man whom Deborah presumed was Jonah emerged from the bowels of the mud and wattle structure with a simple stool. On appraising Deborah, he smiled and hastily fetched a better plastic chair which he proceeded to wipe with his shirt sleeve.

"Around here, they call me old man Olobango." The old man's voice was raspy, buffed by nearly a century of smoking the pipe and drinking banana beer.

"Will you take banana beer?" Olobango asked, raising his drink towards a fascinated Deborah.

"I will be fine with soda please," Deborah told Jonah who disappeared inside and came back with a bottle of Coke.

"Ah! You don't know what you are missing," Olobango said. He took a generous sip and smacked his lips loudly. Then he bowed his head.

"Let us pray" Olobango said.

Suspiciously, Deborah bowed her head but left her eyes wide open.

"To our forefathers: drink something," Olobango said as he poured a few drops to the ground before carrying on. "Our father Nzambaa Nkhu Kawemppe, this one is for you." Olobango poured a few more drops on the ground. "Thank you for life and for these guests. Cut down those who want to cut us down."

"May that be so."

After he wound up his prayer, he took a sip of his beer and adjusted his blanket. Leaning backwards, he reached into his shorts pockets and fished out a banana bark that had been folded into two and secured with sisal twine. Loosening the twine, he shook a pinch of snuff into his palm took it into his nostrils before sneezing noisily and then muttering a swear word.

Obed who was watching this from a distance sighed in distaste.

Deborah watched with bemusement and felt a connection with the strange old man.

"So, who are you and what brings you and your many cars to this land of peanuts, bananas, and sugarcane?" Olobango asked

"I am Deborah Nzhinga from Kawemppe Peoples Movement. I am running for the presidency and would appreciate your vote." Deborah introduced herself.

"You should have told me that earlier," the old man rebuked sharply, causing Obed to inch closer to Deborah.

"I have no liking for politicians and their colorful stories."

Stung, Deborah folded her hands across her chest ready to apologize and take off.

"Did you see those water cans on the roadside as you came this way? They have been standing there for the past four years as a protest over the promise to construct a dam here made to us over ten years ago," said the old man as a mirthless laugh began to play in his gaunt lips

"We have heard it all from politicians, but nothing much changes. So, my girl, what new newness do you think you can bring to the people?"

The old man's pessimism reminded Deborah of the resignation the exploited Xamcom clients had had when her clerks were signing them up for the case. 'We cannot fight a multinational and hope to win' they had said.

Wanting to defend her brand of politics, she opened her mouth to speak, but Olobango forestalled her by raising his hand forbiddingly.

"Wait I finish talking, and then you can talk," he admonished. The cavalier mood Deborah had approached Olobango with was all gone.

The rest of the campaign team had begun converging towards Deborah. When the locals had recognized Deborah, they had left their wares and moved nearer. Olobango, feeling important, straightened his back and squared his shoulders. One of the campaign assistants handed him a microphone.

Olobango blew on it twice before proceeding.

"I was telling our guest here, that I have instructed my grandchildren not to sell a single nut of peanuts to any of those thieves calling themselves middlemen. We will eat them till we cannot stand the taste and use the remainder as animal feed. Those smooth-talking conmen keep on telling us that the market prices have fallen, yet they don't explain they have fallen from where to where. How come we never hear that the prices have risen?"

Olobango's voice, carried by the powerful speakers, reverberated across the darkening plains.

"Mzee Olobango, tell her," one of the ladies urged the old man on.

Olobango skillfully aimed a stream of tobacco laden saliva towards the side walk.

"I have eaten a bit of salt. Therefore, I can say this without fear. If you want, you can tell that young man standing there like a colonial turncoat to come and slice me up. I don't care." He jerked his chin towards Obed. Planting his feet, encased in sandals carved from old tires,, he went on.

"The white man should have waited a little bit longer before he packed his bags to see whether we knew how to handle this new machine called government he had created." Olobango declared and looked at his audience challengingly.

"Ask me why should I speak such foolishness when my back was stamped with a red-hot cow-branding iron severally by the hands of a white man?" Olobango shifted his blanket to expose his back. In the crevices of the soot-black skin, wrinkled up by age, Deborah saw the scars. They were raw cruelty. Olobango closed his eyes for a long time until Deborah thought he might have fallen asleep. But the villagers did not move. They understood the freedom fighter's silent pain. Ruthanne and Lumumba, who had edged nearer, stared at Deborah questioningly.

Eventually, Olobango resumed his speech. "It is because things had a head and a tail when the white man was around. You see that valley down there near River Sinai?" The KPM team followed the old man's skeletal finger but could not see much since darkness had swallowed up the plains.

"We used to grow sugarcane. Low prices drove farmers to burn down their sugar plantations. Why make another man rich when our own children could not attend school for lack of fees?" Olobango asked as he lifted his milky eyes to the crowds.

"Did all of us not stir a spoon or two of sugar into our tea and porridge this morning?"

"We did," the crowd shot back.

"And so did the rest of Wemppean." A puzzled look crossed over his face.

It was Olobango's expression that did Deborah in. The look reminded her of her grandfather Mzee Abraham. One August holiday when she was sixteen years old, she was home for the holidays when the radio announced that the price of coffee had dropped to twenty cents a kilo. She had watched her grandfather, then a healthy giant of a man, shake his head in despair.

The restlessness that had been troubling Deborah crystallized. The injustice her people were subjected to is what had made her to take up law at the university.

"If the population of Kawemppe is increasing as fast as they keep telling us, and we're advising these young men to shield themselves with plastic sacks to avoid making more children—" The crowd laughed spontaneously interrupting Olobango. "It means that the demand for sugar is high, so why should the price be lower when there are more tea cups in which to stir sugar, and porridge bowls in which to sprinkle peanuts?. My daughter, tell me, who is torturing us more? The white colonialist or our duly elected African sons and daughters?" Olobango asked.

"There is something here that is rotten. You politicians may succeed in suppressing our generation, but I doubt whether our grandchildren will allow you to go any further,"

Olobango concluded glumly and handed the microphone to Deborah.

Accompanying journalists who had thought the stopover was quick, whipped out their cameras and began taking their pictures. Jonah, the pub owner whose regular drunks were content to use a tin lamp, realized that his pub was about to make headlines. Hastily, he put kerosene into a pressure lamp he kept for just such special occasions and hung it on the veranda using a metal coat hanger.

Deborah composed herself and attempted a weak smile. "Mzee Olobango and others gathered here today, if I am the last politician you have to listen to before you give up hope for the future, then I want to assure you that my number one agenda is to address what you have just shared with me. Farmers deserve to be well paid for their hard work of feeding the nation. You need to be supported. We will do so by excavating dams, teaching revolutionary sustainable agricultural practices, improving water-harvesting techniques and putting at your disposal Agricultural Extension Officers, who will dispense timely advice every step of the way. If KPM wins the election, we will do so in the first week of assuming office. If we don't win, I will still come back here and help you excavate that dam." Deborah paused to allow the clapping to die down.

"I feel your pain when you talk about middle men exploiting you, hence forcing you to stop doing farming because of the poor returns you get. It is the reason why I studied law. When I see the poor being exploited, it is akin to throwing dirt into my eyes. I fight back. It is the reason why I take the big companies to court when I see them treading on the rights of the people."

"Xamcon!" someone shouted.

"KPM will also guide farmers to form cooperatives so that they can sell their produce collectively and directly to local and international markets at agreed upon prices, thus eliminating the middle men.

"My daughter, finish them all," Olobango yelled, forcing the villagers to cheer ecstatically.

After an hour of talking Deborah fielded questions from the crowd till late at night.

Lumumba Abiola sensed a change in Deborah. Gauging the mood around them, he realized that even the journalists accompanying them seemed to acknowledge that this was not politics as usual.

"Madam, don't leave us like that. Here, we vote according to how heavy your pocket is," a youth chewing a large wad of gum declared as Deborah prepared to leave.

"You big-stomached fool. Are you not tired of stretching your hand and begging for twenty cents from every passing politician? Leave our daughter alone to get us bigger things than food. If you want something to eat, come by my house. I left some cow hoofs boiling somewhere," Olobango rebuked him, sending the crowds roaring.

The next morning, all the dailies carried an almost identical front page: the picture of an invigorated looking Deborah sitting beside an eccentric old man.

# CHAPTER
# 21

GOLDIE'S BIRTHDAY FELL ON July 30. The day brought with it a tide of reasonably warm weather, which seemed to be in solidarity with her birthday plans. "People! You don't want your friends to find the house looking like a cow pen, do you?" Deborah asked the children as she rounded them to picking up the heavy jackets they had discarded carelessly on the sofa. Shamefaced, the kids took their jackets to their rooms and helped Khavere straighten up the place. Goldie, had a legion of friends. In school, she was popular a must invite to all her friend's birthday parties. A large turnout of chatty misses and boisterous masters was expected to attend the birthday party. Deborah had engaged a private caterer for the function.

By midmorning, AJ was having a difficult time balancing between hanging around Jonte and being with Goldie just in case he missed something seriously important like a passing tray of ice cream. Goldie, the perfect hostess, was by the gate receiving her school friends as their parents dropped them off. Common courtesy demanded that the parents should speed off after the drop, but a few lingered gawking at the house of the woman who might soon become the country's president.

Jonte finished setting up the tents and moved to the mango tree near the chicken coop. Dangling precariously from a branch, he began to shake the ripening fruit which fell to the ground and the children scrambled to pick the ripest. "Don't just eat them fwyaaa. You will soil your beautiful dresses. Knead them against the wall to make them squishy then make a small hole at the tip and suck the juice out." Jonte advised as he demonstrated the trick.

"What if there are insects inside, like fat caterpillars?" Goldie enquired

"Then you will be lucky to have some meat protein alongside your juice," Jonte added nonchalantly.

"Yuck," cried the growing little crowd, before they all giggled and went ahead to roll the mangoes on the wall.

Deborah walked past Khavere, who was helping in setting up a bouncing castle, and veered towards the tent housing the busy catering crew of four. Several pots were bubbling on the fire, and buckets of peeled potatoes in a line waiting to be converted into chips stood washed and diced. She picked a chicken wing, marinated and fried, and nibbled on it.

"Monica, this tastes just perfect," Deborah exclaimed, licking her fingers. Monica, the owner of the catering firm 'Licking Finger' beamed with pride. She was a motherly woman who got along well with children.

"Madam, wait till you see the cake," Monica said in a cheery voice that always deepened the curiosity of her clients. She stopped arranging the sturdy plastic glasses she normally used at her young clientele parties and grabbed Deborah's hand. She led her to a mobile freezer and opened it. Resting in the center was a humongous mouthwatering life-size black Cinderella cake. Monica had decorated it in a pink dress and silver slippers. The tiara was flowery calligraphy written in silver: "Goldie Rocks Twelve."

Deborah gasped, "Thank you, Monica. Goldie will be thrilled."

"You are welcome," Monica said proudly before adding hesitantly, "By the way, I want you to know that a lot of people, me included, are voting for you. Deborah squeezed Monica's hands in gratitude and walked away, past the rows of fresh juices, chocolate dip cookies, éclairs, popcorns, and crisps.

Satisfied with the preparations, Deborah hit the shower. She was just about to wet her skin when she remembered that all her phones were downstairs. Goldie's friends might be calling for directions she thought. Wrapping a towel around herself, she ran downstairs to fetch them.

At that moment, Paa drove in, took one look at Jonte surrounded by the screaming children and with quick strides walked to the main house. He yanked the front door open. Deborah, who was about to pick her phones, spun around and stared at the intruder in surprise.

"I can see you now have a live-in playboy." Paa's voice was thick with envious rage. For months Deborah had ignored his calls despite his sending playful messages every day to her WhatsApp messenger.

A few moments elapsed before it dawned on Deborah what Paa meant and she dissolved into uncontrollable laughter.

"Yeah! Isn't he juicy?" she taunted after regaining her senses. She watched Paa's mask of fury crumble with shame, retrieving his irresistible dimple in the process. Then they simultaneously realized that Deborah was nearly naked save for a towel. With all the party's din forgotten, Paa took two steps and stood beside her. They stared into each other's eyes until they felt like they were dissolving into one mass. Deborah's lips parted slightly. Spontaneously, Paa locked his mouth with hers and buried his long fingers in her silk soft hair. A long forgotten and frightening desire began to throb inside her, eliciting a small gasp, and she slipped her hands around his neck. Paa's lips shifted expertly to her eyes before sliding to her ears—the one area he knew she could not resist. Barely containing himself, he backed her to the wall and began kissing her neck and her hair which smelled like jasmine. In one swoop, he lifted her up effortlessly and carried her up the stairs into her bedroom, kicking the door shut with his heel.

"Paa, we will soon regret this," Deborah said breathlessly fighting the giddying excitement that was making her knees weak.

"I don't think so." Paa's voice was husky with desire. With his lips, he began tracing the outer walls of Deborah's ears. Wild electric currents cascaded down Deborah's spine until she reluctantly let open the sluice doors that had been holding the feelings she had been reserving for Paa. Fussed together, their hands frisked each other urgently. Paa tore off his clothes, pausing only briefly to retrieve his protection and the two tumbled down on the carpet.

Josephine pulled in at midday, cradling Zaituni's chubby toddler, with a much happier Dina in tow. She immediately noticed the twinkle in Deborah's eye.

"Aalililili hiiiihaaaaaaaaa, did you or did you not?" Josephine asked cheekily. On her way in she had by-passed a mob of children racing under Paa's jubilant supervision. Paa looked like he had won an international lottery. The answer clicked when she saw Deborah shimmering face.

"You will burst the baby's ear drums," Deborah reprimanded and attempted to pluck the dangerously held baby from Josephine's excited hands with little success. The only visible evidence of the awesome pleasure the place had witnessed in the past two hours was an extra wet towel that had been carelessly thrown into a corner

"This is not the first baby we have seen."

"Spill the beans," Zaituni nudged playfully. She was now much slimmer after her delivery. She headed straight to Deborah's wardrobe and started trying several outfits to make up for lost time.

Josephine handed the toddler to Goldie, who had just walked in, drawn by Josephine's ululation. In no time, the women were sprawled on Deborah's bed. A plate of hot golden samosas lay between them.

"There is nothing to tell," Deborah said sassily and moved towards the large windows.

Below them a dancing competition was underway. Jonte, who was the DJ and photographer of the day, had some nice music playing. Paa, donning a silly paper hat, was acting as the competition's judge. The carnival noises in the compound had Zaituni's little baby now held by one of Goldie's friend like a fragile glass vase, kicking and tweaking her chubby arms excitedly. The caterers had already set up the cake on a table and Goldie looked really happy. Her face was almost cracking into two halves.

Looking at Paa seeming so relaxed, Deborah felt her remaining reservations fall away. She knew she was in love.

The three women who had moved to the window observed the loving look etched on Deborah's face with joy.

"Woiee! Give the man a chance, please," Josephine encouraged.

"I will think about it," Deborah said and pushed the women aside. "But first let us go and cut that cake."

# 22

T HE BEGINNING OF AUGUST brought an unwarranted tide of bad coverage for the KPM camp. One of their devoted female supporters, Mrs. Maggie Zumba, had been murdered. The coverage by Wemppe Gazette was sensational.

*Female Presidency Causes Death in Mnazi County*
*By James Nyundo.*

> *A woman was slashed to death in Mnazi County by a man after she proposed Deborah Binti Nzingha as the best presidential candidate in the coming elections. County police boss Ben Chokaa identified the deceased as Mrs. Maggie Zumba, the chairlady of a local self-help group known as the Nuru Women's Group. The late Mrs. Maggie Zumba, a diehard KPM supporter, was walking home in the company of*

*several villagers after attending a KPM rally convened by political activist and HMA chair Ziphorah Lengo, when an argument with a fellow village mate ensued. The assailant has been identified as one Mathew Pempe.*

*According to an eye witness, Maggie, elated by the prospect of Kawemppe electing its first female president, was discussing with Mathews the pros of such a development. Mathews, unable to sustain his side of the argument, drew a sword from the inside of his coat and, in a fit of anger, lunged at the victim and slashed her neck, killing her instantly. On witnessing the horror, the other witness fled the scene, screaming for help. The body of Mrs. Maggie Zumba lies at the Mnazi General Hospital Mortuary "Police are hotly pursuing leads that will result in the capture of the suspect," police inspector Chokaa was quoted as saying . . .*

Governor Fundi was inconsolable as she huddled in the conference hall at KPM headquarters. She was with a large group of KPM staff planning Maggie's funeral. When she met the vibrant Maggie in Virunga's office, she had developed an instant liking for the lady—especially the boldness she had displayed when she returned Virunga's money. Maggie had been a permanent fixture in most KPM meetings. Remarkably, Deborah who had met millions of women on the campaign trail, could remember the joyful Maggie vividly.

"I have my misgivings. Mnazi County is Virunga's turf, and there are no guarantees as to what may happen to us there. I advise Deborah to skip the funeral altogether," Lumumba Abiola's said. His eyes were red from lack of sleep. He was nursing a cup of strong coffee to clear his head.

Listening to the radio earlier in the week, Lumumba had heard Senator Virunga accuse the KPM party of confusing women and encouraging them to abandon their children and husbands for the campaigns. Lumumba had called in and posed a question. "Senator, are you worried that the preexisting narrative of women and children being left in the house might be changing to that of men and children being homebound?"

"Young man, listen to me. There is no woman who is going to lead Kawemppe any time soon!" Virunga had snapped back, obviously irritated by the caller.

"So, do we want to play the media game that Deborah caused the death of our Maggie?" Jasper Hadithi enquired of the gathering.

The team kicked the idea around for a few minutes before Deborah announced firmly, "I am attending the funeral. Nobody is going to stop me. Not even Virunga."

On the Saturday of the funeral, Deborah arrived in Mnazi County with a convoy of cars and several buses full of her supporters. The press had begun dubbing KPM supporters as "Deborah's army." They had their WOMAN badges firmly pinned to their lapels. The local KPM representatives led them to the Mnazi Church of God. The new arrivals caused audible whispers as the ushers scrambled to get seats for them. Following a beckoning usher, Deborah and the top KPM leaders walked down the aisle towards the front. Like in a slow-motion video, a middle-aged woman sprung from her seat, turned towards Deborah, and unleashed a spray of spit which missed its target by a whisker and landed squarely on Mrs. Ziphorah Lengo's blouse.

"You deserve that," the furious woman shrieked. "You women with money are shamelessly cheating us small women, who have nothing, to destroy our families. Since when did the neck come before the head?" Several ushers were closing in on the furious woman in an attempt to subdue her. Deborah could see the fury in the woman's eyes. They were scorching with hate.

"Maggie has been finished by these women speaking English through the nose. Now we are burying her." The lady's voice was choked with emotion. Within minutes, all hell broke loose. An organized group of women rose up from the front seats, ready to send torrents of saliva towards Deborah. Obed, sensing the tangible hostility, sprung up like a wild lion and wedged his body between Deborah and Governor Fundi. Holding their arms firmly, he turned the two women around and herded them outside into a waiting car, which sped off, leaving a cloud of dust behind.

The rest of the security team, assisted by Jonte's boys, who could easily convert their choir boy demeanor to mean-looking street hustlers, sandwiched the remaining

KPM supporters between them and marched them into the waiting buses and hightailed from Mnazi at full speed, leaving behind an effigy of Deborah bursting into flames.

The chaotic day proved to be the answer to Paa's prayer.

"Can you do me a favor?" Deborah breathed down her phone.

"Anything for you my dear. Are you okay?" Paa was watching the Mnazi funeral fracas on TV.

Deborah felt her body begin to relax. Paa's voice always did that to her. "I am ok. Thanks. But I am afraid that Nana and the kids might not understand that spitting comes with the political territory." Deborah's children were out of school for the August holiday. "Is there any chance you could go to my place and break it down for them?"

Paa had not been Deborah's first choice for help. She had started by calling Josephine, but she was unavailable, as he had taken her science club students for the August Holiday Science Congress in Ufuoni County. Dina was on holiday with her husband in Jamaica, and Zaituni was at the hospital. The baby had developed a fever. That had left out the only other person the kids liked crazily: Paa.

"Consider it done," Paa replied, happy to be of some help to this proud and self-sufficient woman.

As soon as he ended the call, he grabbed his coat and drove straight to Wemppe Meadows. A worried Nana welcomed him. Although Deborah had called to reassure her, Nana was still disturbed. Nana had been watching the funeral service on TV when things turned ugly. To keep the children occupied, Nana had let the chicken out of the coop and instructed the youngsters to graze them like goats.

Paa's arrival was greeted with shrieks and hugs, especially after he produced two king-size chocolate bars.

Paa relieved the tired nurse and began wheeling Mzee Abraham round the compound while explaining the complicated intrigues of politics to Nana. Eventually, the old man slept and Paa helped the nurse put him to bed.

"Now, tell me why a man of your stature is without a wife," Nana asked Paa while handing him a mug full of millet porridge prepared the traditional way, sugarless with a dash of sour milk. They sat on wicker chairs on the cold veranda.

He told her about Gail his American-born wife, now three years dead from drug addiction. Nana was a good listener, and Paa found himself telling her about Lee, his thirteen-year-old son. She nodded in understanding and wondered why Deborah had stubbornly rejected such a decent man.

"How is Deborah coping with all this campaign business?" Paa asked afraid that he might appear selfish with his tales of personal woes.

"We cannot complain. That Obed always delivers her in time for supper or breakfast with the children. My grandchild is a special woman. My only worry is that Deborah might not have anyone to talk to when Mzee and I leave this earth."

Paa took a deep sip of the thick porridge and examined Nana's worried face for a while.

"If she will allow me, I will be there for her," he said hesitantly.

Nana's hands, which had been pruning the hard stems from her favorite vegetable, the amaranth, stopped and grabbed Paa's hand firmly and looked straight at his eyes before asking.

"Do you love her?"

"If only you knew . . ." Paa began before Nana snapped at him.

"Don't read me poetry young man. Do you love her? Yes or no?"

"Yes, I love Debbie very much" Paa replied. He had always called Deborah Debbie.

Nana stared into Paa's eyes for a long time. There was no deceit in them. She let go of his hand.

"Then while she is campaigning for the country to love her, I will campaign for her to love you," Nana added sagely. Ignoring Paa's protests, she reached for the thermos and refilled his mug.

"Drink to your health. I have just told you that that girl has been too long without a man. We don't need any wobbliness from you when the time comes,"

Despite being a notable scribe, Paa lacked the words to counter that. He grinned sheepishly like a drunk for a long time, until AJ came barreling through the door, closely followed by Goldie all dressed up for a trip into town.

"Our campaign is not going to be derailed by a few sick and misguided individuals. If the likes of Senator Marko Virunga and Victoria Maarufu are expecting KPM to back down, then I have got news for them," Deborah said with zest.

It was almost eight at night, and the campaign team was sequestered in her office at the KPM headquarters. Mrs. Ziphorah Lengo, who had showered and put on a different dress, nodded vigorously. Lumumba Abiola brooded next to Marcus, who was for a change, as grave as a judge. Obed who was as inscrutable as usual, shared a sofa with an incensed Juma. Honorable Harakka was leaning on a table.

Downstairs, an army of campaign assistants under the supervision of honorable C.F. Fundi, attended to the phones, which were ringing off the hook. The KPM Facebook page was nearly crashing with KPM supporters going head-to-head with their perceived haters.

"Virunga, Ronald, and Victoria Maarufu are a worried lot. Victoria is becoming more desperate and dangerous by the day. She cannot understand the fact that times have changed and Wemppeans can think on their own without being herded into the political factions she is used to," Governor Fundi said soberly.

Lumumba Abiola effortlessly moved his lithe body toward the muted television, showing the evening news. Deborah's burning effigy was aglow on the screen. He snapped the TV off.

"I totally agree," he said, "but I am sensing something deeper than what meets the eye. As a party, we need to be careful." Lumumba paused, searching for the right words to communicate his message.

"I stand to be corrected, but successful women are sometimes perceived to emit a certain energy that can be interpreted wrongly as a threat. Deborah epitomizes what many a sister might subconsciously want to be but cannot be due to circumstances beyond their control. She has the education, the finances, the independence, and, I am sorry to make this very unfortunate observation, freedom from a husband asking her where she is coming from late at night."

Lumumba was about to explain further when Mrs. Mary Msalaba interjected with some steam. "Why do women encounter double standards, especially when it comes to politics? If a man is educated, rich, and independent, then he is the people's hero, but if it is a woman, she becomes a villain." Several heads nodded in agreement.

"My deduction is that what we encountered in Mnazi embodies the fears of people faced by the uncertainties of change. Deborah is the change women want but cannot get due to their financial or educational limitations. The men feel that Deborah is usurping the existing traditional set-up, where man has been king since the Big Bang, if it ever was." Lumumba paused briefly before proceeding.

"Ladies and gentlemen, we are at a crossroads. One wrong move, and our campaign will be reduced into a men versus women agenda, or a haves and have-nots debate. We need to tread with utmost care. Unfortunately, it is a huge cross that Deborah has to bear." The room grew silent as they digested the comments. No one contradicted Lumumba. As a seasoned journalist and a social scientist of repute, he knew his territory well.

"Why are we allowing people to give KPM headaches? First it was Agrippina, the voter card thief, whom we let away scotch free, and now we are letting those despicable spitting cobras from Mnazi off the hook. I say we sue them," Marcus blurted out in exasperation.

Governor Risper Fundi and Praxedes understood Marcus very well. The KPM agenda had been born of such frustrations.

Deborah who had not spoken the entire time stood up. "We would be playing directly in the vile hands of Victoria and Virunga. That is why Lumumba, Obed, Ruthanne and I are going back to Mnazi County right away. I need to speak with Maggie's family tonight. Get the helicopter ready," she said crisply, surprising the group.

Governor Fundi began to protest, but one look from Deborah stopped her. It was a look she had seen many times. She knew Deborah could not proceed with the campaigns unless she had personally ensured that Maggie's family understood how she valued Maggie's ultimate sacrifice to the KPM cause. Ruthanne grabbed her laptop and checked her phone. A news alert declared that Police Inspector Chokaa had arrested Mathews Pembe, Maggie's killer. She hugged her gadgets close to her body and followed the others onto the helipad. The rest of the team dispersed, leaving the night staff to handle the internet ruckus.

Deborah crawled home towards midnight, after having condoled with Mr. Zumba, Maggie's husband. The grieving widower was sure Senator Marko Virunga was behind the attacks. Despite his grief, he unnecessarily apologized for the attack.

She found Nana having a cup of tea with Paa. Nana was relieved after confirming that Deborah was fine, and she retired to bed. Paa followed Deborah to the children's bedroom and watched her kiss their sleeping foreheads gently. At AJ's bedroom he watched her delicately wipe off some tomato sauce moustache around the child's mouth.

She then made her way to the kitchen. Lining the kitchen counter was a stack of boxes full of assorted foodstuffs.

"Paa, you are too much," Deborah exclaimed, looking at the half-eaten pizzas, chicken, and cake."

Paa leaned on the fridge, looking guilty.

"Who feeds children pizza, chicken, cake and tops all that up with ice cream in one seating?"

"Your grandmother was not amused either." Nana had scolded him the moment he had brought the kids back hauling a mountain of food in paper bags.

"It would be a miracle if AJ doesn't get a stomach upset before morning." Deborah said, shaking her head in disbelief. Selecting a piece of pizza and a chicken drumstick, she placed them in the microwave and stood waiting for them to warm up.

Paa moved behind her, and began massaging her shoulders gently. His every stroke making Deborah to feel more relaxed. Flipping open the box containing the rich chocolate cake with blue berry topping, she swiped a finger over the cream and tasted it. Paa reached for a knife and cut out a slice and began feeding her. The wholesome creaminess of the cake made her close her eyes involuntarily. Paa's strong lips locked onto hers and kissed her deeply. The pinging of the microwave broke the magic of the moment.

Deborah wanted him to kiss her forever, but her heart still held some hurt. How could she allow a man who had made her pregnant twenty-five years ago, before disappearing to America, become a part of her life again?

"Why do you always fight me?" Paa enquired. His strong face was a mixture of hurt gentleness.

Deborah remembered that fate-changing night years ago when Paa had picked her up from the Wemppe University student quarters for what was to be a whirlwind romance before he left for the United States. The car had been garlanded with red rose petals and a tub of her favorite vanilla ice cream rested on the dashboard. Before she had time to realize where they were driving to, they were at the airport boarding a plane—a first for her. Forty five minutes later spent thinking about what would happen if the plane were to crash and Nana got to know about her clandestine campus life, they disembarked at the coastal town of Ufuoni county where they shared a romantic starlit dinner served aboard a dhow anchored in the calm waters of the Indian Ocean.

Retrieving her food from the microwave, she led the way back to the sitting room and sank into one of the jungle green armchairs. Paa pulled a matching poof and sat in front of her.

"You have not answered my question, Debbie. Why do you dislike me so much?"

Deborah looked at Paa keenly. The man looked charmingly innocent. Could it be that he had not received the letter explaining her predicament? Maybe he didn't know that he was the father of a twenty-five-year-old daughter. Paa, who had been watching Deborah's defenses fall by the way, pulled off her pumps. Cupping her feet in his hands, he began to massage her ankles gently.

"Have you ever thought about what would happen to the KPM campaign if the press got a hint of our being an item?" Deborah asked and pulled her legs away from Paa's strong hands. The illicit sensations rushing from her feet to the follicles of her hair were overwhelming.

"It is none of their business."

Deborah knew Khavere, Jonte, Obed and his boys residing in her compound would never leak anything to the media. But she still needed to be cautious. A large sum of money was known to set mouths loose in Kawemppe.

"I don't think so. It is very much their business" Deborah said seriously. She knew that if the news leaked, Wemppeans would celebrate Paa, the widower, for wanting to revive his masculinity. On the other hand, a widow like her would be vilified and labeled weak and somewhat immoral. But that would be nothing compared to the scandal that would erupt if the world knew who their daughter was.

"Paa, thank you for everything, but you must leave." Deborah was reluctant to let him go. But she knew that one more move up her calf with those powerful hands and she would lose her senses. Standing up quickly, she lost her balance and fell into his compact chest. His strong hands steadied her.

Their eyes met and held.

"Debbie, I sincerely wish you would tell me my mistakes so that I can make amends, because by God I do love you." His eyes where blazing with intensity. Bending down, he brushed his lips on her forehead and exhaled painfully. With fast steps, he made for the door and disappeared into the cold dark night. Rooted to the spot, Deborah listened to her pounding heart, while fighting an impulse to run after Paa until she heard his car drive away.

# CHAPTER

# 23

W E NEED TO TREAT ourselves. We have had some rough times lately. How about orchestrating a story that will take people's attention away from Deborah for a change," Ruthanne began. She was addressing Praxedes, Jasper, Richard, and Professor Visomo Majuaa. The professor had joined the KPM team, bringing with him over forty years of political science experience.

"Prof, any ideas?" Ruthanne asked. The seventies tweed coat the professor wore was now back in fashion, making him fit in with the youthful campaign staff who had resorted to calling him Prof.

Professor Majuaa nodded his head slowly. His head had a bald patch in the middle, surrounded by a shock of thick but badly combed hair on the outer edges. It looked like an ancient volcanic crater. Behind the shabby outer shell lay an intelligence that was incisive when dealing with complicated situations.

"Who among our rivals can comfortably carry a skunk if it was presented to them dressed as a doll?" Prof asked. Few ideas came up. Jasper suggested that between Ronald

Maarufu, his running mate Mitambo Mitambo, and the Bishop Ephaphrus in NWS, there must be an aggrieved girlfriend or illegitimate child they could use against them

"Imagine if we were to get an un-acknowledged teenage son sired by Bishop Epaphras?" he asked.

"This if Africa, my friends. The more girlfriends and illegitimate kids a man has, the more manly they are perceived to be," Prof pointed out.

After much head-scratching, Professor Majuaa reached out for a tool that if well-disguised would hand one of the three presidential contenders with rope enough to hang himself.

"How about shooting a documentary featuring the life and times of the flamboyant Mitambo Mitambo?"

"Prof, why promote our rival?" Ruthanne asked surprised.

"The documentary will not be promoting him. That is the catch. You see, the country is experiencing a strangled cashflow because our people are saving to travel upcountry to vote. You all know how we love to migrate to up country cradles near voting time. Right now, Wemppeans are hoarding every available wera. So the documentary will be intended to contrast the lavish lifestyle of an aspiring leader with the modest existence of the citizens."

"That's a brilliant idea," Praxedes said, remembering the idea she once had of Wemppeans getting to view the cream of society up close on TV.

*M2: A Man of His Own Making* aired repeatedly over the first weekend of September on all WAMO channels. Being a cold weekend, many families were stuck indoors in front of their TV sets, watching sickening opulence being flaunted against their simple life. The documentary began with Mitambo swinging the gates of his mansion open. He was dressed like a rock star in an expensive dark brown suit and a pink silk shirt. A few buttons were left loose at the neck to reveal chunky gold chains. Like an excited teenager, he proceeded to strut about his expansive estate giving viewers a tour of his abode. His diamond rings trapped the light and sparkled fiercely for the cameras when he pointed at his fourteen vintage cars. Stroking each car lovingly, he reeled off each machine's make, year of manufacture, and staggering price.

The next stop was by the invitingly blue swimming pool, where viewers were quickly introduced to the family. Mrs. Clarisse Mitambo stood beaming towards the camera. She was a large girl. Her kind face was obscured by the red satiny dress she had worn. It clung to her body like foil paper. Standing beside her were their three meek-looking teenagers. Judging from the speed with which Mitambo waved the cameras away from his family, Ruthanne sensed that Clarisse's weight must have been an embarrassment to her husband's quest for perfection. Being a large girl herself she knew the feeling first hand.

Mitambo waved the crew toward the main door of his palace. Behind him, one of Clarisse's spiky sandals got caught in between two tiles and she tripped, sprawling to the ground. Unruffled, Mitambo strolled on, leaving the kids and the documentary crew to pick up his hurt wife. The camera man, acutely sensing the breaking news moment, stepped back and captured the unfolding scene with dexterity. It was the perfect silver bullet that KPM needed.

Shocked viewers were treated to a minute-long footage of Mrs. Clarisse Mitambo lying on the floor writhing in pain, while her husband swaggered away unbothered, eager to show Wemppeans his gold-coated plates and cutlery.

Monday morning found Dalmas Kinga Nzambe sitting at his usual breakfast spot. He had no appetite and was cringing with horror, watching on TV for the umpteenth time as Mitambo shot the future of his political career down. The media, and especially the radio, were on fire with incensed callers.

"Gold and cars we can tolerate. But if Honorable Mitambo is not concerned about the welfare of his wife, then we cannot trust him with the wellbeing of the nation," commented a peeved female caller.

"He has way too many lotions and colognes for a man. He might prove to be a burden to the taxpayers who will be cushioning his ointments bills," a male caller added.

Onessi, his houseboy approached him with the usual: a platter of boiled maize and red flask of porridge. Dalmas dismissed him, clicked off the TV, and strode out to his garden. The cold sharp air began to clear his muddled thoughts. This prompted him to take stock of his life. Technically, his beloved party DDP was dead under Mitambo's Neanderthal stupidity. The few aspirants vying for seats under the DDP ticket were now afraid of venturing out to beg for votes courtesy of the documentary.

Thrusting his cold hands deeper into his trouser pockets, Dalmas rounded the side of his mansion and paused under an old jack fruit tree. His thoughts went to his four grown children in Australia, who were still relying on him to pay their way. Other children their age were supporting their parents, but his were still sucking their thumbs, waiting for his aid. A line of safari ants working a caravan towards the dry safety of an unused old pickup truck caught his eye. He bent down to inspect. The reflex saved his life. If Dalmas had moved one step further, he would have been fatally hit by a falling giant jack fruit that missed him by millimeters before landing on the pick up's windscreen and shattering it into smithereens.

Startled, he straightened up and moved away from the tree in shock. Neither Clementine nor Onessi came out to inspect. For a long time, Dalmas stared at the shattered windscreen in awe. *I could be dead out on this cold yard, and no one would have known by now. Indeed, life is short, and I must start living*, Dalmas pondered uneasily. The thought caused Dalmas to start seeing his present circumstances with greater clarity. With the tidy sum he had made after handing DDP to Mitambo Mitambo, he decided that he was going to give each of his adult children a six-month allowance. He would cut them adrift after that. It was about time they realized what life was all about.

Resuming his pacing, he rounded a corner and found himself standing directly below Clementine's bedroom. Impulsively, he looked up. There was no sign of life in the upstairs bedroom. The windows were shut and the curtains tightly drawn. Clementine rarely woke up before midday.

"It is over," Dalmas mumbled under his breath. There was no need of carrying on with the public charade they put on every once in a while for the benefit of their few friends. Dalmas decided to give her the mansion and the rental apartments—virtually everything they had acquired together. He would then move in with Bibiana. There was a little house on the outskirts of Wemppe City, which he had spotted that came with a big playground. He could visualize himself playing a game of football with Chad, Bibiana's enthusiastic son. In fact, he had always wanted to take a lazy, slow, smell all the roses, Cairo to Cape tour of Africa. It was about time he did so with Chad hanging on his left hand and Bibiana on his right hand.

The pleasant thoughts cleared the cloud of misery which had been besieging him since he sold DDP to Mitambo. He felt relieved. The feeling was akin to what he felt as a young boy, when he had faced the circumcision knife without flinching many years ago. On second thought, he called Onessi and asked for his breakfast. He needed all the energy he could master to plan for the final act before the curtain fell.

# CHAPTER

# 24

WHY ARE WE PAYING you loads of money when you cannot deliver?" Victoria yelled venomously at Alloys Faya. Her voice matched the cold September chill, which had plunged temperatures to 8ºC, a record in Kawemppe. The newspapers Victoria had turned to for the latest polls from were spread on the coffee table like gambling cards. Their headlines were screaming the latest Mzalendo polls. SASA party's popularity stood at forty four percent, KPM was two points behind with forty two percent. NWS stood at twelve percent. The population of undecided voters had reduced to a mere two percent.

They were at the Maroon House, the SASA campaign nerve center. The SASA Campaign Manager who sat between Mitambo Mitambo and Ronald Maarufu stared at M2 lethally. The fool had gotten them in the current predicament.

Mitambo Mitambo had proven to be a political liability. After Mitambo had solidified his idiocy by appearing in a TV show and flaunting his wealth to hapless Wemppeans stuck in a financial crisis he had not stopped there. At a recent rally in Solanga County, Mitambo had stood to address the nomadic tribesmen, when he went overboard and began to taunt them. Alloys reluctantly recalled the speech.

"My kinsmen, I am your son. Just reassure me of your support. I should not be wasting my time begging for your votes. I should be campaigning in other regions," Mitambo had said in condescending tones at the nomads.

"If you think you are wasting your time with us, why don't you rush to where you are needed most?" a herdsman shielding from the sun under the acacia trees had retorted, provoking a ripple of laughter. It was what Mitambo had said next that had mortified Alloys.

"You all know that I am a rich man. I can buy the lot of you, your wives, plus your cattle with this single bracelet I am wearing," Mitambo had retorted back as he thrust his hand in the air to jingle his latest possession, a diamond-studded bracelet. Hardly had he finished the sentence when a tribal club, a plumb stick curved like a clenched fist, had come whistling towards the dais. In less than the minute it took for the SASA team to evacuate, the insulted Solangians had shattered all the windows of the campaign vehicles. Shah had a broken arm while Luke was still in hospital, nursing his left eye, which had been smashed to a pulp by a flying club. The few points SASA had garnered from the KPM missing voter card incident had long since been restored.

Alloys, weary of the hydra-headed campaign with Victoria hot on one side and Ronald cool on the other, thought quickly. There was no way he was going to get fired by this woman and risk losing his rewards of joining the diplomatic corps. Ronald had promised him a European post should SASA win. Mitambo Mitambo's attempts to dig into Deborah's past for some dirt had not unearthed anything juicy enough to taint her name, despite having hired a detective. In despair, Alloys remembered Senator Lydia Masumbuko once mentioning that the KPM presidential nomination process had not been transparent.

"Madam Victoria, we can arrest the situation. If Senator Lydia agrees to testify on our behalf," Alloys suggested. Tentatively, he explained the KPM situation to his audience and watched as Victoria's annoyance was replaced by curiosity.

"We will promise her anything, including the Solanga County gubernatorial SASA ticket, if she delivers Deborah's head to us." Victoria said firmly and looked at her husband for reinforcement. Ronald stared absently ahead.

"By the way, Mitambo you will not contact any public or private business that can attract the media without express permission from me. Understood?"

"Yes, madam," M2 replied hastily.

"We have to win this election," Victoria said when she met Lydia two days later. They were seated in Victoria's town house taking tea in front of a crackling fire. The friendship between the willowy Senator Lydia and the short matronly Victoria had been forged by politics two years ago. Victoria had spotted the lust for success in her new friend and kept it at bay, waiting for the appropriate time to test it.

"I have heard that the KPM primary nominations were flawed because Praxedes and company crowned Deborah without going through the proper procedure."

Victoria explained her agenda to Lydia and watched her cover bubbling lust with a veneer of indifference.

The statement was music to Senator Lydia's ears. Not wanting to look eager, she concentrated on stirring her tea and thought of the advantages that came with the request. First, she would demand the SASA ticket for the Solanga gubernatorial seat and a waiver of the exorbitant fifty-million-wera nomination fee. Though Lydia was not a native of Solanga County by birth, she was married there and knew that if Ronald Maarufu endorsed her candidature, Solanga people would vote her in.

Within a week, Senator Lydia Masumbuko's lawyers had filed a case alleging that KPM had violated pertinent clauses in the law when they nominated Deborah Binti Nzingha as their flag-bearer. The morning of the hearing found Ruthanne and Lumumba Abiola assembled with their core team at KPM headquarters, tuned in to the morning radio talk shows. A huge pail full of popcorn lay dejectedly in the middle of the table waiting for takers. For several days, the Prof had been supervising several campaign staffers who were monitoring the fifteen radio stations in Kawemppe, listening for any negative vibes against KPM and neutralizing them immediately.

"Lumumba, I think we have got some help here," the professor said.

Lumumba Abiola drew near and began to read the editorial column of The Wemppe Gazette the Prof was pointing at. The paper's cartoonist had drawn Senator Lydia Masumbuko hurling a stone towards KPM house while standing in a mine field.

*Glass house*
*By Elijah Lmbatwa*

*Deborah Binti Nzingha's success with her brand of unusual politics has left many critics confounded. Unlike in America—once a Republican, always a Republican—Kawemppe enjoys fluid party rules that allow politicians to hop from one party to the next.*

*Senator Lydia Masumbuko belongs to the defunct Democratic Democracy party but has been living in the SASA house for the last five years. Her belief that throwing a stone at her neighbor KPM with the hope that Wemppeans eyes will follow the hurled stone and forget to review the ground the senator is hurling it from is absurd. Under the stewardship of the KPM regional electorate body, led by the impeccable Solomon Ngome, Wemppeans watched the KPM party conduct credible primary elections. Deborah Binti Nzingha was democratically voted for as presidential flag-bearer together with a gallant team of representatives. The ruse deployed by SASA hiding behind Senator Masumbuko . . .*

Lumumba Abiola left it at that. He would read the full article later. He reverted his attention to Radio five, where the Lydia Masumbuko vs. Deborah Binti Nzingha case as the media had dubbed it was being tried in the court of public opinion.

"Are women their own worst enemies?" Ananias crooned in his creamy British accent, which drove his audience crazy. He was hosting the show alone, as his co-host Sabina was down with the flu.

"Hello, Ananias. This is Winchester from Makonge County."

"Sir, go ahead and share you views."

"My problem with women is that they are their own saboteurs. When a woman sees another woman progressing, she works overtime to pull her down, just as Senator Masumbuko is doing to Deborah."

"What makes you say that?" Ananias asked

"Isn't it obvious, Ananias?"

"Thank you, Winchester" Ananias drawled.

"I need to hear a lady's opinion. Keep calling"

Louisa, from Ufuoni County, called next.

"Women are traitors and cannot be trusted. Ananias, just imagine, I found out that my boyfriend is cheating on me with my best friend" Louise said.

"Ouch! That must be painful, dear," Ananias empathized.

The next caller was one croaky-sounding Mike calling from the capital, Wemppe.

"Women can be very stingy, cash-wise, Ananias. When we men have money, don't we spend it on our women? But when they have money, we never get to know. Ananias, my wife permanently keeps her purse tucked in her bra twenty-four seven. She cannot part with a coin even when I'm mosquitoes-flying-out-of-my-wallet broke." Mike guffawed at his predicament.

"So how does she use her money?" Ananias asked with genuine curiosity.

"On useless things like taking her already nice hair to the salon, buying clothes, and taking the kids out for fancy foods like pizza, which they can do without," Mike whined.

"And what useful things do you do with your money?" Ananias queried. A moment of silence followed before Mike's voice boomed back.

"Ananias, the problem with you is that you favor women a lot and you will never agree with me." Mike lowered his voice conspiratorially like the entire world was not listening in and asked, "Ananias, can you organize like five hundred weras for me I go to work, 'cause I don't have fare, and if I have to trek, I will reach there at around midday.

"Mike, are you trying to hit me up for drinking money?"

"No, seriously . . ." Mike now sounded pitiful.

"Your wife is a clever woman. Pick up your shoes, dude, and start jogging towards your place of work. That is if you have a job in the first place. Keep talking to me, people. I'm not hearing anything to write home about. Are women their own worst enemies?" Ananias needled his listeners.

Agnetta from Mabanda Moors said woman were loudmouthed and could not keep a secret for long. That is why they create lasting enemies from gossiping.

Justine from Lokamiko County claimed that women were cowards. "Ananias, let a rat enter the house unexpectedly, and the only man in the house whether three years old or ninety and blind will be ordered to battle it out while the women are perched on top of chairs."

Deborah, who was in the company of Josephine, her bestie, and Governor Fundi, laughed loudly at that one. She regaled them with a story about how one rainy day not long ago, a frog had leapt into the house unexpectedly, sending all the women on top of the sofas, leaving a frightened AJ to sweep the jumpy amphibian out with a broom.

The professor thought it was the right time for Cheupe, who was leading the damage control team in charge of Radio Five, to kick in. All the other buzzing radios were switched off. The silence that followed was as loud as that caused by a sudden electricity outage in a discotheque.

"Hi Ananias. This is Stella calling from the town center. My take is that Deborah's track record speaks for itself. Long before she even joined politics, her CLEAN NGO had Wemppeans realize that for power to return to them, they had to start by owning their environment through cleaning and rehabilitating it. Secondly, Ananias, if women are their own worst enemies, how come the likes of Mrs. Ziphorah Lengo, Governor Risper Fundi, and countless other women are vouching for Deborah? The caliber of men and women backing Deborah and the KPM cause speaks for itself."

"Sweetheart, I am with you there, "Ananias agreed.

It was amazing how Stella's phone call changed the schema of the subsequent callers. Wemppeans began extolling the virtues of women. Men praised sisters who had paid school fees for them, and others spoke of female parliamentarians who held stellar development records.

As the debate raged on radio and TV sets across Kawemppe, the high court grounds in downtown Wemppe were filling with thousands of KPM supporters. They were pouring in from all corners of Kawemppe in solidarity with their leader Deborah Binti Nzingha.

Alloys Faya sensed his mistake at around nine in the morning when Victoria summoned him. With no small amount of panic, he cautiously approached his chairman's red-carpeted office and took a seat beside SASA lawyer Jogoo Mapanga. His bosses, Ronald and Victoria, Mitambo, and the eight County campaign coordinators who were present and seated.

"Unless we withdraw this case now, KPM lawyers will expose to Wemppeans over three hundred irregularities we the SASA party have flouted." Lawyer Mapanga said. The political writers led by Paa Isaya and Elijah Lmbatwa, had been equating the shaky ground SASA stood on to the proverbial eye jammed with a log pointing at its neighbor's speck.

Victoria's eyes wandered towards the muted TV, which sat on a low shelf by the corner. On the screen could be seen busloads of men and women in a blur of the gold and purple KPM colours, disembarking from hired school buses. Their saucer sized WOMAN badges pinned on their lapels glistened like stars in the morning sun.

Alloys looked at Victoria with hidden disdain and thought that if Ronald was not going to tame his wife's lust for power, then one of these days she was bound to bring disaster to the SASA house.

Against his better judgment, Alloys opened his mouth and said, "I have been listening to the radio shows for the past week, and the people's court out there is of the opinion that SASA is a big bully taking on the underdog. I suggest we call this thing off right now before we damage our chances further." He wanted to add some more insights. Furthermore, it was his idea to dig up the mud on KPM that had immersed them in their present predicament, but Victoria's deadly gaze caused him to clam up.

A few minutes elapsed while Victoria looked at Alloys like a leper who had not only been invited to the main table for supper but was also commenting about the food. The moment was saved by Ronald.

"I think Alloys is right," Ronald said.

Victoria who wanted to see blood spilled was adamant that the case should proceed, but Ronald overruled her and ordered his lawyer to withdraw the case immediately.

At midday, Lawyer Jogoo Mapanga filed a withdrawal of the case. Soon, the news of the withdrawal began to filter through the crowds of KPM supporters. The large gathering began to dance on the streets of Wemppe. Deborah, Risper, and other KPM leaders led the dance from the front. Obed was not taking any chances with the security arrangements. His boys and Jonte's friends from the slum had ringed the outer edges of the dancing locomotive of humanity. Sophisticated city dwellers, rarely unfazed, could be seen gawking at the passing mob from their office windows.

Being a Friday, most Wemppeans decided to close shop and fall into step with the dancing caravans.

"V-P-M," the women sang.

"Mama," the men replied.

"V-P-M," the women sang.

"Mamaaaaa," sang everyone.

"De-bo-ra-h," the men sang.

"For president," the women replied, accompanied by Jonte's *vuvuzela* which splintered the air at measured intervals.

When the evening rolled in at the Maarufu's town residence, Victoria impatiently surfed several news channels, looking for something other than Deborah's human train which was dominating most news channels in vain. Feeling unsettled, she looked loathingly at Ronald who was asleep in his favorite armchair with his mouth ajar. She felt a volcano of rage well inside her, and for a mad minute, she felt like jamming the T.V remote inside his open mouth. Instead, she roughly woke him up.

"Ronald, I think you should be worried for real. This girl is gaining momentum faster than a wild fire."

Ronald cleared his throat and, halfway awake, mumbled a well-known proverb. "An old bull fights with flair"

Victoria rolled her eyes at her husband's mention of the proverb.

Sensing his wife's distress, Ronald adjusted his seating position and explained. "Deborah has a long way to go. I will start playing my drums when all the other political parties have danced themselves lame. I have been in this game long enough to read trends. We haven't had the presidential debate yet." Ronald had just seen off his top campaign managers. He was tired and wanted to snooze a bit in peace.

His fatigue caused Victoria's ire to ebb away.

"Don't you think it is about time president Jabali paid back the royalty we have served him with over the years? By now, he should be hinting strongly that you are the bride in waiting."

"I don't know why you are fretting yourself over the president's endorsement. I know the man. He will show up just at the right moment," a tired Ronald pleaded.

Victoria often wondered how best to jostle Ronald from his accustomed comfort zone in life. As the son of a colonial paramount chief, Maarufu Skukii, Ronald was used to gliding through life, with doors held wide open for him.

"Okay, I will let you sleep. But my grandmother used to tell me that the possum received the shortest tails of all animals because of being over assumptive. Victoria began to narrate the story just like her grandmother used to tell it.

"Long time ago, all the animals had been called by the maker to go and collect their tails. The lion, cheetah, cow, monkey, and giraffe arrived early and had their tails fixed. Other animals followed suit and got a perfect fit. The possum, never one to be bothered by what the crowds were up to, decided to attend to some household chores before going to meet the maker. Towards midday, Cheetah passed by and asked him, "Possum, aren't you going to get your tail? All the other animals are already queuing for theirs.

"The possum answered noncommittally, 'I have things to attend to first and anyway the maker knows I am on my way.'

"Around three o'clock in the afternoon, the dog passed by possum's place, switching its newly acquired tail excitedly. 'Possum don't tell me you haven't collected your tail yet.'

"Possum answered, 'The day is still young,' and went under a tree for his afternoon nap.

"When he woke up, it was almost dark. Worriedly, he started racing towards the maker's house. When he got there, all the best tails had already been issued out, and the possum got a little butt of a thing which could not wiggle a fly away. He still has it to this day.

"What do you make of that?" Victoria asked her husband.

She was greeted by the light snoring of her husband who was fast asleep.

# CHAPTER

# 25

ON SEPTEMBER 20, AN extremely cold day, Deborah led a group of close family members to commemorate her late husband's fifth Memorial Day. Nzingha's mother, Rael, and her kin stood at a distance with guilt as they stared at the woman they had rebuffed not so long ago with muted respect. Jasper Hadithi and Praxedes had wanted to air the service live, but Deborah had totally opposed the idea.

"Why not?" Praxedes had asked.

"I am not going to milk Nzingha's legacy for any political gain."

Nonetheless, WAMO TV featured a twenty-second mention of the service, and it was an unforgettable scene. The nation watched Deborah dressed in a severe grey suit, stand by Goldie as she placed a bouquet of flaming red roses on her father's grave. AJ followed suit, his lower lip stiff in a valiant effort to stem the tears that were threatening to fall. He placed his favorite plastic toy, a crouching commando, next to the red roses on the cold tombstone, stood back and smartly saluted his father's grave.

Paa, preparing for a rare and much-anticipated interview with outgoing president Jabali, watched the news clip on his office TV and felt his heart catch at AJ's gesture. How he wished Deborah would accept his proposal.

Out of sheer courtesy and dedication to duty, he picked up his jacket and recorder and left for the Wemppe Presidential Palace, all the while fighting an overwhelming temptation to cancel the presidential interview.

President Jabali had been hoping to spend some private time with Paa Isaya as a way of building rapport for a favorable review of his memoir, *The Transitional Man*. The thought disappeared once the much younger journalist was ushered into his study. Paa Isaya wore the most dispirited look the president had ever seen on the face of a member of the fourth estate. The young man was not like his father, the millionaire Isaya Hekima, the president concluded. One could say that Isaya Hekima had a peculiar strain of humility while his son was courteous, and that made a huge difference. The father was bound to get out of his way to please the president. But not his stubborn son, who had refused his father's financial backing and made his way up from a one-roomed office to the newspaper empire he currently owned.

"Mr. President, your critics are accusing you of abandoning Honorable Maarufu in his hour of need? What should Maarufu make of your prolonged silence?" Paa began his interview immediately, as soon as an aide had settled him comfortably in the president's study. Heavily bound books lined the mahogany-paneled study from floor to ceiling.

For almost half an hour, Paa listened absent mindedly at the president speech. Jabali passionately articulated his theory of equal opportunities for the rich and the poor, until he interrupted him with his next question.

"You are teaching two lectures on leadership and governance at Makonge University."

"Correct," the president replied.

People knew that the lectures were a strategy to avoid Maarufu.

"With your hectic schedule, where will you get the time to attend lectures?"

President Jabali laughed good-naturedly. "I simply want to keep my brain from rusting and to impart my experiences to the future generations before I forget them."

They talked about the president's many successes, ranging from fighting corruption cartels to stemming ethnicity. President Jabali acknowledged that more needed to be done.

It was at this juncture that Paa switched the interview to the president's memoirs.

"In your autobiography, The Transitional Man, which I admit is well-written, who is this transitional man you are talking about, when it appears like you have not groomed a successor to take over when you leave office?"

The president considered the question for a while. It reminded him of his daughter Vizuri. As he reiterated his opinion that every Wemppean deserved a chance, the president felt Paa's stare analyzing him. President Jabali knew that behind the harmless stare on Paa's face lay one of Kawemppe's most incisive and brilliant minds. He wished his daughter Vizuri was still around. Maybe the two could find common ground for a future relationship.

Paa could attest that when history was told, president Jabali would be remembered as a visionary giant who had streered Kawemppe from the brink of despair and brougt her back to the highway of change and development. President Meshack Jabali was a true transitional man. Paa would have continued the interview but his mind was still stuck with the picture of Deborah and her grieving children standing next to the cold tomb of her late husband. He brought the interview to an end, collected his tape, and drove back to his office.

By evening he was fit for the mental hospital for thinking about Deborah. Thoughtfully, he drove towards Wemppe Meadows. Deborah and her family were in a subdued mood. He found them watching a collection of videos and picture slides taken when their beloved Nzingha was alive. Feeling embarrassed for intruding on such a private moment, Paa wheeled Mzee Abraham around the compound for an hour, had small talk with Jonte, and left.

"I don't like the direction KPM is taking," Deborah began, surprising her campaign team, who were preparing to rollout to another stadium for a campaign rally. All the buzzing ceased at once, and over twenty pairs of eyes locked onto Deborah in confusion. Governor Fundi looked at her mentee in bewilderment. Her whole body was sore from the grueling campaign schedule Deborah adhered to. *Modern campaigns are not designed for people over sixty*, she thought wryly. The day before, they had held a successful rally on Honorable Maarufu's turf in Lokamiko

Country. Risper had watched enviously as Deborah danced with various women's groups, while shaking her shoulders like she had no bones.

"We need to activate our WOMAN machinery properly. We cannot sell the KPM agenda by standing in stadia and propounding our agenda to faceless people just like our rivals, and hope to be different. We need to get personal and know our voters better. So, ladies and gentlemen let us don our shoes and slap the dew off the grass in every hamlet in Kawemppe"

Professor Majuaa scanned the team critically. Everybody was gazing at Deborah. He had last heard the language she was using with revolutionaries. Rattled from their "filled up stadium comfort zones," the team went to work. Lumumba reorganized all KPM aspirants into manageable provincial, district and village groups and dispatched a program of what was expected of them. Organized groups like All on Board, now numbering over a million, and Mrs. Ziphorah Lengo with HMA, moved into action with specific instructions from Ruthanne to conduct door-to-door campaigns. The professional groups were not left out. Through focused group discussions and recruitments, they began to educate their colleagues on the KPM vision. Praxedes had five out of every eight talk shows on WAMO MEDIA address the KPM agenda. Only Mrs. Clementine Kinga Nzambe's the Independence Women League (IWL) chair and her sixty-eight snobbish madams resisted the idea of knocking on doors on behalf of KPM.

"Cut them off. This is injury time. We don't have space for joy riders," Mrs. Lengo snapped once she heard the news from Ruthanne. Marcus, whose voter management software's could access any voting demographics with the click of a button, hit the delete key over Independence Women League (IWL), and they ceased to be an affiliate of the KPM party.

⟡

# C H A P T E R

# 26

Victoria Maarufu woke up with a start, her eyes popping wide open like exploding pea pods on a hot day. Within seconds, fear surged through her as the latest Mzalendo poll numbers cascaded through her mind. Her husband's popularity was declining by the day. Reaching for her mobile phone, a quick flick indicated it was four in the morning. The phone's backlight illuminated the mummy-shaped outline of her husband asleep next to her. His chest was rising and falling like a slow wave as he drew breath.

How Ronald could manage to sleep so well when his popularity was fatally hemorrhaging and the SASA annual delegates meeting was only hours away was a miracle to Victoria. Even Senator Virunga, with whom she had spent weeks campaigning in the mountainous region of the Amusitu, had alluded to grim realities: if Deborah Binti Nzingha wasn't stopped soon, then their future was not as certain as people had imagined.

A gathering headache began to throb in the back of her skull. Easing herself from bed slowly, in order not to wake up Ronald, she threw on a fluffy robe over her night dress and crept out of the bedroom. At the landing, she flicked on the staircase light. The portraits of her two grown children mounted on the wall near the winding staircase smiled back at her. She paused to scrutinize the pictures.

Victoria was still not clear about the kind of job their son Tabora claimed to be doing back in Bristol. The man had never been consistent with any aspect of his life. He had flopped in college, and his marriage was also gone. Now, she was raising his two small sons. The only thing Tabora did with some consistency was his twice a year begging trips under the pretext of visiting his sons.

Chenna, their thirty-five years old daughter was an associate professor in a Canadian college. According to Victoria, Chenna was her father's daughter, determined on the exterior but naïve on the inside.

*A girl your age is giving us sleepless nights, but you two cannot pause from your self-centered lives to join us in the battle for the presidency. What a shame,* Victoria thought. A pang of anger gnawed deep in her soul. *Those loser genes must be from Ronald's side of the family,* she concluded and walked downstairs to her hotel-sized kitchen. Filling a pot with water, she set it on the gas burner and added in the tealeaves, sugar, and a teaspoon of relaxing cinnamon, then stood back to wait for the brew to boil.

Something drastic needed to be done to save SASA. Despite the hour, she retrieved her mobile phone from her robe pocket and dialed Senator Virunga's number. He picked up on the third ring sounding groggy.

"Senator, I would not have called you, if I could handle the matter from this end. I want you to stop that girl before SASA's goose is cooked."

"What's in it for me?" he asked.

"The running mate post," Victoria replied.

"What?" Virunga asked in astonishment.

"You heard me," Victoria said and disconnected the phone.

Senator Virunga was stunned. He tried to wonder what else the foolish Mitambo Mitambo had done to get booted.

For the first time since meeting the tenacious Victoria Maarufu almost four years ago, Virunga had sensed naked despair in her voice, and sleep deserted his eyes. Lying still in his bed, his mind began kicking about several possible options he could deploy to stop Deborah Binti Nzingha and KPM in their tracks. The answer came to him towards six in the morning. Extricating himself from the cuddly warmth of his second wife's body, he sat up and flicked on the light while ignoring her cursing clicks at the disturbance. His briefcase stood by the corner. He retrieved it and brought it back to bed. After a minute of very noisy rifling, purposed to annoy his wife some more, he pounced on what he was looking for. A copy of KPM's campaign schedule. His beady eyes scanned the nearby dressing table for a pen until they landed on his wife's black eye pencil. He uncorked it and circled out the October 5 Makutano homecoming tour. It was the day KPM had earmarked for Deborah to visit her home town. Satisfied, the Senator decided to sleep for an hour before preparing for the delegates meeting. He rolled his now cold body towards his wife who flinched and moved away.

Ronald and Victoria Maarufu, in the company of top SASA stalwarts, swept into the three-thousand-seat basketball court of Wemppe Stadium to a rousing welcome. Pausing to acknowledge the greetings from their supporters attired in a blur of maroon and cream, they slowly made their way to the VIP area at the center of the court, and the meeting commenced.

The first speakers to address the conference were young and upcoming hopefuls, aspiring members of parliament, senators and governors all newly subscribed to the party by their ability to buy the nomination papers. They had nothing but praise for Ronald and the party. According to them, SASA was the party most likely to form the next government.

Victoria watched a herd of young men prance around importantly, nearly gouging each other's eyes out as they executed one of her fundraising ideas, SASA branded walking sticks. From time to time they gave robust handshakes and slapped each other's backs like people who had already won the battle. *Ronald was partially to blame for creating such a misguided perception*, Victoria thought. But who could blame Ronald? He seemed satisfied with the empty words that president Jabali fed him when their paths had crossed.

Over breakfast, she had sweet-talked him into switching his running mate, Mitambo Mitambo, with the more experienced Senator Marko Virunga. Ronald had gone along with her idea. Twisting her neck, she leaned close to Ronald's ear to confer. "If Risper, Praxedes, and that silly girl had not interfered with our plans, we wouldn't even need to placate Jabali for his support." Victoria spoke loudly to make up for the noise emanating from the delegates. As she waited for an answer, her eye peered down Ronald's ear canal and encountered a frighteningly ripe lobe of wax ready for removal. Thank God journalists couldn't see such things. The fuss they would make!

"KPM is a fading star. We have this thing in our pocket. I keep telling you that an old ox fights with flair, but you don't listen to me," Ronald replied.

After reading Paa Isaya's interview with the president, Victoria was convinced that President Jabali's support could not be banked upon.

"Has Jabali called you today, or is he busy with his governance lessons at the university?" Victoria's tone was sarcastic.

"I know the man well. He said he will come," Ronald answered simply and turned his attention to the dais.

Unconvinced by her husband's assurances, Victoria began to meticulously review the plans she had for the day. What had to be done was unavoidable and it was going to earn her two lifetime enemies before the conference was over. A sharp pain shot through her tummy. She popped an anti-acid tablet in her mouth and began to chew. A few feet away, a jovial Senator Lydia Masumbuko moved about the jammed floor, networking with other delegates unaware of what Victoria had in store for her.

After listening to numerous speeches, Victoria turned worriedly to her benignly smiling husband. It was two in the afternoon, and the president had not arrived. Like a fool, Ronald kept hoping that President Jabali was on the way.

"He won't come. Reframe your speech and make it seem like you had an understanding that he wasn't coming," Victoria advised. Her voice was brittle with disappointment. She scanned the crowds and saw Alloys Faya begin to execute her plan B.

Alloys worked his way around the delegates with a purposeless grin to camouflage the incongruous demands Victoria was making of him. He waded towards the cluster where the aspiring Governors were seated and aimed straight for Senator Lydia Masumbuko. Beckoning her to follow him urgently, he led her straight inside the VIP ladies bathroom reserved for Victoria Maarufu's sole use.

"Senator Masumbuko, we need to iron out a few things," Alloys began, before apologizing to pick up one of his many ringing phones. Strolling out of the bathroom with a phone affixed to his ear, Alloys bolted out the door firmly after him and rejoined the meeting.

Unaware of the trick being played on her, Senator Masumbuko took the opportunity to freshen her makeup. She was in the process of dubbing away excess lip-gloss with a tissue, when she heard the speakers announce that the unopposed gubernatorial contestant for Solanga County was Mitambo Mitambo. Jolted like someone treading on hot coal, Lydia spun around and in one quick step reached for the door knob and jerked it violently before realizing that she was locked in. Like one waking up from a bad dream, Senator Lydia Masumbuko realized that she had been duped. Victoria had used her to wage her political wars and was now discarding her. Limply, she sank down on the floor and let out an anguished scream.

In the adjoining VIP gent's room, a disbelieving Mitambo Mitambo, freshly bundled in by Alloys Faya also listened in disbelief as the speakers announced that he had willingly agreed to relinquish his post as Honorable Maarufu's running mate to the more experienced senator Marko Virunga and instead was now the unopposed SASA gubernatorial contestant for Solanga County. The old gizzards at Maroon House who had promised him the running mate post had shortchanged him. Stepping back, he took a well-aimed kick at the locked door and heard the unmistakable crack of his ankle breaking. Excruciating pain surged up his leg and he slumped to the floor, howling in pain.

When the blazing sun dipped further towards its westerly lodging, SASA's mandarins, consisting of aging party vultures, took over the floor, led by Jonathan Mrwah. The vultures had become very restless after realizing that President Jabali was not going to grace the occasion.

Victoria's face brightened. She knew that Jonathan could use his great oratorical powers to smoke out President Jabali from his hideout.

"SASA hoyeeeee," a visibly angry Jonathan shouted as he swung his fly whisk above his head.

"Hoyeeeee!" the crowd roared back,

"SASA hoyeee."

"Hoyeee"

"Where is Jabali? We need the calabash that we gave him years ago back and filled to the brim."

It took a full minute for the frenzy he had evoked to die down.

"You all know the story of the hare and the fox who were once great friends. When famine hit the land, they decided to kill their mothers and feast on them. Hare convinced Fox to kill his mother first, and for a long time the two persevered out the famine with the meat from fox's mother until it got finished. Then it was Hare's turn to kill his mother. The hare, being crafty, began playing delaying tactics with the fox until the long-awaited rains came and his mother survived with her life intact.

"Jabali, we gave you our mother first. It is your turn to give us yours today." Jonathan spared no words as he called for president Jabali to step out and if necessary coronate Maarufu as the next president of Kawemppe.

Eventually, Ronald Maarufu stood up to address the gathering. A thunderous applause befitting a president in waiting escorted him to the microphones, which were capturing the event live on all TV and radio channels in Kawemppe. For a minute, Ronald stood erect and proud, smiling at his people who were waving ecstatically.

At last he spoke, his voice welling with enthusiasm propagated by the crowd's encouragement. He clenched his fist and thrust his maroon fly whisk into the air.

"SASA hoyeee."

"Hoyeeeeee," the crowd roared back.

# CHAPTER

# 27

NOTHING COULD GO WRONG with a Makutano homecoming. Makutano, a Swahili word meaning "a meeting point," had been coined from the land's geographical positioning, which saw it sandwiched between the banks of river Maru to the east and the hilly regions of Amusitu County to the north. Jonte, the CLEAN team and the All on Board had been camping in the area for two weeks, providing the much-needed direction to the growing excitement. Groups of youths ignored the cold weather and worked all day long, repairing ditches and potholes all across the County. Overgrown bushes had been hacked back and dirt roads swept clean. Makutano grounds, where the homecoming meeting was to be held, had its grass trimmed and numerous waste bins mounted at various points. After school, the voices of children mass choirs could be heard as far as the neighboring Soda Baridi Shopping Center, bursting with song ready for the big day.

A day before Deborah Binti Nzingha's entourage was expected in town, the County was all poised to welcome their famous daughter. Senator Marko Virunga arrived incognito in the neighboring town of Soda-baridi, accompanied by two peculiar looking youths, and took refuge from the cold winds in a dimly lit back street lodge. A waitress served them beers. The senator lowered his huge mass on the only available furniture in the room—a rickety stool—as his company casually flopped on the bed covered with a hideously dirty blanket. The bare yellow bulb cast the Senator's shadow on the wall. It resembled a toadstool mushroom.

"Some of these women walking around with big coconut heads have no idea what politics is all about," Senator Virunga said gravely after downing half a glass of beer in a single gulp.

"True, sir. My own mother normally calls me every election time to ask whom she should vote for," Mrefu, one of the youths, confessed.

Senator Virunga nodded at the short, stunted man approvingly. The youngster had a worldly grasp of the power of violence that many of his peers were yet to get acquainted with. The senator knew that whatever Mrefu lacked in strength, his partner, the ruthless monster Toto, slouching calmly on the bed, compensated for.

"The future of Kawemppe lies in young people like you. You have to mind the country's business. We need to stop this women's nonsense in a fashion that will make women elsewhere think twice before they desert their homes to join the passing KPM bandwagon". Senator Virunga look lingered on Toto's beefy arms. "Is everything ready for tomorrow?" he asked.

"Yes, sir. My boys will be rolling in any time from now with the materials," Mrefu answered calmly like someone giving an update of his sister's wedding preparations.

"Good." The senator's avocado face broke into a lopsided grin. He admired the dangerous schemes that ran through Mrefu's mind waiting for a proper moment to get activated. Reaching for his briefcase on the table, he retrieved two large brown envelopes and handed them to Mrefu, who stretched both hands and bowed down with respect like a beggar reaching for alms.

"Thank you, sir," Mrefu said.

"Boys, don't fail me. I need proper terror, tattered petticoats, tears and broken bones. Nothing less." Virunga gulped his remaining beer. Supporting himself by grabbing the sides of the wobbly stool he stood up. His earlier grin was gone, and in its place was a chillingly dangerous scowl. "Remember I don't want any stupidity on your part finding its way back to me. Do you understand?"

"Sir, I swear that we don't know you," Toto, speaking for the first time, reassured the politician. His soft voice belied the brutality of his bulging muscles."

After the senator's car had disappeared into the cold fog, Mrefu roughly tore the more compact-looking envelope with his fingers. Crisp new bank notes—hundred wera denominations—fell on the bed, and the two thugs whooped with pleasure. They didn't need to inspect the second and bulkier envelope. The strong aroma of marijuana was already starting to percolate the room.

An hour later, a pickup truck full of menacing looking youths pulled into the lodging's parking lot and ejected its sinister looking load. Two of the men speedily hoisted tightly sealed drums from the co driver's seat and dashed them straight to the room Mrefu and Toto were holed up in.


"Don't tell me this animal looks like this on the inside," Nana exclaimed awestruck as Obed helped her into the campaign helicopter. It was her first time to fly.

"Obed, knot my belt properly. I don't want to slide off my seat and land on people's heads below."

"I have you covered, Nana," Obed said smoothly, reassuring the old lady.

"Yippee! I want to be a pilot when I grow up," AJ exclaimed in unchecked excitement once the chopper became airborne. Goldie clung to her mum partially with fear and partially with envy when she saw how unbothered AJ looked.

An hour later, the chopper began circling the wet Makutano grounds, ready to land. From the air, they watched the unprecedented crowds gathered below, chasing after the chopper and giving captain Tanar a hard time as he maneuvered to land. Giant cranes hoisting WAMO TV cameras zoomed back and forth, capturing the moments.

With nostalgia, Deborah's mind recollected her journey—how far she had come. It seemed just like yesterday when, as an example of what educating a girl was all about, the entire village had gathered to bid her farewell. She was the first girl from the locality to ever to set foot in a university to study law. And now, here she was, coming back home to commune with her kin and ask for their votes. Overwhelmed by emotions, she wiped away a tear.

"If you ever see me wanting to fly with this animal again, tie me to a tree," Nana said in relief once Captain Tanar landed.

Immediately, a lanky youth dressed in a full scout's uniform matched towards Deborah and her entourage to ask her to inspect a guard of honor mounted by the scouts. It was composed of students selected from several schools. AJ followed behind his mother, a permanent salute stuck to his head. Goldie, a scout in her own right, fell into a coordinated step behind them. Unruly crowds of school children in warm jackets jostled from the sides, craning their necks curiously to catch a glimpse of Deborah. Some held colorful placards and Deborah managed to read some as she marched by "Deborah We Love You" and "Deborah for President."

The full KPM steering committee and aspirants from the entire republic were present. They had begun trickling in from dawn in a convoy of over seventy buses. Numerous local development committees, of which Deborah was a member, had amalgamated to form the Makutano Professionals Group and were ushering the guests. Mrs. Mary Msalaba and a sizeable congregation of Kilele Girls Government School (KGGS) alumni were present. All the associates and staff of Nzingha & co Advocates led by Aphia had also come to celebrate their former boss. As she greeted them, she watched in amusement as Obed faltered in his ever-sure step as he stared at the stunningly beautiful Geraldine, her former assistant.

After much hand shaking, Deborah sat down, and the choirs began singing. Risper and Praxedes looked at her approvingly. Ndollah had outdone himself. He had dressed Deborah in an indigo maxi dress decorated with gold buttons. A mass choir led by the Makutano branch of Gospel Africa (K) Church, where Deborah had attended services as a child, began singing Deborah's favorite song: "Lead me." She knew most of the members by name. Briefly, she joined the altos and sang along to the delight of the crowd.

Next in line was a mass choir of pupils from various Makutano schools. Their poetic song was quite a sensation. Divided into two rows of brides in white scarves versus groom in red scarves, they took turns in taunting each other in the poem.

"Poor me, poor me."
"You told me that if I marry you,"
"You will build me a stone mansion."
"Sixty years down the line,"
"I still live in a mud thatch hut."

"Have patience, have patience, my dear."
"Money does not grow on trees."

"Poor me, poor me."
"You told me that if remained loyal to you,"
"You would get me piped water. Why then,"
"Sixty years down the road, am I still relying on my faithful donkey
To fetch my water?"

"My dear, my dear, where have you been?"
"Have you not heard?"

"That climate change has robbed us of our waters?"

"Enough!! Enough!! Oooh enough!!"
"Phew!!"
"Deborah Binti Nzingha, our sister, will listen to us."

The crowds broke into a loud cheer, which hushed down quickly eager to hear the next stanza. Suddenly, all hell broke loose. Honorable Harakka, seated behind Praxedes, thought it was one of the trees overwhelmed by its perching human cargo that had caved in. Then he heard the screams of panicked school children as they were being trampled on. Grown men were jumping dangerously over seated women and children trying to escape. A sense of mortal danger gripped him when someone shouted out the word, "bees."

Instinctively, Deborah turned around and enveloped her children between herself and Nana and threw a scarf over their heads. Obed, Zulu, and Ken were beside her in a flash. Obed, who had fought in the gulf and other places, sized up the situation and pried the microphone from Honorable Harakka's shocked hands. The scene in front of him was like a sea of humanity being whipped by the broken blades of a giant blender.

"This is security. Everybody, down, down, down. Don't move. Bees don't sting when it is cold. Please stay down." Obed's voice was authoritative and calm but he could as well as have been talking to himself. Dropping the microphone, he turned towards Deborah. "We have to evacuate you at once," he said.

"I am not leaving," Deborah replied. Obed looked at Deborah's determined eyes and decided to change tact.

Reassuring her children of her safety, Deborah handed them over to Josephine and Dina. Jonte paved the way in the confused melee, firmly holding Nana's hand while Zulu was swatting the air over their heads with a jacket. The frightened lot rushed towards captain Tanar's waiting chopper which took off immediately.

Ruthanne, Lumumba, and professor Majuaa, cowering from the buzzing bees, watched, stunned as Deborah, wearing her trademark calm look, picked up the fallen microphone and began addressing the screaming crowds. Obed stood behind her, all his muscles taut.

"Please stop running. Do not run. Stand where you are or lie down, bees don't sting when it is cold," she said. To illustrate her instructions, Deborah stood ramrod straight. A few determined bees buzzed around her immobile body before they took off. The distressed crowds, witnessing Deborah's bravery, stopped running. Scores of children lay on the ground wailing in pain. From the corner of her eye, Deborah could see Honorable Harakka, Governor Fundi, and Praxedes working their phones, frantically calling for help.

"Those of us who are hurt, stay where you are. Help is on the way," Deborah continued soothingly

"What these beautiful bees are doing for us now is to strengthen our resolve to fight on. When bees pollinate a flower, new life springs forth." With that, Deborah jabbed the air with her fist and began singing the Kawemppe national anthem. The crowd slowly joined her.

That was the pose police Inspector Otto Temmu found them in when he came charging in with his team. With a few unnecessary threats, the inspector managed to direct the crowds towards different exit points. Governor Fundi's medical skills came in handy. Collaborating with uninjured scouts, local nurses and the police, they started to help the injured into the few waiting ambulances

Paa Isaya had been engrossed with work on his computer at his seventeenth-floor office, preparing for a scheduled interview with Honorable Ronald Maarufu the next day, when, as if telepathically, he lifted his head and saw on the muted TV the pandemonium happening at the Makutano rally. Reaching for the remote, he hit the volume key to the maximum and listened to a worried-looking news anchor replace the live broadcast with the breaking news.

"We interrupt our live broadcast to bring you some breaking news. News just in indicates that scores of people have been injured after swarms of bees attacked a mammoth crowd at a KPM rally in Makutano County. I repeat, reports just reaching us now . . ."

Snarling like a caged cheetah, Paa rose from his seat, grabbed his coat and phone and stormed out of his office. If something ever happened to Deborah or her children, he would die, he thought, as he absently took the stairs clearing three at a time.

By the time he hit the tenth-floor landing, he had calmed down enough to realize that not even his powerful motorcycle could get him to Makutano fast enough.

He reached for his mobile phone and called his father.

"Dad, I need a chopper now," he said breathlessly.

Isaya Hekima could not recall a time in his living memory when his stubborn son and heir had ever sought him out for help. Refusing to dwell on the details of the strange request, he simply asked "How many helicopters son?"

"A minute." Paa hung up the call and phoned his journalist pal Prost Bandari, who he knew was covering the event at Makutano.

"The bees have not stung many. It is the panic. We have many people with broken limbs. We may need around eight choppers to airlift the seriously injured people to neighboring county hospitals. Makutano general hospital is almost overwhelmed." Bandari was brief and to the point.

Paa redialed his father number again "How about ten of them. Send one to the helipad on the roof top of my office, and the rest to Makutano municipal stadium please," Paa yelled down the phone startling the pair of guards manning the tenth-floor lobby. Attempting to control his anxiety, he did a quick about-turn and started to race for the helipad on the twenty-second floor of the building.

Isaya Hekima deployed twenty choppers. Nineteen of them flew directly to Makutano while one swung by Paa's office to pick him up. He was partially relieved after succeeding to have a quick word with Deborah over the phone.

At the Makutano general hospital, seriously injured people writhed in pain on the crowded corridors surrounded by abandoned shoes, umbrellas, and tattered clothes. The scenes were bleak and desperate, such that even the ever-curious journalists milling around the hospital had lost their insatiable appetite for news and stopped asking questions. When the helicopters began landing next on the empty fields surrounding the hospital, a fast-thinking surgeon began weeding out the critically injured for evacuation to neighboring county hospitals.

Upon landing, Paa immediately ditched his chopper and jogged towards the hospital, frantically searching to just get a glimpse of Deborah. His journalist eyes missed nothing. Not the scattered muddy clothes, broken twigs, or the shell-shocked people who stood around the hospital, talking in hushed voices. He thought of taking photos, but it seemed almost rude to invade the grave environment pervading the town. The snapshots he had were enough. Before landing, his pilot had circled around Makutano grounds giving Paa different angles to shoot from and record the aftermath of the stampede with his sophisticated camera.

Entering the casualty wing, Paa began wading past worried parents and relatives standing on the muddied corridors. Several beds later, he saw her hunched over a frightened schoolgirl lying on a bed. Alongside her were the girl's worried parents, along with Ruthanne, Prof, Obed, and Ken. Sensing Paa, Deborah straightened up and looked at his eyes directly, giving him a slow-motion nod that seemed to say "I'm okay. Are you?"

He nodded back at her. Their silent transaction only took a split second, and not even the ever-alert Obed noticed it. With his heart banging about his ribcage in relief, Paa quietly slipped outside the hospital and started what he knew how to do best. Sniffing for leads. There was a story behind this tragedy and he was determined to unearth the truth.

He was lucky several pubs later. After coaxing a few patrons with endless bottles of beers, he stumbled upon a bar maid, whose cousin, Gladys, another bar maid in the neighboring Soda Baridi town, had been talking of hosting a strange-looking bunch of youths the previous night. Mounting a motorcycle taxi, Paa raced towards Soda Baridi town and found a mute and hostile Gladys behind her pub counter. After assuring her that he was not a policeman and parting with a handsome amount of weras, Gladys thawed up and began talking.

"Those riff-raff were not locals and I hated them for their uncouthness," Gladys railed. From the moment she had seen the youths, she had sensed trouble. Her curiosity had prompted her to take a few discreet photos on her phone as the goons danced in the lodge's discotheque.

Paa WhatsApped the pictures to his phone and emailed them further into the safety of his cloud account. Thanking Gladys profusely, he returned to Makutano and printed a few photos at a local cybercafé. He then sought out Inspector Otto Temmu who was still recording eyewitness accounts and handed him a few copies.

Eventually, the long day, mired by political thuggery never before witnessed in Kawemppe politics, came to an end. Wemppeans brought indoors early by the cold weather settled in to watch the evening news.

Senator Virunga admired his handiwork from the safety of his first wife's sitting room. She was in the kitchen, preparing his dinner. His boys had definitely executed their job brilliantly, he thought. Once he became the second most powerful man in Kawemppe, his payroll would absorb Mrefu and Toto as his official body guards.

According to the news reporter, scores had been treated and discharged while fifty-six people, forty of them schoolchildren, were admitted to various hospitals with serious injuries.

With pleasure, Senator Virunga watched the President Jabali, emerge from the offices of Makonge University after cutting off a lecture midway, to condemn the evil attack. He called for a speedy investigation.

"It is your fault. All we need from you is your endorsement, and the election is over," Virunga hissed loudly at the president's disappearing image.

His wife peeked in from the kitchen.

"Have you called me?" she asked. Mrs. Hannah Virunga was a tall and plump woman.

"Woman, someone could die here waiting for that supper of yours," the Senator retorted.

"You would surely make it to the history record books, if that someone was you," she countered sarcastically before retreating back to her kitchen.

Ronald Maarufu appeared next on screen, condemning the cowardly act. "I urge the police to hunt down the criminals responsible and bring them to book."

Honorable Maarufu's innocent comment sent the Senator roaring with laughter. "Surely, you don't mean to say that the police should arrest your wife, Ronald. Do you?" Virunga murmured as he shook his head in disbelief. It was obvious that the cultured Ronald had no idea that he was harboring the main culprit in his house. Returning his attention back to the newscaster, the senator's jovial mood soon vacated his face. A news flash from police headquarters announced that police Inspector Otto Temmu had a suspect in custody. Alarmed, the senator sat paralyzed, waiting to find out who the idiot was.

# CHAPTER
# 28

FOR DAYS, DEBORAH ATTENDED numerous counseling and debriefing session organized by KPM to help her, the affected schoolchildren, and the local community cope with the attack. Sometimes she took Goldie and AJ. AJ had acquired a catapult and had a few pebbles ready in his short pockets, just in case someone tried to attack his mother. The two thugs in inspector Temmu's custody had refused to name their benefactor.

According to Professor Majuaa, the bees attack, heinous as it had been, had rattled voters who had been undecided to wake up and actively become keepers of their brothers and sisters. The Kawemppe Election Secretariat (KES) was registering unprecedented numbers of first-time voters. Interestingly, baggy-mouthed politicians acquired better manners overnight, including Senator Virunga whose garrulous tongue was noticeably subdued.

When most of the injured children had been discharged from hospital, Deborah took a rare break to relax and prepare for debate night, which was only four days away. She also used the break to go on her long overdue date with Paa.

Paa throttled his powerful motor cycle towards Deborah's mansion with his heart in his throat. He was afraid that she might cancel their date yet again. After years of hopefully praying for his wife Gail to rally through her addiction, Paa had learned the virtue of patience. But he had to admit that despite Nana's fervent encouragement, getting his first date with Deborah had cost him untold levels of patience. Earlier in the week, he had cleaned his log cabin, located near the edge of the Wemppe forest and restocked it. A tub of vanilla ice cream sat chilling in the fridge next to a marinating leg of lamb. He had borrowed a bottle of rare red wine from his father's cellar. He was sure it would go well with the music collection of rumba and soul CDs stacked next to the stereo.

After a few minutes of waiting, he spotted her chatting with her gateman and smiled in relief. Deborah wore a pair of blue jeans and a black leather jacket worn over a thick white sweater. She looked like a royal Senegalese princess. Feeling blessed, he helped her to a spare helmet, waved at Obed who looked totally unsure about letting Deborah out of his sight, and sped off. After thirty minutes of weaving through the traffic, he detoured into a private dirt road and accelerated.

The impending presidential political debate was causing more excitement in Kawemppe than the hot weather, which had rapidly snuck over Kawemppe like a bout of measles.

The anticipation had further been heightened by James Nyundo, a junior reporter from REKE TV station and a columnist for the Wemppe Gazette. James had been seeking to stamp his authority over the dominance of his seasoned peers and had prepared a provocative documentary on the subject of NWS presidential hopeful Bishop Epaphras.

Armed with a camera and a microphone, James Nyundo had spent two days snooping around Bishop Epaphras up-country roots.

The documentary had featured Bishop Epaphras's gaunt brothers and their children living a pauper's life unaware of how wealthy their uncle was. The Bishop's mother confessed that she had not heard from her son in over five years. Nonetheless, she extolled her son's successes proudly, like any mother would do. As she talked, Nyundo's camera was panning her entire compound and captured the Bishop's half blind father, barefoot and sitting on the bare ground. His feet bore cracks wide enough to house a millipede.

Young Nyundo, being a fair reporter had not stopped there. Posing as a member of OFIS, the Bishop's church, he had gained access to the church's video library. After a day of screening numerous videos, he got what he was looking for. It was a video of Reverend Naomi, Bishop Epaphras's wife, confiding to her followers how blessed she was.

"We don't cook one large meal for the entire household. No way. We have been blessed. We have an in-house chef who caters to the specific appetites of my husband and children.

Wemppeans could forgive the excesses of a worldly man like M2, but not a man of the cloth. For days, they took to social media and questioned the lack of humility in God's servants and criticized the usage of church finances.

It was this state of affairs that had Bishop Epaphras sweating in the hot coastal sun of Ufuoni County on the afternoon of October 30, ready to play his last redeeming card. Prophet Esau Phaladum, of Borderless Christ Church, was holding his annual international crusade and Epaphras had marshaled colossal financial support from his church, towards the crusade. Prophet Esau was a man in a league of his own. He was a simple man who did not care about worldly possessions, money included. He had a following that made many a politician envious. His congregation, drawn from various denominations, normally organized themselves through various groups and raised the resources to cater to the crusade logistics, while the prophet was up some mountain interceding with God on their behalf.

Bishop Epaphras had seen this opportunity and seized it. A month prior to the crusade, Epaphras had taken over the role of overseeing the crusade's logistics. His loudly advertised contribution was hard to miss. Buses from various transport companies dispatched to ferry hundreds of faithful from all corners of Kawemppe bore a large banner screaming "Buses provided by OFIC." Four out of every five chairs in the crusade arena had the emblem OFIC stenciled on the backrest. The event, which was televised live by WAMO Media and REKE TV, had a red footnote flicking under the pictures: "Crusade airtime paid for by OFIC." In return, Epaphras was hoping for just one word from the prophet asking people to vote for NWS.

Not a man to be caught off guard, Bishop Epaphras jockeyed past a cluster of pastors and stood near the staircase leading to the podium. It was a vantage position from which he would be the last person to usher the great prophet onto the podium. That way, he could ensure he got the five minutes he sorely needed to share his presidential vision with the people. Epaphras looked at the mass of Christians swarming under the punishing afternoon sun and felt a tug of envy in his heart. *How could Prophet Esau command such a crowd without bothering to invest even a single cent in any form of advertising?* he wondered. Briefly, his mind wondered off to calculate how much cash the loud crowd in front of him was capable of raising. His arithmetic was cut short by a loud cheer on the left side of the dais. Alarmed, Epaphras thought that the great prophet had used the wrong way, but it was only a popular gospel artist taking up the microphone.

At six foot two, Prophet Esau was a handsome, muscular giant. At sixty-two, he was aging very well. He emerged dressed in his trademark sky-blue robe which contrasted sharply with his dark complexion. Most people thought it was a pity he wasn't married. Customarily, he jogged towards the podium, his clean-shaven head glistening in the sun with his eyes focused straight ahead.

Bishop Epaphras felt the other Bishops and pastors begin to jostle him out of position. He elbowed a few while trying to look like he was not doing so. Cheers rang through the air as Prophet Esau effortlessly ran down the long red carpet Epaphras had invested in. In no time, the prophet was beside him, and Epaphras felt the glow of the prophet's laser eyes fix on him.

"My brother, Epaphras, the Lord is asking you whom you have left his flock with," Prophet Esau said, his snow-white teeth glistening in the baking sun. Moving on, the prophet mounted the center stage and began the service.

For the rest of the crusade, Bishop Epaphras was in a trance. He looked at the prophet balefully and felt like yanking the expensive red carpet he had bought for the podium from under his feet. When the crusade drew to a close at eight in the evening—the prophet had never been known to keep time—Epaphras headed straight to the airport and caught the next available plane back to Wemppe City. He was a very disappointed man.

# CHAPTER
# 29

DALMAS KINGA NZAMBE SAT down for his staple breakfast of boiled maize and sour millet porridge. He was alone as usual with his stack of dailies. The presidential debate to be held that evening dominated the news with pundits predicting possible outcomes. Switching on the TV, he surfed through the channels and stumbled on *Your Good Morning Breakfast Show*. Anita Mzinga was hosting Senator Lydia Masumbuko.

"Anita, since when did getting married outside your tribe or race become a criminal offence in Kawemppe? The reason why I never got the Solanga gubernatorial ticket from SASA was because it was alleged that Solangians viewed me as an outsider who is just married by their son." Senator Lydia's words were laced with bitterness.

Dalmas, who knew the real reason, actually smiled in satisfaction. *Tit for tat is a fair game, Lydia*, Dalmas thought, switching channels. All the anchors were repetitively predicting possible answers the presidential candidates were likely to give to various questions. He switched off the TV and summoned Onessi his houseboy.

Onessi came fast, his face animated with a smile.

"Onessi, you have served me well over the years, and I want to reward you and terminate your service immediately." Naturally, Onessi was shocked. He watched Dalmas suspiciously as he reached for a fat envelope, which he proceeded to hand over to him. Onessi opened the envelope and howled in delight. The money Dalmas had given him was enough to buy a piece of land in his rural Ufuoni County and put up a modest house.

"Thankgu, sir. I has hollowazs know you goot man," Onessi said in Pidgin English. He then engulfed Dalmas in a bear hug.

The embarrassed Dalmas disentangled himself from the hold of his tearfully happy houseboy. "Gather your things. You are leaving in an hour's time," Dalmas said. He watched Onessi race towards the servants' quarters and walked to his own bedroom to pack too. Socks, belts, innerwear, and toiletries were quickly swept into a bag. Another bag accommodated his good shoes. Selecting his few good suits and shirts, he packed them into his best suitcase. Earlier in the week, he had shifted his golf kit and the books he could not live without to the house he had bought for Bibiana. Together with Chad, Bibiana's cheerful son, they had neatly arranged them in the book shelf in their new house.

Taking a machete and an empty trash bag, Dalmas walked through the overgrown garden of his mansion and began collecting flower cuttings for Bibiana's little garden. Bending down, he uprooted huge clusters of creepy verbenas and dug up holsta bulbs. Stubborn fuchsias, dwarf zinnias, cannas, and assorted geraniums disappeared into the bag too. He was sure Bibiana would make a great garden with them. By the time Onessi was ready for home, Dalmas had his car boot full of his belongings.

In nostalgia, Dalmas watched his faithful servant swing his simple bag over his shoulder and energetically walk out of the gate towards the bus stage. Minus Onessi's blaring radio, the mansion became eerily quiet. A few birds that chirped above the trees were a reminder that life must go on.

"The end of an era," Dalmas said softly to himself. After sending his four children their six-month stipend, he had advised them that they were on their own from thence. Clementine asleep in her bedroom upstairs, was unaware of the transition taking place below her. She missed the peaceful look on Dalmas's face as he closed the gate behind him and pointed his loaded car towards his new life with Bibiana and Chad.

Deborah felt the adrenaline rush she always experienced on the eve of a big trial. Professor Jackstone Majuaa, Deborah's mobile university in matters of politics, had practically been living with her. Two days before the debate, the professor had mock-staged the debate at KPM headquarters. Deborah, with two other characters standing in for SASA and NWS, had answered assorted questions fired by Lumumba and Ruthanne in front of an excited KPM staff who had filled in as spectators.

"I hope you will bring the kids. The viewers would love that," Ruthanne suggested.

"I will ask them," Deborah replied,

They loved the idea.

"What will I wear, Mum?" AJ asked, concerned about his appearance.

"Your penguin jumpsuit pajamas. Then you can curtain raise with that donkey song of yours. 'Little donkey, carry your load, and when you get tired, you can always plunge it in the river.' Goldie began waltzing about like a ballerina sending everyone into paroxysms of laughter.

In the late afternoon, Obed drove Deborah and her family to Governor Fundi's residence to prepare for the debate. The makeup artist, a chap called Yakubu, specially sourced by Neema, installed Deborah in front of Neema's makeup table. Yakubu took a few steps backward like an artist working on a canvas and paused to study what he told Deborah were facial contours.

"So, how is your project coming along?" Deborah asked Neema. The latter lay propped on her bed, amused by Yakubu's antics.

"Great, the necessary funding came through." Neema had been waiting for funds to finance her genetic research.

Deborah looked in delight at Dr. Neema, who not a long time back had been a little chubby girl. Now she had grown into a beautiful woman.

"I am so proud of you, Neema," Deborah said. It was not the words but the way Deborah said them that made Neema roll out of the bed and give her a hug.

"And so am I. You have been like a big sister to me, and you will make a fine president." It took all the will power Deborah could master for her to keep her cool.

Yakubu stepped aside to give the embracing women space.

"Someone could swear that you two are sisters. You resemble each other quite a lot," Yakubu said, drawing near Deborah to get on with his job.

"It is the story of our life" Neema said casually. She perched on top of her bed, resuming her watch. She had decided to watch the debate from the house, as she had an early flight back to her lab in Atlanta the next day.

The sheer power of Deborah's stare centered Yakubu's inner Zen. It was not the mean gaze he normally received from some high-flying females. This one glowed clarity, humility, and power. Stashing away the red paints he had planned to use, he pulled out his muted brown and bronze compacts and went to work. In the outer corridor, Ndollah clucked like a mother hen and stomped his feet impatiently. He had just returned from a West Africa shopping spree paid for by KPM and could hardly wait to display the exquisite Ankara and batik materials he had brought back.

Twenty minutes later, Deborah emerged on the stair landing facing the vast sitting room of the Fundi's household. Ndollah and Neema walked behind her like warriors escorting their queen. With pleasure, Ndollah watched the chatter in the sitting room below hush down. Honorable Carey Francis stood up automatically like a robot. Governor Risper, Lumumba Abiola, Professor Jackstone, and Deborah's kids all gaped, transfixed by the sight. Obed, who was rarely ruffled, stared openly at his boss in admiration.

"Mum, you look like the president" Goldie cried out, her face full of admiration as she raced towards her mother.

Deborah was in a standing collar indigo Ankara dress with creamy cowrie shells buttons running down the front.

A tiny head square was jauntily patched on the dome of her head allowing her long hair to fan out around her neck.

"Lumumba Abiola, say something," Ndollah taunted Lumumba below in feigned anger.

"Ndola, you have killed it. Why lie?"

With the fuss over, Deborah huddled with the KPM team, ruminating over last-minute details. Quietly, Ndollah beckoned Khavere, Deborah's house girl, to the dressing room. He proceeded to dress her in a fancy-looking blue outfit as she shrieked in delight. Beside them, Mrs. Mary Msalaba, Ziphorah Lengo, and several KPM assistants took turns at Neema's dressing table, where Yakubu's professional hand made them look ten years younger in a matter of minutes.

"Ndollah, don't you have time to stitch a dress for me anymore?" Neema complained when she saw how the new outfit had transformed Khavere. The complaint was unfounded. Ndollah had made her countless frocks.

"Doctor Neema, even Jesus told his disciples to stop whining aloud when he was around. This particular dress Khavere is wearing is my personal contribution to the debate." No one understood what Ndollah meant until much later.

The debate was held in the colorless mortar and glass buildings of the Wemppe School of Medicine. The main hall, a boxlike space, had been constructed for the basic purpose of providing a roof and a floor for learning. The stage background was jacketed in by a massive blue velvet curtain. Three glass podiums stood obliquely in the horse-shoe shaped stage.

Police Inspector Otto Temmu could be seen restlessly patrolling the compound. He was leaving nothing to chance. All day long, sniffer dogs had combed the campus grounds at intervals, in preparation for the eight o'clock debate. Special Forces, armed to the tooth, had encircled the entire campus compound. A police chopper hidden in a neighboring secondary school was all keyed up and ready for a quick response if the need arose. Inside the hall, news crews personally checked out and tagged by Inspector Otto, hustled about, testing their equipment and angling their cameras and microphones towards the stage.

SASA presidential hopeful Ronald Maarufu was the first to arrive, accompanied by his wife, Victoria. Their cute grandchildren hung on their hands. Honorable Maarufu looked sharper and younger than his sixty-seven years. The midnight navy suit he wore projected him like the president in waiting. Many people watching at home thought he was the right man to take over. Pausing briefly for the photographers, he waved at the audience and walked majestically to his designated podium, his face wearing the satisfied look of a man about to receive his due reward.

The next arrival was the Bishop in a gold suit. His running mate, Orpha Njuzun, and his wife, Naomi, accompanied him all the way to his podium. Reverend Naomi hugged her husband like he was going for war, while Orpha hugged him lingeringly like she was the wife. The two women retreated to their seats. Noticeable hostility was beginning to build up between them.

Deborah brought the rear, with AJ by her side, his eight-year-old chest puffed to breaking point. Goldie and Khavere walked behind them barely containing their giggles at AJ's newly discovered fashion sense. The little boy wore a white shirt neatly tucked into knee length navy khaki shorts, and his black school shoes. There had been a heavy debate about his choice of outfit with Goldie and Khavere proposing he change into something more jazzed up like jeans and a baggy t-shirt but the opposition led by Nana, Deborah, and AJ himself had agreed he looked dandy just as he was.

As Deborah drew close, the whispering that had been going on came to a stop, and necks craned forward.

Photographers tripped over each other as they attempted to get the best shots. Deborah authoritatively walked towards the stage. For the full minute it took her to reach her podium, Paa, who was seated in the audience, realized that he had held his breath. According to him, Deborah looked stunning, authoritative and presidential. She had just the right combinations of dress and makeup to bring out her strong personality. He realized that enchantment was not his alone. Deborah had a magnetic pull on the audience, the host, and definitely the people in television land.

Risper Fundi chanced a peek at Paa and noticed that he was looking at Deborah with funny sheep's eyes. Victoria Maarufu, clapping along with the audience for the sake of civility, also happened to glance at Paa and wondered why the guy was staring at Deborah like a drunk bull.

Gracefully, Deborah greeted her opponents before turning to and smiling at the audience. Ruthanne cast her experienced eye through the well-balanced audience of women and men and smiled with relief. Everything seemed okay.

If the photographers had not been entranced by Deborah, they would have captured the murderous look on of Victoria's face as she was staring at Khavere, Deborah's house girl.

"Ndollah, you are evil," Cheupe yelled loudly back at the KPM headquarters. The entire KPM team was crowded around the auditorium's large flat screen. On the screen was Khavere, Deborah's house help, dressed exactly like Mrs. Victoria Maarufu. The team erupted into a cheer. The first coup of the night had been executed. Ndollah took the friendly reprimand with a sinister smile on his face. He knew Kawemppe's self-appointed fashion police would have a field day comparing the filthy rich Victoria against Khavere the humble house help.

"Good evening viewers. Welcome to our presidential debate, live from Wemppe School of Medicine. I am Prost Bandari. Anita Mzinga and I are co-hosting the debate". The duo sat at the center of the horse shoe platform.

"The debaters tonight are Honorable Ronald Maarufu of SASA party, Honorable Deborah Binti Nzingha of the Kawemppe People's Movement, and Bishop Epaphras of the New Wine Skins party," "Anita said before Prost took over.

"Like a football match, we have ninety minutes for this debate. In the first half, we will allocate two minutes to each question's answer. The second half will be an interactive session in which you will ask each other questions and take a few from the audience. As the referees, Anita and I will come into play once in a while to nullify offside goals." The four contestants smiled at Bandari's humor.

"So, let us kick off the debate. What three major issues will you tackle first once elected into office?" Anita asked. "Let us begin with you Honorable Maarufu.

"Thank you, Bandari, Anita," Ronald began. "First, you all know that the economy has not been performing well in the last five years. Once in office, I will increase government spending, in order to re-build our institutions to their former glory. Two, I will strengthen our relations with our neighbors and improve our foreign trade, and three, I will take the nation's security a notch higher to ward off elements that are posing a danger to our nation."

"Honorable Deborah," Prost said.

"Thank you, Anita and Bandari. This country needs someone whose schema of reality is in tandem with the people's concerns. Our children need affordable quality education delivered by well-remunerated teachers. Our youth need help with their innovations so that we can create new cottage industries. Our middle-aged population, sandwiched between forking out school fees for their kids and taking care of their aging parents, should be supported by keeping the wera stable so that they can afford a favorable lifestyle and improve their standard of living. Wemppeans earning minimum wage need access to cheap transportation services and shopping alternatives. Our neglected senior citizens need free food rations and free and comprehensive medical services. If I take care of those issues, then not only will Kawemppe's security improve, but we will grow our economy with double digits. That is what my KPM government is planning to do."

"Bishop Epaphras," Anita called out

"Thank you all. First, I will review the developmental goals of every county, and have them match with the people's needs. Two, I intend to overhaul the health care system and replace it with a more inclusive package that will cater to preexisting conditions and our elderly populations. And third, I will implement programs that will aim at inculcating the moral values we have lost as a people and made us to institutionalize corruption.

The contestants fared well in the first half of the debate. It was the second round that drew blood.

"Bishop Epaphras despite the fact that the Wemppean church has a branch in every street of the republic, its impact in terms of education, health, charitable work, and even imparting the moral teaching you told us about earlier is dismal. What difference do you think you will make in the political space that you could not do within confines of the church?" Anita asked at the onset of the second round.

The Bishop grew evasive and began citing some five-year school program his church had implemented. Stung by the truth pastor Nehemiah had been pointing out all along, the Bishop turned his guns towards Deborah.

"Honorable Deborah, it is a well-known fact that women tend to cry and sulk when confronted with difficulty issues." A few in the audience sniggered at this and the Bishop awarded them with his own grin. "In matters of foreign policy, will this be your style if, for example, we differ with our neighboring country like, say, Gumbotswi?" Deborah's laughter at the Bishop's question was not a little apologetic giggle but a full belly laugh.

"Indeed, women tend to see issues differently from men. Sometimes, we cry. Other times we consult our friends and come up with an action plan. That is how our maker wired us. Men, on the other hand, are known to bottle up issues and allow matters to boil over internally while acting like all is well on the outside. Even this very minute as am speaking, I know there is a man hopelessly lost in this city, burning fuel, and still too proud to ask for direction." As she waited for the laughter to die down, her voice and body language became all business.

"As the commander-in-chief I will diligently safeguard the sovereignty of Kawemppe with more zeal than when I went for the multinationals. Every Wemppean in this country knows my ceaseless quest for justice. I am sure that they must have noticed that when I faced those multinationals, or a swarm of bees hurtling my way. I did not cry or sulk." The answer yielded the first applause from the audience that night.

"Honorable Maarufu, please explain what you mean when you say that you will tighten Kawemppe's economy," Deborah enquired.

Ronald turned his face to Deborah.

"As a country, we need to sacrifice more and tighten our belts to foot the huge budget facing us." Paa could discern tones of condescension creeping into Ronald's voice.

"Sacrifice what?" Deborah asked abruptly, cutting into Ronald's rehearsed answer. She knew she was defying the warnings of the Prof and Lumumba Abiola not to appear too forceful or abrasive and send the wrong message to her voters.

Her voice filling with concern, Deborah went on. "A good number of our children, brothers, and sisters, are jobless. Our people are sick and stuck in inadequately staffed hospital with, if any, inferior medicines. What more tightening of the belt are you asking of us when we have long surpassed the proverbial limit the wasp was said to have attained with his belt?" Deborah paused briefly and stared at Honorable Ronald Maarufu. "Let me ask you, sir: what is the price of a two-kilogram packet of maize flour?" Deborah posed. All eyes riveted towards Honorable Maarufu.

"It has been a while since I last shopped, but I think it is around the neighborhood of a thousand weras, if I am not mistaken."

Even Inspector Temu who was not paying any particular attention to the debate joined in the collective loud gasp the audience emitted. Risper watched Victoria wince.

Deborah let the moment linger. Ronald, perplexed by his answer, attempted to shrug it off.

Lifting her hands like a surrendering POW, Deborah caused a tense moment at the KPM headquarters before proceeding. "Sir, a pack of maize flour is one hundred weras, not one thousand weras. If you ventured out of your comfort zone from time to time and met everyday Wemppeans, you might realize that people are at their wits end. If you don't know what Wemppeans are feeding on, then you cannot suggest tightening of belts as a financial strategy."

Sensing that no one was about to challenge her, Deborah spun towards the cameras and left a perplexed Ronald alone.

"For the remaining debate time, Ronald Maarufu attempted to salvage his vision but you could tell the steam had left him.

When Bandari brought down the curtain, all eyes at the KPM headquarters turned towards the professor. He gave a thumbs up sign, and the staff broke into jubilation.

"Bring out the champagne," Marcus yelled at Ndollah. There was no champagne, as Irene Cheupe, the campaign's financial manager, ran a tight budget. Two crates of beer emerged and plastic glasses. Plates piled high with popcorn, crisps, and peanuts began circulating. Frugal Irene placed a phone call to a neighboring butchery and ordered some goat roast. Music blasted from a powerful speaker. The jubilation became even rowdier when Deborah walked in an hour later. Full of pleasure, Professor Majuaa, who was sipping beer straight from the bottle, watched as Deborah trooped in and proceeded to congratulate the staff.

"You do know you are the best team to work with in this election. I am proud of you. You have been working harder than termites, so we are all having a weekend off. Let us meet here on Monday morning, hale and hearty, ready to continue doing what we do best."

With only twenty days remaining before the elections, Bishop Epaphras held a meeting with his usual panel of pastors.

"Despite the bad press we have been getting, we are still in the race. Seasoned parties like DDP have given up along the way," Bishop Epaphras began. "It is obvious that KPM and Deborah Binti Nzingha are going to win this thing. But that is not the reason I have called you here. I want us to put our heads together and start strategizing for the next elections five years away."

The Bishop wanted to plan ahead. The billionaire Dwayne Kirby Hershel was still interested in helping him out.

"I want your suggestions on how we should proceed. Where do we begin?"

The pastors, afraid that the Bishop might be baiting them for their opinion, kept quiet for several minutes. Eventually, pastor Nehemiah began talking.

"Bishop, I think we need to bring power back to the church by building political self-confidence in our followers. We need to start by economically empowering our members. If in a certain parish our children are learning from under trees for lack of classrooms, the church should build classrooms for them. If our herders in dry parts of the country are fighting for water, we the church should sink bore holes and excavate dams for them. The church should lead from the front. Like you said at the debate, we need to inculcate in every Wemppean, man, woman, and child, the vital virtues of integrity, respect, and empathy for their fellow man."

No man at the table dared to snigger when Pastor Nehemiah began outlining his vision.

"I believe that we have the capacity to take charge of the country. Every church in Kawemppe can at least boast of having professors, teachers, nurses, housewives, pastors, doctors, herders, engineers, company CEOs, and many other professionals. We have the necessary manpower to fully instigate true change with diligence and integrity, shunning corruption and ethnicity.

"Bishop, I strongly believe elected leaders are the reflection of a society. The trending wave of leadership seems to favor female presidents and unaccountable dictators. I believe religious leaders are next in line. Someday soon, the world will have harmed itself so badly, it will desperately need the empathic ear of religion to rescue itself. The question is, will we be found ready?" Nehemiah argued.

Although the speech was beginning to take an unorthodox turn, Bishop Epaphras pulled out his notebook and began to take notes.

# CHAPTER 30

I n Kawemppe constitutional law is a clause that requires polling companies to cease their predictions twenty days to the election date. The law had been necessitated by a need to protect Wemppeans from briefcase pollsters who had a penchant for posting fictitious polls favoring the politician who paid them the most. The last Mzalendo polls had KPM leading the pack and even a whooping seven points above what the professor had predicted. The favorable prediction did not stop Honorable Solomon Ngome and Mrs. Ziphorah Lengo and the WOMAN machinery from spreading over Kawemppe like white on rice.

Feeling a sense of elation, Deborah took a day off, a sunny Friday, to attend the annual alumni party organized by KGGS.

It turned out to be a hen party with wine, music, roasted ribs served with jacket potatoes, and hilarious laughter. Both the young and the not-so-young alums caught up with old times. Deborah had arrived home late in the night and attempted to catch some late-night news.

There was a developing story of the downfall of aspiring senator Mitambo Mitambo, who had been arrested for corrupt dealings in stadia contracts. Tired, she had switched off the telly and gone to bed.

Deborah had hardly laid her head on the pillow when she was woken by the persistent ringing of her cell phone. Her mind still sleepy, she had tried ignoring it, but the caller kept on. Grudgingly, she dug under her pillow and retrieved the offending handset, pried one sleepy eye open, and stared at the caller ID. It was Governor Risper Fundi.

"Hello?"

"Sorry, Deborah. I know I must have woken you up, but please come over to my house right away." Risper's voice was faltering. Within seconds Deborah's head cleared up. The backlog of sleep she had been hoping to clear over the weekend rolled away like the retreating tongue of a chameleon that had just captured an insect. With her heart beating erratically, she sat straight up on her bed. Risper's call could only mean one thing. Their past had caught up with them.

Freshening up in a flash, she pulled on a free-flowing kitenge dress and exited the house quietly. She did not want to wake up the watchful Obed. Apprehension tightened around her throat, like one choking from a starchy chunk of sweet potato, as she drove straight to the governor's mansion.

The governor's security waved her through without delay. Before she could park her car properly, Risper had emerged from the house, her face deathly white.

"Come with me to the attic," she called out, practically propelling Deborah up the stairway that led to her study.

Risper dropped the bombshell after closing the door behind her tightly. "Our past is out. Unbeknownst to us, Neema has been experimenting with our DNA profiles, attempting to discover a cancer cure for her eh . . . dad. Her research has proven to her beyond doubt that we are not related to each other in any way. Last night, she flew in with her brother Faraja, and they want to know about their roots."

Deborah sank into the same chair she had sat on eight short months ago when Risper and Praxedes had declared her presidential worthy and buried her face into her palms.

"How are they doing?" she asked.

"Somewhat okay. They have gone out for a walk." Risper said and exhaled laboriously.

Faraja, Fundi's only son had called home soon after Neema had let him in on the findings. He was not particularly keen to know about his past, but Neema was. Risper and Francis had told them to come home immediately as the matter could not be discussed over hackable phones.

"Can you imagine what damage the SASA party machinery and especially senator Virunga's vile mouth can do to us if they got wind of this? They can pollute Wemppeans to think that we have denied them some vital information, which is none of their business." Risper's face was deeply lined with worry as she said this. She went on. "Sorry, I know I sound hollow, like I am just thinking about me, myself and I, rather than Neema and Faraja's welfare."

Vividly, Deborah recollected the genesis of her current quagmire. The day she discovered she was pregnant, she had run to Isaya Hekima's home to let Paa in on the new developments. Paa had less than a day before departed for further studies in America. Deborah never got past the gate. Paa's frosty mother had dismissed her at the door. In desperation, she had written Paa a short letter explaining her predicament and left it with the sneering woman.

Three months later, when it was apparent that Paa was not going to respond to the letter, she decided to do the unthinkable: abort. The whole idea of abortion was illegal in Kawemppe. Deborah knew she was going to die at the delivery table just like her mother. Thoughts of how the scandal would rock her village and probably kill her poor grandparents assailed her for days. On the same day, Wemppe University had been closed down, following the deadly riots demanding the resignation of the dictator President Ochao, which left activist Amos Juma paralyzed. Deborah had been walking scared near Wemppe hospital when she spotted the white-washed gynecology clinic of one Dr. Risper Fundi. Falteringly, she had walked in and encountered her liberator. That evening, when the dictator President Ochao had punitively declared that all universities be closed for a year, Debora had informed her grandparents that she had gotten a job and she couldn't go home. She had then moved her personal effects and taken refuge in the Fundi's household away from her university pals and any other meddling eyes. It was a period she recalled with remorse.

"I should have told Neema long time ago that I am her biological mother, and gotten over with it." Deborah cursed herself.

On second thought, she knew she could not have done that when Neema regarded Risper as her mummy.

After five years of barrenness, Risper had secretly conducted numerous fertility tests, which proved that Francis was sterile. He could not sire a child. After discovering the hard truth, Risper had made up her mind to make Francis a father and began working on a strategy. In Kawemppe and Africa in general, if such news leaked out, it could ruin a man's esteem and reputation. More so if the man was a politician.

On the sixth year of their marriage, Honorable C. F. Fundi was due to take a yearlong government posting overseas when Risper began mimicking bouts of morning sickness. Refusing to accompany him, she was left behind. On the expected due date, she had given birth to a baby boy, Faraja.

Faraja had come to Risper in the form of a homeless and very pregnant street girl who had been fatally stabbed by her drugged boyfriend. As the surgeon and his team struggled to save the teenage mother, a very "pregnant" Doctor Risper had eased the baby out through an emergency caesarean section. Taking advantage of the confusion that was going on in the theatre, Risper had swapped a mummy of bed sheets resembling a dead infant with the newborn. She had walked away with the healthy infant, whom she had quieted with a pacifier and hid it in an empty drawer in her office, leaving her radio on to disguise any noise.

The mother had never woken up. By the time the operating team regrouped, the presumably dead infant had been handed over to an orderly who took it to the incinerator. A month later, C.F. Fundi had flown home to the joyful welcome of Faraja, his healthy first-born son.

Neema had been an easy birth. The timing was perfect. Faraja had turned five years old, and C. F. Fundi was travelling to Leeds, U.K for his yearlong post-graduate studies. It was the same week a nauseated Deborah had walked into Doctor Risper Fundi's private clinic in a state of panic. Risper had choreographed her assumed second pregnancy around Deborah's real journey and personally delivered the baby through a careful cesarean section that left no telling wounds on the mother.

"Does Francis know?" Deborah asked when the silence grew unbearable.

"He has known all along that he is impotent and is grateful that I did not embarrass him."

If a person was to barge in at that hour, he would have been shocked at the defeated looks on the faces of the two most powerful women in the land.

*What am I going to say to her?* Deborah wondered. *That I gave you away because the timing was not right? That traditions and religion at the time forbade an out-of-wedlock child? Or should I say that your father left me and the only option left was for me to give you up for adoption?*

Even to her unsettled mind, the excuses sounded hollow. Sighing, she realized that she had to face her demons. The chicken had come home to roost. She was going to tell Neema the truth. That unlike millions of other women who were raising their children singularly at the time, she had handed the task to a more deserving woman.

"I have not told Neema that you are her biological mother yet." Risper's voice caught as she spoke the words.

Deborah moved towards her mentor and embraced her in a bear hug. "Trust me, if I were to do this all over again, I would still choose you as my child's mother. You did a good job."

"So, what do you think we should do now?" Risper asked after a long while,

"Tell her the truth." Deborah's voice was full of clarity.

"Pardon me for asking this, but who is her father?" Risper enquired.

"Paa Isaya, and he doesn't know."

Risper's mouth fell open in surprise. She now understood why Deborah appeared so aloof to Paa's naked admiration.

"I need to inform him first. I will be right back."

"Don't be long."

Risper watched Deborah stroll hesitantly outside the mansion. She was glad they had a campaign-free weekend. They could use the time to sort out the matter without interfering with Ruthanne's schedule.

Nana was patiently spooning amaranth porridge to Mzee Abraham in the verandah when Deborah drove in. The beauty of the sunny Saturday morning scorned the aching pain bottled up in Deborah's heart. Obed, who was jogging along the perimeter of the compound, looked at her broodingly. He had cautioned Deborah about leaving the compound without a security escort, and now she had breached their security arrangement. Ignoring him, Deborah entered the quiet house. She went straight to her bedroom and called Paa.

With schools closed for the long November–December holidays, Goldie and AJ had migrated to Zaituni's place to play with the baby, whom they regarded as one big live doll.

AJ had gone along after being reassured that the baby was all grown now and she wasn't going to pour saliva all over him again.

Paa received Deborah's urgent phone call in his apartment. He was preparing some eggs for breakfast while reading his rival paper, the Wemppe Gazette, which had covered extensively how Mitambo Mitambo's stolen stadia stash had been recovered from septic tanks in the outskirts of Wemppe City. His son Lee was with his grandparents. He thought he sensed some subdued excitement in Deborah's voice. Wolfing the eggs down, he splashed some cold water on his face, gargled some mouth wash and dabbed a little after shave on his chin before changing into a clean shirt. *Maybe she has accepted my proposal*, he thought optimistically as he reversed his car carelessly like a teenager on his first drive.

His enthusiasm was met at the door by a stony-faced Deborah. She led him past the chicken coop to the outer garden out of earshot.

"Are the children okay?" he asked with concern.

"They are fine at Zaituni's," Deborah replied and let Paa stew in a lengthy silence as she worked out how to broach the subject.

"You are spooking me, Debbie. What is it?" Paa asked, unable to stand the silence. He moved closer to Deborah and circled his hand around her waist and drew her closer.

"Paa, I need a very clear answer from you now. On the day you were to leave for America for your studies at North West University, did your mother give you any letter from me?"

"None at all, Debbie. As ridiculous as this may sound, I have always wanted to ask you this same question. Did my mother give you the numerous letters I sent to you through her?"

Deborah stared at Paa's face for signs of guile, but there were none.

"No, she didn't," she said at last. "It is the reason I have called here. There is a story you need to hear. We have a baby girl together."

"What? Are you kidding me? I mean, where is she?" Paa almost yelled.

"Don't you want to know who she is?"

"Very much, who is it?"

"Doctor Neema Fundi."

"No," Paa gasped clenched his fist and punched the air. His clear eyes acquired a deep red glint and a thick throbbing vein appeared at the center of his forehead.

"Yes, and she wants to know her roots as soon as possible."

"This is unbelievable. Neema is my daughter. No wonder she is your carbon copy." He smiled, revealing his dimple.

"She has you dimple." Deborah said.

"Oh, my ancestors!" Paa said when the political implication of the news unfolded in his mind. "Debbie, what have I done to you? If this news gets out, it will be a Molotov cocktail hurled at the heart of your campaign. With nineteen days left to the elections, this is pure gold in the hands of Virunga. Can you imagine trying to explain to Wemppeans that Neema Fundi, the daughter they have known all along to belong to Governor Risper Fundi, the

KPM party running mate, is actually the real daughter of the presidential candidate Deborah Nzingha? That, my dear is an overwhelming revelation for many a Wemppean to digest."

Paa could name numerous qualified leaders, the majority of whom were women, who despite having clean track records in social justice affairs, had been destroyed by well-aimed ad hominem arguments. If honorable Ronald Maarufu did issue a statement like "Deborah and Risper are evil, untrustworthy, and secretive; they don't deserve to be leaders,' he would derail a few Wemppeans and possibly shift the political scales to his favor.

"Debbie, I am too sorry to even ask you for your forgiveness. But please forgive me. I now get the whole picture and understand your ambivalence towards me. Will you forgive me?"

"I do," Deborah said easily.

Paa dropped her hand gently and flushed out his car keys.

"Let's do this correctly. Give me an hour. I will be right back."

"Where are you going?" Deborah asked, alarmed.

"My mother has some explaining to do."

"Don't be harsh with her. Whatever happened, happened, and it is not the end of the world," Deborah called out after him.

Deborah watched Paa drive off her compound like a bat out of hell, prompting Obed to pop out of his quarters to investigate whether there was a problem.

At the Fundi household, Faraja and Neema were walking back home after inspecting the vast estate on their morning walk.

"Honestly, Sis, personally, I don't think I want to know who my birth parents are," Faraja said as he rounded a corner and came upon a thick lantana bush. Its black fruit was ripe and plentiful. It was evident from the bird poop on the leaves that the birds enjoyed feasting on them. He swiped a few berries on his hand and smelled them before tossing them away.

"As a matter of fact, I also don't want to know. Come to think of it, I am just reacting to the initial shock of the sudden loss of identity. Furthermore, what difference will it make?" Neema asked as she paused under a cluster of young eucalyptus saplings.

As an industrial psychologist, Faraja knew that accepting the sudden sense of lost identity was more difficult than the mergers he oversaw on a regular basis where he walked thousands of newly laid-off employees through the motions of accepting the change and restarting their lives afresh. Considering that they had accidentally learned about their roots, they were justified in wondering what was so wrong with them that they had to be given away.

"I cannot remember any single day mum or dad acted like we weren't their biological children. They loved us unequivocally," Faraja added

He walked along the bushy path he knew so well. When he was a small boy, his dad had taken him out most Saturdays to hunt for squirrels.

"Faraja, I feel happy as I can possibly be. If we were adopted, it is what it is. I am not going to dig up my past, period," Neema said.

"In that case let us go put Mum and Dad at ease. Our parents have and always will be Francis and Risper Fundi, and you are my sis, whom I love very much," Faraja stated and quickened his pace towards the mansion.

Half an hour later Paa returned with a parcel of letters. He found Deborah where he had left her, seated on the grass.

"Mother is beside herself with remorse." He said as he lowered himself next to Deborah.

He took a single yellowed letter addressed to him and handed Deborah the rest of the bundle. Paa opened his carefully, and began reading. It was the letter Deborah had written under the scornful gaze of his mother some twenty-five years ago. Deborah knew it by heart.

*My dearest love, Paa,*

*I write this missive with a heavy heart. Though we said our goodbyes, before you leave you have to know what befell me. I would have loved to break the news one-to-one, but your mother stood in my way. I am buckling with fear. Somewhere, inside me, I feel the flutter of a new life. A conjoined innocence, a beautiful feeling of you and me. How I wish I could be with you as we bask in*

*its growing sparkle. My heart is flooded
with longings to be with you. I know
that as soon as you get this letter, we
will be together,*
    *Here or there. Mostly together,*
    *And with our baby,*
    *Waiting anxiously,*

          *Yours, Debbie*

Paa finished reading folded the yellowed letter and placed it in the inner pocket of his jacket. Deborah's heap of letters lay untouched on the table. What was the point of un-ringing a rung bell?

"Debbie, forgive me. I am so sorry that things have turned out this way."

"You are beginning to sound like AJ when he gets keyed up on something. I am past what happened otherwise wouldn't have let you anywhere near my life?"

The answer seemed to pacify Paa.

"Thank you for saying that." Paa replied, brushing a stray strand of hair from Deborah's face.

"You are radiating peace," he said as he looked into her eyes.

"Sure. I do feel at peace, and I have also decided not to let the important practicalities of life to pass me by." Deborah was not wasting any chances. Starring keenly at Paa's eyes, she asked, "Paa Isaya, will you marry me?"

Paa's jaw slackened involuntarily, before turning into a big smile, which brought out his bewitching dimple. Still staring at Deborah, he dropped to one knee on the grass and in slow motion took Deborah's hand.

"I would love to marry you more than anything in the world—and right away."

"How serious were you about wanting to marry me right away?" Deborah asked sincerely

"Dead serious." Paa's tone was tender.

"Can we do this before the Election Day?" Deborah enquired. She reached for Paa's hand and intertwined her fingers with his.

"Whatever you say, my love" Paa replied and gently kissed her on the lips.

"I will have Josephine take charge of the matter. But first, let us go see our daughter."

"Absolutely," Paa said, afraid of destroying the moment with the unnecessary words bubbling in his mind. "Let us go see our daughter." he jumped up and helped Deborah to her feet.

Deborah's phone began ringing. It was Risper.

"You are not going to believe this, but Neema has decided she doesn't want to pursue the matter, now nor ever," Risper announced.

"Is she certain?"

"Cocksure."

"Then I respect her decision. Once again, please know that if I was to do this all over again, I would still entrust her to you," Deborah assured Risper.

"Thank you, and see you on Monday. the show must go on," Risper said and terminated her call.

"I don't know exactly how I feel. I was looking forward to meeting my daughter, but since she is happy with her decision, let her be," Paa replied thoughtfully after Deborah had explained the new turn of events.

They fell into companionable silence for a long time.

345

CHAPTER

# 31

TOTO THE THUG HAD cracked under interrogation. He had placed the blame of the bee attack on an unmentioned senior official within the SASA party. The inspector's hunch was that the rogue Senator Virunga, now Honorable Ronald Maarufu's running mate, was the mastermind behind the attack. Inspector Otto, using one of his old tools of trade, had secured Toto a cash bail, then sent one of his undercover deputies, Kassim, to misinform Toto that he was a walking bullseye.

"The police have a bullet with your name on it. Find somewhere quiet and lie low," Kassim, who passed himself around Wemppe City as a garbage man fully kitted in tattered murky cloths and a huge dirty sack of waste to boot, whispered to Toto.

For inspector Otto, the ruse had worked well in the past. Faced with uncertainty, most criminals tended to run back to their masters to get advice and survival cash. Apart from Kassim, whose dirty sack concealed a lethal machine gun and an automatic pistol, Inspector Otto assigned four other undercover cops to trail Toto day and night.

Otto took on senator Virunga in person. For days, he trailed the senator in his bullet-proof police car just to spook him. The effort had borne some fruits. Wanderlust dried up, the senator seemed to be permanently holed up at his first wife's house. To inject more pressure on the suspects, Inspector Otto made a habit of strolling into the luxurious SASA headquarters every morning and interrogating everyone he met.

Panicked by inspector Otto's sudden interest in him, Senator Virunga called Victoria Maarufu.

"Madam, I think our stew has too much salt," he said, speaking metaphorically just in case his phone was being tapped.

"So, where do I come in? Did you want me to instruct you about which meat you were to buy and how much salt you had to use? I did not know what you were cooking in the first place," Victoria snapped back.

Listening to the mocking tones emanating from Victoria, Virunga lost control and boomed out his answer. "Woman, listen. A person who has tasted the stew cannot claim not to have eaten it. We are in this fire together whether you like it or not."

"In that case, Zinjathropus, let us wait and see who will cry first!" Victoria retorted angrily.

"Woman, switch on your TV right now, and you had better have your handkerchief ready," Senator Virunga growled and disconnected the call.

Victoria snapped the TV on at once and watched in disbelief as flashing red letters filled the screen declaring breaking news: River Maru Restored. The live pictures showed President Jabali standing on the banks of the mighty Maru, addressing journalists. Several bulldozers were mercilessly tearing down Mr. Cho's projects. Mr. Cho and his engineers, in handcuffs, were being matched to waiting police cruisers, escorted by a contingent of police officers.

"No stone will be left unturned in fighting corruption," the president said. "There won't be any sacred cows to spare. I; Meshack Jabali will not favor anyone, no matter who they are or how close they are to me."

For some strange reason, Victoria sensed that the president was addressing her. Her heart began to beat erratically. She reached for a vial of aspirins on the side table, shook out two tablets, and swallowed them dry. One tablet lounged on her throat causing her to choke. For several seconds she coughed and cleared her throat until the tablet went down. The effort left her eyes welled with tears.

Rising up, she reached for her flask of warm lemon water and sipped some to sooth her throat. Her mobile phone which was lying on the bed began to ring. It was Ronald, so she picked it at once.

"Khosiya, come to maroon house, and I mean right now."

The fury in Ronald's voice was frightening. He only called her by her native name, Khosiya, when he demanded instant attention, and that was rare.

Victoria dialed Alloys Faya, the campaign manager, to find out what was going on.

She learned that President Jabali had called and given her husband a tongue lashing, worth of a schoolboy. He had accused honorable Maarufu of harboring corrupt thugs like Mitambo Mitambo and had declared that that was the reason he would never endorse Ronald for the presidency.

*It is over. Mr. Cho must have implicated me*, Victoria thought as she hung the call. Instinctively, Victoria glanced at the wall clock, it was nearly noon. A quick plan was forming in her mind. She had to flee to the neighboring country of Gumbotswi, where she had many friends who owed her favors. Using the helicopter now would give away her escape plan. If she started the journey right away by road, she could make it to the border before seven in the evening. She could ditch her car and arrange for one of her friends in Gumbotswi to pick her up.

As a precaution, over the years Victoria had acquired four passports in different names just in case the need arose. She also had an old-fashioned phone that was registered under one of her former house girl's names. She packed the passports, the phone, items of clothing, and her expensive jewelry in a simple duffel bag. She had enough money stashed in different international banks under different names to afford her a movie star lifestyle in any city in the world. All she needed was enough cash for the road trip in which she intended to drive herself.

Victoria planned to weather the remaining fifteen days to the election hiding and hoping that her husband would win the election so that she could get back. If Ronald lost, she knew that she would become a fugitive, because there was no way Victoria Khosiya Maarufu was going to rot in anyone's jail. She changed into jeans and a t shirt and laced on her gym shoes. She wrote Ronald a brief note telling him not to search for her, placed it on the nightstand, and pinned it down with her ditched phone. Hurriedly, she walked outside towards her land cruiser.

"I am going to the gym," Victoria said as she waived her body guard away. She reached for the vehicle keys from the driver and drove off the compound. The two men were stunned. Madam rarely left the house without at least one of them for company.

With the election a short ten days away, the entire team at the KPM headquarters was on red alert, despite things on the ground never having been better. Lumumba Abiola was briefing the team.

All WOMAN groups are burrowed deep in the villages, pulling in stray votes with tremendous success. Mrs. Ziphorah Lengo and her HMA network are on a door-to-door show-me-your-voter's-cards mission. Our adverts are airing exclusively on all WAMO Media stations courtesy of Praxedes. Honorable Solomon Ngome, former Speaker Robert Harakka, Seth Pasakhwa, and Commander Pillar Shinyanga are handling the arising matters from KPM aspirants from the eight counties with unrivaled acumen. Mrs. Mary Msalaba, Josephine, Aphia, and Dina are manning various professional groups and giving daily updates. Jonte and the All on Board team are dotted all over the countryside sweeping and rehabilitating streets, rivers, and roads.

Lumumba concluded his report.

"Ok, team. I hate to lose an election after working this hard." Deborah's tone entertained no nonsense. "This may sound like overkill, but we need a fresh panelist, possibly a maverick to spur with our competitors on the talk shows."

Lumumba, who sat facing the entrance of the hall looked through the glass windows, and froze. "I think our maverick just walked in."

The team turned and stared at the entrance. Vizuri Jabali, President Jabali's daughter, was just walking in.

"Let me find out, whether she will take up the post" Lumumba said and headed towards the reception to meet Vizuri.

After his release from jail, Toto had searched high and low for his friend Mrefu for days on end. Mrefu seemed to have disappeared without a trace. The city was partially empty, the majority of the population had fled to their up-country villages to await voting day. Panicky and without money or Mrefu's guidance, Toto was like a loose cannon. Broke and desperate, he decided to go visit Senator Virunga at his home. Toto knew both the first wife and the second wife's residences. He remembered how the senator had once said that weekends were reserved for his second wife. Being a Wednesday, he decided to chance on the senator's first wife's home. Being broke meant that he had to walk there. Unknowingly, he dragged along the company of five police officers. Two officers followed him on mountain bikes. One was on foot, while Kassam and his partner crawled after them in an inconspicuous tinted Subaru. Luckily, the senator's residence was on a slightly busy street, so no one paid attention to a beefy youth sitting outside the gate, two cyclists repairing the tire of a bike, and a Subaru parked under a tree.

At exactly eleven in the morning, the gate of the mansion swung open, and the senator's cruiser emerged. Senator Virunga spotted Toto immediately.

He ordered his driver Simon to stop at once and got out consumed in fury.

"Idiot, bloody fool. Who told you to come here? The senator approached Toto, spewing expletives.

He gave the youth a hard slap across the face and shoved him roughly.

Toto had never failed to avenge a personal attack.

From the cover of the Subaru, detective Kassam, who was filming the scene on his 64-pixel phone camera, zoomed in on time to catch Toto's unrestrained ham of a fist smack the senator dead between his eyes. He didn't need to hear the sound of the nose break. Virunga reeled backwards, and slowly like a drunk Goliath, he toppled and fell on the road.

The officers with the bicycles arrived first. They stopped the senator's bodyguard cum driver, who had drawn his pistol, from shooting Toto.

After determining that the senator would rally through, Kassam called his boss, Inspector Otto. He then WhatsApped the video with the senator going down to his journalist friend Prost Bandari.

Vizuri Jabali was an instant hit. For six days, she ruled the airwaves on behalf of KPM like the pro that she was. At no time did she try to steal the limelight from Deborah or rub in her first-daughter privilege on her viewers. Her only competition, was the video of senator Virnga going down after being punched by Toto which had gone viral.

The prof had her running back and forth to different radio and TV shows for good measure.

The KPM team had rigged Deborah and Risper on a last tour—a countrywide lap. They had been campaigning in Ronald Maarufu's backyard, Lokamiko County, when the news of senator Virunga's arrest broke.

"I told that fool not to throw stones at a bee hive—that he'd get stung—but he didn't listen. Now, he is politically done, and it will take a miracle for Ronald Maarufu to find a suitable running mate," Risper remarked.

"That is not even news. I have heard from a very reliable source that Victoria Maarufu has fled the country. Apparently she was the mastermind of the River Maru disaster and the bee attack," Praxedes said.

Deborah, who was napping in between the two women, as their vehicle sped to yet another campaign meeting quipped, "Let them have it. They did injure a lot of innocent people."

With Mitambo Mitambo and Senator Virunga cooling their heels in jail, Ronald Maarufu began grasping at straws to stay afloat. Minus Victoria's quick thinking, he took two sweet days before he started to scout for a running mate. In the Kawemppe constitution, electioneering stopped four days before voting day. Ronald tried to woo Bishop Ephaphras and his NWS party, but the bishop was determined to have his presence felt politically. Eventually, against his campaign manager's advice, Ronald settled for Lydia Masumbuko with less than twenty-four hours to spare. Lydia was a hard sell.

The next day on Radio Five's *Ananias and Sabina Breakfast Show*, Vizuri Jabali called Lydia's appointment "a death knell." The newspapers and other TV pundits picked the vibe, and all day long, the situation in the SASA party became officially known as the death knell.

While Ronald Maarufu was running out of ideas to breathe life into SASA, Ndollah, Deborah's stylist, was bursting to the brim with creativity. He had made what he called, "D-Day special numbers" for Deborah. Three outfits from which Deborah could choose from. Most of the KPM ladies already had an outfit marinating in their wardrobes, waiting for the day, courtesy of Ndollah.

# CHAPTER

# 32

ALL CAMPAIGNS CEASED AT six p.m. on Saturday, November 30. Chagga Batuta, the chair of KES, took over the airwaves and read his riot act. No more campaigns. No pundit or advertisements of a political nature on TV, radio, or the internet. The people needed time to think and make up their minds on who they wanted as their leaders. Chagga Batuta was short, stout, and brown with a booming voice. He was also an internationally celebrated lawyer.

The wedding was held the next day in the afternoon. It was short and simple. It was held on a tiny island owned by Paa's family, which was only accessible by helicopter. Josephine had done a splendid job as an amateur wedding planner. Under her stewardship, the two families had met severally to get to know each other as per Kawemppe tradition. Infact Josephine concluded that Lee, Goldie and AJ were getting along well.

Thirty close family and friends had been flown in. The smartly dressed guests had only one rule to adhere to: they were to keep mum about the wedding until the election was over. Deborah glowed in a smart, creamy A-line dress Josephine had found for her. Together with Paa, Lee, Goldie and AJ they made a beautiful blended family.

The next four days saw Praxedes physically living with Ziphorah Lengo in her house, afraid that the latter might try to carry out some injury time vote hunting escapades and land them in trouble with KES. Chagga Batuta ran a ruthlessly honest ship. The Fundi's, Rtd. Commander Pillar Shinyanga, Seth Pasakhwa, Solomon Ngome, Bishop Priscilla Timotheo, and Mary Msalaba, Prof, and the regular staff spent the time holed at KPM headquarters, strategizing. They brainstormed over different scenarios and possible appointees for different government posts. Deborah, whom they had banned from the office for at least two days, with instruction to rest, got the daily reports via email in the evening. Select members of the WOMAN team and All on Board, led by Jonte, had been appointed as presiding agents to man polling stations and ensure that every vote had been cast and tallied. Nothing was being left to chance. Agents from the SASA party were desperate and capable of doing anything to derail and discredit the voting process.

Lumumba and Ruthanne had the chopper at their disposal, just in case some irregularity was noted in some far-flung hamlet and they needed to hop over in a beat.

On December 4, all the polling stations opened up at exactly five in the morning. The excitement in the air was palpable. In some polling stations, voters had begun forming lines as early as three to cast their votes. Deborah cast her vote at eight in the morning, accompanied by Paa,, Lee, Goldie and AJ, Nana, Khavere, and Mzee Abraham. The cameras clicked away as Deborah smiled and slipped her vote in the ballot box. With nothing else to do, they went back home. Across the country, Wemppeans sat on their verandas and under the trees with radios and TV blaring at top volume. Some individuals could be seen tallying up the results with the help of notebooks and calculators. Deborah skipped the TV coverage and instead retired to her bedroom for some reflection. This proved to be impossible. Her girls, Josephine and company, had come over immediately after casting their votes. The ruckus they were making together with Paa, the children and Nana was contagious. Deborah retired to the garden to meditate and pray.

By two o'clock, Nana and Josephine began to ululate as KPM showed a clear and steady lead against SASA and NWS.

The prof called at four, unable to contain his excitement. His voice was a bit squeaky. "Madam, this one is in the bank. I think you had better start getting ready, because by eight in the evening the show will be over."

After the prof's call, things moved on fast. The newly promoted Inspector Otto arrived with a contingent of presidential guards and began securing Deborah's residence. Deborah had made it clear that Obed and his boys were staying. While Obed showed the cops around the compound, Otto introduced Deborah to her official bodyguards.

As the sun dipped westward, a carnival mood began to descend on the country. By six o'clock, cheers, whistles, and the occasional blare of a *vuvuzela* cracked the air from a distance.

Risper called. "Get ready and come down to the headquarters."

Deborah went into her bedroom, knelt down, and said a brief prayer. Her girls helped her change into one of Ndollah's masterpieces, a purple and gold maxi Ankara skirt and a matching top with a square neckline. She added a red double-strand Masai bead necklace, which matched her shoes and head scarf.

"Congratulations, my love. You don't just look like a president. You *are* the president," Paa whispered into her ear when she emerged.

Ronald Maarufu called at seven to concede defeat

Five minutes later, President Jabali called. "Madam President, congratulations. I am so proud to have you as my successor," he began. They talked for several minutes, and despite herself, Deborah caught herself grinning like AJ.

Nana prayed, and they left the house in a convoy of ten chase cars. Deborah's limousine was buffeted in the middle by security. Paa rode with the children. AJ, Goldie, and Lee were over the moon. Nana, Josephine, and the girls were in different vehicles.

Deborah and her entourage walked in at the KPM headquarters at seven sharp. Miriam Makeba's "Allutta Continua" was playing, and the cheers were deafening. Risper waiting upfront watched Deborah dance all the way to the front, in vigour of a boxer who knew the game was over. Everyone thought Deborah was singing along, but she was mouthing a private prayer.

"I honor my promise to Phyllis Mngamata Jones, no more tribalism,Olobango, the middlemen time is up, Wemppeans I got your backs." occasionally she paused to give high fives here and there.

"She looks like a stateswoman," Ruthanne gushed out at Lumumba.

"She is a stateswoman," Lumumba replied proudly.

All TV stations were zoomed in at the KES headquarters. Chagga Batuta seemed ready to announce what the country already knew.

Deborah Binti Nzingha was the president elect.

# ACKNOWLEDGMENTS